> "Love, luck and betrayal . . . a sprawling epic
> following two feuding families over three
> generations . . . guaranteed to keep you
> turning the pages!"—*Catch-Up*

Alexandra had set her sights high. She would use her
brains and her nerve to rise to the top of a world that
rewarded the strong and destroyed the weak.

FEARFUL RISKS . . .

She thought Robert Alexander would help make that
dream come true. In his arms she learned what it was to
be a woman. In his hands she learned what it took and
what it cost to make the right moves and take the fearful
risks of the money game.

TO DO ALONE . . .

Then came the shattering discovery that turned her
dream into a nightmare. She woke to the knowledge that
what she had to do, she had to do alone. She would have
other men, but only as instruments of pleasure. None
would ever wrest from her again the lever of power.

A WEB OF VENGEANCE . . .

Now it was her turn to teach Robert how well she had
learned his lessons . . . as she wove a worldwide web of
vengeance and desperately tried to keep her heart from
melting in passion's flames again. . . .

"STEAMY . . . FAST-PACED . . . a huge saga of families in conflict against a background of social change." —*Everywoman* magazine

"INTRIGUING . . . HOOKS YOU STRAIGHT IN . . . a good story with an excellent background history . . . people, places and events spring to life in detailed description." —*Ivybridge Gazette*

"AN ABSORBING SAGA OF FAMILY SECRETS AND REVENGE."—*Today*

NETTA MARTIN

World to Win, Heart to Lose

A SIGNET BOOK

SIGNET
Published by the Penguin Group
Penguin Books USA Inc., 375 Hudson Street,
New York, New York 10014, U.S.A.
Penguin Books Ltd, 27 Wrights Lane,
London W8 5TZ, England
Penguin Books Australia Ltd, Ringwood,
Victoria, Australia
Penguin Books Canada Ltd, 10 Alcorn Avenue,
Toronto, Ontario, Canada M4V 3B2
Penguin Books (N.Z.) Ltd, 182-190 Wairau Road,
Auckland 10, New Zealand

Penguin Books Ltd, Registered Offices:
Harmondsworth, Middlesex, England

Published by Signet, an imprint of Dutton Signet,
a division of Penguin Books USA Inc. First published in Great Britain by Penguin
Books Ltd. under the title *Tycoon*.

First Signet Printing, December, 1993
10 9 8 7 6 5 4 3 2 1

To John and Anne, for being a
marvelous son and daughter
—and my best friends.

ACKNOWLEDGMENTS

First and foremost I have to thank my husband Jack for all the years of love, laughter, and support.

A very special thanks to Peter Mayer of Penguin who suggested the idea for this book, commissioned it, and encouraged me through the long years of its creation. Thanks are due as well to editors Fanny Blake and Clare Alexander for their help and advice, and also to Pamela Norris and Maureen Rissik.

Although *World to Win, Heart to Lose* is a work of fiction it does have a historical background encompassing many varied events over the years 1930 to 1988. I owe a great debt to the following friends who checked my manuscript: Sir Eric Yarrow, formerly of Yarrow Shipbuilders, and past Chairman of the Clydesdale Bank; Professor Brian Baxter of Strathclyde University; Colin Brown, ex-Chairman of the Scottish Stock Exchange, and Colin Roebuck, former Senior Operations Supervisor, Shell Offshore.

I am also indebted to the following: John Wright, Operations Manager, Buchan Oil Field; Margaret Spencer, BP; Clive Callow, oil analyst; George Ritchie of Stonehaven for sharing with me his experiences with the Royal Naval Patrol Service during the war; Trevor Sprott, former Director of Physical Planning, Grampian Regional Council; Alan Campbell, Principal Economic Research Officer with Grampian Regional Council; Bruce Lenman, Lecturer in Scottish History, and Richard Saville, Lecturer in Economic History, both at the University of St Andrews; D. R. Dare, Deputy Chief Planner of the Scottish Development Department; Andrew Haigh; Douglas Cockburn; Ruby Turberville of Aberdeen; Henry Milne and the staff of the Aberdeen *Press and Journal*; historians, economists, and sociologists at the universities of Glasgow, Aberdeen, Edinburgh, and St Andrews; librarians in district libraries in Renfrewshire, Inverclyde, and Strathclyde, who went to an enormous amount of trouble to find the books I wanted; Rosemary Watt, Curator of the Burrell Collection, Pollok Country Park, Glasgow; and Baron and Baroness Leslie of Leslie Castle.

PART I

The Armstrongs: 1938-43

PROLOGUE

Alexandra Meldrum woke early in her penthouse apartment in New York. She switched on the light and saw it was only five o'clock. It was too early to get up, but she was too excited to go back to sleep. She pulled the silk sheet closer to her face and snuggled down under it. She loved warmth. Frank felt the same way. It was probably a legacy of their upbringing in the chilly north east of Scotland where they had run barefoot across the moors to save the cost of shoes.

Her lips curved in a smile at the thought of the half-brother who was so dear to her. Today was the day he was out on the North Sea platform with her daughter; she was glad Frank was there to protect her. Not that Catherine appeared to need protecting. Her columns in New York magazines and papers, and her television series in Britain were famed for their courage. Catherine's visit to one of the safest oil production platforms in the North Sea would make good copy.

As would Alexandra's takeover bid for Armstrongs. She could imagine the headlines already: "Crofter's daughter becomes one of the richest tycoons in the world." In the process she would destroy the only man she had ever loved . . . But why should she feel guilty? It was time Robert Armstrong paid the price for his double treachery all those years ago. Time all the Armstrongs paid for the misery they had caused the Meldrums.

Alexandra glanced at the clock calendar on the bedside table. Friday the thirteenth. The date did not worry her. She felt this was one of those times in her life when nothing could go wrong.

Later she was appalled at her lack of prescience.

ONE

Aberdeen, 4 August 1938

On the morning of the royal visit, William Armstrong had a precognitive flash of insight about the woman who was to become his mistress; in the moment between sleeping and waking it crossed his mind that his secretary might have an ulterior motive in pursuing him so assiduously. He had no way of knowing that his decision to dismiss that idea as absurd would have far-reaching repercussions in his own generation and the one that followed.

Since William was blissfully unaware of what the future held he smiled happily as he lay in bed and thought about his slim, red-headed secretary. She had told him that she had come to Aberdeen simply because she was tired of the rat race in London. He was immensely flattered at her obvious interest in him; she flirted, smiled at him provocatively, and brushed her breasts against him when she leant over his shoulder. She was a minx.

The previous day she'd whispered in his ear, "You've given the office a holiday tomorrow, William, but if you want to work for an hour or two, I'll come in and keep you company . . ." The seductive gleam in her eye had left him in no doubt about her meaning.

William felt himself hardening as he thought about it. Would he go? Of course not. He was a respectably married man . . . He turned round in bed and looked at his wife. He called Isobel his little wren because she was brown-haired, brown-eyed, and pleasantly plump. He'd first met her at a little nursery school which he and his brother Toby had attended. Toby, in his typically disruptive way, had poured paint on a drawing Isobel had done and William had rushed to console her. That was the beginning of a friendship which culminated in marriage, much to his brother's amusement. William frowned. He wouldn't think about Toby, not this morning.

William slipped out of bed, careful not to disturb his sleeping wife. He cast a critical glance at himself in the dressing-table mirror. Since he had turned 40 he had noticed a glint of gray in his dark hair and a thickening in his waist and buttocks, but he was still a fine figure of a man. Had to be. Otherwise young Margot wouldn't be trying to seduce him.

Reluctantly he tore his thoughts away from his exotic secretary and padded over to the window to see what the weather was like. Today was a very special day of celebration. Their Majesties King George VI and Queen Elizabeth and their two daughters were sailing into Aberdeen Harbor in their yacht, the *Victoria and Albert*. Since it had been twenty-four years since a royal yacht had graced the harbor with its presence, Aberdonians were concerned that the city should present its most flattering face.

"What's it like, William?" a sleepy voice asked. His wife was awake now and as anxious as anyone to hear the verdict on the weather.

"It's snowing."

Isobel Armstrong leapt out of bed and rushed to the window in dismay, only to see sunlight slanting on to dry pavements.

"William!"

"You have to admit it was a good way of wakening you. Why don't you hop back into bed?" he went on. "I'll bring breakfast up to you."

"You spoil me."

His conscience appeased, William bounded downstairs to the kitchen. When he had filled the kettle and put some bacon under the grill, he went to the front door and picked up the Aberdeen *Press and Journal*, and the *Glasgow Herald*. The headlines in 1937 had been dominated by the Spanish Civil War, but in 1938 the papers were concerned with Germany's avowed need for *"Lebensraum"*: living space. Adolf Hitler had declared at the Nuremberg rally the previous year that, without colonies, Germany's space was too small to guarantee that the people could be adequately fed. Since then he had annexed Austria and seemed to be looking towards Czechoslovakia, which Britain and France had made vague promises to defend in the event of its invasion. William grunted. Unlike some of the national papers, the *Glasgow Herald* was taking a stand against appeasement. He agreed with them.

"Do I smell bacon burning?" Isobel asked as he edged into their room with the breakfast on a tray.

"House next door. The man there is a terrible cook."

"And my man's a terrible liar! What's in the papers today?"

"The Czech problem and whether it will lead to war."

"I can't bear to think of another war. Are you worried about it?"

"Of course not." William smiled at Isobel reassuringly. He was old-fashioned and did not consider it a wife's place to discuss such things, but it so happened she was right: he was concerned about war and its consequences for the family business. During the Great War there had been a huge upsurge in demand for ships, and all the shipyards in Scotland had geared up their production to meet it. Unfortunately once the war was over the shipyards were saddled with too much equipment and too few orders.

"Oh William, no long faces today," Isobel complained as she finished her breakfast and began dressing. "For goodness' sake put away the papers and let's enjoy the royal visit. The boys have been looking forward to it. Where are they, by the way? The house seems unnaturally quiet."

"I heard them stealing out early on. Probably gone to see all the preparations."

II

The preparations for the royal visit had been extensive. For days workmen had been putting up flags and bunting in the city's main thoroughfares, but by midday it was the harbor area that was drawing the crowds. Matthews Quay where the royal barge would berth was barely recognizable. Its drab, functional face had been landscaped with palms, shrubs, and a decorated awning. Although it was barely twelve o'clock, hundreds of people from near and far had already gathered there and others lined the North Pier and Pocra Quay. Excitement and speculation mounted as the sun rose higher in the sky and the arrival of the royal yacht drew near.

Not all the citizens of Aberdeen were gathered by the quay. Across the navigation channel on the headland of Girdleness, crowds swarmed on the rocks, along the breakwater and on the greensward in front of the Old Torry Fort. Like many other families, the Armstrongs had chosen Greyhope Road as their vantage point.

"It's coming. There it is." Seven-year-old Robert Armstrong jumped up and down in excitement as he spotted a smudge on the horizon. Lean and dark, he was the mirror image of Adam, his twin brother. But, although the boys' physical appearance was almost identical, their characters were diametrically opposed and they seemed to spend most of their spare time arguing or fighting.

"That's a trawler," Adam said scornfully.

James at 17 was the eldest of the Armstrong brothers. He peered into the distance through his father's high-powered binoculars. "Take a look, father."

William Armstrong studied the shape on the horizon. "It's the royal yacht. Different shape altogether from a trawler," he added.

Adam flushed. He should have known. Trust Robert to get it right. Isobel Armstrong intercepted Adam's venomous glance at his brother and turned anxiously to her eldest son.

"Sibling rivalry," James whispered reassuringly.

Isobel smiled up at him, delighting in his golden good looks. James had left school and was about to take his place in the family business.

Scattered cheering broke out as the yacht came into sight, but it was restrained as if the spectators were holding back until the royal family could see them.

"In 1848 your great-grandfather watched Queen Victoria and Prince Albert sail into Aberdeen harbor in the first royal yacht," William said softly to his sons.

"You've told us about it before," Adam muttered.

"Not for a long time," Robert protested. "Anyway, I've forgotten," he added diplomatically. "Was the yacht like this one?"

"No, it was a wooden paddle steamer and the whole town

came out to see it. A salute was fired and the royal couple stepped ashore and passed under a triumphal arch . . ."

"And our great-grandfather was one of the people presented to the Queen," Robert interrupted.

William nodded. His grandfather had been the founder of Armstrongs, building ships and exporting a variety of goods to distant lands. Unfortunately he had been so enchanted by his fine sailing ships that he had failed to keep pace with the faster clippers being built by his rivals, the Meldrums, and eventually they had taken over his yard. In time the Armstrongs got it back again, but then the Meldrums won control of the Armstrong quarries and rebuilt Drumcraig Castle on Deeside, a ruin which the Armstrongs had always coveted. As the fortunes of the two families kept being reversed their hostility became more deeply entrenched. William had been 8 when Luke Armstrong had won possession of the Meldrum castle and moved his family into it.

Luke had been such a fierce, unyielding man that William had decided early on that the only way to survive was to appease his stern father. Toby had taken the opposite stance and consequently had never been out of trouble. He had been expelled from his school and arrested for stealing.

"Toby is no longer my son," their father had said vehemently. So why had he bequeathed Drumcraig Castle to Toby in his will? That was one mystery William had never been able to solve. When he had asked his brother about it Toby had laughed in his face and told him it served him right for being such a toady. Since then William had forbidden Toby's name to be mentioned by his family.

William became aware of Robert's hand tugging at his sleeve. "What's he saying father?"

William peered through his binoculars. The royal yacht had anchored and the harbor master was standing in a nearby lifeboat.

"The harbor master will be reading an address giving the city's birthday greetings to the Queen."

"She's not replying."

"She is. It's just that we can't hear her. Look, that's it finished."

The minutes of waiting seemed interminable and then the King and Queen followed by the two princesses stepped down the gangway to the royal barge which was positioned at its foot. As the barge came past the breakwater, the crowd roared their appreciation and frantically waved their flags. After the formalities of landing were over, the sound of cheering mingled with music as the royal family were ushered into their car and driven away. Their destination was Deeside and Balmoral Castle.

It was time for William to take his family home. He listened with only half an ear to their chattering as they trooped into his car. He couldn't stop thinking about his secretary. One phone call from his office and Margot would come running. Could he risk it? Would Isobel ever find out? William felt himself flushing and tried to concentrate on his driving.

The road to Aberdeen was like a room after a children's party: untidy, colorful and still charged with a lingering excitement. Bunting fluttered bravely in the wind, discarded papers and streamers blew along gutters, and children armed with flags waved them frantically whenever they spotted their friends.

The crowds made their progress a slow one. As the heat built up in the car William wound down the window and gazed out at Torry, the suburb of Aberdeen which was the center for trawl fishing. The residents of Torry were like an extended family with the wives helping to mend the nets and bait the lines for their menfolk. Footdee, or Fittie as it was called, was another fishing community which kept very much to itself.

William hadn't lived in either enclave, but he had served his time on a trawler to avoid working for his father. It was only when Luke Armstrong died that William abandoned his seagoing life to take his place in Armstrongs. Fortunately he proved to be a quick learner and when his acumen saved the firm from a disastrous whaling venture the board elected him Chairman. Immediately he started expanding the shipbuilding side of the business; a fortuitous move in view of the recent increase in orders as the Admiralty was preparing for war.

When a traffic jam caused the car to stop again the passengers groaned. William leaned on the wheel and wondered if he'd ever have the courage to seduce Margot Gossamer. James suggested taking a different route, the two younger boys started to argue, and Isobel declared that if she didn't get everyone out of the car, frustration would end up spoiling their happy day.

"Why don't we leave your father to it and walk the rest of the way home? You don't mind, William, do you?"

"No, of course not," he replied as a traitorous thought surfaced. This would be the ideal chance to slip into the office and summon Margot. The image of her long white legs danced in front of him, and he groaned. For a moment he thought of calling his wife back, but the words wouldn't come.

III

While Adam and Robert raced ahead to see if they could find any of their friends, James and his mother walked slowly up Market Street and turned into Union Street, the city's main thoroughfare. Even in bleak weather, Aberdeen's mile-long Union Street had a dignity and grandeur which commanded attention. Three- and four-story Regency houses formed the main facade, their elegance enhanced by the arched gateway and Doric columns of the Kirkyard of St. Nicholas.

The leaves of the trees which draped over the front of St. Nicholas were a fresh mint-green, and scarlet and pink roses blazed from unexpected corners. Isobel and James turned off Union Street to walk down the steps to the Terrace Gardens where Isobel stopped to catch her breath. They sat for a while on a bench, enjoying the sunshine. James mentioned a play being performed at His Majesty's Theater and suggested she might like to go to it. Isobel smiled contentedly. She had always felt a special affinity with her eldest son. Sometimes she caught herself imagining what it would be like to be married to someone like James. Were such thoughts incestuous? Briskly she decided they were not.

When they emerged from the comparative quiet of the Terrace Gardens back into Union Street Isobel and James were at once absorbed into a carnival atmosphere of sound and color.

"I wonder if your father's gone to the office," Isobel speculated. "The business is still doing well, isn't it?"

"Better than ever," James replied, as he admired the way the late afternoon sun shed an amber glow on the stately pillars of the Music Hall. "Father was telling me that since 1935 when the Defense White Paper signalled the start of rearming, shipyard orders have doubled."

Isobel looked back along Union Street and for a moment the faces, flowers and flags shimmered in the light like a mirage. Everyone said that all the young people were drifting south to the bright lights of London. She wondered if there would ever come a time when the trend would be reversed, but she doubted it. Aberdeen had limited appeal for the rest of the world.

When they came to the western end of Union Street they stopped to appreciate the view dominated by the castellated facade of Christ's College. As they approached Rubislaw Terrace they heard shouts of anger from behind the wall which separated the gardens from the road. "Sounds like Adam and Robert," Isobel said wearily. "Do go and see what they're up to."

She went into the house and ordered up afternoon tea from their housemaid before wandering through to the sitting room to read the papers. A little while later James came in. He looked angry. "Robert fell over and Adam was kicking him in the side—quite viciously! Adam has a nasty streak in his character."

"Let's hope he grows out of it," Isobel replied. She put the paper aside. "I'm not going to read any more, James; the news about a possible war is alarming."

"Don't worry," James said gently. "When Neville Chamberlain meets Adolf Hitler they're bound to come to an agreement."

Later when his mother had disappeared into the kitchen to see to the evening meal James lingered by the window, gazing out at the other houses in the terrace. Their gray, granite splendor seemed immutable, but James knew Aberdeen was changing as was the rest of Scotland. If war broke out these changes would accelerate. He had reassured his mother's fears about war with a platitude. There would be thousands dispensing similar platitudes throughout the country. Truth can be a hammer, he thought, but when the future is a sheet of glass which might be shattered at any moment, it isn't a hammer you want to hold in your hand. In this summer of 1938, evasion of truth was becoming a national pastime. His father had remarked on that fact the other evening when they were alone together.

James looked at the clock on the mantelpiece. His father really shouldn't work so hard.

IV

When William Armstrong's family had extricated themselves from his car earlier that afternoon, he had felt a charge of excitement that had nothing to do with the royal visit. There was a frenetic atmosphere in Aberdeen, but he felt detached from it. Everyone outside seemed to crave a communal joy, whereas he wanted to crawl like a snail into a shell where he could be alone with his anticipation of seeing Margo.

At the junction at the top of Market Street the traffic was at its busiest. To his left, Union Street marched graciously to the west end. His family would be walking along there at this very moment, but he felt detached from them as well. He flicked his indicator to the right and as the traffic started moving again he drove along the east end of Union Street past Shiprow and the Athenaeum. This was old Aberdeen, his favorite section of the city, and he looked towards the lead-covered spire of the Tolbooth and tried to imagine what it must have been like to have been imprisoned there in the seventeenth century. He was glad the building had been preserved. He much preferred the ancient steeple of the Tolbooth to the taller one of the Town House to the west of it.

When he drew up outside the office he noticed that his hands were trembling. Inexperienced hands, he acknowledged nervously as he climbed the stairs. The only woman he had known in the biblical sense of the word was his wife. That thought halted his steps on the stair, and he mopped his brow with his hanky. His wife's well-rounded body was as familiar to him as his own. She was a compliant partner, but she had never shown much interest in the sexual side of marriage and for a long time now he had been able to find sexual fulfillment only by visualizing another body beneath his own: a mysterious woman who would thrill to his touch and would fire his own eroticism. The mysterious siren beckoning him to undreamt-of delights had never had a face until Margot Gossamer walked into his life.

He continued up the stairs in a dream and opened the door

to the main office: it was empty. He was conscious of the
silent typewriters and empty work spaces as he walked past
them towards his office. As he pushed open the door, shock
waves rippled up and down his body. Margot Gossamer was
standing by the window. She was wearing a black skirt and a
high-necked Victorian blouse, a demure outfit which was totally at variance with her glinting blue eyes and the wild tumble of red hair which cascaded round her shoulders.

"I had a feeling you would come today," she said lightly as
she moved towards him: past the antique desk with its tele-
phones, past the stand where he hung his hat and coat, and on
to the chaise longue which he had brought into the office to
give it a more furnished look. He watched as Margot sat down
and kicked off her shoes. "I wonder if you could help me," she
said softly. "A strand of my hair seems to be tangled up in the
top button of my blouse. Look . . ."

Hypnotized, he walked forward to where she was sitting.

"I'm sure you can undo it for me," she breathed as he bent
over her.

But he couldn't. The knot of hair was wound round so
tightly that it resisted his efforts.

"Try undoing the other buttons," she said calmly. "That
might help."

With fingers that suddenly seemed to be made of cloth he
did as she suggested and freed her hair. A second shock went
through his system as he realized she was wearing nothing underneath her blouse. His fingers touched velvet skin and erect
nipples.

Margot smiled up at him and he saw that she had planned it
this way. Anger fuelled by guilt swept away his hesitation. He
tore off her blouse and pushed her roughly back on the couch.
As their lips met he felt her undressing him: unfastening his
trousers, taking off his shirt, pulling at his underpants. Then
she moved under him and eased off her skirt and underwear.
After that he was hardly conscious of what she was doing because by then he was fondling her breasts and pushing himself
into the golden-red patch of hair between her thighs.

"We've plenty of time, William," she whispered.

But he was beyond caution. He was driven by demons
which made him press faster and more fiercely until his juices
exploded inside her. His heart pounded against her chest as he

clasped her tightly to him, his senses dizzy with pleasure. He heaved a great sigh of satisfaction, exulting in his feeling of virility.

V

Margot lay curled in William's arms, irritated by the narrowness of the chaise longue and the restrictions imposed by it. Still, it had served its purpose. As she saw the sated look on William's face her eyebrows rose. My God, he had a lot to learn; he was obviously used to satisfying himself with no thought for his partner.

"I feel so ashamed," he said in a muffled voice. Margot's lips curled. She'd soon fix his guilt. With an expert twist of her body she reversed their positions so that she was the one on top. She murmured in his ear and began stroking the hairs on his chest and under his arms. Her fingers moved lower to his thighs and legs, and she drew her scarlet-painted nails lightly across the surface of his skin. Then she bent forward and fastened her mouth on the hardness at his center, amused by his shocked expression as she moved down on him. Obviously William's notions of sex were old-fashioned; the missionary position every time.

He tried to push her away, but as she massaged him in her mouth and tickled the pouches beneath his penis she could feel him casting aside his doubts and giving himself up to a pleasure she sensed he'd never experienced before. "Aaah!" he cried. "Oh God, don't stop!"

She didn't stop until his seed gushed into her mouth. He shouted out in excitement before falling back exhausted. Margot stretched like a cat, luxuriating in her powers. As she turned on the chaise longue her eye was caught by the photograph of William's wife on his desk. She was a plump country girl. Unimportant. Why on earth did people bind themselves in marriage, Margot wondered idly. It was no part of her plan. She had other ambitions.

Two

I

November 1938

William moaned in ecstasy and then cried out in despair. He was making love to his secretary on the drawing-room floor of a friend's house and his wife had just walked in.

"William, it's time to get up. William, William, William . . ." He felt a hand shaking his shoulder and opened his eyes. He was lying in his own bed in his own house and his wife was bending over him. "It's not like you to sleep in when you're going out on the trawlers. Were you dreaming? Or was it a nightmare?"

That was the problem. In his relationship with Margot Gossamer he found himself unable to distinguish between the two. The passionate coupling in his office on the day of the royal visit to Aberdeen had proved to be the first of many. William had to laugh at his original concern about how to handle an affair. It was always Margot who arranged the time and place, and she delighted in seducing him in places where he would normally never have dreamt of making love: the office, a friend's house, a country park. Yet although he was alarmed at her lack of caution he was also aware that the danger sharpened the edge of their appetite.

He showered, shaved and hurried downstairs to the kitchen. Isobel put a plate of bacon and eggs on the table as he drew up his chair.

"It's not too late to change your mind," she said.

"All our skippers are committed. Besides, I want to go."

That at least was true. It would be a relief to be away from his mistress for twelve days. Lately Margot had begun pestering him about promotion. Some weeks after their affair had begun she had persuaded him to make her his personal assistant. He had realized then that she was ambitious, but the scale of her ambition wasn't revealed until she confided that she would eventually like a seat on the board. When he had dismissed her suggestion out of hand she had shown her claws: a menacing hint about what his wife would say if she found out about them.

His appetite gone, William pushed aside his unfinished plate of bacon and eggs, and excused himself from the table. He picked up his kit bag and made for the front door.

"Aren't you going to kiss me goodbye?" Isobel exclaimed.

He bent and kissed her on the cheek, but when she hugged him and whispered, "I love you. Good luck!" he drew back. It was unbearable to have such unqualified warmth and sympathy from the woman he was betraying.

II

At the harbor he stood for a moment enjoying the tang from the sea breeze before continuing his walk towards Point Law where the trawlers were berthed. Although catches had improved in the last year or so and Aberdeen was still one of the top ports in Britain for high-quality white fish, the trawling fleet of 1938 was on the edge of obsolescence. Many of the old trawlers had to confine themselves to the north-east coast and their owners were reporting daily that these seas were overfished. What was a fishing port to do if there weren't enough fish in the sea anymore? There was no other industry that could bring a similar prosperity to a city like Aberdeen. Nor could anyone foretell what effect a war would have on the trawling fleet. It was the worsening situation in Europe that was making William take an occasional trip in one of his own trawlers. One of the conditions of being in the Royal Naval Reserves was that he had to maintain his seagoing skills; he had to be fit to take command in the event of war.

William cursed as he stumbled on some wooden crates piled on the dockside and headed towards the *Clarion*, the trawler he was skippering. There were 255 steam trawlers in Aberdeen; the *Clarion* was one of the newer ones. William was proud of her. The next few hours were spent checking and servicing equipment and gear, and taking on food, ice and fuel until they were ready to sail out on the flood-tide.

The crew's first task at sea was to prepare the huge net which was kept open by trawl doors: wooden boards shod with iron to scrape along the sea bottom. Steel warps connected the otter boards to the trawler and there was a complicated system of ropes which ensured that the fish would be trapped in the net. This was hauled to the surface by a powerful winch. Preparing the net, ropes, pulleys, and winching gear were important tasks and William made sure his crew carried them out efficiently.

The trawler began to roll when she met the first heavy swell caused by a stiffening wind, but William was not concerned. A steam trawler was designed to have the maneuverability of a tug and the sea-keeping qualities of a lightship.

The *Clarion* had been steaming for a few days when William sensed they were nearing the fishing grounds. Gulls were wheeling overhead and there was an air of mounting expectancy on board. Suddenly the trawler was "on fish," and contemplation was at an end. The *Clarion* was broadside on to the wind and rolling so heavily that the bulwarks were nearly under water, but after endless minutes the otter boards came up over the side, followed by the net which spilled its silver harvest the minute the cod end was released.

The gear was shot again, and the crew settled down to gutting and sorting the fish and packing it in ice. Shooting, hauling, gutting, sorting: as soon as one cycle finished it was time to begin another.

As suddenly as they had come the fish disappeared. As skipper, it was William's decision whether to steam to another patch or wait it out in the hope the fish would come back. The stiff breeze became a gale and as it worsened William decided to take a chance and shoot the trawl in the hope that the plunging waves would push the fish into the net. It was a reckless decision, but in trawling such recklessness can reap rewards. William shouted in triumph when his gamble paid off. The deckhands grinned at each other, delighted that the skipper hadn't lost his touch.

Twelve days after departure the *Clarion* steamed back to Aberdeen with her hold full of fish. The trip had been one of the most successful of the year and William felt so exhilarated by the experience that he had difficulty settling down to work in the office. Margot, sensing his elation, suggested celebrating his return by having lunch at the Palace Hotel. Normally he avoided being seen alone in public with Margot, but at this moment he felt in no mood for caution. Anyway, even if someone told Isobel that her husband was being unfaithful she wouldn't believe it.

III

Isobel was at the hairdresser's in Aberdeen when she discovered her husband had a mistress. She was sitting under one of the hair dryers which was facing away from the counter and she had pushed the hood back so that she could cool off for a while. Idly, she picked up a newspaper and then became aware of voices chattering at the counter; a backward glance revealed two typists who worked at Armstrongs. She hadn't seen them having their hair done and concluded they must have popped in to buy a beauty product.

The receptionist wasn't at her counter and the two girls seemed to be enjoying a good gossip.

"You should have heard the row Margot Gossamer gave me this morning because I was ten minutes late," one of the girls complained. "Just because she's William Armstrong's mistress she thinks she can lord it over the rest of us!"

"I don't know what he sees in her," the other girl replied. "She's built like a beanpole."

"Must be a comfy beanpole; that affair's been going on for months! It's the wife I feel sorry for!" the first girl replied as the receptionist returned. Having justified their malice with feigned compassion the girls bought some shampoo and left the shop.

Isobel shrank into her seat, her cheeks burning. How dare they suggest her husband was having an affair. William would never be unfaithful to her.

"I think you're dry now, Mrs. Armstrong."

Isobel walked tightlipped over to the dressing-out cubicle.

"Are you all right? You look a bit peaky." Peggy, the hairdresser, sounded concerned.

"I'm feeling a little faint, Peggy. If you could just finish me off quickly . . ."

It seemed an age before she was able to pay her bill and stumble out into King Street. The buildings glistened in the pale winter sun, but Isobel looked at them through a haze, her mind frantically trying to find a way out, something that would convince her there was no truth in the typists' gossip. Instead she remembered that her husband hadn't made love to her in months. Had drawn away from her when she'd hugged him before his fishing trip. Hadn't even bothered to give her a card or present on her birthday in August this year. Come to think of it he hardly ever suggested an evening out. An overload of work at Armstrongs had been William's excuse and she had accepted it. Like many wives she was always more concerned about assuaging her husband's guilt than expressing her own hurt.

She thought about the typists' gossip and decided it was the jigsaw syndrome in reverse. Usually the last piece in a jigsaw completes the picture, but in this case that one fragment had instantly drawn all the others together.

When William arrived home that evening she felt like hurling accusations at him, but instinct warned her that confrontation might be playing into Margot's hands. She would have to be much more cunning if she wanted to keep her husband. For the next few days she wandered about the house not knowing what to do with herself. Her younger sons sensed her strange mood and kept out of her way, but James, the child of her heart, was concerned about her gloom.

"What's wrong, mother?" he asked one evening when he found her staring into the fire.

"Headaches, that's all. Come and sit down and tell me what you're doing at the office these days."

As he talked she thought about Margot Gossamer. William didn't have film-star looks and he was old enough to be Margot's father, so why had she fastened on him? Was she using William to secure further advancement in Armstrongs?

"Mother! You've asked me to talk about the office and you're not even listening."

"I am. How did you learn so much about the business so quickly?"

"Years of listening to table talk; I must have absorbed more

than I imagined. And of course father has been coaching me at
every opportunity. I've been groomed for the job."

An idea began to form in Isobel's head. Perhaps she too had
absorbed more than she imagined about the business. Perhaps
she too could be "groomed for the job" . . . "James, didn't you
mention that your father had written a series of articles for a
shipbuilding magazine about Armstrongs? Telling how it
began, what's happening now, future prospects . . ."

"I didn't know you were so interested."

"I wasn't, but now . . . What would you say if I asked you to
give me business tuition every moment you can spare?"

"Why on earth would you want to do that? It's not as if
you'll ever work in Armstrongs."

"If war broke out the firm would be short-staffed. I could
make myself useful." And if war broke out and she had secured a niche for herself in Armstrongs she might be in a position to oust her husband's personal assistant. The idea of
giving Margot Gossamer her comeuppance might sustain her
in the months ahead.

She hadn't thought of a way of doing it yet. But she would.

IV

William and Isobel were lying in bed musing over a very satis-
factory Christmas Day. The food and festivities had put
William in a benign mood, but he was jolted out of it when
Isobel stunned him by announcing that she wanted to start
working at Armstrongs in the New Year. William couldn't
have been more surprised if she'd suggested dancing naked in
the streets. His wife had always seemed perfectly contented
looking after her home and bringing up her children. "What
about the twins?" he asked.

"They're at school all day and they always seem to have
something on afterwards. Anyway, I can arrange to be home
before they are."

"But you don't know anything about the business."

"Oh yes I do! I asked James to start coaching me a few
weeks ago. The Personnel Department is the one that interests
me. I think you'd be surprised at how well informed I am."

William felt a tremor of unease. Did she know about Margot? Did James? Neither of them had given any indication that they suspected him of infidelity. No, no, he thought, Isobel can't know about Margot; otherwise she'd be having hysterics instead of calmly discussing her job prospects.

"Ask me about Personnel," she said.

"Isobel, it's late. Let's go to sleep."

But she wouldn't, so he humored her by quizzing her about the Personnel Department. He was astonished by her knowledge of the way the department was run.

"One of the girls in Personnel is leaving after Christmas," Isobel said carefully. "I know you're still looking for a replacement. Please, William, give me a chance. Don't I deserve it?"

Her innocent remark stung like an arrow and before she went to sleep he agreed to give her the job.

Isobel started at the office on 1 January 1939 and showed such an astonishing aptitude for the job that she was soon promoted within the department. The only person who wasn't pleased by Isobel's rapid progress was Margot Gossamer. She had begun by thinking the whole idea a huge joke that would embarrass William. When the reverse proved the case and praises were heaped upon Isobel's head for her tact and diplomacy, Margot became shrewish and tried to denigrate Isobel's efforts. This made William angry, but Margot always knew how to charm him back into a better humor.

V

By the summer of 1939 Hitler had made Czechoslovakia part of the German Empire. The British Prime Minister stated that war would break out if Germany invaded Poland, but no one expected this to check Adolf Hitler's rapacious appetite for conquest. Preparations for war accelerated. The iron and steel industries were working flat out, the Clyde shipyards once again rang with the sound of riveters, and the armed forces extended their field of recruitment. James Armstrong was about to sign on with the Gordon Highlanders, and William now had a command in the Royal Naval Patrol Service.

A few days before William went to sea, he arranged to meet Margot Gossamer at an empty cottage on Deeside. It was owned by a gamekeeper who had left the day before to join the army. William brought champagne and smoked salmon and they sat on the rug in front of the fire feasting, drinking, and making love. It was when Margot was impaled on his penis that she murmured in his ear that she was determined to sit on the board as well as on him.

"You're outrageous!" he gasped in his moment of orgasm. And of course she was. But she was also in deadly earnest and impatient about his continued prevarication. He promised that he would discuss appointing her to the board of Armstrongs the first time he came home on leave. He dreaded the thought of it because he sensed that once Margot became a director of Armstrongs she would start making life unpleasant for the people she disliked. Like his wife. He didn't want that. He lusted after his mistress, but he loved his wife. It was bad enough that he was betraying Isobel; he didn't want her humiliated at the office into the bargain. Yet what was he to do? Margot was determined to become a director of his company.

The night before he left William took his wife out for dinner at the Caledonian Hotel in Aberdeen. Isobel was radiant and William couldn't help congratulating himself on the way he juggled the demands of wife and mistress and kept them both happy.

"I've slimmed down and smartened up, haven't I, William?" Isobel said as they left the dining room and went into the lounge to have coffee and liqueurs.

"Yes," he said absently, "you look very nice. I've been thinking . . . I'm not too happy about you working at Armstrongs. War's going to break out any day now and I think you'd be safer at home. I mean you've done marvelously well, but . . ." His voice trailed off as he saw the resentment in his wife's brown eyes. "Tell you what, let's forget about business and talk about your birthday. You've been keeping me in suspense about what you want as a present."

He smiled at her benevolently. Isobel had announced that she wasn't going to tell him until they finished their meal and had added mischievously that at least he would be feeling mellow, when he heard what she wanted.

"I can see you're going to spin this out till the very last

minute. So, Isobel, what's it to be? A fur coat? A gold necklace? You can have anything you want."

"Promise?"

He promised. He felt it would be a relief if she asked for something extravagant; it might appease his conscience about his ongoing affair with Margot. His wife put down her coffee cup and cleared her throat a little nervously. "For my birthday I'd like a sizeable parcel of Armstrong shares, and a seat on the board as Director of Personnel. That's James's job and he'll be leaving it soon to join up."

William choked on his coffee, then burst out laughing. "For a moment there I thought you were serious."

"I am."

"But my dear . . ." He leaned across the coffee table and clasped her hand. "You're simply not qualified."

"Neither was James. He was given the job after he proved to have a flair for it."

"I couldn't praise your work too highly," William said quickly, "but you can't compare yourself with James. I gave him a sizeable parcel of shares to ensure the family are in control of stock. His shares gave him priority."

"As mine will do," Isobel replied tartly. "Why d'you think I'm asking for them? Ours is still a family business and the largest shareholders have the power. You can't deny that when you and James have each gone to war Armstrongs will need another board member."

William signalled the waiter to bring him a brandy and tried to keep calm. He would have to choose his next words very carefully.

"I'll concede you have a claim, but there are others who have a stronger one. Take Margot Gossamer for example; she's been with Armstrongs for a long time now. For the past year she's been my personal assistant. I rather think the board would prefer . . ."

"I have a confession to make," Isobel interrupted. "As the Chairman's wife I'm in a privileged position. So . . . I decided to use that position to lobby the board. Would it surprise you to hear that although the board respect Margot Gossamer they don't like her arrogance? If it comes to a vote, I'll win. I've checked."

For a moment William was too startled to speak. Imagine Isobel canvassing his board . . . Christ, it was incredible!

"Let's talk about this some other time," he said irritably and began to rise from his seat.

"No, William, we decide it now—if you want me to come home with you, that is."

"What on earth d'you mean?"

"I mean that I'll move out of our home tomorrow if you make the wrong choice. It's Margot or me, William," she added softly.

Dear God, he thought, appalled by the hurt in her eyes. "How long have you known?" he asked, his voice thick.

"Months."

William threw out his hands. "So why did you keep quiet about it?"

"I thought you might get tired of her; that the affair would fizzle out."

"I'm leaving tomorrow," William said desperately. "I don't have time to organize anything."

"Yes, you do. You can phone our lawyer to arrange the share transfer and James already has your proxy vote."

"He knows too? About Margot?"

"Yes."

"Bloody hell!" William muttered. What a mess. The sooner he was out of it the better. "Welcome to the future member of the board!" he said in a resigned voice and bent forward to kiss her. "By the way," he added, "how do you intend to deal with Margot? Have you thought about that?"

"I've been thinking of little else for the past ten months," Isobel murmured. "Was it Francis Bacon who said that revenge was a kind of wild justice?"

William shuddered. He couldn't imagine what Isobel had planned for Margot, but he was glad he wasn't going to be around when it happened.

VI

Isobel's appointment was confirmed at a board meeting chaired by her son, James, acting temporarily as his father's deputy. Isobel asked if her appointment could be kept secret for another week. A few eyebrows were raised, but no one objected. After all, as well as being William's wife Isobel had become the second-largest shareholder. It all added up to a position of power.

After the meeting was over James took her to one side. "Mother, I realize you have every reason to loathe Margot, but if you sack her she'll probably sue for wrongful dismissal."

Isobel smiled. "Don't worry, James, there are more ways of skinning a cat . . ."

VII

Margot Gossamer was humming as she walked along Union Street towards the office. Before William had sailed he had promised to discuss her promotion to company director the first time he came home on leave. Once a directorship was secured she'd work to strengthen her position on the board. There was no reason why she shouldn't go even higher . . . William was so dazzled by her she could manipulate him into doing anything she wanted. Margot's lips curled. Men were such easy game. She was able to rouse William to such heights of passion that he couldn't refuse her anything. He'd even given her an extra week's holiday so that she could go down to London to shop.

As she pushed open the swing doors of Armstrongs she saw James in the foyer.

"Margot, I've been looking out for you." James draw her aside and spoke in a whisper. "I've got a bit of news: a new member of the board has just been appointed. The vote was unanimous, by the way. The announcement will take place at noon."

Margot's cheeks flushed with pleasure. Dear William! He'd been so eager to please he had brought her promotion forward. James grasped her arm and led her along the corridor till they were standing outside her room. "As you know I'm Acting Chairman in my father's absence and cousin Harry will take over when I enlist."

"Yes, yes, I'm very well aware of that," Margot replied irritably. Really, at times James was a bit thick!

"I must talk to you about your new position in the firm,"

James went on, "but I have to attend a meeting and I won't be free till eleven. I'll leave you to your own devices till then."

Margot was amused to see that someone had put a "Do Not Disturb" sign outside her room. She pushed the door open and automatically threw her shoulder bag towards the occasional table which stood in the corner. It wasn't there . . . As she bent to pick up her bag she noticed the dove-gray carpet and the pink walls. Everything was new: all the furniture, the furnishings . . . Margot steadied herself against the desk and rubbed her eyes as she looked at the framed photograph of William and Isobel and their three sons which took pride of place on her desk.

"Quite a transformation, isn't it?" a voice said from the doorway.

Margot whirled round and found herself facing Isobel Armstrong. She looked at her critically, taking in the smart suit and the slimmed figure.

"The board decided that their newest member should have a newly decorated room," Isobel said pleasantly. "I organized it."

Margot's lips curled. "Thank you, but I'd have preferred to do it myself. The decor is . . . rather dated. And I'm afraid I don't care for a family photograph on my desk."

"Don't you? It's one of my favorites." Isobel walked round the desk and sat down in the chair behind it. She leaned back, testing her weight. "Very comfortable. Margot, you'll have to excuse me, I have a lot of work to do."

"Well, do it in your own room," Margot said rudely.

Isobel's brown eyes stared back at her. "But Margot, this *is* my room. I was appointed Personnel Director a week ago. The official announcement is at noon. Didn't James mention it? I asked him to look out for you at reception."

"*You* asked him!" Margot exclaimed, her cheeks flaming. "I just don't believe this is happening. Before he left William promised me the post of Personnel Director."

Isobel tapped her pen on the blotting paper. "Yes, I rather gathered that. But company chairmen *do* change their minds if a more suitable candidate arises."

"And you're more suitable than me?" Margot hooted. "Don't make me laugh. The board . . ."

"Have already made their decision," Isobel intervened, "and

it was unanimous. I particularly asked James to mention that to you."

Margot sat down heavily on the chair which stood in front of the big desk. She'd been set up. The little bitch had planned every part of it and was enjoying the prospect of giving her the push. Well, she wouldn't get away with it.

"If you sack me I'll sue," she threatened.

Isobel raised her eyebrows in surprise. "You're so good at your job, Margot, I have no intention of sacking you. Though your title does present a few problems . . . James and Harry each have excellent secretaries of their own."

"I was much more than a secretary to your husband!"

"Indeed you were," Isobel repled coldly. "Let's just say that the services you gave William won't be required by the new chairman."

"How dare you!" Margot exclaimed as she stood up. "I presume that you've finally found out that I'm William's mistress."

"*Was* William's mistress," Isobel said softly. "From now on you'll find that your role is confined to the office. Talking of which, you have a choice: you can either use the room along the corridor where I've put all your belongings . . ."

"That cubbyhole next to the men's toilet!" Margot shrieked. "You couldn't swing a cat in there. I wouldn't *dream* of using it."

"Then we'll find you a chair in the typing pool."

"You'd like to see me relegated back to the typing pool, wouldn't you?" Margot said viciously. She picked up a piece of paper on Isobel's desk and scribbled on it furiously. Her eyes were wild, her cheeks flushed. "There!" she shouted, throwing her resignation on Isobel's blotter. "You thought you'd have the pleasure of gloating over me, didn't you? Well, I have no intention of playing into your hands."

"But that's exactly what you have done!" Isobel murmured to herself as Margot stormed out. She allowed herself a congratulatory smile as she surveyed her room and contemplated Margot's comeuppance, but as her eyes strayed to the photograph of William on her desk some of the lightness went from her heart. William was on patrol in the North Atlantic and that morning in the news she had heard that the prospect of war was increasingly likely. She prayed fervently that William's trawler would not be a U-boat target.

THREE

I

It was dawn. The U-boat was no longer registering on the asdic, but William sensed it was still there, lurking somewhere beneath the gray waters of the Atlantic. It would be waiting for a convoy, or at least something more worthy of its attention than the *Topaz*, the battered old trawler which William had commanded since the outbreak of war three months before.

The *Topaz* was part of the Northern Patrol, a unique fleet of ships which had been requisitioned to detonate floating mines, challenge all ships and keep a lookout for the submarines which had started harassing the Atlantic convoys. Initially this task had been assigned to merchant cruisers, but it had taken too heavy a toll of them. Within weeks of the outbreak of war nine merchantmen had been torpedoed and the War Office decided to replace them with converted drifters, whalers, paddle steamers, and fishing trawlers like the *Topaz*. They formed the strangest assortment of fighting ships in the world. Most were weather-beaten, garishly painted, and armed with ancient guns which had been used in the First World War.

Officers in the Royal Navy were almost as disparaging about the Northern Patrol as their German counterparts. The men commanding the ships were mainly trawler skippers like William Armstrong, but the crew comprised a motley mix of civilians and fishermen who thumbed their noses at Royal Navy regulations and turned up for work wearing tea-cozy hats and jackets that looked like jumble-sale discards.

William's crew on *Topaz* were no exception, but he counted himself lucky because several of his men had worked on Armstrong trawlers and were used to the rough seas of the North Atlantic. Like most fishermen the men on *Topaz* were superstitious and wouldn't have dreamed of sailing without the presence of their lucky mascot, an ill-favored black cat rejoicing in the name of Princess. The crew were so concerned for her safety that they had blown up a Durex and tied it around her neck as a lifejacket.

William glanced down at the cat. She had coiled herself in a tight ball at the feet of Lofty, his first mate, who was standing on the bridge beside him. Princess might need her lifejacket today: the seas were swelling ominously. William and his mate had to brace their feet against the bridge as the trawler bucked and rolled like a rodeo seahorse attempting to unseat her rider. Neither was concerned about the ship's stability. Fishing trawlers had been specifically designed to withstand anything the sea could throw at them—another plus in their favor as patrol boats.

William scanned the horizon with his binoculars and swore as he saw the periscope of a U-boat surfacing briefly before disappearing below the waves. Lofty had seen it too. "Didn't show on the asdic, skipper." William cursed loudly once more. If the asdic wasn't working his orders were specific: proceed to the nearest port for repairs. Lofty handed him a map and they pored over it for a few minutes before William stabbed his finger at the Faroe Islands. "We'll have to make for Thorshavn."

"Aye, so we will," Lofty replied laconically.

Nothing ever worried his first mate, William mused, as he studied the map in more detail. Lofty led a charmed life and in the three months they'd been together on the *Topaz* there hadn't been a single incident. But even as this consoling thought flashed through his mind, a gigantic wave rolled over the trawler and the cat which had skittered through the door of the bridge suddenly disappeared over the edge of the boat.

"Princess!" Lofty yelled, his legendary calm disappearing in a moment. He rushed to the edge of the trawler's deck and peered anxiously down at the water, but there was no trace of the animal—nor any hope of finding her. The cat's Durex lifejacket would be useless in the mountainous waves.

Lofty's face was gray. "Our luck's run out!" he cried.

"Shut up!" William yelled, but from the furrowed brows of the rest of the crew it was evident they agreed with the first mate. Despite the roaring noise of wind and waves the atmosphere on *Topaz* was muted as she sailed towards Thorshavn.

As the trawler rose on the crest of another huge wave there

was a yell from the lookout and all eyes turned towards the islands looming ahead: volcanic pillars enclosing precipitous bays. *Topaz* signalled her identity to the coastal stations and repeated an earlier signal about the sighting of the U-boat. It looked as if the entrance to Thorshavn had already been swept for mines because *Topaz* was given permission to steam into the harbor where a freighter was already at anchor. Close by was her watchdog, a naval corvette nearly three times the size of *Topaz*.

Under other circumstances the crew might have felt enlivened by this unexpected call at the Faroes, but the disappearance of their lucky mascot bit deep into their superstitious psyches and hardly anyone smiled or talked. Ridiculous to act like this, William thought angrily, it was only an ugly old cat! But as the long hours passed whilst the experts repaired the asdic his uneasiness increased. There was an immediate lightening of the atmosphere when the repairs were finished and the *Topaz* chugged her way out of the harbor closely followed by the freighter and the corvette.

Topaz was veering to starboard when alarm bells sounded out like klaxon calls from hell. A U-boat had been sighted and the crew guessed the freighter would be the target.

"Jesus Christ!" the lookout exclaimed in horror. William's throat convulsed with fear as he realized that the *Topaz* was between the freighter and the submarine. His trawler was going to catch the full force of one of the torpedoes which had been aimed at the freighter. William wrestled with the controls of the *Topaz*, but the trawler was built for strength not for quick maneuvering and he watched aghast as the white streak of foam in the water came closer and closer.

"Abandon ship!" he yelled and moments later the torpedo slammed into the side of the trawler and blew her out of the water. The noise of the explosion was punctuated by the tearing sound of metal, fractured pipes, hissing steam, and terrified screams.

William felt himself sink below the waves. When he surfaced he saw other men floating nearby.

"Are you all right, Mac?" he yelled as he recognized his engineer. When Mac made no response, William swam over to him and then drew back in shock. The engineer was already dead, as were the lookout and the sparks.

"Skipper!" a voice yelled. William swivelled around in the water and to his relief he saw his second-in-command floating towards him. "Look, skipper, the corvette's coming straight towards us!"

"Rescue," William thought dazedly before the awful truth dawned. He forced himself up in the water and yelled at the top of his voice: "Lofty! Everyone! Get out of the corvette's way. It's laying depth charges!"

In a situation like this the Admiralty's ruling was precise: the enemy must be destroyed regardless of survivors. The corvette was obeying orders and trying to sink the U-boat by laying a pattern of depth charges. William remembered someone describing the effect of depth charges on men swimming or floating in their vicinity: brains and stomachs spilling into the sea, balls feeling as if they'd been kicked by a Clydesdale horse.

"My legs don't work," Lofty screamed. William grabbed him and tried to keep his head above water as he steered them both away from the oncoming corvette. He caught a glimpse of a life raft bobbing on the waves. If he could get to it they might still have a chance.

"Hold on!" he shouted desperately as he felt his second-in-command slipping from his grasp, but the wash from the corvette swept Lofty out of his arms and he disappeared. A moment later an explosion from a depth charge erupted close by. William felt every one of his organs shudder as his body was catapulted out of the water. Through a red-rimmed mist he saw that he had been thrown near a floating spar. He reached out and hauled himself up on to it and it was at that precise moment that he looked down in the water and saw Lofty's fragmented body strewn on the waves like pieces of firewood. William retched violently and felt his hands losing their grasp on the floating wreckage, but by then he was beyond caring what had happened to him.

II

"Use your knife and fork," Isobel said angrily as she came into the room and saw the Karmigan brothers eating the bacon with their fingers. "I keep telling you to mind your manners."

"I know, missus, you go on and on. Dead boring, so it is!"

Having delivered their verdict the two evacuees from Glasgow continued to stuff the bacon into their mouths with their fingers.

"Missus, ye look awful no weel; I'll pour you a cuppa."

"No!" Isobel shrieked as Billy reached for the teapot. She was learning that whenever Billy Karmigan offered his services they should be refused. The last time he had lifted the teapot he had spilled its contents over her new carpet. The stain was still there. Isobel was beginning to regret the impulse that had prompted her to offer lodgings to evacuees. There were hundreds of city children whom she would have found perfectly acceptable; it was her bad luck that she had been given the Karmigan brothers.

Initially the Karmigans, like many of the evacuees, had been given lodgings at a cottage on Deeside. Billy and Lennie had taken one look at the rolling green acres and been appalled when they discovered them empty of football posts. There was room for ten Rangers and Celtic teams. So where were all the people? When the farmer and his wife pointed out the cows the brothers summed up the situation in four words: "Cows can't kick footballs." The Karmigans decided there was no future for them in the country and ran away.

They were caught, brought back and immediately ran away again. They explained that they were trying to get to Aberdeen. None of the children there had been evacuated since the town had been designated a "neutral area," and the Karmigans had decided this was where they wanted to stay.

Isobel heard of their plight through the WVS and offered to take the evacuees into her home. On the first day with the Armstrongs the Karmigan brothers were aghast when they saw that Isobel had laid out fresh clothes for them. They explained to her that in Glasgow they were sewn into their clothes at the beginning of winter and did not wash properly till the following spring.

"No wonder you smell to the heavens!" Isobel cried. Nor was she mollified when she was told by the WVS that the Karmigans had been brought up by a granny who could not afford new clothes and no doubt that's why she had resorted to the working-class tradition of "sewing-up."

"It's the most disgusting idea I've ever heard!" Isobel exclaimed.

Billy and Lennie were amazed when they heard "sewing-up" wasn't a custom practiced in Aberdeen, but they were happy because the place was full of people and there were several football clubs. The boys were so delighted to be back in civilization again that they showed their appreciation by breaking into the house next door and stealing a joint of beef. They laid it on Isobel's kitchen table and expressed disbelief at her outrage. Robert and Adam thought it all a great joke until they started scratching and discovered that the two Glasgow boys had given them fleas. After that it was open warfare.

There was a crash and when Isobel whirled around she saw that Billy had broken a cup. "You little varmint!" Isobel exploded, her patience in shreds. "That's the fifth this month. Get off to school with you. And don't forget your gas masks."

"Right, cheerio, missus."

"And don't call me 'missus'!"

"Have they gone?" Adam asked as he poked his head around the kitchen door. He was joined a few minutes later by his brother.

"That bacon looks good, mum," Robert said as he sat down at the kitchen table. The twins were 8 and ate everything she put on the table. She had lost her own appetite the day she heard William's trawler had been torpedoed, but she still clung to the belief that he had survived. The boys were blithely convinced that their father was indestructible, yet, whenever letters were delivered or the doorbell rang, fear and tension showed on all their faces.

III

When William regained consciousness the nightmare of flaming water, burning oil, grinding metal, and screaming men closed in on him and everything became dark again. When he woke once more blurred faces bent over him, whispering that he was in the hospital.

"What happened?" he croaked.

The told him. The gunboat's depth charges had found their mark and the submarine had been blasted out of the water, spewing out German bodies to mingle with the Scottish ones from the trawler. The rescue team kept pulling bodies from the sea, but there was no trace of William and he was reported missing. A month later they discovered he had been washed ashore and was being tended by a senile old woman who believed he was her son. She cried bitterly when they removed him to the hospital.

"What about the rest of my crew?"

"You're the only survivor."

William thought of his mates on the *Topaz*. "Surely someone else survived with me?" he pleaded. When the men in white coats shook their heads he turned to face the wall. "You can go home soon," the doctors said. When he told them he did not want to go home they looked puzzled. William heard them saying. "What are we to tell his wife?" But it was of no interest to him.

IV

Isobel wept tears of gratitude when she heard that William was alive and she immediately flew down to London to the specialist hospital where he was recovering. To her distress, William wouldn't talk to her or acknowledge her presence. She wept and pleaded at his bedside, but he treated her like a stranger and the doctors gently informed her that her husband did not want to return home. The psychiatrist explained that William was suffering from "survivor guilt."

"You'd be best to return to your family in Aberdeen," he said soothingly. "We'll let you know if the position changes."

V

When William finally agreed to come home to Aberdeen it was obvious to Isobel that he was still far from well. He spent his time huddled in a chair staring into the fireplace and drinking glass after glass of whisky. He had not kissed her since he had returned and when she tried to cozy up to him in bed he pushed her away.

At first Isobel wondered if her husband was still hankering after Margot Gossamer. Although Margot had resigned from Armstrongs and was working in a factory it seemed that she still cherished ambitions to get William back into her life. She wrote letters which Isobel burned, made phone calls about which William never heard, and turned a deaf ear to Isobel's demand to stop trying to contact him. It appeared that Margot, stubborn as ever, regarded her removal from William's life as a temporary setback.

Although Margot's persistence alarmed Isobel she began to wonder whether it could be put to some use. Perhaps contact with his mistress might provide the shock William needed? Of course there was always the possibility that when he heard Margot's voice he might be attracted to her again, but Isobel felt the risk was justified. Anything was better than watching him sink deeper and deeper into apathy. The next time Margot rang, Isobel handed the phone over to her husband. William was hunched in a chair by the fire, staring into space. "It's Margot Gossamer, your former mistress," Isobel said brightly. "I've a feeling she wants to resume your relationship."

"Margot? What the hell do you want? I don't want to speak to you again," he barked, and banged down the phone.

"You used to be so keen on Margot," Isobel ventured, wanting to push him as far towards reality as she could.

"I was a damn fool," William muttered, "and I felt guilty about it. I still do."

Isobel dropped to her knees by his chair. "Oh, William, you've no idea how glad I am to hear you say that!"

"Leave me alone," he said gruffly and reached for his bottle of whisky. Why do I bother, Isobel wondered as she stood up and went out into the hall. But she knew the answer: she loved the man William had once been and she wanted him back.

The doorbell rang. When she opened the door and was faced with a policeman she put her hand to her throat in anticipation of a disaster. William was safe, but James was with the Gordon Highlanders somewhere in Europe. She missed him dreadfully.

"Is it my son?" she asked, her voice hoarse.

The policeman looked surprised. "Your son? No, it's your neighbor, Mrs. Blackstock. She says that one of the Karmigan brothers has put a huge sign outside her gate."

"What does the sign say?" Isobel asked nervously.

" 'Help yourself to my fruit and vegetables. Free teas!' " The policeman avoided her eyes and gave a cough which sounded suspiciously like a chuckle. "People have been queuing up to get in!"

Isobel stamped her foot in rage. "Those Karmigans! What am I to do with them? They're the terror of the town."

"I know," the constable said feelingly. "When anyone comes into the station and says it's an emergency, I never know if it's Adolf Hitler or the Karmigan brothers! There is also that matter of the missing wheelbarrow—to pinch it from the provost was a bit of a cheek. No chance of them going back to Glasgow?"

Isobel shook her head. The anticipated bombing of Britain which had prompted the evacuation in the first place had not happened, and after three months of what came to be called the 'phony war' most of the evacuees had gone home to Glasgow, but there was no home to go back to in the case of Billy and Lennie Karmigan. The granny who had looked after them had been taken into the hospital, and since there seemed to be no other relatives the authorities had decided that it would be better for the boys to stay in Aberdeen until a solution could be found for them.

"The Karmigan brothers are still at school," Isobel said to the policeman. "I'll deal with them when they get home."

"Beg pardon, ma'am, but they're home. Mark you, they scampered when they saw me. I'll call again later," he added as he walked down the steps and round the corner to where he had parked his bicycle. A few moments later Isobel heard an outraged yell and knew at once that his bike must have disappeared. This time the Karmigans have gone too far, she decided grimly. She went back to the sitting room to tell William about their latest act of mischief, but as usual he refused to take any interest in their doings. As far as William was concerned the evacuees did not exist.

He cut across her story impatiently. "What's for supper? Can't you produce something decent?"

William hadn't taken kindly to the introduction of food rationing. When Isobel had told him that each person was allowed only four ounces of butter, twelve ounces of sugar and four ounces of bacon and ham, he had snorted indignantly and said that that wasn't enough to keep a sparrow alive, and he took a dim view of Woolton Pie made with potato pastry, sugarless puddings, and meatless soup.

"Fish," she replied, thankful that at least fish wasn't rationed. The Armstrong trawlers which hadn't been converted for war use were making big profits—as was their shipyard. Unfortunately William did not want to hear about Armstrongs. He kept saying that the board were quite able to run the company without him.

The war was William's only interest and when he wasn't drinking he was glued to his wireless set. Isobel was surprised by his enthusiasm because the news was depressing. Hitler's blitzkrieg in Poland had been followed by his invasion of Denmark and Norway.

William had been particularly interested in news that filtered through about the activities of the Royal Naval Patrol Service. At the end of April the BBC reported that the Northern Patrol had joined the fleet warships and were helping the British Expeditionary Force give the Norwegians some relief. One of the trawlers had brought down a German plane with nothing more than twin Lewis guns; another had intercepted German wireless transmissions and this had enabled an armed party from the flagship to go ashore and capture a Norwegian fifth columnist.

But the story which stirred William Armstrong's imagination concerned the trawler that was deliberately placed against a blazing pier so that the fire could be fought and an ammunition dump prevented from exploding. The day after William heard about this exploit, which won its skipper the VC, he went down to the fishing harbor for the first time since he had come home. When he returned to Rubislaw Terrace, instead of sitting by the fire he began pacing around the house.

"What's wrong?" Isobel asked quietly.

"I stood at the harbor this morning looking out to sea—I don't think I'll ever have the courage to go out in a ship again. It looks as if I'll have to sit out this war at home."

But as it happened fate had a surprise in store for him.

FOUR

I

Since William had come round to the view that Neville Chamberlain was making a mess of the war he was delighted when Winston Churchill replaced Chamberlain as Prime Minister, but his face grew gloomier as he listened to the news each day and realized that the Allies were in danger of being defeated. Hitler's armies invaded Belgium and Holland, and the British and French forces began retreating to Dunkirk. There were rumors that the thousands of men who were being forced back to the beaches of Dunkirk would be slaughtered on a scale unparalleled in human history.

William and Isobel found it difficult to sleep the night they heard the news and at six o'clock the next morning William could stand his bed no longer and went downstairs to make a cup of tea. A few minutes later Isobel joined him. They were sitting in the kitchen when there was a thunderous knocking on the front door. Isobel glanced round in alarm, wondering if she had infringed blackout regulations, but when William opened the door he was confronted by one of the Armstrongs trawler skippers.

"It's just come through . . ." the man said, his voice practically incoherent with excitement. "Everything that can float is to go to Dunkirk to try to pick up our boys on the beaches. Get on your jacket, William, you're not going to sit this one out!"

William's face was a mask. Then his lips parted in the biggest grin Isobel had witnessed since his return from the Faroes.

"Pack a kitbag, Isobel, with some food. Sandy, how quickly can we get to the south coast? Isobel, hurry up, my love."

Isobel choked back tears. William had said "my love." She hadn't heard these words for a long time. As she drove them down to the harbor they realized there had been a pandemic mood-change in the city. Faces at the harbor were brighter, steps were quicker, and voices excited. The prospect of some positive action to help the stranded soldiers was acting like an electric charge.

II

William never forgot his first sight of Dunkirk. Tracer shells and star shells arced over the sky in brilliant flashes of color, and flak lighters seemed to explode like Catherine wheels as they poured out round after round of ammunition. Ships erupted in flames as they were hit by bombs, and huge fountains of water spewed up from the sea; it was like a fairground in hell.

William was skippering the *Mirabel*, a drifter belonging to his own company. It had seen action in Norway, but for the past week it had been in Aberdeen for repairs. Off Dunkirk the transports were waiting to receive troops from the smaller boats which had the job of steaming in as close to the shore as possible. "Stuka" dive-bombers were being used as airborne artillery, and through the smoke and flames William glimpsed a line of men wading through the water trying to reach a flotilla of small craft.

"Going my way?" a Cockney yelled as he clambered on board a boat which had formerly been used for water skiing.

When the *Mirabel* steamed into Dunkirk harbor the crew made her fast to the mole and threw a scaling ladder against it. Immediately a crowd of soldiers materialized from behind a wall of smoke. Some were bleeding badly, others limped or were supported by colleagues, all of them had grimy desperate faces. They tumbled down the ladders on to the deck and kept coming down until there wasn't an inch of free space left.

As the *Mirabel* made her way cautiously out of the harbor there was a mighty explosion of sound as fuel tanks on the shore were ignited. William looked in vain for the transports which had been lying offshore and decided they must have left with a full load of men; the *Mirabel* would have to make her own way back to Britain. His ship was so heavily laden that he worried about her stability and he was immensely relieved when he sighted the English coastline.

As soon as the men stumbled ashore at Ramsgate, the *Mirabel* was loaded up with fresh stores and William set off once more. On the second return trip from Dunkirk they passed a minesweeper which had been torpedoed by a U-boat. The men swimming in the water yelled for help, but the *Mirabel* was already overloaded and they had to steam past them. On the next trip the *Mirabel* arrived at Dunkirk after dusk to find a night sky streaked with flames and a seemingly endless succession of shells. The Germans were pressing hard towards the beaches, and orders were given that all craft must return to Britain.

William slept for two days when he came home. When he awakened he made love to Isobel for the first time since he had returned from the Faroes. As release came coursing through him, William murmured his thanks. "You're a wonderful woman," he whispered. "I don't know how you've had the patience to put up with me these last few months!"

Isobel murmured that she loved him and cuddled into his side.

As she drifted off to sleep there was only one dark cloud remaining on her horizon. William had survived Dunkirk, but for weeks there had been no word of James . . .

III

James flung himself into a foxhole as a shell exploded nearby. When he raised his head a hail of bullets whistled past his ears and he could hear screams piercing the thunder of the guns.

When Belgium had surrendered to Germany on 28 May 1940 the gap that was opened in the war front became a door through which the Reich poured regiment after regiment of troops. Thousands of British soldiers had been rescued from the beaches at Dunkirk, but the men of the 51st Highland Division were not so lucky. Two of the brigades, including the one to which James Armstrong belonged, found themselves stranded at St. Valery high on the hills of the Normandy coast. They were within sight and sound of the sea, but were unable to get to it as Rommel and his Panzer troops tightened the net around them. Finally they were forced to surrender, but rather than face the probability of years as a prisoner of war, James had decided to make a break for freedom.

There was a lull in the firing and then a great thunder of guns to the north gave him hope that the enemy's attention had been diverted by a surprise sortie. He risked moving out of his foxhole and began inching forward. When there was still no response from the enemy he quickened his pace, slithering on his side along the rough grass, heading in the general direction of the outskirts of St. Valery. If he could manage to slip through the circle of Germans he might make it to the hills beyond and a friendly village. After that the Resistance would help him escape. The dunes and beaches were silent as he hauled himself to his feet and began running.

After heart-stopping moments sprinting across open terrain, he threw himself into a thicket only to find himself facing a German gunner. Without hesitation, the man started pumping bullets into his body. James slumped to the ground, his hands clutching the jagged hole which had once been his chest.

IV

It was a drowsy summer Saturday and Isobel was sitting in the back garden in a deckchair. A gentle breeze rustled the leaves of the silver birch above her head, and a blue tit flitted in and out of the branches, a phosphorescent smudge of blue and green. Isobel smiled at the little bird benevolently, feeling warm towards all living things. She thought she heard a bell and when she turned her head towards the house she saw William walking slowly towards her, holding a piece of paper. A telegram?

Please God, forgive me for having a favorite son, Isobel prayed as she ran to meet her husband. Please God, don't let it be James. But her husband's stricken face told her the answer.

"Lt. James Armstrong killed in action on 4 June. Deepest regrets. Lt. Col. R. A. Bannerman."

Someone was moaning, a plaintive keening howl like an animal in pain, and Isobel realized the sounds were coming from herself. She was conscious of a rising fury against fate. "Why did it have to be James?" she cried, anguish in every line of her face. Out of the corner of her eye she glimpsed the flash of the blue tit as it settled on a branch nearby. "And why are you still alive?" she cried bitterly, lunging at it with her hand. "Why is anyone still alive?"

FIVE

I

As the war continued the Karmigan brothers progressed from mischief-making to the black market. Soap, paper, silk stockings, matches, needles, cosmetics, and tobacco were commodities in demand. The Karmigans "acquired" some of these goods and found suppliers for others, and word soon got out that if you wanted anything and didn't have too many scruples, the Karmigans would find it for you. There was only one rule to which Billy Karmigan adhered: his customers had to pay for everything in cash. "Cash down!" he would say firmly. He said it so often that Cash Down Karmigan became his nickname.

"I've just got hold of some commercial petrol," Billy whispered to his brother one morning.

"But commercial petrol's dyed red," Lennie protested, "so we can't sell it to the punters."

Billy grinned. "We can so. If you filter the commercial stuff through a gas mask the red dye disappears. We're going to make a stack of money out of this lot!"

"We'd better watch the missus doesn't find out," Lennie said nervously. "Since her son got killed she's gone a bit funny. She's just walloped me on the bum with her hairbrush!"

II

With William back in the Royal Naval Patrol Service the full responsibility for the Karmigans lay at Isobel's door. She was furious when she heard rumors about their black-market activities, and she was equally annoyed that neither she nor the police could catch them in the act, so when she noticed the boys out in the back yard having an earnest discussion she decided to play detective.

"Right, that's it," she yelled when she caught them filtering commercial petrol. "I'm calling the police."

Unfortunately by the time the sergeant arrived the petrol had disappeared.

"I think you was imagining things, missus," the Karmigans said cheekily.

Isobel decided enough was enough. Within the week she'd managed to get the Karmigans transferred to Drumcraig Castle on Deeside which had been turned into a home for displaced evacuees whose relatives had been killed or wounded. The temporary owners of the castle were reluctant to be burdened with the town's troublemakers, but Isobel placated them with a generous donation and a promise to host a party for the children at her own expense.

III

As the months passed Isobel felt guilty that she had not kept her promise and she finally got round to organizing a party for the evacuees at Drumcraig in the spring of 1943. The party had such a horrific ending that she never really recovered from it, and her mind began to feel like a fragile spider's web which was gradually being torn apart. She tried to sublimate the terrifying memories of the party by throwing all her energies into her work at Armstrongs and as a consequence became increasingly impatient with distractions. When Robert and Adam were about the house they always seemed to be asking for food, or demanding to be run to rugby, football or swimming. Weekends were even worse because they brought their noisy friends in to play.

"I'm trying to catch up on some work," she screamed at them as they clattered past her study one Saturday morning. Adam ran on, but Robert came into the study, looking far older than his 12 years. "Mum, can't Adam and I help?"

"Yes, you can both grow up and go away to university so that I can concentrate on my career," she snapped. At the sight of Robert's stricken face Isobel opened her mouth to apologize, but the words wouldn't come. She looked up and saw

that William had heard this exchange and she felt consumed
with guilt. "Leave me alone. Everyone leave me alone . . ."

Isobel knew she was in the grip of another depression—a
bad one. The black bat had settled on her shoulder and, to add
to her worries, she was losing her grip at work. She got up and
looked in the nearest mirror. Her eyes were wild and red-
rimmed; she felt she was going mad. It was hopeless. Everything was hopeless.

IV

Every time William came home on leave he could see the
change in his wife. He was also concerned about the effect her
attitude was having on Robert. Adam didn't seem to care, but
Robert was taking it very much to heart.

Another problem in William's life was Margot Gossamer.
Whenever he appeared back in Aberdeen, Margot phoned him,
pleading to get back her job at Armstrongs. He told her that
was out of the question, but still she kept pestering him. It was
all very stressful, he thought, as he made lunch for the boys on
one of his leaves. Afterwards he played football with them in
the garden and then sat down to have a well-deserved whisky
in the sitting room. He was listening to the news when the
phone rang. It was Margot suggesting a meeting.

"No," William replied firmly, "I'm having problems at
home. Isobel's having one of her depressions and the least little thing tips her over the edge. This morning she was nearly in
hysterics because of the noise the boys were making."

"I understand," Margot said sympathetically. "All I'm wanting is a job. I can't get a decent one because I didn't get a letter of recommendation from Armstrongs."

"I'll put something in the post."

"No, William, I want to see you face to face about the letter.
Ten minutes of your time? Surely after all we had together,
that's little enough to ask?"

"All right," he said uneasily. "There'll be no one at Armstrongs around seven. I'll wait for you at the side door and we
can go inside and have a talk. Just a talk, mind; and then you
must promise not to contact me again."

"Right," she agreed quickly. "See you at seven."

William put the phone down and went straight to Isobel's study. She glared at him. "I told you I don't want to be disturbed."

"Isobel, I'm worried about you. Let me call the doctor."

"No."

"Don't you think you should get away from these papers for a while and eat something? I gave the boys their lunch, but it's after six. They'll be hungry for their supper. I'll be going out soon, by the way—I've got a business appointment."

Isobel's head jerked up. "But this is Saturday."

"I know, but it's something that can't be cancelled."

V

Isobel went through to the kitchen and quickly fried fish and chips, the boys' favorite. When she summoned them to the dining room they took one look at the food and groaned, "Not again! Dad made us fish and chips at lunch time."

Isobel's control snapped. "Well, starve then! See if I care!" she shouted and threw the plates at them. The boys ducked and fled from the room, and Isobel sat down at the table and put her head in her hands. This was the worst depression she'd ever had. If only James had been here to comfort her. She missed him more than ever. Sometimes she had this vision . . . James standing at a gate with his arms outstretched waiting to welcome her. The vision used to be at night, but recently it had started coming during the day as well. She was always wretchedly angry when she recollected where she was and realized that James was not with her. Would never be with her . . .

The phone on the worktop in the kitchen trilled loudly. Isobel frowned when she recognized Margot Gossamer's voice.

"Thought you'd like to know," Margot said in her breathy whisper, "that I've had the last laugh. Your husband's business appointment this evening is with me."

"I don't believe it."

"Come to the office and see for yourself. But don't expect too much chat. We'll be . . . rather busy. Bye!"

The bitch! She probably thought Isobel wouldn't have the nerve to come to the office, but she bloody well would . . . Isobel threw on her coat, banged the front door behind her and jumped into the car. She drove like a maniac until she reached Armstrongs' office in the center of Aberdeen.

The big front doors were tightly shut. That bloody bitch was telling lies, Isobel thought angrily, but as she walked around the building she noticed one of the side doors was open, and when she glanced up she could see a light in William's office. Quietly she stole up the stairs. She could hear voices in William's office as she approached it, and the door was slightly ajar. She put a hand to her mouth when she saw William and Margot standing in the middle of the floor. William had his back to her, but Margot was facing the door. Margot was in tears, but she gave a faint smile when she saw Isobel and whispered something to William. The next moment he was kissing her.

Isobel managed to tiptoe back downstairs without making a sound. Blindly she pushed open the door, fumbled for her car keys and then drove off out of Aberdeen; past the suburbs, the villages, and out along the coast road which ran parallel to a steep cliff. When she reached the highest point of the road she put her foot on the accelerator, wrenched the car wheel to the left and drove into space. Down, down, down . . . till the car crashed into the rocks far below where the sea foamed against them.

Before she lost consciousness Isobel was sure she could see the gate and James waiting on the other side . . . She died with a smile on her lips.

VI

On the day after Isobel Armstrong's funeral Adam went out to play with his friends; Robert was nowhere to be seen. William found him huddled in the crotch of an oak tree in the garden. "Come down, lad," he said kindly. "Let's have a talk. You can cry if you like."

Robert bit his lip. "I'm not going to cry. But I want to know the truth. Mum drove the car off that cliff deliberately, didn't she?"

"The coroner," William began, but Robert clutched his arm.

"I've heard what the coroner said. I want to know what *you* think."

William was conscious of the strength of his son's clasp and the fire in the brown eyes. Robert had grown up overnight. "I think she committed suicide," he said despairingly.

"But *why*?" Robert demanded. "We loved her. *You* loved her."

That was true, William thought bleakly. He'd come away from the interview with Margot Gossamer feeling rather pleased with himself. He'd given her the recommendation she wanted, but when she'd suggested resuming their relationship he'd been brusquely dismissive. Margot had started crying and had gone on crying until suddenly she'd jerked up her head as if she'd seen someone at the door. "Kiss me and I'll forgive you," she'd whispered. So he'd kissed her. He left immediately after that and drove home.

But by then Isobel had gone.

"Why?" Robert asked again.

William wondered where to begin. James's death should have made his wife cherish her remaining children, but the reverse had been the case. Once James had died Isobel seemed to resent her other sons for surviving. Her love for James had been so obsessive it had bordered on incestuous . . .

William knew he couldn't tell Robert that; he'd have to find another acceptable explanation for his mother's behavior.

"What I can't understand," Robert said gravely, "is that mum used to be so loving. She was interested in everything we did, spent all her free time with us. She couldn't do enough for us, dad, and we were all so happy. I don't know when things started to change. Was it after she started at Armstrongs?"

William seized on the lifeline. "Yes," he said at once, "that's it. Eventually your mother just couldn't cope with all the pressures. They crowded in on her and made her feel life wasn't worth living."

"Why didn't she remember that we loved her? Needed her?"

"When you get very depressed, Robert, you don't think or act rationally. When a wife and mother decides to have a career it can cause all kinds of problems."

It was a facile explanation intended to comfort, but it left a scar on Robert's psyche which never really healed.

PART II

1950

SIX

I

Glasgow

At the end of his shift Frank Meldrum was unusually morose with his workmates. He was having lunch with Alexandra in a Buchanan Street restaurant and he was worried in case his half-sister had got herself into trouble. She was 19 years old and had grown into a beautiful woman, the kind of woman who aroused men's lusts. She had reassured him recently that she was still a virgin, but had then given him cause for alarm by declaring that it was time she became a woman in every sense of the word. They'd laughed about it, but today he was not amused. When Alexandra had phoned him the previous evening she had told him she had found an easy way of making money. She said she would explain everything over lunch and he added in a teasingly confident voice that he would be shocked by her news.

Frank picked up his gear. An easy way to make money. Well, there was only one way beautiful girls could make money easily in postwar Glasgow . . .

Usually he was one of the first to hurry towards the yard gates, but today he sat on a pile of planks and tried to decide what he'd say to Alexandra if his worst fears were confirmed. His eyes ranged round John Brown's shipyard. During the war the Clyde yards had built and repaired more vessels than all the shipyards of the USA put together. After the fighting was over the shipbuilding industry had been given a further boost by the lack of competition from countries like Japan and Germany whose economies had been crippled. In Scotland new ships were being built, old ones were being repaired and people who weren't making ships' components were selling them. John Brown's had welcomed him back, but despite the shipbuilding boom he was one of the lucky ones. He belonged to an ex-servicemen's association and knew that many ship-builders' plumbers, joiners, and electricians were having diffi-culty finding jobs. It was Scotland's perennial problem: no matter how much work there was available, there was never enough to keep employment levels high.

He felt doubly lucky because his work afforded him so much pleasure. Even now in the aftermath of rain, John Brown's shipyard had a special magic for him. The watery sun was warming the atmosphere, and tendrils of mist were rising from the river and curling round the giant cranes which watched over the yard like prehistoric birds of prey. He no-ticed that their harsh lines seemed to soften as they were em-braced by the river mist, as well they might since it was to the river they owed their existence.

Men had sailed ships here since the earliest inhabitants had crafted primitive canoes, and in the eighteenth century Ameri-can-built vessels belonging to the Glasgow tobacco-lords had voyaged to the colonies where goods were bartered for to-bacco. It was when the Americans declared their Independence that the Scots began building more of their own ships. The transition from wood to iron, and iron to steel, together with the advent of steam propulsion, helped forge the Clyde's repu-tation as one of the greatest shipbuilding rivers in the world. The story of Clyde shipbuilding had captured Frank's imagi-nation when he was a child. It still did.

Some of the men on their way towards the yard gates stopped for a moment and watched the big man with blond hair gazing up at the gigantic cranes. "Catching flies, Frank?" they asked.

"I was just thinking."

"Thinking? That's a dangerous habit!"

"Aye, but our Frank wants to be a politician," someone else said. "That's why he's practicing sitting on his bum!"

The men laughed as they went on their way. Frank picked up his gear again and followed them through the gates toward the tram stop. He didn't mind their teasing; he knew they were as concerned as he was about certain aspects of shipbuilding. There had been thousands of riveters on the Clyde in the Thir-ties, a decreasing number in the Forties, and now in 1950 they were numbered in hundreds; the riveters were being made re-

dundant by electric welders who had no need to join bits of
metal together when they could fuse them with an electric arc.

Fortunately for him, there was plenty of work for joiners.
They were the ones who had to transform the steel-lined
spaces of the big ships into cabins and living spaces which
were warm and welcoming. He'd never had a chance to work
on a really luxurious vessel so he hoped the rumors were true:
the men were saying that John Brown's might build another
Queen. There was even a whisper that the yard had been given
the order to build a new royal yacht. Alexandra would be fas-
cinated to hear that choice bit of gossip.

As he jumped on the tram Frank couldn't help feeling apprehensive as he wondered what Alexandra was going to tell
him. He loved his "little sis" and felt responsible for her; after
all, he was nine years older than she was. Although he knew
Alexandra must be haunted by the horrors of her past she
made a point of never referring to it. Her mother, her father,
the croft in Aberdeenshire where she had been born and
reared, and Drumcraig Castle: all were forbidden topics of
conversation. Especially Drumcraig Castle where her mother
had suffered a death that was the stuff of nightmares, and
Alexandra had been there watching . . .

Yet somehow she had endured all the traumas and emerged
stronger and braver because of them. "I think about the past a
lot, but if I never speak of it the horror is diminished," she had
said to him once. "The only way I can survive is to pretend
that my life began in 1943."

Nineteen forty-three was the year Alexandra returned to
Glasgow from her mother's funeral in Aberdeen. She was almost 12. It was arranged that she would continue to make her
home with Abigail Roberts, a Glasgow headmistress who had
employed Briony Meldrum as her housekeeper. Alexandra's
school fees and books were covered by the scholarship which
she had won and she paid Miss Abigail a weekly rent from her
mother's savings.

The tram screeched to a halt and Frank moved towards the
front as more people clambered on board. He was full of admiration for his half-sister. When she realized that her mother's
savings were disappearing she set about earning money in her
spare time. She tutored children younger than herself, offered
her services as a babysitter, delivered papers and helped in a

grocer's shop on a Saturday. Cooking was Alexandra's hobby and she enjoyed preparing elaborate dinners for Miss Abigail. When a neighbor sampled one of them she asked Alexandra if she'd cater for a party she was having. The party was such a success that Alexandra soon received other commissions and her hobby became another source of income.

Aye, Alexandra had always been a hard worker, Frank thought. So what the hell was this lark about finding an easy way to make money? He was worried about something else. In the last few weeks Alexandra seemed to have undergone a personality change. She sounded reckless and lighthearted, and kept talking about having to take risks in life. He felt sure it was all tied in with her new way of making money. He didn't like the sound of it. Not one little bit.

II

A driving wind was forcing the citizens of Glasgow to bow their heads as they walked towards the city center. Faces glimpsed under rain hats and waterproofs were for the most part gray and somber, but there were exceptions. As Alexandra Meldrum hurried across George Square the thought of the money she had accumulated in recent weeks gave her such a charge of joy that she laughed out loud. Startled passersby turned their heads to gaze at the girl with the sparkling green eyes and luxuriant chestnut hair. She was tall and shapely, and exuded an air of happiness.

Alexandra grinned, aware that she wasn't conforming to the notion that private pleasure should not be revealed in public places, but she did not *want* to contain her happiness, she wanted to shout it to the skies. She hadn't felt so excited since she had won a place in the Glasgow University Bursary Competition in her last year at school, entitling her to free education.

As Alexandra walked she allowed her mind to roam back over the years. Miss Abigail had been delighted that her protégée had performed so well in the university bursary and had started making plans for the future, but her own was destined to be shortlived; in the summer she died from a heart attack. Miss Abigail left her house and possessions to the twin sister who had been Alexandra's teacher at the school on Deeside. Miss Agatha was very upset. "You did all her housework and shopping, Alexandra. It was very remiss of Abigail to leave you out of her will. I intend to send you money myself."

Alexandra thanked her former school teacher, but proudly declined the offer of financial help. "I'll be fine on my own. The bursary money will pay for everything and I'll be able to stay in one of the halls of residence."

Alexandra had been dismayed when she discovered that the residences were already full. She began trudging around lodgings which were on the university list, but there were no vacancies. Just as she was beginning to despair she went to view a house in Park Terrace. The terrace was like a hilltop balcony, commanding breathtaking views of the spires and towers of the art gallery, the university, and the green slopes of Kelvingrove Park. Alexandra had leaned on the balustrade which guarded the terrace and looked down on a peaceful scene: young couples wandering arm in arm, students hurrying to lectures, old men dozing, children playing. In the stillness Alexandra heard a blackbird singing and suddenly a flock of starlings rose in the sky and winged their way across the sooty tenements of Partick towards the giant cranes of Clydeside. She turned back to the terraced houses and knocked on one of the doors. It was opened by a lady wearing an apron who introduced herself as Mrs. Thom.

"I haven't liked the look of any of the students they've sent me so far," Mrs. Thom began unpromisingly.

"Have you been baking?" Alexandra asked as she noticed Mrs. Thom's floury hands. "I love cooking—in fact I cater for parties." When Alexandra saw the immediate spark of interest in Mrs. Thom's eyes she pressed her advantage. "I could cook for you occasionally."

"Would you now?" Mrs. Thom said eagerly. "In that case you can have the room."

"But of course, if I did some cooking and baking for you, I'd expect to pay a lower rent." Alexandra countered swiftly.

Mrs. Thom's jaw dropped. "You've a nerve, I must say. Still, I like a lass with spirit. Come in and we'll talk about it."

Alexandra moved in a week later at half the rent Mrs. Thom had intended to charge. She was very much aware, however, that her budget would be tight and decided the solution was to

keep earning money with her part-time jobs: tutoring, babysit-
ting, and cooking. Since Alexandra was often allowed to take
home leftovers from her catered dinner parties she got into the
habit of sharing these with her landlady. This was such a treat
for Mrs. Thom that she gave Alexandra bits and pieces from
her own store cupboards. It was a very amicable arrangement
which resulted in Alexandra spending very little money on
provisions.

Money, Alexandra kept thinking; one day, she determined,
she'd make so much she'd never have to worry about it again.
One Friday evening she was cooking for a wealthy estate
agent and his wife who lived in Bearsden. After the guests departed, Rosemary and Brian Bannon began chatting to her
about their agency business in the center of Glasgow. When
Alexandra mentioned that she intended looking for a holiday
job over the Christmas holidays Brian Bannon asked her if
she'd like to help out in his office.

"But I don't know anything about estate agents," Alexandra
exclaimed.

"No, but I've a hunch you'll be a quick learner."

Alexandra's trial run at Bannons Estate Agency was so productive that they asked her to come back at Easter and when
her Easter stint was over Brian suggested she work during the
summer holidays. The following year when the pattern was repeated Brian Bannon said he'd be delighted to employ her in
the agency on a permanent basis. Alexandra felt it was a
pointer to her future; an indication that her forte lay in business rather than in the cloistered world of the university.

She enjoyed showing clients around houses, discussing surveyors' reports, and negotiating prices. Yet she didn't want to
be acting for other people all her life; she wanted to be part of
the property scene in her own right. Some of the agency's
clients bought houses and commercial buildings in poor condition, renovated them, and then sold them on at a profit.
Alexandra knew that this was what she'd love to do. If only
she had more money . . .

When she began her third year at university, Alexandra took
a long look at the savings she had accumulated over the years
from part-time jobs and estate agency work. Four hundred
pounds! At one time she would have considered that to be a
fortune, but she knew it wasn't enough if she wanted to be-

come a property tycoon. And she did. Each night when she went to bed she hugged this new ambition to her chest like a cuddly toy, savoring the warmth it brought her.

Sometimes when she saw buildings for sale at bargain prices she longed to buy them, but her training at the agency held her back. Buying property was only the first step. You needed money to renovate it and employ staff, and while you were waiting for a buyer you had to have enough cash to provide for yourself and your employees. There were cases in papers in the papers every other week of construction firms which had been caught short by cash-flow problems and she didn't intend to be one of them. Alexandra decided she would need to double her capital before she could launch herself into the property market and she had no idea how she could do that.

And then out of the blue she had discovered an easy way of making money . . . She couldn't wait to tell Frank about it. The rain was still sheeting down like stair rods, but Alexandra's high spirits refused to be quenched by the downpour as she walked through Glasgow's city center.

"I'm rich," she whispered gleefully to the statue of Queen Victoria in George Square. Alexandra felt it fitting that the old queen should have a prominent position in a city renowned for its Victorian architecture. James Watt, who had revolutionized the steam engine, was another of her favorite statues. His expression bore the faraway look of someone who knew his own destiny. Today Alexandra felt an affinity with him.

The Italianate block of the City Chambers loomed to her right. Queen Victoria had declared the City Chambers open in 1888 and district councilors still gathered there to discuss current issues.

"Good morning!" Alexandra said happily as she bumped against a little man with a flat cap on his head.

"What's good about it?" he replied sourly.

Alexandra's eyes glinted. She was willing to bet that by the evening the man's face would be wreathed in grins. Friday and Saturday nights were pub nights in Glasgow and after a few pints the punters would be laughing and joking and telling funny stories. Sometimes she thought all Glaswegians were embryo comics. The trouble was they often shared that opinion and became embarrassing exhibitionists. But she loved them. On this wet windy Saturday when her financial prospects looked so promising she loved everyone. Alexandra quickened her step. She didn't want to be late for her lunch with Frank.

III

Frank was the first to arrive at the café. He leaned back against the door and as he looked down Buchanan Street he saw a tall rangy girl hurrying towards him. Frank smiled. Daisy O'Malley was a medical student who worked with Alexandra at Bannons Estate Agency. He liked Daisy and her independent attitude to life. Although Daisy's mother was wealthy and her father was a doctor Daisy had insisted on working in the holidays "just like all the other students." Frank approved of that, although he didn't approve of the political stance she sometimes adopted.

"I thought you might have left," Daisy said as she came up beside him. "Alexandra's been delayed."

"Are you joining us?" he asked.

"Wish I were! But I've promised to meet my mother and buy a new dress for tonight's party. Poor mother. She'd like a pretty daughter she can dress up like a doll; instead she's saddled with a Plain Jane."

Frank studied her and acknowledged to himself that Daisy had cause to have reservations about her looks. She was tall and lanky with mousey brown hair and very dark eyes and her face undoubtedly conjured up equine images. He had no idea what her figure was like since it was usually swathed in baggy trousers and sweaters. Nor did she bother with make-up. But when she smiled her face lit up, her eyes twinkled and she made you feel good. Everyone liked Daisy. Frank did as well; she was a great pal for anyone to have.

"Once I've pacified my mother," Daisy went on, "I'm going with my father on his rounds. His patients are great, but their houses are damp and disgusting—a disgrace to Scotland."

"The government knows that, but it'll take time to improve living conditions in the Gorbals."

"How much time?" Daisy asked indignantly. "Nye Bevan promised the country that the housing shortage would disappear by the next election, but the houses in the Gorbals are in a worse state than they were before the war."

"Aw, come on, Daisy, Scotland's in the middle of a boom. I know the Gorbals is falling down, but in other places Labour's spent a lot of money on low-rent housing."

"That's because so many socialist politicians are in the construction industry. They're hoping all this low-rent building will make people vote for them next time around."

"That's libelous!" Frank protested. Then he saw the twinkle in Daisy's eyes. "You're baiting me!"

"Half-joking, half-serious," Daisy admitted, "but some of your Labour councilors aren't lily-white and everyone knows it. As for the boom, why are some people predicting that it won't last?"

Frank frowned. "I suppose they're concerned because Glasgow's still caught in the old trap: the steel industry's too dependent on shipbuilding. If that declines it will affect the whole country."

"So the sooner the Conservatives sort things out the better?" Daisy asked provocatively.

"They haven't a hope of getting in at the next election," Frank was saying forcefully when he felt a tug at his elbow. He looked around and saw Alexandra grinning up at him.

"Are you two arguing about politics again?" she teased. "Daisy, you're suppose to be in Sauchiehall Street meeting your mother."

"I was passing this way and I thought I'd let Frank know that you were going to be late," Daisy replied hastily. She turned to Frank again. "Why don't you change your mind and come to my party tonight? Ah well," she went on when Frank shook his head, "perhaps I'll be able to tempt you another time."

IV

Alexandra allowed herself a small smile as she saw the telltale blush on Daisy's face as she fled. She guessed that her friend had come up Buchanan Street with the express purpose of waylaying Frank. Poor Daisy was well and truly smitten! But although Frank enjoyed her company he didn't seem to be attracted to her. Still, Daisy was trying hard. Knowing Frank's preoccupation with politics she used every meeting with him to turn the conversation in that direction; at least when she did that she knew she held his interest.

"I'm hungry, let's eat," Frank said impatiently, pushing open the café door. Alexandra followed him inside and they managed to find a table for two by the window where they could have some privacy. They ordered sausage and chips, rolls, and a pot of tea.

"I've got lots of news to tell you," Alexandra said the minute the waitress moved away. "I don't quite know where to begin—except that I've met some interesting men recently."

"Get it over with," Frank said abruptly.

"Why are you sounding so cross? Okay, I'll begin at the beginning. You know this 15-year-old boy I've been tutoring for two years? Well, I've become friendly with his older brother. Alan Gillian is quite strange-looking: piercing blue eyes, white hair, eyebrows and eyelashes. Almost an albino."

Frank's face was a study. "You can't be attracted to a man like that!"

"Oh, his looks don't matter," Alexandra replied, "but his brain does. His father told me Alan is the sharpest stockbroker in the country. Anyway, after I've finished tutoring his young brother, Alan runs me back to my digs and before I go inside we sit and chat. I tell him about university and he tells me what's happening in the stockbroking world."

"I hope he hasn't persuaded you to invest in stocks and shares. That's for experts—or people who've got plenty of cash to spare."

"Alan would agree with that. He says that if you dabble on the stock market you've got to be prepared to lose money on occasions."

"That will rule you out, little sis! You hoard your money!"

Alexandra put her tongue out at him, but when she started talking again she couldn't keep the excitement from her voice. "A few months ago I asked Alan if there weren't any occasions when money could be made very quickly."

She stopped talking for a moment as the waitress arrived with two plates of sausage and chips. "What was I saying?" she went on. "Oh, yes, Alan began telling me that people can make money quickly if they have access to insider information—about forthcoming mergers and takeover deals."

"You're losing me."

"If a small publicly quoted company is suddenly taken over by one of the giants, then usually anyone holding shares in the small company will benefit because the price of its shares will rise. Of course, to make money at this kind of thing," Alexandra went on, "you have to mix with wealthy, influential men."

"And you do?" Frank asked incredulously.

"I cater for their dinner parties. And Frank, you'd be surprised at how indiscreet tycoons can become when they've wined and dined too well!"

"So you eavesdrop on their conversations?"

"My ears are pinned back from the minute I arrive."

"I thought you were in the kitchen cooking the food."

"I serve it as well. A few weeks ago I heard a drunken director mention to his neighbor at dinner that his company was about to be taken over by one of the multinationals, so I asked Alan Gillian to buy £400 worth of shares in that company."

Frank choked on the cup of tea which he had raised to his lips. "Four hundred pounds! That's a small fortune. My God, Alexandra, you must have been out of your mind!"

"I was—till the takeover went through and the shares rocketed in value. Alan Gillian sold them for me when they were at their peak and I made a profit of £600. I couldn't believe it," Alexandra added, her green eyes glittering. "In a few weeks I've made more money than I've earned in the past two years!"

"An easy way of making money," Frank said faintly. "And here I was thinking . . ." He took out his handkerchief and wiped his brow.

Alexandra frowned. "You didn't think I'd taken to the streets?"

His flush of color confirmed his guilt, but Alexandra couldn't stay annoyed with him for long. Frank's concern and anxiety for her had been writ large on his big kindly face from the moment he saw her at the café entrance.

"I thought I might launch myself in the property market," she went on, "but seeing you here today has given me a better idea. Why don't I use my capital to set you up in business?"

"As a cabinet-maker?"

"Why not! There's a big demand for utility furniture and you could progress to making good reproduction pieces when there's more wood available."

"You've got more tricks in that head of yours than any conjurer. I'm not interested, sis. I enjoy working at the shipyard and being involved in union politics. I'd hate to go into business."

Alexandra looked so disappointed that he bent forward and gave her a quick kiss on the cheek. "That's for being the most generous sister in the world. I can hardly credit that you'd hand over your life savings to me instead of spending it on something *you* want to do."

"You're sure you're not interested?"

"Quite sure! But thank you anyway." He glanced up and noticed the queue at the door. "Since we've both finished eating maybe we'd better leave room for someone else." He pushed back his chair and signaled to the waitress for the bill.

Once they were outside the café they saw that it had stopped raining. The buildings in Buchanan Street were shrouded in that eerie half-light caused by dark clouds.

"Where are you off to?" Alexandra asked.

"I'm finished for the day, so I'm going back to Govan. The secretary of the ex-servicemen's association is coming around for a drink."

"You're a spoilsport not coming to Daisy's party tonight."

"I'd be out of place with a bunch of students."

"It isn't just students. Daisy's mother has invited some of her friends' sons from Edinburgh."

"In that case I'm definitely not coming. You know what they say about Edinburgh? The best thing out of it is the Glasgow train! You're away back to the estate agency, I suppose?"

"I said I'd work till five. Then I'll have to whizz back to my digs and get ready for the party."

V

Bannons Estate Agency had a quiet Saturday afternoon and Alexandra had plenty of time to rifle through their list of properties. Bungalows, mansions, terraced houses, flats, commercial property, warehouses: they were either too expensive, or she felt they wouldn't give her a good return on her investment. Alexandra knew what she wanted and suddenly she saw it: an empty tenement block in Edinburgh which was going very cheap. It must be in extremely bad condition, she thought, but it might suit her purpose very well. She picked up the details and put them in her handbag; she would map out her campaign on Monday.

Meantime this was only Saturday and she had an important night ahead: Daisy's party. Alexandra was looking forward to it with a certain amount of trepidation because she had made up her mind that by the end of the party she would have lost her virginity. Since she'd come up to university she'd been too busy studying or beavering away at her part-time jobs to have time for romance. She'd been out with several boys, but had never allowed a relationship to get past the kissing stage; yet she kept being tantalized by snippets of gossip from her fellow students who talked about "ecstasy of orgasm." When Alexandra had been up at the university signing on for the autumn term she'd talked to a girl who was in the middle of her first love affair. She told Alexandra that you weren't really a woman until you had gone "all the way." The conversation had made Alexandra feel inadequate and she had decided there and then that the sooner she went "all the way" the better. Daisy's party was the perfect place for it to happen.

Alexandra was getting ready for the party when the phone rang. It was Daisy. "Listen, I've just had a phone call from a friend to say he's bringing a good-looking guy to the party: Adam Armstrong, of Armstrongs, Aberdeen. That's where you come from. So give me the lowdown."

"I'd rather not," Alexandra groaned. "I met Adam years ago. He's rich, arrogant, odious."

"He could have improved . . ."

"He hasn't."

Alexandra's face was set in somber lines as she replaced the receiver. A few days previously she had been having lunch with friend in the union when Adam had sat down at the same table. He had looked closely at her when he heard the name "Meldrum." It seemed to act on him like a goad and he'd spent the rest of the lunch hour making fun of her humble background.

"Don't pay any attention to him," a girl whispered in her ear. "Adam's a nasty bit of work."

Alexandra thought the same. It was a pity he was coming to the party.

SEVEN

When Robert and Adam Armstrong finished school they were accepted by Glasgow University to read law. To their dismay their father announced that they were to lodge with their mother's Aunt Ethel in her home in Jordanhill, one of the outlying suburbs of Glasgow. Her husband had just died and she would be glad of their company.

"Oh no!" Adam groaned when their father left the room. "Remember Aunt Ethel? Small, severe-looking—a broomstick with glasses. And her house . . . Placards on all the walls extolling virtue and chastity and denouncing the demon drink."

Robert asked his father if they could discuss other lodgings, but his request was brushed aside.

"The decision is made," William Armstrong said brusquely.

Robert wasn't cowed by his father's overbearing tone. "Adam and I are 17—old enough to look after ourselves. We definitely do not want to lodge with Great-Aunt Ethel."

"In that case you stay in Aberdeen!" William retorted. "Glasgow is well known for drink and debauchery and I don't want my sons to be corrupted. I went through to see Aunt Ethel last week and I feel sure she'll be a restraining influence on you."

A restraining influence was the last thing either of the boys wanted, but their father was adamant: they accepted his terms—and his money—or they remained at home.

Reluctantly the brothers packed their bags as term time approached and caught a train from Aberdeen to Queen Street railway terminus. From there they carried their bags to the nearby bus station. The bus conveyed them to Woodend Drive.

"Aunt Ethel lives here," Robert said to Adam, pointing to an avenue on the map bordered by the playing fields of the local school. "I seem to remember we go straight up this road and turn right when we come to the school, then we carry on to the top of the hill."

They picked up their cases and began walking along Wood-end Drive. Their father had explained that the expansion of Glasgow westward had extended at the beginning of the twentieth century towards outlying suburbs like Jordanhill.

"This place stinks of respectability," Adam said disgustedly.

It was a view that was reinforced when they were admitted inside the portals of Aunt Ethel's terraced house at the top of the hill. It was exactly the way they remembered it: the walls were lined with texts aimed at improving mind and morals. "The end of the world is nigh" proclaimed the largest picture.

The brothers exchanged doom-laden glances. They realized Aunt Ethel was watching them closely as she showed them to their rooms on the first floor: two single bedrooms each furnished with a bed, desk, wardrobe, chest of drawers, and a wooden chair. Every item of furniture looked as if it had been designed by an ascetic monk.

"Not very welcoming, is it? Aunt Ethel said grimly. "Nothing in this house is intended to please or comfort. My late husband did not believe people were put on earth to enjoy themselves. Now, boys, why don't you unpack and then come downstairs for tea."

"I'm not staying in this dump," Adam said angrily to Robert when their aunt had left the room.

When they went downstairs they saw that the dining room was dominated by a placard decrying the sin of gluttony. Surprisingly the table below the placard offered a sumptuous afternoon tea: chocolate cake, biscuits, sponge cakes dripping with jam and cream. The brothers sat down and ate rapidly in case this unexpected bounty disappeared as unexpectedly as it had arrived. Robert shot an appreciative smile at his aunt when he'd had his fill. "That was great. You must work wonders with the rationing."

The smile Aunt Ethel gave him was positively evil. "I get lots of things on the black market! My late husband—God, do not bless his departed soul—would not have approved of this little feast."

Admission of black-market corruption followed by religious

blasphemy? Robert and Adam gazed at their great-aunt, intrigued to hear what she would say next.

Assured of their undivided attention she continued with evident enjoyment. "Horatio, the auld skinflint, used to say that when half the world was starving it was sinful to eat luxuries like cream and chocolate. So here's to the starving world!" she proclaimed, biting deep into her cream-filled black-market chocolate cake.

The boys gaped at her. "You know, Aunt Ethel," Robert began tentatively, "we weren't really looking forward to coming here."

"I'm not surprised," Aunt Ethel replied, "but I've been looking forward to having *you* in the house. I kept up all the placards because I knew they'd impress your father, but I want you to help me take them down. After that you can go down to the shops and bring me some bottles of gin, whisky, and brandy. I've a good mind to become an alcoholic!"

She smiled at the stunned look on their faces. "Did I tell you that my husband Horatio—God, do not bless his departed soul—was teetotal and never uttered a swear word in his whole life? Your father imagined that I shared Horatio's views. I don't. I suffered them. But from now on I'll do as I please. Damn! Hell! Bugger!" she finished triumphantly.

Robert and Adam burst out laughing.

"You won't tell your father?" Aunt Ethel begged.

"We won't say a word," Robert promised. "Anyway, it's your house, and you should be allowed to do what you like in it."

"Precisely!" Aunt Ethel replied. "Horatio, the auld skinflint, saved all his money, but I'm going to blow the lot. I might even buy a small car."

The boys looked at her. "Can you drive?" they asked with new respect for their eccentric relation.

"No, but I'd love to have one sitting outside on the road just to make the neighbors gossip."

"We've both passed our driving tests," Robert said hopefully. "We could take you shopping."

"Splendid! And in return you can have the use of it yourselves."

"Bravo!" Adam declared, warming to his aunt by the

minute. "What about the list of rules which our father drew up? Dictated!" he amended cunningly.

Aunt Ethel rose to her feet and rummaged in a drawer in the desk. She drew out a neatly typewritten piece of paper. "Down with rules and regulations!" she declared and threw the sheet of paper on the fire with a theatrical flourish.

Robert and Adam could hardly believe their luck in the months that followed. Aunt Ethel allowed them to come and go without question and turned a blind eye to noisy parties and girlfriends. They each joined university societies, played rugby and golf, and generally led a sybaritic existence mainly undisturbed by their studies which neither of them found particularly arduous.

One Saturday evening in their last year at university Robert wandered through to his brother's room. Adam was laying out all his socks, ties, and shirts to decide which ones to wear.

"You're going to a lot of effort for Daisy O'Malley's party," Robert remarked. Earlier that evening they'd had a call from a fellow-student in the conveyancing class. He said he'd been asked to round up extra men for the party; Robert had refused but Adam had accepted.

"I've got better things to do now than go to Daisy O'Malley's party," Adam said smugly as he checked through his ties. "An hour ago Belinda Belgrove finally agreed to come out with me."

"I'm impressed," Robert acknowledged. And he was. Belinda was a stunning blonde American who had attracted a lot of attention since she had enrolled for an arts degree. She told anyone who cared to listen that her forebears were poor Scots who had gone to America and made a fortune from steel. Since she chose to live in a luxury hotel while she was studying she was known as "the millionairess."

"Hey, that's my best tie," Robert said suddenly as he watched Adam select a bright red one. "That's the one the girls like."

Adam's lips curled. "You go out with girls, but don't bed 'em. Lily-livered, are you? Or scared they'll find you wanting?"

Robert moved quickly across the room and gave Adam a clip on the jaw which knocked him to the floor.

"Save that poisonous tongue of yours for someone else!" he said before he went back to his room.

Moodily Robert kicked at the rug in front of his desk, feeling more restless than ever. He wished he hadn't turned down the invitation to the O'Malley party. At the time he'd thought it would be another boring evening, but the one stretching ahead of him looked equally dull. He glanced at the clock. The hell with it, he'd go.

As he showered and changed he began whistling, completely unaware that Daisy O'Malley's party would irrevocably change his life.

II

Daisy's mother came from Melbourne in Australia, but she loved films and film stars and Alexandra always thought the O'Malley home looked as if it had been flown in from Hollywood. She felt sure she had seen one like it in a Cary Grant picture. Cary had been chasing a girl across Europe and they had ended up in a Californian-style ranch house with a colonnaded entrance, picture windows, and a beautiful garden overlooking a golf course. At night the garden had been hung with lamps, just as this one was.

The party hadn't begun. Daisy had asked Alexandra to come early to give her moral support, but it had taken Alexandra nearly an hour to get to Whitecraigs using public transport.

"Welcome!" Daisy squealed when she saw her friend standing on the doorstep.

"Your dress is lovely," Alexandra lied, as she assessed the yellow taffeta creation festooned with frills and bows. "Do you hoover this or rake it?" she added as her feet sank into the shag pile carpet. It was a well-worn joke, but it always made Daisy giggle.

In Daisy's bedroom the carpets, hangings, and wallpaper, and *en suite* bathroom were decorated in pale pink. "Mother keeps vowing that when daddy retires they'll go back to Australia," Daisy commented, "but I doubt if Australians would like this kind of decor. Come on, leave your coat here and we'll go downstairs. The study's been converted into a bar and there's a buffet laid out in the dining room."

The furniture had been cleared from one of the sitting rooms and the carpet rolled up to reveal the newly polished parquet floor on which everyone was going to dance. A band was busy setting up its instruments in one corner. Alexandra's favorite place in the house was the huge open-plan drawing room. Table lamps cast soft pools of light on gleaming mahogany furniture, valuable ornaments, and sumptuous sofas and chairs. French windows led out to the garden. A small elegant lady with upswept dark hair came gliding forward. "Alexandra, how nice you look in that blue dress! Come and sit beside me on the couch."

"Mother, you mustn't annex Alexandra."

"Darling, you'd better go and see the boys about the music. They're arguing already about which numbers they'll play."

"They are?" Daisy turned on her heel and headed towards them.

Mrs. O'Malley settled herself back on the couch and gave Alexandra her full attention. "Now, my dear, just before your arrived Daisy told me you were thinking of going into the property business. I've dabbled in that myself over the years, so I'm agog to hear what your plans are."

Alexandra's face flushed with pleasure at Mrs. O'Malley's enthusiasm and she began telling her the details of the tenement block which she had seen in the estate agency.

"Who is going to renovate this property for you?"

"My brother's a member of an ex-servicemen's club and he keeps saying there are lots of skilled tradesmen who can't get jobs. I thought I might be able to use them as an inexpensive workforce."

"What a splendid idea! But remember, once you employ them, you've got to keep paying their wages each week."

"I'm going to the bank on Monday. I'm hoping the manager will give me a large loan." Alexandra hesitated and then decided to hold nothing back. Since she'd become Daisy's best friend Mrs. O'Malley had taken a great interest in everything she did. "I've saved £400 from Bannons and my part-time jobs and this week I made £600 on the stock market."

"You did? How clever of you! Tell me more."

When Alexandra had explained the background to her first stock-exchange coup Mrs. O'Malley looked thoughtful. "My dear, I think you're going to do very well indeed. I'm so sure of it that I'm going to help." She rose from the couch and walked across to a mahogany escritoire. When she came back she handed Alexandra a card. "Tell your bank manager that I'll stand guarantor for your company for a year."

"I don't know what to say," Alexandra stuttered, quite overcome by Mrs. O'Malley's faith in her. "How do you know I won't let you down?"

"I'll make sure you don't by recommending you to my accountant, Fyfe Walker. Who's your lawyer?"

"I haven't got one yet."

"Hmm. Mine is too stuffy and old-fashioned. I've invited quite a few lawyers tonight—sons of friends. Aha! I can think of someone who would be ideal for you. Boyd Brown. Comes from Edinburgh. I hoped he might make a good match for Daisy, but . . ."

"Mother, what have you been saying about me?" Daisy asked as she sat down beside Alexandra.

"We've just been discussing a few business details," Mrs. O'Malley replied. "I've decided to give Alexandra my backing," she added as she got up from the couch and walked away to talk to the barman.

"Does your mother usually make decisions so quickly?"

"Always," Daisy said firmly. "The story is that she decided to marry my father five minutes after meeting him."

"But choosing a husband . . . well, it's a bit different from investing in someone else's ideas."

Daisy giggled. "It's much harder to get rid of a husband than a business partner. And don't be fooled by my mother, she's knife-sharp."

"I'm sure she is," Alexandra agreed.

"Bet she's already safeguarded herself by recommending her own accountant. Next, she'll steer you towards a good lawyer."

Alexandra nodded. "She's going to introduce me to Boyd Brown. I gather she tried to do a bit of matchmaking there."

Daisy groaned. "Mother's getting desperate because I've never had a boyfriend. Why d'you think she's throwing this lavish party for me? *And* inviting sons of some of her best friends. Like Boyd Brown. Yuk! He may be a brilliant lawyer, but he bores the pants off me. And talking of knickers," Daisy added as she leaned back on the couch, "you're not seriously thinking of taking them off for anyone . . . I mean, you've been chuntering on about this for weeks."

"Daisy, I've never gone all the way."

"So what? You're talking about the finishing line. Me, I haven't got past the start."

"I just want to find out what it's like," Alexandra said slowly, "and then get on with the rest of my life."

"Speaking as the ultimate non-expert, may I point out that you can't take sex the way you take an exam!"

"Why not?"

"Oh God, that's the doorbell!" Daisy cried. "You go, I can't face anyone."

"Of course you can!"

Alexandra took a firm grip on Daisy's arm and marched her to the door. When they opened it they were engulfed in a mass of laughing, shouting friends.

The party had begun.

The music from the band grew louder as the pace of the party quickened. Voices were raised, drink flowed freely, and everyone seemed to be having a good time. Alexandra had been determinedly chatting up boys ever since the party began, but she hadn't found one that appealed to her. She decided to go and hunt out Boyd Brown, the lawyer Mrs. O'Malley had recommended.

"He's in my father's study reading a newspaper," Daisy said. "I told you he was dead boring."

Boyd Brown turned out to be short and square with horn-rimmed spectacles that dominated a rather serious face. But when Alexandra mentioned that Mrs. O'Malley was prepared to lend her name as guarantor for Alexandra's projected property company Boyd's interest quickened. He absorbed the full story of Alexandra's ambitions and outlined the steps which would need to be taken before Meldrum Enterprises could come into being.

"Given your capital and Mrs. O'Malley's collateral you'll have no problems with the bank loan," he said. "Phone me when you're finished at the bank and I'll start doing searches on the tenement and send out a firm of surveyors. Better have a full structural survey in case there's dry rot or woodworm."

"If the tenement does have rot, would you recommend I don't buy it?"

"Depends how bad it is, but whatever the surveyors' report you'd be best to try and get a top joiner or cabinet-maker on your team."

"To assess the state of the wood?"

"And to advise on the renovation. The woodwork can make or break a reconstruction job."

"My half-brother's a joiner," Alexandra said slowly, "but he wouldn't want to become involved. The only other joiner I've ever met is Malcolm Semple. He was an apprentice joiner with Frank at John Brown's shipyard. They joined the army together during the war. Frank always said Malcolm Semple was a genius with wood."

"A genius on your team would be useful," Boyd commented dryly. "Where does he hang out?"

"He used to live in Edinburgh, but I've no idea where he is now."

"Forget him, then. I'm sure you can find someone else."

Alexandra remembered how kind Malcolm Semple had been to her on the one occasion they had met. She had been 9—and terrified. "I'd really like to trace Malcolm," she said thoughtfully.

"Surely you can ask your brother to help?"

Alexandra shook her head. "When Malcolm became an officer Frank lost touch with him."

"Any idea which school Semple went to?"

"Fettes. And wait, I remember now. I think Malcolm's father owned Semples."

"The paint people? They went bust a few years ago and then the old man died. Read about it in the *Scotsman*. Tell you what, you've given me enough to make a few inquiries. Edinburgh isn't like London; it's not too difficult to trace people whose parents have been in the public eye."

"You're being wonderfully helpful. I'm so glad you're going to be my lawyer." Alexandra leaned forward and kissed him on the cheek.

When she left, Boyd remained on the couch and tried to analyze the feeling which this girl had induced in him. He couldn't. But he knew that whatever Alexandra Meldrum did with her future he wanted to be part of it.

* * *

The noisy exuberance of the party had been replaced by soft music and quiet chattering as couples settled in secluded corners to exchange kisses and intimate gossip. Daisy's parents had retired to their bedroom suite on the top floor of the house.

Alexandra was at the buffet helping herself to spaghetti, stuffed potatoes and green salad. When her plate was full she glanced around for somewhere to sit, but the room was packed. She propped herself against a piano which was tucked into one corner. The pianist smiled at her as his fingers stroked the keyboard, playing a selection of old and new melodies.

"Hello there, beautiful girl," he said in an accent she couldn't place. "I'm Jan."

"Alexandra."

She felt embarrassed as Jan's eyes lingered on the scooped neckline of her blue dress, which revealed more of her breasts than she had realized. It was uncomfortable eating spaghetti with Jan's eyes traveling down past her waist to her long legs. After a while Jan stopped playing and came over to stand beside her.

"You play very well," Alexandra said politely.

"I do lots of things very well, pretty lady."

"Where are you from?"

"Amsterdam. I'm spending a year in Glasgow at your famous art school. You've finished your supper: why don't we find a seat somewhere and we can get to know each other better?"

Alexandra looked around. "Seats seem to be in short supply."

"We'll find one," he said confidently and led her through the crush into the next room and then to the study beyond it where a bartender was dispensing drinks. Jan spotted a small couch in a corner at the back of the room. "Just made for two," he said as he sat down and pulled her on to his knee. Alexandra was about to protest when she remembered that her main objective in coming to this party had been to try and lose her virginity. Since Jan was already stroking her knee with one hand and squeezing her waist with the other it looked as if she wouldn't have to try very hard.

"Tell me about yourself," she said nervously.

"What's to tell? I'm an artist and I like beautiful women."

His right hand began caressing her breast and as he turned her body towards his own she felt the hardness between his legs press into her side.

"I don't believe in wasting time at parties, do you?" he murmured. "Let's find some place quieter. I'm told there are some vacant bedrooms upstairs . . ."

Alexandra's mouth was dry and her hands were clammy. This was what she wanted, wasn't it?

No, she thought, it wasn't. She pushed herself free and stood up. "Sorry," she said breathlessly. "I've remembered I'm meeting someone else." She looked around wildly and through a sea of faces glimpsed a familiar head of impossibly white hair. Alan Gillian, her stockbroker, was standing at the bar, a long-handled cigarette holder in his hand.

He turned around as she approached. "Where's the fire?"

"In Amsterdam! A Dutchman just gave me a pressing invitation to go upstairs to one of the bedrooms."

"How enterprising. Wish I'd done the same. Unfortunately you've got me labelled in your mind as stockbroker, consultant, moneymaker." Alan gave a theatrical sigh. "You don't see me as a beddable human being," he said dolefully.

"I do!" Alexandra protested.

"Really?" His ice-blue eyes glinted. "Well, then, why don't I volunteer to be the one to take you upstairs?"

"Oh, men! You're all impossible," Alexandra said crossly. "I'm going outside to get some fresh air!"

She saw a wrap on a chair by the window and slung it round her shoulders as she ran out of the house into the garden.

The night air was chilly and Alexandra pulled the wrap tighter around her shoulders as she wandered aimlessly along a path lined with Leylandi conifers. Alan's teasing had touched a raw nerve. But while one part of her was chastising herself for cowardice, another was acknowledging that Daisy had been right and that, at least in her own case, it wasn't possible to pigeonhole passion as a subject to be explored objectively. Perhaps it wasn't true that the most potent aphrodisiac was the brain. She was gazing up at the stars as she walked and, failing to see a small urn blocking the way, she stumbled to her knees.

"Let me help you up!"

Alexandra looked up at the man standing over her. He was

tall. Dark-haired. She had noticed him at the party talking to an attractive blonde and had thought he seemed vaguely familiar though she couldn't place him.

"Have we met before?" she asked hesitantly.

"I don't think so, yet there's something about you that seems . . . Here, let me help you to your feet! By the way, I'm Robert Armstrong."

"And I'm Alexandra Meldrum."

The names jolted their memories at the same time.

They had been 11 years old and had both been present at a party for evacuees in Drumcraig Castle on Deeside. Alexandra remembered Isobel Armstrong arriving at the castle flanked by her two sons. Robert had been friendly and polite when he had been introduced to Alexandra and her mother, but Adam had ignored their outstretched hands and made some remark about the family feud with the Meldrums. His mother had been positively hostile and had tried to order Briony around as if she were a kitchenmaid before she sailed off to the Great Hall.

Alexandra had been on the point of running after her to demand an apology for her mother when Robert suddenly appeared at her side.

"I'm sorry about that," he said. "When mother's been working hard at Armstrongs she gets a bit bad-tempered. I'm sure she didn't mean to be so rude."

His brown eyes were so anxious that Alexandra felt her own temper evaporating. "It's okay. Maybe she'll apologize to my mum later on. Can you help me carry some of those things to the kitchen?"

She didn't have a chance to speak to him again until she was sent to the outhouse in the garden to fetch more lemonade for the evacuees. In her haste she didn't notice a stone statue on the path and she fell and grazed her knee. As she was trying to wipe away the blood with her hands Robert appeared. He too had been sent to help bring in more lemonade.

"Let me help," he said. As he cleaned the graze with his hanky, Alexandra noticed that it was already bloodstained. "I've just bumped my head and I'm still feeling a bit woozy." he explained. Then he pulled her to her feet. "You're beautiful," he said shyly.

Alexandra's eyes shone. No one had ever called her beautiful before. In a sudden rush of gratitude she bent forward and kissed his cheek. Robert took her in his arms and kissed her on the mouth. "Gosh," he said. "You're the first girl I've ever kissed. It feels good. Can I kiss you again?" He kissed her again and Alexandra felt her knees trembling.

"Come on, you two, where's the lemonade?" a voice called from the castle.

The moment passed, but as they looked at each other in the garden in Whitecraigs they both remembered it as if it were yesterday. Their eyes darkened as images of the fear and horror which followed that first meeting flickered in their minds. It was Robert who broke the silence. "That night at Drumcraig Castle . . ." he began.

"I don't want to talk about it," Alexandra said, panic-stricken.

Robert grasped her hands. "Neither do I. Nor do I want to talk about our families. I mean, I *know* the Armstrongs and Meldrums have been feuding for centuries, but we're the new generation. We should start afresh . . ."

Alexandra gazed up at him. His black wavy hair outlined a face made distinctive by a proud Roman nose and a determined chin. Yet his aura of strength and power was shaded with compassion and kindness and Alexandra felt an inexplicable ache of intimacy and longing. Yes, she wanted to be friends with him. "Is it possible for us to blot out the past?" she asked hesitantly.

"We'll fill the present with so many memories we won't *want* to remember it." Robert said forcefully. "Our future starts now. You know, I nearly didn't come to this party," he mused.

"Is Daisy a friend of yours? I haven't heard her mention you."

"She wouldn't. A classmate in conveyancing told me Daisy needed extra men for her party. My brother Adam intended to come and then went somewhere else. I turned down the invitation." He smiled at her. "I'm glad I changed my mind. Let's take a walk around the garden and banish our mutual ghosts."

He put his arm protectively round her shoulders. "Just in case you fall again," he said lightly.

Robert began regaling her with stories of his Aunt Ethel and her fall from grace. Then he started talking about his future with Armstrongs. She found his enthusiasm entertaining and felt an immediate chord of empathy when he mentioned his uneasy relationship with his brother. Alexandra in turned chatted to him about Frank, her landlady, her university studies, and her part-time jobs. She did not mention her ambitions in the property market: these were still so newly minted in her mind she wanted to keep them to herself.

They walked round and round the garden oblivious to the party still going on inside the house, but as the night chill deepened Alexandra began to shiver. Robert took off his jacket and draped it around her shoulders.

"It's strange," he said as they walked towards the French windows, "we met once when we were children and haven't seen each other for years, yet somehow I feel I've always known you."

"I feel the same," Alexandra replied. All those years ago there had been magic in the moonlight.

Then and now.

Robert pulled her closer as they came to the door and tipped her chin with his finger. "You're beautiful," he said with a kind of wonder, echoing the remark he had made as a boy. These days Alexandra was constantly being told she was beautiful, but the compliment had never impinged on her nerve ends. Now she felt them tingle at Robert's words and a sudden rush of warmth through her body brought color to her face.

"Maybe we'd better rejoin the party," she said and pushed open the French window.

"Wait," he urged. "Who brought you here?"

"I came by myself. Bus and tram. Daisy's mother has ordered a taxi to take me back to Park Terrace."

"Cancel it. I've got my aunt's car."

"All right," Alexandra agreed meekly.

On the journey back into town the frenetic flow of conversation which had kept them talking in the garden was stilled and they sat in a companionable silence which was punctuated by occasional exchanges of information. Alexandra felt she was caught up in a dream. "It's a pity the party had to end," she sighed as Robert stopped outside her digs.

He switched off the engine. "For us the party's just beginning," he said and took her in his arms. His lips were warm and strong, his hands firm as he pressed her close to him.

Reluctantly she pulled away. "I'd better go in."

"I'll phone," he said. "I'll plan something special—to celebrate our reunion."

I'm in love, Robert thought, as he pulled up outside his aunt's house in Jordanhill. He went to bed straight away, hoping to dream of Alexandra. But instead out of the darkness loomed an old nightmare which sometimes came back to torture him: Drumcraig Castle. Resolutely he forced it from his mind.

EIGHT

I

Alexandra spent a restless night dreaming of Robert and worrying about the old feud between the Meldrums and the Armstrongs. Her mother used to say that the Armstrongs never failed to bring bad luck to the Meldrums. Would history repeat itself?

Near dawn she fell into a deep sleep and when she wakened she felt unexpectedly refreshed. Daylight had diminished the problems which had haunted her dreams. The sins of the fathers shouldn't be visited on their children and the notion of fate as an abstract force which could command your actions was ridiculous. She would cock a snook at fate and relegate the ancient enmity between the Meldrums and Armstrongs to the past.

When Robert phoned later that morning and proposed taking her on a surprise outing she agreed joyfully.

"Where on earth are we going?" Alexandra shouted as Robert's car raced along the Boulevard leaving Glasgow's suburbs behind.

"Bet you a pound you'll never guess. An outing you'll remember when you're old."

"Do you plan to be around then?"

"I do," he said in such a forceful way it sounded like a promise.

Alexandra studied him as he was driving. Broad forehead. Aggressive chin. A man very much in command of himself. A powerful man. Not just physically but in character. She felt an ache in her belly at the thought of his big capable hands resting on her body instead of on the wheel of the car.

Mountain peaks and a stretch of water glinted through banks

of trees. "You're going to lose your bet. We're going for a drive past Balloch along Loch Lomondside."

"Wrong. We're leaving the car right here," Robert said as he eased it to a halt beside the jetty.

As Alexandra got out of the car she felt a smirr of rain on her face. The gray sky made the waters of the loch look cold and menacing. "What now?"

Robert pointed to a small motor cruiser anchored beside the jetty. "It belongs to a friend. He's lent it to me for the day."

"Isn't it dangerous to cruise up Loch Lomond in November?" Alexandra exclaimed as Robert helped her on to the boat.

"Can be very dangerous. Especially with someone like me. Wait, I've got to get something out of the boot of the car."

When he returned he was carrying a small grip. "Hold tight." Robert said as he settled himself in the cockpit and put the key in the ignition.

"I hope you know what you're doing."

"You're forgetting I've grown up with boats. Compared with a trawler this is a toy. Anyway, I've been on this one before."

The engine roared into life and the bow of the cruiser powered through the water. Through the cascades of spray Alexandra was able to catch fleeting glimpses of the scenery on either side of the loch: trees, mountains, and isolated hillside cottages which seemed to undulate with the boat's movement.

"Been on Loch Lomond before, Alex?" Robert yelled above the sound of the engine.

"No one calls me that," Alexandra exclaimed.

"Then I'll be different from everyone else!"

He put his foot on the throttle when they left Balloch behind and as they flashed past the island of Inchmurrin Alexandra strained her eyes to catch a glimpse of its castle. Spray spiralled around the boat like a gauze curtain, emphasizing their isolation. Robert kept his hands firmly on the wheel, but every now and then he glanced down at her, his eyes alight with an excitement which she knew was mirrored in her own. When they came to the stretch of water between Balmaha on the east side of Loch Lomond and Luss on the west Robert shouted out the names of the islands which were scattered like mounds of moss: Inch Fad, Inch Moan, Inchtavannach . . .

"We'll have something to eat at Luss," he shouted and guided the cruiser towards the shore.

The rain had stopped and a watery sun was beginning to glint on the houses lining the waterfront and on the treetops on the slopes beyond. There was a fairy-tale atmosphere about Luss, Alexandra decided. She could imagine roses climbing the cottage walls in the summertime, gardens scented with hollyhocks and goldenrod, and children fishing by the harbor. Looming above the loch was the massive shadow of Ben Lomond. Three thousand feet high, Alexandra remembered. From its summit you had a bird's-eye view not just of Loch Lomond, but of the Argyllshire hills and the Grampian mountains.

Robert guided her towards a small whitewashed cottage on the edge of the village. There was a brass knocker on an oak door and when Robert gave a sharp rap a genial bearded giant came to greet them. Robert introduced him. "Sandy Dochart. An old school chum from Robert Gordon's, my school in Aberdeen."

"Delighted to meet you," Sandy said, giving Alexandra a warm handshake before taking their jackets and scarves and hanging them on a coatstand by the door. They followed him through the hall to a door at the opposite end marked "Restaurant." He pushed it open to reveal a big airy room with windows overlooking the loch. It was furnished with chintz-covered couches and chairs, and pretty table lamps.

"Sandy runs this as a restaurant in the summer months," Robert explained.

"And in the winter?"

"It's closed. Unless someone makes a special request."

"He knows what he wants, does my friend Robert," Sandy said with a grin. "I've set up a table for you in the corner by the window. You're up to time, so the meal's all ready."

"You planned all this?" Alexandra asked Robert.

"Phoned up Sandy this morning. He's a good cook—you'll enjoy your lunch."

A few minutes later Sandy brought in steaming bowls of lentil soup flavored with ham and pea.

"Delicious," Alexandra said appreciatively.

"Wait till you taste his casserole of beef."

The beef was served with home-grown potatoes, sprouts and

peas. Pudding was a crispy cake flavored with Sandy's own heather honey.

"It's a bit like Greek baklava, isn't it?" Robert commented.

"I wouldn't know: I've never been to Greece. In fact I've never been out of Scotland," Alexandra replied as she forked the cake into her mouth. When Robert looked surprised she grinned at him. "You mustn't forget that we come from different backgrounds. Rich boy. Poor girl."

"Don't talk so daft. Your grandfather was a superb mason. Drumcraig Castle was his masterpiece!"

"I never discuss my past," Alexandra said huskily. "Frank and I have a pact that we only talk about life after 1943, when I came back from Aberdeen to Glasgow after my mother's funeral."

"What about your father?" Robert began.

"My father is the *last* person I'd want to mention!"

Robert saw the hurt in Alexandra's eyes and put down his pudding spoon. "If you haven't mentioned him to anyone else, make me special," he challenged. "You don't need to tell me it all. Just a hint of why you feel the way you do—to put me in the picture."

"All right," Alexandra replied in a flat voice. "I slept in the kitchen bed and heard everything that went on between my mother and father in the room next door. My father was a brute, a sadist. He abused my mother, beat up my half-brother Frank, and knocked me out of the way whenever I passed. I hated him. We all did. And I have a suspicion that in the end he was . . ." She choked and put her head between her hands.

Robert stood up quickly and coming round to her chair took her in her arms. "God, I'm sorry, Alex. I'd no idea there were such horrors in your past. Please forgive me and I'll never bring up the subject again." He held her close as she sobbed, drying her tears with his hanky. Then he settled her gently in her chair and, and sitting down on his own, began talking about the Armstrong family business in an effort to distract her. "Father wants Armstrongs to stay the way they are. I want to expand the Armstrong empire. Adam says he agrees with father and since I hear the board are divided there are going to be lots of battles. But I'll *enjoy* that," Robert added, his eyes gleaming. "I like tension and confrontation at business."

When she made no reply he squeezed her hand. "But I'm

looking forward to peace and quiet when I make a home of my own—with a wife and family who'll be waiting for me. I can't understand women who allow other people to look after their children while they're out at work. Anyway, women aren't good at the cut and thrust of business."

Alexandra's eyes widened. "Why, I do believe I'm sitting opposite an old-fashioned male chauvinist!"

"I knew you were a perceptive woman the minute I saw you," Robert said with a laugh.

"What would you say if I told you I wanted to be a property tycoon?"

"I'd walk right out of this restaurant and never see you again. I might be chivalrous enough to leave you the boat, though," he chuckled. "It's a long swim up Loch Lomond back to Glasgow!"

Alexandra tried to join in his laughter and hoped he could not see how false her own was. Obviously she would have to choose another time and place to tell him that she *was* going to be a property tycoon and that a new company called Meldrum Enterprises was about to be formed.

She felt reluctant to leave the cozy comfort of the white-washed cottage, but after a leisurely coffee Robert thought that it was time he paid the bill. Sandy shook their hands and said he hoped it wouldn't be too long before they came back.

"I really like your friend," Alexandra said as they walked towards the jetty where the cruiser lay bobbing on the waves.

"Don't get too fond of him—or of anyone else," Robert commanded. "I'm the jealous type."

Yes, he probably was, Alexandra decided as she looked into the dark eyes. A strong man. And one with decided convictions.

"Where now?" she asked once they were back in the boat.

"The most picturesque spot on the whole of Loch Lomond," Robert replied. He steered the cruiser towards the center of the loch and switched off the engine. "Balmaha on the east side, ma'am, Luss on the west."

It had started raining again, but even the rain couldn't spoil the magnificence of the mountains and forests which overlooked the loch and its many islands. The water was a ribbon of metallic gray and blue, stretching as far as the eye could see in either direction. While Alexandra was gazing at the scenery Robert was busy pulling out the grip he had stowed away in the galley. With a flourish of his wrists he produced two beautiful crystal goblets and a bottle of Bollinger.

"Money no object," he declared. "At least not for today."

Robert uncorked the champagne, solemnly presented Alexandra with the cork and poured out the sparkling wine. "Champagne in the rain. Here's to forever!" he said as they clinked glasses.

"Here's to forever!" Alexandra echoed, trying not to let him see the tears of happiness pricking her eyelids.

Robert kept looking at her as they drank and when their glasses were empty he refilled them till the champagne was finished. Then he took her in his arms and kissed her. "You're soaked. Come into the cabin."

She felt the warmth as soon as she stepped inside and he gestured her to stand in front of a heater in the corner. She warmed her hands and watched him tugging at the handle of a couch by the porthole which he soon converted into a double bed. She was both relieved and disappointed when he made no move to pull her down on it. Instead he rummaged in the locker and produced a towel. "I don't want you to catch a chill," he said. He dried her face and hair and then threw the towel aside and began kissing her with a passion and urgency which took the strength from her legs.

When he started to ease off her clothes she began to tug at his tie and the buttons on his shirt. Every now and then they stopped fumbling with their clothes to cling together for another kiss. It was only when Alexandra realized that they were both naked that her sense of modesty returned. She drew back from him and tried to cover her breasts and the fluff of chestnut hair between her legs.

Everything that had happened and was about to happen seemed distilled in the sudden silence between them and Alexandra thought in panic that perhaps this wasn't the right time, the right place . . .

"Have you ever . . . ?" he began.

She shook her head just the tiniest fraction. "And you?" she asked.

Shame fought with pride. Honesty won. "I was waiting for someone special," Robert confessed.

Joy sliced through her uncertainty and she knew then that everything was going to be all right. "So was I!" she exclaimed and they kissed, hugged and laughed, relieved that their inexperience was mutual.

As Robert picked her up and laid her gently on the bed she noticed a star-shaped mole on the inside of his wrist and kissed it. He kissed a childhood scar on her leg. Then he stood back. As he looked at her Alexandra felt that wherever his gaze rested, her skin flamed. Robert bent closer and his lips began kissing and caressing her neck, her breasts, her thighs and the mound between them. He lowered himself on top of her, probing with his fingers for the space between her legs. As she moaned and began pressing upwards, she felt the pressure of his fingers replaced by the insistent pulse of his manhood.

"I know you're supposed to take it slowly the first time . . ." Robert gasped, but he was so overcome by his own need that he kept pushing and pushing until she cried out in pain.

"Oh God! Alex, I'm sorry!" he shouted. But she clasped him closer, straining her legs and her body to embrace every part of him.

Sensation threatened to overwhelm her. "Yes!" she shouted. "Oh yes!" she cried, as she felt herself climbing upwards till she swirled dizzily off the peak: spinning, tumbling, hurtling . . . Lost in space . . .

"My love," he gasped. "I imagined . . . but I never guessed . . . just how good it would be."

They lay for a while, dazed and happy until once again she felt his fingers and lips exploring her body. This time their passion ignited even more fiercely until Alexandra felt she was burning up with it.

Neither of them wanted to leave the confined space of the cabin, but when Robert looked out of the porthole and saw the darkening sky he whispered in her ear that it was time to leave. Alexandra dressed herself quickly and began brushing her hair. There was a mirror on the side of the cabin and she looked intently at her reflection. Had she changed? Could the mirror tell? As she twisted her head this way and that, and bent closer to look at her eyes she was sure she could see a new maturity in them.

"Here's to forever!" Alexandra whispered. But she felt a momentary chill as she said it. It was obvious from the way

Robert had talked that he envisaged a future with a wife and family. Her perspective was diametrically opposed to that. She was greedy for love, but marriage was no part of her plans. Once you were married you had to stay at home and look after your husband. She wanted to travel the world and build up an empire, and she'd never be able to do that if she conformed to Robert's idea of a wife.

Would Robert be content to have her as his mistress? She'd be happy to settle for that. But would he? She glanced at him as he dressed, a big powerful man with muscled hairy legs and a broad chest, and she trembled with renewed desire. Robert sensed her need immediately and promptly carried her back to bed again.

NINE

I

Alexandra knew she had been right to put the old family feud between the Meldrums and the Armstrongs at the back of her mind. She and Robert were not only ideally suited to each other, they were totally, crazily, obsessively in love. When they weren't walking or talking or lying in bed they sallied forth to enjoy the lighter aspects of university life: like "Daft Friday," the day when students were traditionally allowed to roam the streets around the university getting up to all kinds of silly pranks. The tradition dated back to a misguided concept that if you allowed students to have twenty-four hours of nonsense they would behave for the rest of the year. Although the authorities had long since been disabused of that idea, the custom remained firmly fixed in the student calendar.

On the morning of Daft Friday, Robert and Alexandra arrived at University Avenue warmly clad in jeans, sweaters, thick gloves, and waterproofs: defense against handguided missiles like bags of flour, a favorite student weapon. Paper streamers festooned lamp posts, unseasonal confetti floated in the air and rude signs began appearing in unexpected places. By midday Robert and Alexandra had participated in all kinds of silly stunts which ranged from adorning statues with jockstraps to making barriers with lines of brassieres.

"Are you hungry?" Robert asked.

"Starving!"

"Right, let's finish with Daft Friday. We'll get something to eat in Byres Road."

"The meat ration is miserly," Alexandra grumbled as they walked down University Avenue.

Meat wasn't the only thing in short supply: rationing still applied to butter, bacon, cheese, sugar, tea, and sweets. The shortages meant that Alexandra had to use great skill and ingenuity for her dinner party menus. She still enjoyed cooking but since she'd met Robert she had become reluctant to spend Friday and Saturday evenings in other people's homes and she had asked two students if they'd like to help out. The arrangement was working so well Alexandra was thinking of expanding her catering service, but first she wanted to get Meldrum Enterprises successfully launched. Fortunately Boyd Brown was doing all the hard work. The minute she had secured the bank loan he engaged surveyors to go over the tenement in Edinburgh, assessed their report, and then advised Alexandra to buy it.

She had been so jubilant the day her offer was accepted she wanted to rush round and share her news with Robert. Unfortunately he had been up in Aberdeen and when he returned to Glasgow he was in a furious mood because he had quarrelled with his father about business. He also seemed to be annoyed about a relationship William had with a former assistant, Margot Gossamer. But why shouldn't William Armstrong have a relationship with another woman, Alexandra wondered. His wife had been dead for seven years. Still, she felt it wasn't the right moment to tell Robert her plans.

It never seemed to be the right moment and Alexandra sensed intuitively that she was afraid to tell Robert in case his disapproval shattered their cocoon of closeness. Today, she decided, I'll tell him today over lunch.

Low prices and well-cooked food had made the café at the corner of Ashton Road and Byres Road a favorite with students.

"You might have to wait for quite a while," the waitress said as she scanned the room and failed to find an empty seat.

"We'll wait." Robert pulled Alexandra into the crook of his arm and they leaned against the wall in the corner where they could talk without being overheard.

"No meat on the menu," Alexandra whispered as she scanned the sheet of paper handed her by the waitress, "but they've got mushroom vol-au-vent and chips. I could eat three platefuls!"

"Greedy pig!" He kissed her gently on the nose.

She smiled up at him. Ordinary everyday things like walking or having lunch acquired a special magic when you were with someone you loved.

"If you want to look like Belinda Belgrove you'll have to diet," Robert teased. The American "millionairess" was notoriously slim. "Don't frown at me. You're the one I want to marry."

"This is a serious proposal?"

"Very serious. Points 1 to 99: I love you forever," he whispered.

"What about point 100?"

"Point 100 is that when I leave university and join the family business I'll need a very supportive wife. There's going to be a lot of infighting between my father, Adam, and myself. I'm glad you've given up your tutoring; pleased too that someone else runs your catering service. I hope you'll give that up as well."

"I don't want to get married," Alexandra began, but Robert wasn't paying attention.

"It was my mother's obsession with her career which ruined her health and her marriage," he was saying earnestly. "My father told me that. I've made up my mind that when I marry I'll have a stay-at-home wife whom I can love and cherish, not a career woman who pays other people to look after her home and her children."

"There's a table free," the waitress called, and they moved across to one which looked out on to Byres Road.

Alexandra gazed through the glass at the passersby. Robert had made his prejudices so clear. If she insisted that she wanted to stay single and build up her career he would want nothing more to do with her. So what was she to do? She couldn't bear to lose Robert, but neither could she bear to give up her fledgling company. She'd just have to carry on as she had been doing: keeping Robert happy by acquiescing to his old-fashioned ideas and at the same time continuing to build up her business.

It hadn't been too difficult keeping her extra-curricular activities secret from Robert; his final-year law studies now entailed such a heavy workload he'd already mentioned he might have to see her less often until after the exams. She was more fortunate with her own course. When she had abandoned the idea of doing an honors degree Alexandra discovered that she needed only two more passes to complete an ordinary MA: one in science and one in philosophy. She had chosen zoology and moral philosophy: two classes a day, no tutorials. She was finding her last year at university incredibly easy.

"I'm sorry I won't be able to see you till Friday," Robert said as the waitress brought the mushroom vol-au-vents. "I'm really behind with my work."

"I'm busy too," Alexandra murmured. And she was, although her workload had nothing to do with university. She had hired a foreman and a group of tradesmen from Frank's ex-servicemen's club and they had started renovating the Edinburgh tenement. Boyd had managed to contact Malcolm Semple and Alexandra was going through to Edinburgh to see him on Friday morning.

She felt the pressure of fingers on her hand and realized Robert was studying her face. "You're miles away." He smiled at her so fondly she felt tears of affection pricking her eyes.

"I love you," she whispered. And she did.

Robert would find out eventually that she had been deceiving him, but surely he would understand?

"Just as well you didn't bring Aunt Ethel's car today," Alexandra said with a giggle as she looked out of the window into Byres Road and glimpsed a professor's Rover being adorned with tin cans.

"Adam's need was greater than mine," Robert replied. "He's out with Belinda."

"I hope she realizes . . ." Alexandra began, then curbed her tongue. Since she'd started going out with Robert, Adam had shown his disapproval of their friendship by trying to hurt Alexandra with well-aimed jibes. When they made her angry she would mutter to herself: don't get mad, get even.

And some day she would.

II

"What's this I hear about you having a date with Belinda Belgrove?" The student who was walking beside Adam as they headed for the conveyancing class wanted to know if the rumor were true.

"I've been out with her twice, but I shouldn't think I'll date her again."

"You should hang in there. God, if you married a girl like that, you'd never have to work again."

Adam mulled over that tantalizing prospect as he walked across the quad. On his last visit to Aberdeen his father had mentioned almost in passing that Robert was probably the one who would succeed him as Chairman. Adam had been dismayed. He did not relish the idea of being under his twin's rule for the rest of his life. He found it difficult to concentrate on the conveyancing class. Although he hadn't admitted it to his friend, his two dates with Belinda hadn't exactly been a success. She hadn't been impressed by the modern restaurants where he'd taken her for a meal, or by the film they'd seen, and each time she had repulsed his efforts to kiss her goodnight. He had decided to cut his losses and enjoy himself with other girls, but his friend's remarks were making him wonder if he should try a bit harder.

After the lecture was over Adam made straight for the library to plan his campaign. He wrote down all the snippets of gossip he had heard about Belinda and decided on his tactics. After lunch he sought her out as she was emerging from her English class.

"Hi, Adam," she said with a noticeable lack of enthusiasm.

"You're looking wonderful, Belinda. Listen, those restaurants where I took you for a meal were awful. Let me try and make it up to you. There's a lovely old hotel in a small village outside Glasgow. The Buchanan Arms has tartan carpets and wonderful views of the mountains and moors."

"Is that right? What about the food?"

"Terrific. Why don't you let me take you there for dinner? Saturday night?"

"Well . . . yeah, I like the sound of that hotel. Give me a call."

The evening went well. Belinda loved the tartan carpets, the discreet service and the excellent meal. They had coffee on the covered veranda overlooking the countryside and Belinda sighed contentedly. "I've really enjoyed this evening."

After that Adam made sure Belinda enjoyed every outing: theaters, ballets, concerts, and sightseeing trips around Scotland. He fussed over her and kept surprising her with sprays of flowers, and chocolates. Since his father's allowance did not cover his vastly increased expenses he decided to confide in Aunt Ethel.

"You've a £50 overdraft? You're very wicked, Adam, but don't worry, I'll see you right."

Aunt Ethel not only paid off his overdraft but lent him another £50 into the bargain and offered to help him out in future if he ran short. "Horatio would not have approved," she said gleefully. She shook her fist at the ceiling. "Are ye up there, ye auld skinflint? I hope you're watching me being imprudent!"

Adam bestowed a grateful kiss on his eccentric great-aunt and made up his mind to take the old girl for everything she had. "By the way, I'd rather you didn't tell Robert about this," he begged.

After that Adam felt free to step up his courtship of Belinda. One evening he presented her with two very expensive books which had caught her eye in John Smith and Son in St. Vincent Street. Belinda was thrilled. "I adore Scottish castles."

"Then why don't I take you up to see the castles in the north east?" Adam suggested.

He borrowed Aunt Ethel's car and they spent a weekend touring the castles on Deeside. Belinda was ecstatic. "We don't have anything like this in the States," she said on the day they visited Crathes Castle on Deeside. "God, I'd give my soul to own a Scottish castle."

Adam felt his pulse racing as he said casually, "My grandfather owned Drumcraig Castle. I'll drive you to a viewpoint."

Belinda gasped when she caught her first sight of Drumcraig. "And your grandfather owned that? My, I'm so impressed I don't know what to say. It's like a castle out of a fairy tale. Did your father live there too?"

"He grew up in it. Unfortunately the castle was left to his brother Toby. When he sold the castle I gather there was only a scullery maid-cum-housekeeper: Alexandra Meldrum's mother."

Belinda goggled. "Alexandra's mother was a scullery maid? Doesn't Robert worry about her humble origins?"

"No," Adam said shortly, "but I do. I don't like her friendship with my brother. She's a social climber."

"Never mind Alexandra, who owns Drumcraig now?"

"Elphinstone. I might buy it back from him one day."

"Adam, the more I get to know you, the better I like you. I'd no idea you were a man of such substance!"

Adam enjoyed that compliment and decided to reinforce it by joining one of the most prestigious clubs in Glasgow.

"The Automobile Club?" Belinda exclaimed when Adam first mentioned his plans to join. "There's nothing special about the AA. Or is there?"

Adam smiled at her tolerantly. "The AA is quite different from the Royal Scottish Automobile Club. You'll see."

On the day he received his letter of acceptance Adam arranged to meet Belinda for lunch. He arrived early in Blythswood Square and ran lightly up the steps of the club, which had an imposing frontage designed to convince the world that only citizens of consequence should be allowed to pass through its portals. Adam nodded to the concierge before selecting a chair in the reception area which would afford him a clear view of the entrance.

He glanced down at his watch. Belinda was late, but he did not mind. During the past few weeks his feelings for her had changed. Although he was still attracted to Belinda's wealth and the prospect of living in idle luxury, she had added a new dimension to their relationship by her behavior in bed. The minute Belinda took off her clothes she displayed a vulgar streak of sensuality that fired his lust as nothing else had ever done.

He was mad about her.

"Hi there, honey! Sorry I'm late. My, isn't this regal?" Belinda exclaimed as she walked through the door of the club and admired the marble pillars, ornate ceiling, antique furniture, and valuable paintings. Belinda's blond hair gleamed, her eyes shone, her skin was alabaster-smooth. Adam could see everyone looking at her and he felt a proprietary pride as he took her arm and led her into the dining room.

Belinda exerted herself to be charming to Adam over lunch, but her thoughts were with his twin. When she had first been introduced to the Armstrongs it was Robert who had stirred her senses, and although he hadn't responded to her flirting she still hankered after him. The brothers were physically almost identical, but Robert emanated a ruthless virility which Adam lacked. At the moment Robert seemed to be enamored of his new girlfriend, but Belinda intended to prise him away from Alexandra. Nor did she have any doubts about succeeding. Her father always said that what Belinda wanted Belinda got.

And she wanted Robert.

Alexandra was in Queen Margaret Union when Belinda came up and suggested a foursome for lunch on Friday.

"Sorry," Alexandra replied quickly, "I'm tied up on Friday—going through to Edinburgh to see a girlfriend."

That was the story she'd given Robert. It was the first lie she'd ever told him. It wasn't to be the last.

TEN

I

A winter chill had the land clenched tight in its grip and the clarity of the air was defining the Edinburgh landscape in crisp, clear colors. It was the type of morning that Malcolm Semple loved and he was barely conscious of the cold as he walked along Princes Street toward the Waverley Steps where he had arranged to meet Alexandra Meldrum. He had been flattered that she had gone to such trouble to trace him, but he wasn't ready to accept a job on her lawyer's say-so. Boyd Brown seemed a decent enough chap, but before Malcolm agreed to work for Alexandra he wanted to find out how she had turned out.

He had met her in 1941. He and Frank Meldrum had both been 19 and working as apprentice joiners at the time in John Brown's, but they were expecting their call-up papers. Because Malcolm was about to go off to war his father had lent him the car for his afternoon off, and he had taken Frank and his half-sister on an outing to Bingham's Boating Pond near Anniesland Cross in Glasgow. Alexandra had just been a kid then. 9? Or was it 10?

13 March 1941: a night Scotland would never forget.

"We've got number five," Alexandra said excitedly as she clambered into one of the numbered rowing boats. The men each took turns at showing their prowess before they handed the oars to Alexandra. She promptly dropped one of the oars in the water and was about to dive in to retrieve it when Malcolm restrained her.

"Christ, Frank, your sister's too daring for her own good," he said in alarm as he hauled her back. "Hold the oars tightly,

Alexandra, and push them gently into the water. Back and forwards. Back and forwards. That's better!"

"I think I spy Treasure Island," Frank said with a knowing wink at Malcolm as he pointed to an old tree stump on the bank. Alexandra entered into the spirit of the game and had a wonderful time rowing towards imaginary destinations. Half an hour passed very quickly.

"Come in, number five, your time is up," the loudhailer boomed from the bank.

"Not already!" Alexandra complained.

" 'Fraid so. Come on. You can row to the shore," Malcolm suggested.

"Gosh, thanks, you two, that was great!" Alexandra giggled as she jumped out of the boat.

"So where now?" Frank asked. "Come on, sis, it's your treat. You choose where to go."

Alexandra confessed that she was desperate to see John Brown's shipyard where Frank and Malcolm worked. The three of them were in high spirits as Malcolm drove along Anniesland Road to Yoker and then Clydebank. They weren't allowed to take Alexandra inside the shipyard because of wartime security, but Malcolm hoisted her up on his shoulders so that she could see the giant cranes and the huge hulls of the ships which were being built. After that they treated her to a fish supper at a café and debated what to do next. Alexandra had never eaten chips from a newspaper before. "They taste different," she said solemnly as they walked back towards the car.

"Look!" she exclaimed as they passed the La Scala cinema. "Shirley Temple and Jack Oakie are starring in *Young People*. I've never been to the pictures. Couldn't you take me?"

Frank looked at Malcolm and shrugged. "Yeah, why not," he said, "but I promised to have Alexandra home by nine, so we'll have to leave the flicks at 8:30."

But at 8:30 Malcolm and Frank were as engrossed in the film as Alexandra. It was only when the air-raid sirens went off shortly after nine that they realized how late it was and made for the exit. The commissionaire standing at the door frowned. "Hey, you lot, you shouldn't go out there!"

"Don't worry, Alexandra," Frank said reassuringly when they stood outside and looked up at the sky. "It's a bombers' moon up there. The Jerries won't be coming to Scotland, they'll be making for London."

It was a view that was echoed in many homes that night and it was only when a flare illuminated the area round the High School that Clydebank realized its turn had come. The German pathfinders were dropping incendiaries to serve as markers for the first wave of bombers which arrived in the wake of the flares. There was a tremendous explosion and the three threw themselves to the ground. Frank looked towards the towering flames shooting up from the Dalmuir area. "I think they've scored a direct hit on Beardmore's Diesel Works."

"Christ, watch out!" Malcolm yelled, as a bomb dropped on a block of flats and bricks began showering in their direction. "There's a pub down the road, we'd better make for it."

They ran as hard as they could, but just as they turned the corner they saw the pub building explode into flames and there was a great whoosh of sound as the walls tumbled.

"What are you lot doing out here? Get into a shelter," an air-raid warden yelled at them. He pushed them towards a flight of steps which led to a big Anderson air-raid shelter. Frank held tightly on to Alexandra's arm as they bent their heads and went down the shelter stairs. Faces glowed eerily at them, illuminated by the makeshift lighting. Although the thickness of the shelter muted the noise of the falling bombs they could all hear the screeching wail of the explosions nearby. When Alexandra put her hands over her ears, Malcolm slipped his arm round her. "Snuggle close to me."

Suddenly the shelter door opened and a man with a blood-stained face staggered in. "Got hit by falling masonry. It's the shipyards the Jerries are after. If any of us survives tonight it'll be a miracle."

Malcolm hugged Alexandra tighter. "We'll get out of this all right," he said reassuringly. "And you know what? One day when you're all grown up I promise to take you dancing."

"Will it be somewhere abroad with lights and chandeliers and ladies in long dresses?" Alexandra asked eagerly. Everyone in the shelter laughed including the doom merchant who was predicting nemesis for everyone.

"Cross my heart and hope to die," Alexandra persisted.

"Here!" a young woman exclaimed. "Enough talk about dying."

"Cross my heart and hope to die," Malcolm whispered.

The bombing seemed to go on and on and eventually Alexandra fell asleep in Malcolm's arms.

At 6:25 in the morning the All Clear sounded, and they stumbled outside. Clydebank was a town in ruins. Street after street had been completely gutted; gable ends of houses gaped open beside spaces filled with bricks and stones and chimney stacks. Smoke and dust swirled in everyone's faces lending a surreal aspect to the landscape. Everywhere there was shattered glass, broken bits of masonry, remnants of household furniture and clothing, and blood from bodies which had been ripped apart by shrapnel.

As corpses began to be pulled out of the rubble and wrapped in canvas bags, people surfaced like moles from the air-raid shelters; bewildered by the empty spaces where streets had once stood, appalled at the extent of the devastation. Malcolm heard later that only eight houses in Clydebank had been left standing. The wail of ambulances and police cars mingled with the screams of survivors who were trapped beneath the rubble. Worst of all was the sickening smell of burning human flesh.

Alexandra gasped when Malcolm pointed to the remains of his car: there was nothing left except charred tires and smoldering upholstery. Someone directed them to a mobile canteen and they were given blankets, hot drinks, and transport home.

"Are you ill?"

Malcolm looked at the woman standing beside him and forced his mind back to the present. He was in Edinburgh on his way to meet Alexandra, but the memories of the Clydebank blitz had been so vivid that he had stopped walking and was standing still, pressing his hand to his forehead.

"Just a headache," he said lightly to the passerby, "but thanks for asking."

Malcolm smiled and continued on his way to the Waverley Steps. Yes, his first meeting with Alexandra had been momentous. She had been so plucky, hadn't cried once. He hoped she hadn't turned into an obnoxious brat, because he liked the sound of the job she was offering him. When his parents had died, the family business had gone into liquidation and when Malcolm returned to Edinburgh after the war he had been forced to rent a small flat and start looking for work. His training as a John Brown's joiner had stood him in good stead and he had accepted a job in Paddy's Antiques near the Royal Mile. He loved working with wood, but the job didn't pay well. He needed to make more money.

Malcolm glanced to his right at the amethyst shadow of Edinburgh Castle perched up on the crags overlooking Princes Street. The castle was like some character in a Wagnerian opera, its closed gray face presenting a dramatic contrast to the greens and golds in the valley gardens separating the castle from Princes Street. Reluctantly Malcolm turned his thoughts back to Alexandra. Imagine wanting to be a tycoon at the ripe old age of 19! She would probably be so eaten up with ambition she'd look like an old hag. He would know soon enough; the ten o'clock train from Glasgow was due any minute. He positioned himself at the top of the Waverley Steps: flight after flight of steep stairs which ascended from the railway station to Edinburgh's main thoroughfare. Malcolm had said he'd be wearing a bright red scarf so that Alexandra could identify him.

Two boys raced up the flight of stairs. Behind them came an old couple who took the steps one at a time. A crowd of tourists chattering noisily had to make way for a girl with a long thin face and determined mouth. Malcolm groaned. Was this Alexandra? He felt immense relief when she passed him by with barely a glance and he could turn his attention to a beautiful girl with a glorious mane of chestnut hair. She looked so confident and held her head so high he wondered if she was a celebrity of some kind.

"Malcolm Semple?" she asked as she came forward to greet him.

"Alexandra? I can hardly believe you're the little girl I met on the night of the Clydebank blitz."

"I can still remember how kind you were. I'll always be grateful for that."

"Your lawyer's been telling me about all your ideas, but he never mentioned that you'd grown into such a stunner!"

"And I wasn't told why you insisted on meeting here instead of in my lawyer's office," Alexandra countered.

"On my days off I like to be in the fresh air, so when I heard you hadn't been to Edinburgh before I thought I'd take you on a tour—the Royal Mile and Edinburgh Castle."

"And by the end of it you'll know whether you want to work with me? Well, maybe we'll both talk more freely in the open air."

"How's Frank?" he asked. "I wish we hadn't drifted apart."

"He's fine. Still working in John Brown's, but becoming increasingly involved in union politics."

They walked along Princes Street and after Alexandra had admired the castle he led her down into the valley and then up the hill to the road known as the Royal Mile. Malcolm explained that in olden times in this area it had been important to have secure defense against raiders and this had been provided by the marshland of the Nor'Loch and the rock of the castle. When the citizens ran out of space for their dwelling houses they had been forced to build upwards.

"These houses are incredible," Alexandra said as she craned her neck to look up at the tenements, some of which rose to ten stories. "They're so narrow, the rooms must be very small, but oh, how I'd love a room at the top. There must be superb views from up there."

"Spoken like a duchess," Malcolm teased. "The aristocrats always lived at the top of these houses and the poorer people lived in squalid condition on the ground floor. They both shared the same winding stone staircase."

"I'm glad there was some equality in it!"

"Ah, you're a political animal, are you?"

Alexandra laughed. "One politician in the family is enough, especially as my best friend shares Frank's interest." She began entertaining him with anecdotes about Daisy. "Daisy's such a tonic that it's a pity they can't prescribe her on the National Health!"

Malcolm smiled. He was beginning to feel optimistic about the outcome of this meeting. They stopped for a moment to admire the elegant spires of St. Giles Cathedral and, as they continued their progress up the Royal Mile, Alexandra talked about Meldrum Enterprises.

"My team of workmen are already restoring the tenement. There's a foreman in charge at the moment, but I wish you'd agree to become building manager. The Edinburgh project is going to be the first of many."

"You've still got to sell the tenement."

"Yes, but Boyd says that shouldn't be a problem if the tradesmen make a good job of it."

"And you want me to make sure they do?"

"Exactly. You're the master craftsman. The genius with wood. But I'm hoping you'll spread your talents wider and keep a lookout for other properties that might be suitable."

"By 'suitable' I take it you mean cheap properties in a state of disrepair, which Meldrums can renovate at cost and then sell on at a profit?"

Alexandra grinned. "Precisely! If I can just get a good launching pad everyone concerned will make a lot of money."

Malcolm's glance was whimsical. "From what you've said so far, it's not a launching pad you need, it's a ball and chain to keep you anchored to the ground."

"You could act as my ball and chain. You could wheedle licenses out of authorities and make sense of the mass of paperwork which has started overwhelming me."

"And you'll take responsibility for my mistakes?"

"I'll be the boss," Alexandra turned to him, her eyes concerned. "Does that bother you?"

"Not at all."

And it didn't. He had spent three years as a prisoner of war and the experience had drained him of ambition. The attraction of Alexandra's proposition was that he would have money without too much responsibility.

The one o'clock gun boomed out from the castle as they came to the entrance. Malcolm wanted to show her St. Margaret's Chapel, the only building left standing when Robert Bruce's nephew, the Earl of Moray, recaptured the castle from the English in 1313. "It's appalling the way the Scots and English wasted so many years fighting each other. One generation seemed to hand down the blood feud to the next."

"A bit like the Armstrongs and Meldrums," Alexandra remarked.

When they walked out to the battlements Malcolm surveyed his native city with affection. "This is a wonderful time to see Edinburgh. On a frosty day like this the whole city sparkles. Look, the spires and steeples of the churches are like black and white etchings."

"You're a poet *manqué*," Alexandra teased.

"Accused and found guilty. But I'm also a realist, so let's talk business again for a while. My friends in the trade tell me the biggest problem at the moment is lack of building materials and the scarcity of timber. Any idea how you're going to get around that?"

"I've been talking to people about this, so has Boyd. And Alan has used his contacts as well."

"Alan?"

"I forgot I haven't told you about Alan Gillian. He's my stockbroker. He's taking a great personal interest in Meldrum Enterprises."

Malcolm whistled. "I've heard of him. You're building up quite a formidable list of business associates. Sorry, I interrupted you. You were about to tell me about building materials."

"I gather we can find plenty of them in old aircraft hangars, ships that no one wants, army buildings that are being knocked down . . ."

Malcolm held up his hand. "Slow down there. You need big money to acquire those things you've mentioned."

"I'm not planning to buy all of them at once, but as my capital accumulates that's where the experts say I should look. You'll be marvelous at persuading people to buy and sell."

"What makes you so sure about that?"

Alexandra blushed. "I'll be honest. When Boyd traced you he made further inquiries; he talked to people who knew you at school and before you joined up, and made contact with men who were in your regiment. Boyd discovered that you've kept up with friends and acquaintances from the days when your father owned Semples Paints. He told me that you still have valuable contacts in the building industry and in local government."

"I have. It's just a pity that they're not offering me jobs."

"Why d'you think that is?"

God, this girl is direct. Malcolm thought. He shrugged. "I want to work as a furniture craftsman. There aren't many well-paid vacancies in that field."

"Your old friends in the army say you can sell snow to Eskimos."

I could, Malcolm mused, but that was before I was a prisoner of war. Somewhere inside that camp the old Malcolm

Semple had died. Could this girl bring him to life again? Her drive and determination were invigorating and he was beginning to understand why Boyd Brown had been so certain that Alexandra would succeed.

"You'll create an empire if you carry on like this," he joked.

"I intend to," she replied immediately. "Malcolm, please say you'll join Meldrum Enterprises?"

"I'll think about it if you promise to have a bit of lunch with me."

Alexandra nodded her agreement. They found a small restaurant in the Haymarket and dallied over a simple meal of soup and chicken. When the waiter brought coffee Alexandra pleaded her case. "Once you're my building manager you'll be your own boss. You'll have lots of freedom."

"When you look at me like that I find it difficult to say no."

Alexandra's face was a sunburst of smiles. "Thank you. I feel happy at the thought of working with you. If you phone Boyd he'll arrange when you can come through and see him to agree a contract."

"All very businesslike."

"Yes, it has to be."

Malcolm studied Alexandra. She was bright, beautiful, and a joy to be with. There was an aura about her that drew people's attention and made strangers smile. She'd make someone a wonderful wife . . . Was that what he needed? A wife who was strong enough to drive away his demons? Malcolm smiled back at her, thinking that he couldn't remember when he'd last felt so optimistic about the future. He just hoped he could live up to Alexandra's expectations.

II

When the train arrived back in Glasgow Alexandra walked to Buchanan Street bus station and caught a bus to Charing Cross. As she walked up the hill to Park Terrace she reflected that it had been a very satisfying day in Edinburgh. She felt convinced Malcolm was going to be a tremendous asset to Meldrum Enterprises.

Frank would be as well. Although he wasn't going to take an active part in the company he had promised to be on hand to give her advice. Dear Frank. Since he had started to gain prominence in union politics he had become much more confident. He'd smartened up his appearance as well and seemed to have no difficulty attracting girlfriends. Alexandra grimaced at the thought of the giggly blondes whom Frank seemed to prefer. When was he going to realize that Daisy was worth ten of them?

ELEVEN

I

Every city has its back streets where murky half-light, strange odors, and flickering shadows conjure up images of evil. In Glasgow politicians liked to point to the Gorbals as a district where it was unwise to venture after dark unless you wished to be divested of your purse, your virginity, or your life. In the Gorbals, cats with tails were visitors . . .

One evening Daisy borrowed her father's car to take Frank to see a Bob Hope film in Shawlands, and they took a detour through the Gorbals on their way home. Frank looked out of the car window at the broken windows, rotten roofs, and dislodged masonry in decaying tenements. He was always shocked at how awful it was. There were few people about, but he sensed Daisy's car was coming under scrutiny. He shifted uneasily in his seat, torn between admiration of her bravado, and anxiety in case they were accosted by one of the street gangs who had made this area infamous. His worst fears seemed about to be realized when a group of men and women who had been standing outside a tenement building came rushing towards them. "It's all right," Daisy said calmly, "some of these people are my father's patients. They'll have recognized his car."

Daisy wound down the window and was assailed by such a clamor of voices that she put her hands to her ears. "One at a time, you noisy buggers," she shouted.

"It's Willie's wife, missus. Her time's come, and she's awful bad, Can ye help?"

Daisy nodded. "Come on then, Frank, you come too—unless you want to stay here."

Frank took one look at the grim faces round the car. "I'll come."

"Just because I'm training to be a doctor, they think I *am* one," Daisy said by way of explanation as they went into the close and began climbing the stairs. The walls of the stairway were covered with graffiti and the toilets on each landing gave off such a powerful stench that Frank put a hand to his mouth.

As they climbed higher he could hear agonized screams. One door on the top landing was open and Daisy went through it to find the source of the noise. Beside a tiny kitchen was a single room with a drop-down bed which jutted out into the center of the floor. On the bed a woman was writhing in pain, although her face lightened when she saw Daisy. "The doctor's daughter . . ." she said with relief. "It's ma first, miss, and it's no . . ." She screamed as she was racked by another contraction.

Daisy leaned over and held the woman's hand until the spasm passed. "Your name's Agnes, isn't it?" she said softly. "Let me have a look at you and I'll see what I can do."

Frank averted his gaze from the bed to the door where a crowd of interested onlookers had gathered.

"Aye, she's awful bad," one woman commented. "The wean's probably roon the wrong way, or the cord's roon its neck, poor mite." The other neighbors knew she wasn't being nasty, she was simply exercising the Glaswegian prerogative of enjoying every second of a potential disaster.

"Get that prophet of doom out of here," Daisy shouted.

Frank assumed his sternest expression, pushed everyone back and firmly closed the door.

"She was right," Daisy whispered to him after a while. "The baby's round the wrong way."

"Can you do anything?" he whispered back.

"I'll have to try. I know what these people are like; they won't call a doctor or a midwife when I'm here."

Frank looked round for the woman's husband and was horrified to see that he was drunk. "I'll shjust leave youse to it," he said and left the room.

"Drink is the problem the Welfare State will never solve," Daisy whispered to Frank as she went through to the kitchen and began filling the pans with cold water which she put on to boil. "It's not just free handouts they need in Glasgow, it's education," she added as she washed her hands in a sink engrimed with dirt.

"And new houses," Frank said, gazing at the damp peeling walls, the rotting floorboards, the cracked ceiling. He pulled open the larder door and was shocked to see how little food it contained.

He had only a blurred memory of the events that followed: the screams, the tears, the cries of pain, and through it all Daisy's calm presence as she manipulated the mother's stomach to turn her baby and then eased her through the increasingly strong contractions.

"Breathe deeply. Push. Breathe deeply again. I can see the head," Daisy said eventually. "Stop pushing now, Easy does it, that's right, that's it . . . The baby's coming, Quick, Frank, give me a hand.

The cord was cut, the baby was washed, and Daisy handed the wrapped bundle to her patient. "There you are, Agnes, you've a fine baby girl."

"I'll call her Daisy," the mother said gratefully.

Daisy called out to the women hovering near the door, and they came in at once and helped to make the mother comfortable as she attended to the baby's needs.

Afterwards in the car Frank looked hard at the girl he had somehow taken for granted. Tonight he had seen her in a different light. "You were so kind, so caring with that woman," he said gravely. He reached over and kissed her.

His kiss seemed to surprise Daisy. "Watching a birth can be pretty unnerving," she said shakily, "especially here in the Gorbals, where there's so much poverty and crime. There are bad men here, Frank, murderers." She shivered. "I hate the thought of being near men who have blood on their hands. But I really want to try to make life better for the others. Their wives, their families . . ."

Frank felt his emotions imploding until he gasped for air. He had his father's blood on his hands. If Daisy ever found out . . .

"Fancy a cuppa at my house?" she asked.

He inhaled deeply and steadied himself. "Fine," he said casually.

Frank had never been to her parents' home in Whitecraigs although he had heard Alexandra mention it, but when he stepped over the threshold he drew in his breath. Daisy made a pot of tea and brought it into the drawing room, where she found Frank sitting slumped in an armchair, looking uncharacteristically despondent. "What's wrong, Frank?"

"That drunken man . . . the father. He was such a brute—so uncaring."

"Did he remind you of your own father?"

"Yes, but . . . I don't want to talk about him."

"You've got a hang-up about your father. I wish you'd tell me about it."

"Well, I won't. We belong in different worlds, Daisy." He gestured at their sumptuous surroundings.

"That's nonsense! Frank, I like you. Won't you stay awhile?"

He knew from the way she looked at him exactly what she meant. But it wasn't on. Daisy was a great chum, but he'd be best not to get too close to her. She was too good for the likes of him. A murderer . . .

"I've got to go," he said abruptly.

He refused Daisy's offer to drive him home, saying he'd prefer to take the tram.

When he had left, Daisy banged her fist against the front door in frustration. The luxury of her home had frightened Frank away and she wasn't sure she'd be able to get him back. Restlessly she paced the room. Her eyes strayed to the telephone. She would ask Alexandra's advice. She picked up the receiver and then put it down. Alexandra would be in Jordanhill with Robert. They might even be making love . . .

Daisy put her head in her hands and wept.

II

Alexandra was putting the finishing touches to the decorations in the living room. Aunt Ethel was upstairs in the bathroom engaged in the marathon task of washing her hair and dressing herself up for bringing in the New Year.

"We've got half an hour on our own before Adam and Belinda come back," Robert said as he took the decorations out of Alexandra's hand, "so why aren't we doing something more interesting?"

"Can't think what we can do," Alexandra said provocatively as Robert eased off his clothes and began undressing her.

"Improvise then!" he replied gaily and tossed her panties to the top of the Christmas tree. He pulled her down on to the floor.

"Why aren't you leaping up and accusing me of stealing your virtue?" he asked as he traced a kiss which began at her throat and travelled down to the silky space between her legs.

"Because my virtue was stolen one evening . . ." Alexandra gasped as his tongue began probing, " . . . after a young gentleman took me out on Loch Lomond. And after that . . ." She gasped again as his fingers took over from his tongue.

"After that?" he asked.

But by then he was driving into her and her own body was rising and falling to meet his, and their lips and legs and arms were adding to the passion which bore them upwards on a great wave till they surfed over the top into a world where nothing mattered but the scent and sound of their lovemaking.

The loud ringing of the doorbell echoed in their ears. Alexandra raced round the room picking up her clothes as Robert struggled into his jeans and shirt.

"Why aren't you using your key?" Robert asked his brother as he opened the door.

"Forgot to take it with me," Adam replied laconically.

"Belinda, you look smashing!" Robert said and kissed her on the cheek.

Belinda pouted her lips. "I thought everyone kissed each other properly at New Year in Scotland!" She put her fingers to his chin and drew his mouth to hers, lingering on his lips.

"Mmmm!" he said. "Better not let Alexandra see us doing that."

"She's already seen you," Alexandra said with great restraint as she came forward to greet them.

"Where's Aunt Ethel?"

"Doing her hair. We haven't seen her for . . . a little while." Alexandra's lips twitched as she caught Robert's eye.

When Aunt Ethel came down she looked as if she'd been dragged through a briar bush backwards. "Your hair's lovely," they all exclaimed and Aunt Ethel preened and sat down beside the fire. For the rest of the evening they regaled her with anecdotes about the university until she was quite pink with laughter.

When the clock hands approached midnight Aunt Ethel set

out whisky and crystal on a silver tray and turned on the radio to listen to the bells. As the last strokes of 1950 rang out, they raised their glasses.

"Happy New Year!" they chorused and exchanged kisses.

"Here's to forever!" Robert whispered in Alexandra's ear.

"Here's to forever!" she whispered back, and clinked glasses with him before putting down her glass and folding herself into his arms.

They were all singing as they drove away from Jordanhill towards Hyndland where most of their friends stayed in digs or rented rooms. Robert parked the car outside a terraced house and unlocked the boot. He picked up a piece of coal wrapped in brown paper.

Belinda looked at it. "What on earth's that for?"

"First foots in Scotland are supposed to carry a piece of coal in one hand and a bottle of whisky in the other. The coal is a symbol of the warmth you hope the house will enjoy in the New Year."

"What does the whisky symbolize?" Belinda asked as he banged on a door in Westbourne Gardens.

"Who's caring?"

They were greeted with a fanfare of noise and dragged into a party which looked as if it had been going on for weeks. More drinks. Shortbread. Crackers. Streamers. And jokes that got raunchier as the night wore on. From that house they went to another. And then another . . . until Belinda wondered if anyone ever went to bed on New Year's morning. By the end of Robert's first-footing tour they were all a little drunk.

It was nearly dawn before they arrived back in Jordanhill. Aunt Ethel had retired to bed, but she had left a tray for them set out with cups and saucers and a plate of mince pies. Alexandra heated up the mince pies and made some coffee. She kicked open the sitting-room door as she came in with the tray.

"I've had the loveliest time," Belinda said happily as Robert stirred up the embers of the fire. "We should all make a wish, shouldn't we? What's yours, Alexandra?"

Alexandra wasn't prepared to say. Wishes were private. "Can't think of anything I want."

"Not even Drumcraig Castle?" Adam asked provocatively. "I thought you might have nurtured grandiose ideas about buying it for the Meldrums."

"Drumcraig?" Belinda mused. "Adam, isn't that the castle you showed me on Deeside? The one that belonged to the Armstrongs?"

"The Meldrums had it first," Alexandra snapped. "They rebuilt it."

"I'd really like to own a castle like Drumcraig," Belinda said dreamily, as she gazed into the fire.

"Well, we'll have to see what we can do," Adam replied. He was gazing at Alexandra as he said it and she could see the challenge in his eyes.

It was light before Adam left to take Belinda back to her hotel, and Robert and Alexandra finally stumbled into bed. Robert pulled Alexandra towards him and brushed a lock of hair from her eyes. "Did Adam rile you with his remarks about Drumcraig? You know, we've been so close, yet I know hardly anything about your childhood. What it was like to live on the croft . . . ?"

"We had this conversation before—on Loch Lomond. I told you a little then. About my father. Wasn't that enough?"

"Enough for me, Alexandra, but not for you."

"I don't understand. What do you mean?"

Robert pulled away from her as he tried to concentrate his thoughts. "I'm no psychologist, but I just feel it can't be good for you hiding away your childhood inside a big box . . ."

"It didn't do Pandora much good when she opened her box."

"But you're much stronger than Pandora," Robert said as he began kissing her again, effectively ending the conversation.

That morning there was a wild abandon in Alexandra's lovemaking as she kept urging them both on to greater efforts.

"God, girl, you've exhausted me," Robert said at length and almost immediately sank into a deep sleep.

Alexandra lay awake. Robert had talked about her past being hidden away in a box. Now his words had broken the seal and the memories were spilling out, and this time she did not try to hold them back. For the first time for years she allowed herself to think back to the tales her mother had told her. About her life with Aunt Bessie. Toby Armstrong. The castle. The croft. The brutality . . .

PART III

Briony's Story: 1930-39

TWELVE

I

1930

In the attic room of a tenement high above the city of Aberdeen a girl was lying on a pallet bed. Rounded breasts strained against a thin shift, black hair tumbled over a rough blanket which was her only covering. There was a soft virginal quality about the girl's beauty which gave her the appearance of a sleeping Madonna; an impression instantly dispelled when she wakened. The mutinous line to her mouth owed nothing to Madonna-like tranquility.

Briony crossed to the window and gazed out at the city where she had been born. Aberdeen was a temptress not always disposed to display her charms. If you caught her in a fickle mood when fingers were frozen and flowers flattened by icy blasts from the North Sea, her buildings could seem as bleak and gray as the Cairngorm and Grampian mountains which defined her boundaries on the south and west. Yet within the space of minutes the sun could highlight the glitter of granite on the buildings giving the city an illusion of grandeur.

Briony watched as the early morning sun drew beads of light from the masts of the trawlers grouped round the harbour, brightening the tiers of houses rising beyond the fishing quays, and silvering the steeples and towers in the center of the town where gracious houses from a bygone era mingled with modern buildings. Her father, Fergus Meldrum, had loved this town in the north east of Scotland.

Briony was roused from her reverie by a noise behind her. Aunt Bessie was standing in the doorway, arms akimbo. "Daydreaming instead of getting on with my housework?" she asked sarcastically.

"I was thinking about my father."

"Your father!" Aunt Bessie exclaimed scathingly. "All he did with his life was work away at that castle."

"He was proud of Drumcraig Castle. And so am I!" Briony retorted, her eyes flashing with anger.

Drumcraig had once been a collection of crumbling stones on Deeside, an area of rolling moor and lush woodland fifteen miles from Aberdeen. The ruins belonged to Fergus's cousin Hamish who had accumulated wealth from granite and shipping. He gave Fergus a good wage for doing the restoration work on Drumcraig Castle. Unfortunately just as the castle was completed Hamish suffered a series of strokes and he began making mistakes at work which proved financially disastrous. As bankruptcy loomed, Hamish became fearful that his creditors might seize his beloved castle. He signed a disposition conveying it to Briony's father and placed the disposition in his lawyer's safe. He died a week later of another stroke.

After the funeral Fergus Meldrum went to see Hamish's lawyer, Willie Snodgrass, expecting to be told that he was now the legal owner of Drumcraig Castle. To his surprise the lawyer claimed that Hamish had changed his mind, there was no disposition in his safe, and Drumcraig Castle had become part and parcel of the Armstrong business which had bought up Meldrums. For Briony's father that was a terrible blow. Losing the castle was bad, but losing it to an Armstrong was even worse since the Meldrums and Armstrongs had been feuding for over a century over their shipping and quarrying interests. Fergus was convinced that the lawyer and Luke Armstrong between them had somehow cheated him out of the castle, but he had no way of proving it since there was no trace of the disposition that Hamish had signed.

Fergus had lost his castle and his job. His skill as a mason ensured that he found other employment in Aberdeen in the years that followed, but he spent much of his spare time trying to discover the whereabouts of the missing disposition. All to no avail. His only solace was meeting Beth McDougall, a fresh-faced country girl from Skye who had come to Aberdeen for a holiday. Fergus asked her to marry him in 1911 and they set up house in a small rented flat in Urquhart Road. Briony was born there the following year.

Fergus found great pleasure in his child especially when she became old enough to listen to his bedtime stories—which invariably featured Drumcraig Castle and his quest to get it back. It became Briony's own family fairy tale and she would listen avidly as her father described every single room in the castle and its contents. When she was 8 years old she solemnly made a vow to her father that one day she would get the castle back for the Meldrums. Beth overheard and her sorely tried patience snapped. She told father and daughter that she'd had enough of Aberdeen and Drumcraig, and wanted to go back to Skye. Reluctantly Fergus agreed.

His spirits lifted a little when he was recommended for a job in Skye which offered a tied cottage as part of the agreement. They lived on the island for the next ten years and although Fergus never saved any money he was happy plying his trade as a mason. And as a bonus he had a bright, beautiful daughter who shared his anger that he had been cheated out of his inheritance. He began to nourish hopes that once Briony left school she might be able to train as a teacher. Briony wanted that as well, but it was not to be.

The day before her eighteenth birthday her parents went to the mainland to buy her a present and were killed by a hit-and-run driver. Briony was devastated. After the funeral the factor told her that she would have to move out of the tied cottage to make way for the new mason. Her parents' friends rallied round and offered to put her up till she found work, but Briony no longer wanted to stay on Skye. She longed to return to Aberdeen, the city of her birth. Yet where could she go? It was January, it was freezing cold, and she had no money.

In desperation she wrote to her father's sister in Aberdeen and asked if there were any jobs in the city. Briony wasn't sure if Aunt Bessie would reply because she had never been close to her brother, but her aunt wrote back by return offering her a proposition. "You can do housework for me in exchange for your bed and board," her aunt suggested.

Briony had agreed, but when she arrived in Aberdeen she found out that Aunt Bessie expected her to get up at six each day and work till eight in the evening. Briony gritted her teeth, countered her aunt's insults and tried unsuccessfully to find another job. Unfortunately Aberdeen seemed to be having the same problems as the island of Skye and hundreds were unemployed. The position was the same throughout the country.

The previous ten years had not been good ones for Scotland. By 1918 the Great War had inflicted a heavy loss of life amongst the young men who should have been the seed corn for her future, and when the postwar slump finally hit Scotland in 1920 the country was ill-equipped to deal with it. By 1926 the miners were being laid off in increasing numbers and when the General Strike failed and the miners were defeated, an air of despondency permeated the cities. The following year everyone began to hope that the economy might improve, but the collapse of the American Stock Exchange in 1929 brought on another slump.

Now it was 1930 and times were even harder. Even the granite industry in Aberdeen was in recession. Briony had heard that foreign firms were producing lower-priced granite because they were paying their workers less than the men in Scotland. Consequently a lot of granite was being imported for monumental work. To make matters worse new methods of road-building and surfacing meant there was not the same demand for the pavement slabs which used to be the mainstay of the granite trade. The seventy-five granite manufacturers who had dominated Aberdeen in 1920 had been reduced to fifty-three in 1930.

Briony couldn't help thinking that her father would have been distressed to hear how badly the industry was doing. To him a piece of granite had been a thing of beauty. He had shown her how the rough stone from the quarry was hammered and levelled and cut, and had explained that dressing the granite by hand, and shaping and carving it demanded great skill. He had given her a piece of polished granite from the famous Rubislaw quarry in Aberdeen and told her to cherish it. She still had it. She wished it was a lucky charm that would get her a job. Every week Briony left her aunt's house and trailed into town to Collies, the employment agency, but the answer was always the same: no work and no prospect of it.

Briony was desperate because she felt she could not endure one more day slaving for her acid-tongued aunt. She looked up at her as she stood arms akimbo in the doorway and decided there and then that she'd had enough. Without a word of explanation she began packing her few possessions in a battered old grip.

"And what d'you think you're doing, miss?" Aunt Bessie exclaimed, her mouth agape.

"I'm leaving. You can find another slave to torment!"

Aunt Bessie loomed above her, a bombazine-clad battleship of a woman, her face mottled with fury. "How dare you speak to me like that!" she spluttered. "And how can you leave? You keep telling me that Collies have no jobs."

"I'll find something," Briony said as she closed the grip, slung it over her shoulder, and stumbled out into the hallway at the top of the tenement.

"You'll come to a bad end," Aunt Bessie called after her as Briony ran down the flights of stairs to the ground floor, slamming the tenement door behind her as she left. Briony crossed the road and tried to control her tears of anger and frustration as she approached the new house which was being built for a wealthy merchant. She had struck up a friendship of sorts with one of the masons who was building it and he always made a point of speaking to her as she passed the house on her way to the shops.

"What's up, lass?" Angus asked.

Briony shook her head and went on her way. Angus the mason was just a casual acquaintance. If she told him what she intended to do he would be shocked.

THIRTEEN

I

June

The gates of Drumcraig Castle had once been ten feet high and made of the finest wrought iron. Now they were broken and hanging loose on their hinges. When Briony pushed them she felt the stickiness of rust on her fingers. The driveway which had been lined with scarlet rhododendrons, pink azaleas and blue hydrangeas was overgrown with wild flowers: cow parsley and yarrow wrestled for space with broom and wild bramble, and the gravel was covered with moss and weeds. The trees were too well established to suffer from the same neglect. Above her the cathedral-high firs leaned towards each other filtering out the light and sending shadows dancing in every direction.

The heat of the late afternoon sun had faded, but Briony wasn't cold. She was wearing the only coat she possessed and had been glad of its warmth on the train journey from Aberdeen to Deeside and on the long walk from Peterculter station to the castle entrance.

The driveway seemed endless, but suddenly as she turned a corner the embracing branches of the trees drew back and she was confronted by a vast sweep of sky so densely blue it looked like fabric. And there, pinned to one corner of it like a brooch, was Drumcraig Castle standing proudly on top of its own small hill.

Strictly speaking Drumcraig had no right to be called a castle since the original building had been constructed in the seventeenth century as a home, albeit a fortified one. Her father had shown her pictures of other tower houses of that period and she had not been attracted to the square gray buildings because they looked so grim and forbidding. Drumcraig was different. Although it had the typical slit windows, loops and gunholes of a fortified house, the castle was a tall slender tower of rose-colored granite which rose upwards towards the sky and ended in a profusion of turrets, domes and parapets, so finely fashioned they seemed ethereal. Fergus Meldrum used to say that Drumcraig was symbolic of Scotland: a continuing compromise between austerity and romance. But to Briony, Drumcraig was a castle straight out of a fairy tale. It reminded her of the story of the imprisoned princess who let her golden hair tumble down the tall tower so that her prince could climb up it and rescue her.

Briony sat down and leaned back on her elbows to savor the view that had enthralled her father for much of his life. She still felt a child's wonder that he had created this masterpiece from a pile of ruins. The finest granite graced the exterior, and sculptors, cabinet-makers and other craftsmen had been enlisted to create an interior that was a triumph of craftsmanship. Or at least that's what the castle had been like in Hamish Meldrum's day. Now it belonged to Toby Armstrong and he had let it fall into a state of disrepair. Briony had heard people in the shops talking about Toby's scandalous behavior. Most agreed that he was a drunk and a wastrel and was living on credit from his bank. There were other rumors as well. Toby, it was said, took advantage of any pretty girl who came his way. He was only 31, but people predicted he'd die young if he carried on behaving in the way he was doing.

"Well, he won't take advantage of me," Briony said to herself as she walked towards the front door. She was here because she had decided that before she left Aberdeen she would try and solve the mystery which had broken her father's heart. Somewhere in the castle would be a drawer containing the deeds of Drumcraig—and the missing disposition. Briony had made up her mind to find it. The problem was gaining access to the castle. If Toby Armstrong had been advertising for servants Briony would have applied for the job instantly, but everyone said Toby had no money to pay staff. Lying in bed this morning Briony had suddenly realized that she could use this knowledge to her advantage.

Briony put down her suitcase when she reached the massive iron-studded door and gave a firm pull on the bell. Above her the slim tower stretched to the sky. Standing so close to the castle she could hardly see the turrets and parapets at the top of it. She could hear the bell echoing in the castle, but no one came to the door. She walked round the walls, but there was no one in sight. Briony came back to the front entrance and gave another pull at the bell. This time she heard footsteps and there was a creaking sound as the door slowly opened. She took a deep breath to steady her nerves.

A man emerged from the shadows. He was wearing shabby brown trousers and a stained shirt. He had dirty hair, a paunchy figure and an aggressive manner.

"Who the hell are you?" he asked belligerently.

"I've come to see Mr. Armstrong."

"I'm the only Armstrong around here. What d'you want?"

"I've come to apply for a job."

He looked puzzled. "I didn't advertise in Collies."

"I know, but someone told me you might employ me. You see, I'm willing to work for nothing."

He scratched his head. "Why on earth would you do that?"

"I was staying with my aunt in Aberdeen and we quarreled," Briony said evenly. "I need a roof over my head. In return for bed and board I could act as your cook or your housekeeper. It's just to tide me over for a few weeks . . ."

Toby shook his head. "Extraordinary! Still, never look a gift horse in the mouth, as they say. If you're fool enough to work for nothing I'll be delighted to employ you. What age are you? What's your name?"

"I'm 18, and my name's Briony."

"Hmm. Used to have a dog called Briony. Had to get rid of her. I suppose you'd better come in."

Briony followed him, her heels clicking on the uncarpeted stone floor. There was dusty everywhere and she noticed cobwebs on the windows and on the doors leading off from the hall. Toby Armstrong pushed one of the doors open, revealing a room which was circular, stone-walled, and unfurnished apart from a bed, a cheap chest of drawers, and a small wardrobe. A dirty pair of curtains hung lopsidedly over the window. There was no carpet.

"Your bedroom. And there's a bathroom." He gestured to a stained closet and a basin which were acting as home to beetles, spiders, and dead flies.

"I suppose I'd better show you the rest of the castle," Toby said grudgingly and led her out to the hall again. He gestured upwards. "There are seven floors, with three or four rooms on each floor. From the seventh floor, there's a stairway to the outside turret. The doors in this hall lead to the sitting room, dining room, and my study. I expect you'll want to see the kitchen."

He kicked open a door with his foot and Briony walked into a square room which was empty apart from a range for cooking, a cold-store larder, a small table, and two chairs.

"One girl walked out when she saw where she had to work," Toby said with a gleam in his eye.

"I don't blame her!" Briony retorted before she could help herself.

"Aha!" he exclaimed. "So the wench has some spirit after all! Good, I hated those mousey little creatures from Collies."

Briony stored that nugget of information in her mind as she followed him up the flagged stones stairway which led to the imposing Great Hall on the first floor. She remembered her father telling her that the Great Hall had been used in the olden days for recreation and for sittings of the barony court. It was a huge room running the full length and breadth of the castle. There was an impressive fireplace, and from the corner of a high ceiling decorated with figures and flowers a balcony jutted out into space.

"That's the musicians' gallery," Toby said helpfully.

"I know . . . I mean, it looks like one," she added hurriedly. She would have to be careful or she might betray the fact that she knew all about the castle. She had imagined that she would recognize every detail of it, but it had changed beyond her wildest nightmares. The tables and chairs of dark carved oak which Fergus had so lovingly described were still there, but the curtains were torn, the carpets faded, and there were empty spaces on the walls which had once held fine paintings. Streaks of dirt covered every piece of furniture and furnishing in the room and the mirrors were so encrusted with grime she could see nothing through them. It was like a scene from a Dickens novel. Everywhere was the patina of neglect.

As Toby led her through the rest of the castle she saw the same sad story wherever she looked. There were floor after floor of rooms with impressively carved ceilings, but the woodwork was disgraced by dust and the dirty and dilapidated furniture and furnishings failed to highlight its magnificence. If rumor was correct and Toby Armstrong was living on credit from the bank he certainly wasn't spending any of it to maintain Drumcraig Castle. Briony peered through one of the narrow windows and saw that the beautiful landscaped gardens had become jungles of grass, the pools were choked with weeds, the pergolas had crumbled and so had the statuary.

"Come and see the view from the top!" Toby commanded, indicating the spiral staircase in the corner of a room which led to her father's favorite place in the whole castle: an open-air balcony projecting from the highest turret. The approach to it from the seventh floor was like the entrance to a loft and the steps were so steep she had to crawl up on her hands and knees. With a final heave she pulled herself up on to the balustraded platform. The sun was beginning to set, but it enhanced rather than diminished the view of distant mountains, castles and the long silver thread of the River Dee. It was as beautiful as Fergus had always said it was.

"The finest view in Scotland," she murmured, remembering her father's words. Briony felt a chilly finger clutching her stomach the minute she had spoken. It was going to be much more difficult than she'd anticipated to conceal her knowledge of this place. Hopefully Toby Armstrong would not notice.

"You've been here before?" he asked, his eyebrows raised.

"I meant I've often heard it described," she said quickly and truthfully, but she could see he was suspicious of her. Briony turned away and began negotiating the steep flight of steps down to the seventh floor. In her haste she stumbled and would have fallen but for Toby's firm hands which clutched at her waist and brushed her breasts.

"A nice plump little pigeon, but what are you up to?" he murmured in her ear.

"Would you like me to make you something to eat?" she asked quickly, as she slipped from his grasp.

"With what? There's not much in the larder. Maybe I'll go into Aberdeen tomorrow and get fresh provisions. But right now I'm going to get myself good and drunk!"

Briony viewed his retreating figure with disgust. How could Toby's father have left Drumcraig to a son who was such a disgrace to the Armstrong name?

II

For the next month Briony used every opportunity to search the castle for the missing disposition, but she could not find it and although she coaxed Toby to drink heavily in the evenings she was not able to make him reveal secrets about his past. The only indiscreet remarks Toby ever made were about his father. He made it plain that he and his father had hated the sight of each other. That made Briony more confused than ever. If his father had disliked Toby so much, why hadn't he willed the castle to Toby's brother, William?

Briony felt she had to find out soon because her relationship with Toby was changing. He had stopped going into Aberdeen in the evenings and instead often asked her to sit and talk to him. He had also started working beside her in the garden and in a dozen different ways he was showing her that he enjoyed her company. In an effort to please her he had curtailed his drinking and smartened up his appearance. "Look at me, Briony, and tell me what you see," he said one evening after dinner when he had announced yet again that he wouldn't be going into town.

Briony studied her employer. A healthy diet and moderation in his drinking habits added to his hard labors in the garden had made him lose his paunch very rapidly. His hair was newly washed, and he was wearing a hunting jacket and a cream shirt. He was a fine figure of a man, but she wasn't going to tell him that.

"I'm your housekeeper. It's not my place to comment."

Toby looked hurt at her cool tone. "I think I'll ride into Aberdeen after all," he said abruptly. "I'll stay the night there."

Briony felt a pang of conscience at the way she had extinguished his high spirits, but she relished the prospect of a night spent at Drumcraig on her own.

Some time later she heard the clip-clop of a horse's hooves and when she peered through the kitchen window she saw Toby riding down the driveway. This was her chance. She had searched the castle before when Toby had gone to Aberdeen, but since she never knew when he would be coming back she had never dared go through the drawers in his bedroom. But if Toby intended staying away for the whole night she would have plenty of time to make a really thorough search. If she

did not find the disposition this evening she would leave
Drumcraig and admit defeat.

Briony took off her apron and went into the hall, but she felt
reluctant to go straight to the fifth floor where Toby slept. Instead, like a child prolonging an anticipated treat, she began
going through the castle, room by room, floor by floor, reac-
quainting herself with all the features which had brought her
father such joy. Every now and then she stopped to stroke the
wood on the panelling, trace her fingers along an intricate
carving, or lean her cheek against a balustrade.

At last she reached the King's Room on the fifth floor
where Toby slept. A faded blue carpet covered most of the
stone flags, but she had to step carefully to avoid the holes and
tears. The biggest space in the room was taken up by a huge
four-poster bed with a draped canopy above it in moth-eaten
blue silk. Tonight Briony was more interested in the three
chests of drawers and the big mahogany desk which stood in
one corner. If Toby had any secrets that's where he would
keep them. She worked her way methodically through the
drawers, feeling with her fingers for a scroll or piece of paper
which might be hidden underneath the clothes. Toby had very
few belongings and some of the drawers were empty. Others
contained newspaper cuttings, childhood letters, and photographs. When she held one picture up to the window to look
at it more closely she realized the light was fading. She put the
photographs and letters back where she'd found them and hurried over to the huge mahogany desk.

Briony gave a cry of delight when she came across the
deeds of the castle in one of the desk's compartments, but
though she studied them closely she could find no reference to
her father. She wept then, bitter tears at the loss of a dream, at
the abandonment of her own hopes, at the waste of time and
energy. As she wiped her eyes she saw a small drawer in the
top right-hand side of the desk. She tried to pull it open, but it
was locked and resisted all her efforts.

Disconsolately she wandered round the room before sitting
down on the big four-poster bed. It looked much more comfortable than her own . . . She got up and walked to the closet
off the bedroom. When she emerged she was washed and
cleaned. And naked. It was getting dark and the moon was
sending silver shafts of light into the shadowed corners of the

room. Shivering, Briony lit the candle beside the bed and slipped between the sheets. Tomorrow she would leave Drumcraig for good, but tonight she would pretend she was lady of the manor and sleep in the master's bed.

"One day the Meldrums will own Drumcraig again," she said to the empty room.

"An interesting thought," a voice replied.

Briony shrieked, imagining that a ghost from the past had come to haunt her, but when she looked towards the door the light from the moon fell on Toby's face. "What are you doing here?" she gasped.

He came forward and sat on the edge of the bed. "This evening I set a trap for you. I let you think I was spending the night in Aberdeen, but once I had ridden out of sight, I doubled back on my trail. I've been watching you ever since."

"I didn't see you," Briony protested as she pulled the sheets round her neck and huddled down in the bed to cover every inch of her nakedness.

"You were too busy touching and stroking all the things you love in this castle to be aware of anyone. It was easy enough to keep out of sight. And when you came up to this room," he continued, "you were so intent on finding my secrets that you didn't even shut the door. I've been behind it looking at you."

Briony felt suffused with warmth as she realized he had seen her naked. "Go away," she said angrily.

He edged nearer. "I'm not moving from this spot till you tell me the truth. I remembered some weeks ago that Fergus Meldrum had a daughter called Briony."

She looked at him. "Why didn't you tell me you knew?"

"Because it was obvious that you were up to something, and I wanted to know what it was. I've watched you searching the castle in the past few weeks, and tonight you've been searching again. What are you looking for, Briony?"

Briony tightened her lips and said nothing.

"All right," Toby said mildly, "if that's how you want it . . . If you don't mind, though, I'm getting ready for bed."

To Briony's dismay he began taking off his clothes.

"Please, let me get dressed."

"I have no intention of letting you get dressed until you tell me what you're looking for." Toby unfastened his tie and began unbuttoning his shirt. When he bent down to untie his shoelaces, Briony wriggled out of his reach and ran for the door. But even half-dressed and shoeless he was a match for her. He caught up with her easily, swung her up in his arms and carried her kicking and screaming back to the bed. "You're going to stay there until you talk," he said firmly and with that he removed the last of his clothes and slipped into bed.

"I won't tell you anything," Briony said, but when he pressed closer her defiance crumpled. "All right, all right, but please move away from me."

"Tell me from the beginning . . ."

Briony turned her face away from his as she recounted the story of her childhood, her father's obsession with Drumcraig, and his conviction that Hamish Meldrum had conveyed Drumcraig Castle to him before he went bankrupt.

"So you were searching for the disposition," Toby said thoughtfully.

"Yes. Is it in that locked drawer? The one I couldn't open?"

"The answer to your question may or may not be in that drawer and I'm not saying whether it is or isn't the disposition. If you want me to tell you the whole truth you'll have to bribe me." He kissed her quickly before she could make any protest.

"Don't do that," she cried out, as she struggled against him.

"Why not? I can see you like it. And you like me. Oh yes, I've noticed. Over the past few weeks you've become fond of me. Though you're not willing to admit it yet."

"I hate you!"

"No, you don't. Anyway, I like you. In fact, these last few weeks *I've* grown very fond of *you*."

"I'm not listening," Briony replied, muffling her face in the pillow.

Roughly he pulled her round. "I'll make a bargain with you. If you let me make love to you, I'll tell you the truth about your father and my father and the whole sorry business."

"You won't. You'd lie your way out of anything."

"That's true," he admitted, "but not this time. Think of it, Briony. In half an hour you could find out all you've ever wanted to know about Drumcraig. So let me kiss you."

Afterwards she tried to remember at what point she decided to give in to him. Was it when he made his promise to reveal everything to her? Or was it when she felt his mouth and hands drawing her into some hidden world from which she could not escape? She cried out in pain when he entered her and tried to push him away, but then the heat in her belly made her clasp him closer. When Toby began moving rhythmically inside her she was overcome with a multiplicity of sensations which alarmed and delighted her as her nerve ends responded to the pressure. Afterwards she turned her face towards the pillow, appalled at her body's treachery.

"I've kept my side of the bargain," she whispered. "Now it's your turn. Tell me about Drumcraig."

Toby turned over on his back and clasped his hands under his head so that he was staring at the ceiling. "Hamish Meldrum conveyed Drumcraig Castle to your father right enough, but my father bribed Hamish's lawyer, Willie Snodgrass, to keep the disposition in his safe instead of sending it to the Keeper of Records in Edinburgh to be registered. If a property isn't registered with the Keeper, then the new owner has no title to it."

"But Hamish . . ." Briony began.

"Hamish never found out that the disposition hadn't been sent to the Keeper. I don't know how my father intended to keep the matter secret. Or for how long. But fate played into his hands. Hamish died and my father persuaded Willie Snodgrass to tear up the disposition. No record in the Keeper's office. No document. Which meant your father had no claim to Drumcraig."

"So your father really did cheat mine out of his inheritance?"

"I'm afraid so. My father was a bastard!" Toby went on, his tone flat and clipped. "He made my life miserable and turned my mother and brother against me. I never thought I'd be offered a chance to get revenge until Willie Snodgrass died and his widow came and told me the whole story. She hated the idea that her husband had defrauded the Meldrums and wanted to clear her conscience."

"But why did she come to you?"

"Because I was the Armstrong outcast! That meant I would be ready to believe her. I really don't know what she expected me to do, but after she confessed she panicked and made me promise I'd keep her secret. I agreed, provided she would write out her story on a sheet of paper I gave her. I made her sign and date it."

Briony looked at him doubtfully. "What was the point of making her do that when you had promised not to show it to anyone?"

He laughed. "You don't think I kept my promise, do you? I informed my father about the widow's confession and told him I would make a public scandal of the matter—unless he left me Drumcraig in his will."

"You blackmailed him!"

"And enjoyed every minute of it," Toby agreed.

"And the widow's confession?" Briony asked, hardly daring to hope.

"An incriminating piece of evidence. After my parents died I burnt it."

"So it's not in the locked drawer? You've tricked me!"

He put his hands round her face. "I haven't tricked you. I promised to tell you the truth. And I have."

"But it's no use to me without proof—which you've destroyed," Briony said bitterly. "Drumcraig is lost to the Meldrums."

"If you marry me, I'll deed you Drumcraig as a wedding gift."

"You expect me to believe all that?"

"I've got an unsavoury reputation, I'm a congenital liar, and my prospects are worthless. No, maybe you wouldn't marry me."

"Is it possible that you're serious about this?"

"Why shouldn't I be? You're the well-educated daughter of the mason who rebuilt this castle and a relation of the man who owned it."

"But why . . ." she began, and then stopped.

He touched her chin with his finger. "I know exactly what you're thinking. Why would that rascal Toby Armstrong propose marriage to a girl when he would much prefer to have her as his mistress?"

"I wouldn't *agree* to be your mistress!"

"Precisely! That's why I think I'll have to marry you."

"That's the most insulting proposal I've ever heard."

"I agree. But since you'd sell your soul for this castle, marriage might seem a small price to pay."

III

Despite her protestations on the night Toby seduced her, Briony stayed on at Drumcraig as his mistress. He told her they could exist, albeit frugally, on the annuity left by his grandfather, but unless he made or borrowed money to clear his debts they would have to leave the castle. There seemed to be no question of selling it; Drumcraig was in such a deplorable condition structurally that nobody wanted to buy it.

Toby begged Briony to have patience for a few months until he could find a way out of his financial muddle, and it was his frankness about his affairs that convinced Briony he meant to marry her. He was equally candid about deeding Drumcraig to Briony as a wedding gift. He confessed that blackmailing his father into giving him Drumcraig was an action motivated solely by revenge. It would be no great sacrifice to deed the castle to Briony; it meant very little to him.

Toby's candor made Briony warm to him more and more, but there was another reason why she stayed on at the castle as his mistress. She had been deprived of love and tenderness in the months she had slaved for her aunt; Toby supplied both and this unleashed a passion in Briony that she had not known she possessed. Soon their lovemaking was not confined to the evenings. Often during the day Toby would slip his arm round her and, once they started kissing, inevitably they ended on the bed or on one of the couches in the Great Hall. But hand in hand with happiness was guilt at the way she was behaving: at times she felt consumed by it.

Briony tried to keep her guilt and the desperate state of Toby's finances in the forefront of her mind, but it was difficult to know how to solve either problem. Unexpectedly it was Aunt Bessie who pointed the way to a solution. One morning towards the end of October when Toby had gone to Aberdeen for the day, a carrier arrived at Drumcraig bringing Briony a letter from her aunt. She had fallen ill with heart trouble and been given a month to live. "My daughter can't leave her job in London," Aunt Bessie wrote, "but if you come and nurse me, Briony, I'll will you a substantial sum of money. But you have to come right away or I'll get someone else."

Nursing her evil-tongued aunt was the last thing Briony wanted to do. On the other hand a substantial sum would not only clear Toby's debts, but could help restore the castle to its former glory.

"I'll come," she said to the carrier. Within ten minutes she had packed her bag and written a brief note of explanation to Toby. She wished fervently that he was there to tell her whether she was doing the right thing, but he was not due back until nightfall.

FOURTEEN

I

In her dying as in her living Aunt Bessie displayed her contrary streak: she lingered on far beyond the doctor's expectations. When she had first begun to feel ill she had persuaded the post office to put all correspondence addressed to her house into one big sealed envelope and deliver it once a week. She felt it would be bad for her heart to have someone knocking at the door or ringing the bell each day.

Unfortunately Briony made the mistake of telling her aunt that she was expecting letters from Toby Armstrong because she had "an understanding" with him. Aunt Bessie's face paled with fury. "I've heard of Toby Armstrong's reputation; he's a scoundrel. Whilst you're under my roof you'll have nothing to do with him. I'm going to write forbidding him to come calling. And if you write to him I'll cut you out of my will," Aunt Bessie went on with barely concealed venom. "If you want your legacy you'll give me your undivided attention for the next few weeks."

Briony was furious. She wanted to defy her aunt, but she couldn't bear the thought of losing the money which she and Toby needed so badly. I can't write, but he will, she thought.

"Any letters for me?" she would ask when she handed over the weekly envelope of mail to her aunt.

"None. That scoundrel has obviously forgotten all about you. Didn't I warn you?"

Briony's confidence did not waver. One of these days she'd get a letter from Toby. Perhaps he was looking for a job and reluctant to write until he found one. But she did feel lonely . . .

Fortunately the men building the new house opposite her aunt's tenement were still there and Angus the mason was al-

ways ready to pass the time of day with her. His surname was
Meldrum, a common enough name in the north east, although
he wasn't even remotely related to her. Nor did his family
cherish any dreams about Drumcraig. Angus told Briony that
his wife had died a year before, leaving him to bring up 8-
year-old Frank on his own. When school was over Frank
would come to the building site, cowering behind the scaffolding if anyone spoke to him.

Briony felt sorry for the fair-haired boy. "When I go shopping for my aunt I could take Frank with me," she suggested to
his father. Angus Meldrum shrugged and said she was welcome to take him any time she wanted. During the long weeks
of her aunt's illness Briony's friendship with little Frank deepened. On the way to the shops she told him stories and made
jokes about the builders. To her delight, the boy began to respond to her sense of fun and tentatively started asking her
questions. Angus Meldrum said he was delighted to be rid of
his son of a while. "The little bugger's always been a nui-
sance."

His choice of words made Briony uneasy, especially as his
son was listening. Surely his father could have phrased it in
another way? Still, she shouldn't condemn a man because he
hadn't the same facility with words that she had. Nor did
Angus Meldrum seem to have the ability to make friends with
his fellow workers. He said he felt ill at ease with them because they were city folk and he was a countryman. Yet he
seemed happy enough to talk to her and always asked about
her aunt. Briony was grateful for his company. "I don't think it
can be long now," she said to him one morning, "Aunt
Bessie's very weak."

The following morning when the doctor came in, Aunt
Bessie lurched forward, then dropped back on to her pillow.

"That's her finished at last," the doctor said callously as he
removed his finger from her pulse. "I'll get the lawyer to notify Margaret, Bessie's daughter."

The lawyer came out to the flat to see Briony the next day.
Sidney Thornton was a gentle silver-haired man with a diffi-
dent manner. He seemed embarrassed as he explained that
Margaret, Aunt Bessie's daughter, had decided not to come up
from London to her mother's funeral. "She told me she
couldn't get time off from her secretarial job, but I know it's

because she and her mother never got on. Margaret's a hard woman," he went on. "When I told her about her mother's death, her only comment was to tell me to put this flat on the market and get as much money for it as possible. She said she'll pay you to stay on as caretaker till a buyer is found."

After Aunt Bessie's sparsely attended funeral the lawyer came back to the flat. "You must be a saint to have nursed your aunt the way you did," he said as Briony poured him a cup of tea.

Briony was too honest to deceive him. "I'm not a saint," she replied quietly. "I loathed Aunt Bessie. I came back because she offered me a substantial sum if I would nurse her."

The lawyer's eyebrows arched. "Well, I hope she gave it to you, because she hasn't changed her will in years. She's left everything to her daughter. You're not even mentioned in the will."

Briony stared at him. "But Aunt Bessie wrote me a letter, making me a promise . . ."

The lawyer leaned forward eagerly. "You've got the letter? If there was proof of her intent it would make a difference."

"I threw the letter away . . . I never thought to keep it. Didn't Aunt Bessie even mention it to you?"

When the lawyer shook his head Briony leant back in the chair and closed her eyes. All the nursing . . . All those weeks away from Toby . . .

"Why would she break her promise like that?" the lawyer asked.

Briony did not like to tell him that Aunt Bessie's only enjoyment in life had been spiteful pleasure in causing someone else's unhappiness. She would have been mightily pleased at the idea of luring Briony back under false pretences.

"My father always said his sister's mind was warped," Briony managed to say at last.

"And what will you do now?" Sidney Thornton asked. "I presume you have some place to go?"

"Of course," Briony replied quickly. Her heart lifted at the thought of Drumcraig. She would go to the castle and wait there for Toby. She could not understand why he had never written to her. She became aware that Sidney Thornton was waiting for an answer to his question.

"Drumcraig Castle," she began. Then stopped. She couldn't

tell the lawyer about her marriage plans. Toby was the one
who would have to make the announcement. "I was housekeeper at Drumcraig Castle to Toby Armstrong," she said quietly. "I'm sure my post will still be open."

The lawyer frowned. "But my dear, haven't you heard?
Toby Armstrong sold Drumcraig Castle and then he went to
England. I don't think he's coming back."

Briony felt her senses spinning. "No, it can't be. He
wouldn't. You see . . . You must have got it wrong . . ."

"My dear, I'm so sorry if this is bad news for you. Actually
it's still confidential. The sale has definitely gone through, but
the announcement won't be made public for another few
weeks. Being a lawyer I heard it on the grapevine. Let me
speak to the new owner."

"No, please don't do that. I have . . . other plans."

Sidney Thornton seemed relieved. "I'm delighted to hear it.
No doubt there's some young man waiting in the wings for
you."

When the lawyer had gone Briony flung herself on to her
attic bed in despair. How could Toby have let her down like
this! And yet, hadn't she always known that he might? She
burst into a paroxysm of weeping which exhausted her so
much that she finally fell asleep, still fully clothed. She woke
in the middle of the night, cold and frightened. If she was to
act as caretaker to Aunt Bessie's flat she had only a few
weeks' grace. Briony took the calendar off the hook and found
herself flipping back through the happy months she'd spent at
Drumcraig. Working in the gardens during the day, walking,
cooking, talking, followed by evenings of pleasure in Toby's
bed. Hours and hours of lovemaking with never a thought for
the consequences . . . Briony felt the color draining from her
cheeks as she looked at the dates on the calendar.

Her courses hadn't come this month. Or the month before . . . She rocked on the bed keening like a child as she tried
to come to terms with this new disaster. Toby's baby, she
thought, Toby's baby. But Toby had deserted her.

This time her grief was too deep to allow sleep as a salve.
When dawn came her eyes were red-rimmed, her face drawn,
her clothes crumpled. Mechanically she washed and dressed
and went through to the kitchen to make herself some breakfast. The toast stuck in her throat, and the tea had no taste. She

sat for a while trying to steady her nerves and make a decision about her future. A job was the answer, but the employment agency had none to offer.

Briony let herself out of the flat, and walked slowly down the stairs and crossed the road. The men on the building site were packing up for lunch. Angus Meldrum and his son walked over to where she was standing and she found herself telling him that she would soon have no roof over her head. He nodded sympathetically and then suggested she come with them round the corner to have a bite to eat at the café.

Briony sat opposite Angus and Frank, listening to the mason as he talked about his own plans. The new house was finished and he was going back to his croft on Deeside. He explained that when his wife was alive she looked after the croft whilst he was out plying his trade as a mason. "There's plenty of work for a mason on Deeside. Castle country, they cry it. And they're aye needing repaired."

"I like the castles," little Frank piped up, his eyes fixed on Briony. "Balmoral, Drum, Crathes, Craigievar. Drumcraig's the nearest; it's only two miles from the croft."

When Briony's eyes brightened, the mason looked at her curiously. "Ye like castles?"

Briony nodded, then dropped her head in despair as she remembered her predicament. "I don't know what I'm going to do . . ."

"We could get merrit!"

Briony was too stunned to say a word. She had never really studied Angus Meldrum. Now she took a good look at him. He was six foot three in height with big powerful shoulders. His eyes were as black as his hair. Was that why he was called Black Angus? Of course she couldn't marry Black Angus. She'd only started speaking to him because she passed the building site on her way to the shops.

"I'd like fine to have a mother again," Frank piped up.

The words sent a chill right through Briony's body. She was going to be a mother in seven months' time. How could she support a child without employment of some kind? Yet how could she look after her child if she went out working? It was hopeless, hopeless.

"I'd help you feed the hens on the croft," Frank said, his eyes becoming anxious as Briony sat silent. Briony allowed herself to envisage a whitewashed cottage on Deeside with roses growing round the door, the baby in its pram, and little Frank by her side. Safety, respectability, security. And somewhere nearby, Drumcraig Castle. At least she could go and look at it occasionally.

She hesitated, wondering if she should tell Angus Meldrum she was expecting another man's child, but when she looked at him closely she could see there was something forbidding about the set of his jaw and a strange fire in his dark eyes. No, she couldn't tell him the truth. If she married him she'd have to pretend that he was the father of her baby. She hated playing a trick like that on a man, but what else could she do? She would tell him later and if he loved her it wouldn't matter. He must love her, or he wouldn't be asking her to be his wife. Briony clenched her hands under the table. Angus was offering a solution to all her problems . . .

"If we could marry right away," she said slowly . . .

"Aye. I'll dae that, no bother at a' . . . So ye'll hae me?"

Briony closed her eyes tight and nodded her acceptance.

II

"That's it done, then," Angus declared after the ceremony in the registrar's office. He flicked the whip over the horse's back and they began the journey to his croft which was situated twelve miles outside Aberdeen.

Although Angus had refused to take her out to see the croft before they were married he had made her aware of its past history. He told her that the lairds who owned the land in the Highlands used to parcel off the best sections into communities run under their jurisdiction, but ignored the stony strips scattered in between until the squatters claimed them. The first settler on the Meldrum croft would have tethered his cow to a bush, cleared the boggy ground and then sent his woman to go "thigging": begging for seed corn to sow for next year's harvest. At that point the laird would have moved swiftly and charged him rent. Angus had waxed indignant about the injustice of the system. "My ancestors had to pay a rent for the privilege of using a house and ground they had built from nothing, and I've got to do the same."

Briony roused herself from her reverie. It was winter now, but in the summertime the ripe corn gave the hinterland of Aberdeen a golden glow.

"Does crofting give you a comfortable living?" she asked.

Her new husband gave her a strange look and grunted, "Dinna be daft, woman."

Briony wondered what she had said amiss. The rich red farming soil of the Mearns lay to the south and the fertile agricultural country of Formartine and Buchan to the north. If Angus's croft lay in between, surely it too was prosperous? Her new husband looked uneasy for a moment and then admitted that Stoneyground Croft lay in poor soil. He hadn't told her that before the wedding in case she took fright and changed her mind about marrying him. He needed a wife, he said. Throughout the north east, it seemed, there were many like him: masons, saddlers, blacksmiths, and tailors who used the cash they earned to subsidize their crofts.

He pointed out farms on the hillsides: sparkling white cottages just as Briony had imagined. She began to feel more cheerful as Angus recited the names of the villages they passed: Cults, Bieldside, Murtle, Milltimber, Peterculter. The trap crossed the bridge over the Leuchar Burn, and up a long winding road which eventually became a dust track. Late afternoon gave way to evening and the track rose higher into the hills until there was nothing to be seen but bleak, deserted moorland.

"There it is!" Angus said.

Briony's spirits plummeted as swiftly as the hawk she had seen earlier diving down for prey. The croft was a dingy gray cottage surrounded by a clutter of sheds and barns. The yards were muddy and there wasn't a flower in sight. It was so far removed from Briony's vision that she could have wept.

"All mine," Angus said proudly, as he handed her down from the trap. "Stoneyground's been in the family for four generations."

"It looks as if it's falling down," Briony said bleakly.

"Well, it's going to be yer home, so ye'd best get to like it," Angus snapped back at her.

Briony bit her lip. This wasn't the way to start her married life. "I'm sure it's a fine house," she said quickly. "Why don't you show me round?"

Mollified, he took her arm. The house was built of stone and clay with a thatched roof where she could see hens picking at the heather between the straw. Inside, it was not much more than a but and ben: a kitchen at one end, a sitting room at the other and in between a big double bed in a closet. Briony averted her gaze from it and looked round the parlor. A faded Rexined sofa and a battered armchair stood on a wooden floor which had two tattered rugs as a covering. There was a chest and a cabinet, but like everything else in the house they were old and chipped. Angus had told her that he had inherited his possessions from his father and it was obvious he had seen no need to change anything.

"I'll make curtains for the window," she said brightly, trying to sound more optimistic than she felt, "and perhaps you could buy some new furniture."

Her husband made a noise somewhere between a grunt and a snort and led her into the kitchen. Before they were married he had told her that in the old crofting days the fire was in the middle of the room and caused so much smoke that everyone coughed and spluttered. He was proud of the fact that the kitchen in his croft had a "hinging lug": a wooden canopy which stretched above the fireplace and contained the smoke. There was a sink, a few cupboards, a larder, and a boiler for the washing.

"What do I use for cooking?" Briony asked.

Angus pointed to the iron rod that swivelled out from the fire and told her it was called a swey. He explained how to adjust the links on the swey to make them go nearer the fire.

"For mair heat," he added, when Briony looked at him blankly. "Now see if ye can make my supper. I've put some food in the larder."

There wasn't much: cold meat, bread, eggs. Less than she'd found on her first day at Drumcraig.

Briony stopped in the act of slicing bread and closed her eyes. She must stop thinking about Drumcraig and Toby. She would have to banish the thought of her old life, otherwise how could she survive her new one?

Angus Meldrum looked incredulously at the meal she placed before him. "Meat *and* eggs? Aye, lass, ye've a lot to learn . . ."

After the meal Briony washed up and went through to the

parlor. Angus was sitting at an old wooden desk sorting through some papers. What a grim room, Briony thought, and what a dull lonely life it must have been in the past year for Angus's son with only his father for company. "Where does Frank sleep?" she asked.

Angus jerked his head upwards towards the loft. Briony climbed the stairs to the loft and looked round in disbelief at the jumble of broken furniture, old clothes, and rusty farm implements. In one corner was a stained mattress.

"That loft is a pigsty!" she exclaimed when she clambered down from it. "How can you let your son sleep in such a place?"

"Frank's only a laddie, it disna matter where he sleeps," her husband replied as he tidied away his bills.

Briony sat down in the old armchair and surveyed her new domain. "I'm going to clean this place from top to bottom," she announced. "I haven't any materials in the cupboards. You'll have to go back to Aberdeen tomorrow and buy them. I'll make out a list of all the things we need."

Angus rose to his feet and pulled her roughly out of her chair. "Ye havna been listening. There's nae spare cash."

"But the money you earn as a mason . . ."

"Pays for animal feed, machinery, stock. The croft takes it all."

"Well, that's stupid," Briony retorted angrily, as she shook off his hands. "If you gave up this croft you could enjoy a reasonable standard of living. So sell it. Why condemn yourself to penury?"

His hand came up and delivered a stinging blow to her cheek. "Ye and yer fancy words," he roared, his face bright red with anger. "Stoneyground has been here for generations," he went on. "I'll work ma fingers to the bone to keep it. Aye, and ye'll dae the same. Why d'ye think we got merrit?"

"I thought you wanted my company . . ."

"Company!" he snorted. "I wanted a wife to help run the croft."

"Then you're an ignorant fool and I'm sorry I married you," Briony sobbed. "And you won't sleep in my bed tonight!"

The mention of bed was a mistake. As his eye traveled over her she saw his anger turning to lust. He reached out his great hand and clutched the bodice of her green dress. She tried to move away, but he increased the pressure of his hand and ripped the buttons off her bodice. He was drunk from the whisky he'd been taking freely since his supper, but still very strong and he was able to pull down her dress and the petticoat underneath it.

"Stop!" she shrieked, but he kept pulling at her clothing until she was completely naked. She began backing away from him with her palms outspread over her breasts to hide herself from him. He smiled then, and his smile was more terrifying than his anger. He strode towards her reaching for her breasts, squeezing them with his fingers.

"Angus, please . . . You're hurting me," she gasped, but her pain and fear seemed to incite him and he squeezed harder. When he took her breast in his mouth and she felt the edge of his teeth, her legs began to give way and she sank to the floor. Instantly he was on top of her, but Briony began fighting back and by chance her knee caught him in the groin. He let out an agonized yell and rolled away from her.

When he began moving back in her direction Briony saw that he had picked up his belt and was wrapping one end of it round his wrist. "I'll hae ma rights," he said as he bent over her. She shrieked in agony as the belt slashed down on her unprotected flesh, but her cries became fainter and fainter as he carried on thrashing her. Only when she was still and silent did he put the belt aside. She lay half-conscious on the floor waiting for another blow, but it never came. He picked her up and carried her to the bridal bed in the closet off the kitchen. Roughly parting her legs, he began pushing between them, harder and harder, until the pain made her lose consciousness.

When Briony came to her senses she saw that Angus was lying snoring by her side. She was too frightened to move so she lay still until sheer exhaustion helped her drift into an uneasy sleep. Dawn light was filtering through the croft windows when she woke again. Every part of her body was aching, but she stifled her sobs in case they wakened the man sleeping at her side. Now she knew why his workmates called him Black Angus!

She slid out of bed, put on a coat and her outdoor shoes, and stole outside to the privy to relieve herself. She peered down at her body to examine the wounds her husband had inflicted the night before. The bleeding had stopped, but the cuts were red and angry-looking and she winced with pain every time she moved. She put her hands protectively over her stomach and vowed that if her husband had harmed her baby she would kill him.

Once she was back in the house again, Briony crept quietly into the parlor and lay down on the couch, pulling her coat round her for warmth. Panic had made her rush into marriage with a man she hardly knew, but she would not stay with him. When it was lighter, she would slip out of the house and begin walking back to Aberdeen.

She groaned as she remembered that she had nowhere to go in Aberdeen, no one to turn to. Aunt Bessie's doctor? Or the lawyer Sidney Thornton? No. Despite their sympathy, they would take the old-fashioned attitude to marriage: once you make your bed you have to lie on it. They would advise her to go back to her husband, even more so if they heard she was expecting a baby.

Briony felt scalded by her thoughts. A baby. She could never tell a man with Angus's temper that she was expecting someone else's baby. Gritting her teeth to stop herself wincing Briony managed to put on her clothes and drag herself across to the kitchen table. Angus was now awake, and she watched her husband as he took some handfuls of oatmeal from the tub which stood by the back window and put them in a pot. Briony was silent as she watched him and wondered how he could have abused her so badly. Maybe it was the whisky . . .

There was a further shock in store. Over a simple breakfast of brose, oatcakes, butter, and strong tea, Angus explained that after his wife had died, he had hired a farmer's daughter to look after the croft. Now Briony would do the work. She was expected to feed the animals, milk the cows, hunt for the eggs which the hens often laid in strange places, look after the vegetable garden, and weed the fields when she had time to spare for the other chores: cooking, washing, ironing, and housework.

I'm going to be a slave, Briony thought in dismay, just the way I was at Aunt Bessie's. She fixed her husband with her gaze. "I'm not going to do all that," she declared stoutly.

"Ye'll do it," he said grimly, "or rue the day."

III

After her husband suggested she work hard or "rue the day" Briony seethed with fury. How dare he threaten her like that! Yet if she refused to work hard for him she was aware that he would not think twice about beating her into submission, and that might damage the baby she was carrying. Toby's child. Until the baby was born Briony decided she would just have to endure life as a crofter's wife.

Adapting to the exigencies of life on the croft proved even harder than she had anticipated. Few visitors ever called at Stoneyground apart from traveling seed merchants or tradesmen. The croft's isolated position on the hilltop was one reason for the absence of company, Angus Meldrum's attitude was another. Early on in their marriage, well-meaning neighbors had called on the newly weds as was the custom in the north east, but Angus had been so rude to them that they had not called again. Admittedly he had given notice on their wedding day that he wasn't expecting any of his former workmates to come and see them, but Briony had not expected him to widen that embargo to everyone in the district.

The two strong ties which bound Briony to the croft were her pregnancy and Frank. After his day at school in Peterculter Frank hurried home to help her with all the chores and every day she could see him becoming happier and healthier.

"You'll stay?" he kept asking anxiously.

She promised him that she would, even though she loathed the nights when her husband demanded his rights. Angus seemed to enjoy Briony's cries of pain as her dry, unaroused vagina protested at his rough entry. In time she found a way of making the experience more bearable: whenever her husband pulled her to him in bed she tried to imagine she was with Toby.

Although she had been bitterly disillusioned by the way Toby had abandoned her she could not help remembering the happy times they'd once had at Drumcraig Castle. It was these she recalled as she lay beneath her husband. The memory of Drumcraig was her lifeline to sanity. The castle was only two miles away from Stoneyground. She had never been back although she heard that a new owner had moved in, and had refurbished the castle. Her husband often asked her what she was thinking about as he pushed and prodded at her intimate places. "Just thoughts," she would reply enigmatically. She was daydreaming about Drumcraig, but she did not tell him that. Sometimes he was so determined to get a response from her that he prolonged his thrusts until she screamed.

Briony knew she would have to tell him soon about her pregnancy. She had kept herself slim, but even an unobservant man like Angus was bound to notice sooner or later. She intended to bring up the subject tactfully, but in the end she blurted it out after supper one evening when Angus was leafing through some seed catalogues.

"I'm expecting a baby."

"So quick?" Her husband smiled, obviously pleased with his prowess and never doubting for a moment that the baby was his. "I hope the bairn's better than my brat. Frank's feart o' his ain shadow."

Briony looked up and saw Frank standing in the doorway, biting back his tears. "Frank isn't cowardly, nor is he a brat!" she protested. "When the bull came towards me one day it was Frank who frightened him away, and he's good with that mad billy goat!"

Her husband snorted. "Frank's like his mother: stupit!"

"My mother wasn't stupid," Frank protested, "and she was only scared because you hit her."

Angus Meldrum turned puce with rage. He seized his son, threw him over the back of a chair and walloped his backside with his stick. "That'll larn ye. Awa' up tae the loft."

"Angus, please, you've hurt the boy. He needs . . ."

"He needs another thrashing and ye'll get one as well gin ye go after him. I'm awa' tae feed the beasts."

Briony waited until he was outside and then hurried up the steps to the loft. She went across to Frank's bed and gathered the weeping boy in her arms. "There, there, Frank. Your father doesn't mean what he says."

"He does!" Frank cried. "He hates me, and I hate him because he was cruel to my mother. And if he's cruel to you, you'll go away."

"I won't desert you," Briony said as she hugged him. Nor would she. Once the baby was born she intended to leave the croft and she would take Frank with her.

IV

1931

The baby was starting to whimper. Briony clambered down from the closet bed and tiptoed across the stone floor to look in the cot. It had been a very easy birth which was hardly surprising since the baby weighed only five pounds. The nurse had said Briony's baby was premature, and the birth had probably been hastened by all the heaving and lifting which was the normal lot of a crofter's wife. Briony had not replied. If it had been Angus's baby it would have been early, but it was Toby's baby and it was on time.

Briony sat down to suckle her daughter, her mind absorbed by her husband. After a year of marriage she was aware that there was something warped about Angus Meldrum. He had a sadistic streak which enabled him to enjoy other people's pain; it made her dread the prospect of resuming marital relations with him. She had vowed to leave Stoneyground when her baby was born, but little Alexandra was so fragile she was frightened to move away. And besides she had no money of her own. She had to find a way of earning some . . .

V

"Hae you ony milk to spare?" a voice called from outside the croft. Briony opened the door and saw a gypsy, with skin as brown and leathery as the bark of a tree. Briony filled a bowl with milk and handed it to her. "There's still some porridge in the pot. Come and take it by the fire. I could do with some company this morning."

"Ye're a kind girl," the gypsy said as she supped her porridge. "Kinder than the new Master o' Drumcraig. He chased me away."

"What's he like?" Briony asked curiously.

"Tall, red-heided, clipped moustache. Arty-looking. But ye should hear what a servant lassie told me about him." The gypsy bent forward and began whispering in Briony's ear.

After the gypsy left Briony began thinking about the Master of Drumcraig. Reputedly he was a millionaire who had spent thousands restoring the castle. Briony had assumed he would be very respectable, very upright, but according to the gypsy . . .

Briony bit her lip. If she had any pride she would not have anything to do with such a depraved man. But didn't poverty cancel out pride? The gypsy said he paid his women well. I could force myself to endure it, Briony thought defiantly. It couldn't be any worse than what she had to suffer from her husband. And she could buy so many things for the baby and Frank with the money . . .

FIFTEEN

I

1934

Frank stripped off his clothes, but instead of going to bed he took the muscle builder from its hiding place under the eaves. Briony had bought it for him from her "sewing money" and he'd been using it ever since. He hadn't transformed himself from a seven-stone weakling to a champion of the world as the advert had promised, but the nightly exercises had certainly developed his muscles. He was much bigger than the other 12-year-olds in his class, but he wouldn't be satisfied until he was stronger than the old bastard. He couldn't remember when he'd first started thinking of his father as the old bastard, but the name was appropriate. Ever since his mother had died his father had enjoyed thrashing him. One day, Frank resolved, he would be ready to test out the power that the exerciser had given him. Then he'd teach his father a lesson . . .

Once he had finished his work-out he hid the muscle builder beneath the eaves and lay down on his bed. His thoughts drifted back to the events of the week before. Mr. Elphinstone of Drumcraig Castle had offered to take three local boys down to Glasgow at his expense to watch the launching of the *Queen Mary* and Frank had been one of the boys chosen. It had been his first outing in an automobile, and his first experience of staying in a hotel for two nights. Best of all had been the magic moment of the launching. Sparks flew out from the great hull as it began to move, huge waves spilled over the *Queen Mary* as she slid into the water and the crowds cheered so loudly Frank felt his eardrums were going too split.

"I'd like to work in a shipyard like John Brown's," he'd said to Mr. Elphinstone in the car on the way back to Aberdeen.

"Come to me when you're 16 and I'll arrange it."

Frank thought it would be great to work in a shipyard in Glasgow. He couldn't wait to get away from Stoneyground and he was secretly hoping that his stepmother would go with him. He could not imagine that she was happy with Angus Meldrum as a husband. The insulation between the loft and the room below was so poor that voices carried very easily. Frank would lie in bed at night clenching his fists as he heard his stepmother's cries. He would go rushing down from the loft and square up to his father, his fists clenched, but father always got the better of him. It was after one of those sessions that Frank had decided to buy a muscle builder with the money Briony gave him. One of these days he was going to give the old bastard a beating he'd never forget.

He often wondered what Alexandra thought of it all. Fortunately she was only 3 and slept through the night. During the day, when her father thrashed Frank or beat Briony, Alexandra would run up and hit him, and when he pushed her away or smacked her Alexandra would scream at him in childish rage. Frank couldn't help grinning at the thought of his half-sister. Alexandra did not appear to be frightened of anyone or anything and Frank was glad about that. She would need to be fearless to survive life at Stoneyground with her father.

At least the old bastard wasn't around all the time. Whenever he finished one job Mr. Elphinstone used his influence to get him another. Yes, Frank thought, as he turned over on his side and drifted into sleep, the Meldrum fortunes had certainly changed for the better since his stepmother had gone to work at Drumcraig.

II

Briony rose early. By the time she had prepared the breakfast Frank had milked the cows and fed the cattle. He always gave her a bit of extra help on the day she went to the castle. Monday was washing day and, after Angus left for work and Frank cycled off to school, Briony scrubbed and pounded and squeezed until all the clothes were cleaned to her satisfaction. Alexandra trailed after her wherever she went, getting her hands and feet wet in the soapsuds and generally making mischief. Once the clothes were hung out on the line Briony baked a pie for the evening meal. She put the potato peelings and the other garbage into the hens' pot which hung by the fire where it stewed quietly, exuding a pungent smell.

Her chores finished, Briony changed into a blue skirt and blouse and dressed Alexandra in her best pinafore before setting off for Drumcraig. When Briony had started going to the castle each week she had pushed her daughter in a cumbersome old pram. Fortunately Frank had managed to find a secondhand pushchair and the two-mile walk to the castle had become easier.

Ellen, the housekeeper, was looking out for them. She was a tall bulky woman with iron-grey hair cut in a mannish style, but happily she loved children and she had volunteered to look after Alexandra whenever Briony was with Mr. Elphinstone. Ellen had been housekeeper at Drumcraig Castle to Luke Armstrong, Toby's father, until she'd left to look after her elderly mother who lived in Cornwall. When her mother died Ellen stayed on in Cornwall, but she didn't settle and eventually she packed up and came to look for work in Aberdeen. She registered with Collies and they recommended her to David Elphinstone. He liked the idea of continuity and employed her immediately.

Ellen was thrilled when she heard that Briony had worked as Toby's housekeeper for a while. "Master Toby was my favorite, but a right rascal," she said fondly. "I wish I'd known he'd fallen on hard times. I'd have worked for him for nothing, but by the time I did come back to Aberdeen, Master Toby had emigrated to America."

"I wasn't his housekeeper for very long," Briony said quietly, "but I liked him too." She hadn't intended to tell Ellen that she and Toby had fallen in love, but the light in her eyes betrayed her.

Ellen pursed her lips when she heard how Toby had vanished without contacting Briony. "Master Toby was aye wild and feckless. He must have taken a notion to sell the castle and he wouldn't think of the hurt he was causing you. I've a good mind to give him a scolding. He started writing to me, you know, when he heard I was back at Drumcraig."

Evidently Toby had started a restaurant in Chicago with the proceeds from the sale of Drumcraig Castle, but it hadn't been a success and he had lost most of his money. Presently he was working in New York in a restaurant where he had hopes of a partnership. Ellen said sadly that Toby was always full of dreams, but didn't seem to have the backbone to make them work.

"Look at the scamp! Isn't she growing fast?" Ellen exclaimed as Alexandra scrambled out of her pushchair and rushed into the castle and up the stairs. Ellen's quarters were on the second floor of Drumcraig where she had a bedroom and sitting room. The four floors above that were occupied by David Elphinstone. The seventh floor of the castle had been converted into a studio because the light was so good. None of the servants was allowed to go beyond the fifth floor of the castle except Ellen. She looked after the master's bedroom on the sixth floor, but even she wasn't allowed to go near his studio at the top of the castle. David Elphinstone was only in his late forties, but all the servants—from the youngest to the oldest—treated him like an elderly rajah whose commands must be obeyed.

"Are you going upstairs to do your sewing?" Alexandra asked when they had all climbed the stairs to Ellen's sitting room. As far as Alexandra—and the staff—were concerned, when Briony went up to the top of the castle it was to work on the tapestries that Mr. Elphinstone had laid out for her. If any of the servants suspected what the master was up to they never talked about it; the kitchen maid had gossiped to the gypsy and she had been sacked.

"Yes, I'm off to do my sewing," Briony agreed. She kissed her daughter goodbye and climbed up flight after flight of steps until she reached the seventh floor. When she knocked on the door a voice bade her enter. She saw David Elphinstone standing at the window, his red hair now long and tied back in a ponytail, his blue eyes gleaming with merriment as he held a picture to the light. "Remember this one? It was the first I ever painted of you."

Briony came across to his side and looked down at the painting which was entitled "Motherhood." In it she was wearing an old blue dress unbottoned to reveal one breast swollen with milk. Her baby was suckling at her engorged nipple, her eyes closed, her face peaceful as she neared the end of her feed. Briony was looking down at her daughter with an expression of such tenderness that even she found it moving.

"It's a beautiful picture," she said slowly. "You know when I first came here three years ago . . ."

"I know. When you drew aside your dress you were shaking so much I couldn't paint until you'd calmed down."

Briony laughed, remembering how terrified she had been, how sordid she had felt at the thought of selling her body for money. On that first day after he had indicated that the session was over, she had waited tensely, sure that she would be expected to share David Elphinstone's bed. Instead he had dismissed her.

At first she had felt shy about posing nude, but she soon got used to it. David Elphinstone had painted her holding flowers in her arms, reading a book, eating a peach with the juice dribbling down her breasts, putting her lips to a rose petal . . . Sometimes he draped swathes of material round her shoulders; at other times he liked to paint her naked body against a wall or window. The paintings took months to complete since he always made sketches before taking up his oils.

He touched her skin frequently as he arranged the angles of her body to suit his picture, but he had never made any attempt to seduce her. Since he liked to talk whilst he was working they got to know each other very quickly and she learned that a talent for figures had led him towards a career in the city where he'd made his fortune. He told her once that he'd had four great loves in his life: making money, Drumcraig Castle, painting, and a beautiful young girl who had run off with someone else.

"She looked just like you," he said.

"Is that why you like painting me?" Briony had asked.

"I'd like you to recline against this couch," he said, ignoring her question. "There, lie back against the blue velvet." When he was satisfied with her position he picked a pink rosebud from a vase and placed it delicately on the hair between her legs. "You really are an excellent model; the other girls are so restless."

"Then why do you employ them?" she found herself asking with the familiarity of three years of friendship.

"They satisfy my baser needs," he replied without a blush, confirming her suspicion that he took them to his bed. "Does your husband still think your only purpose in coming here is to sew?"

"If he knew I was posing for you like this he'd k . . . he wouldn't like it," Briony finished lamely.

"But he likes the extra money you bring home each week?"

"It helps to pay for food and clothes." And some day, she thought, my secret nest egg will help to pay for Alexandra's education and Frank's apprenticeship—and my own escape . . .

"What do you dream about as you pose for me?" he asked.

Almost the same question put by her husband, she thought. And the answer—although she did not reveal it—was the same: she dreamed about Drumcraig Castle and wondered if she would ever be able to fulfill her vow to her father and restore it to the Meldrums.

Once the sketch was completed Briony went downstairs to find her daughter. Ellen came running towards her brandishing an envelope. "A letter to you from Toby."

Briony's eyes widened. "But how . . . ?"

"Wheesht now," Ellen said placatingly as she drew her to a chair by the fireside. "A few months ago I decided it was time I gave Master Toby a few home truths. So I wrote him a nice long letter bringing him up to date on all that's happened to you. So now, as well as a letter to me, there's one for you. Here, take it."

Slowly Briony reached out for the blue envelope and as she read its contents she felt the warmth start at her toes and rise up through her whole body.

DEAR BRIONY (Toby wrote),

Ellen has told me your story. Now read mine and then you'll maybe feel more kindly towards me. When you left Drumcraig to nurse your aunt, I waited a week and then wrote you a letter to see how you were getting on. Your aunt forbade me to come visiting "because of the poor state of her health." When I wrote again she sent a stiff note telling me that you had decided to have nothing more to do with me. I didn't believe her and the following week I sent you another letter. This time your aunt threatened me with the police if I didn't stop pestering you. Well, I didn't know what to do, but I thought I'd better leave it a while to see what happened.

All the same I felt depressed and lonely and I started drinking and gambling again. The bank manager called me into his office and introduced me to David Elphinstone. Elphinstone had been coming up to Aberdeen on holiday for years and had actually visited Drumcraig when my father was alive. When he heard I was running out of cash he told the bank manager he'd like to buy the castle. I know you loved that castle, Briony, and I know I promised to give you the deeds as a wedding present. But your aunt was making out you'd finished with me, my creditors were pressing, and Elphinstone was offering me a large sum of money. Far more than the castle was worth. He said if I signed straight away he'd give me half the money in cash. That was too tempting an offer to refuse, Briony—you can't be too surprised that I accepted. I thought that once your aunt died I would sort things out with you and buy you a beautiful house as a wedding present to make up for losing the castle.

But first I decided to go to England on holiday for a few weeks. And yes, I'll admit it, I fell into my old habits and stayed away too long. I did keep writing to you but you never replied. When I eventually came back to Aberdeen you aunt's lawyer contacted me, and you know what he gave me? All the letters I'd written to you which you aunt had kept stuffed in an old deed box. The lawyer said he felt ashamed of his client, but by the time he discovered the letters your circumstances had changed and he thought it better to say nothing about them.

I was shocked when I heard you'd married someone else, so shocked that I decided to emigrate to America. Now I hear from Ellen that you aren't happy with the man you picked and still cherish your love for me. You've no idea how that gladdens my heart. Ellen will tell you that I've made a new start in New York. I've told my friend Felix Danziger all about you. He knows I want to come back to Scotland to make a new start with you.

III

For months after Briony received her first letter from Toby she floated on a cloud of euphoria. Toby was coming home and they would find a way to be together. But it was a long while before she heard from Toby again and when he wrote he had disappointing news: his new venture had failed and he had turned to gambling once again as a means of making money. Failure was to be a recurring theme in the years that followed. Toby rushed from one business exploit to another and eventually Briony was forced to admit that she loved a man who seemed incapable of keeping his money or his promises.

And then came the day when Ellen suddenly appeared at the croft with dreadful news.

"Toby dead?" Briony whispered. "I can't believe that."

"It's true. Toby and his friend—that Felix Danziger he mentions in his letters—they were playing cards and . . ." Ellen mopped her eyes as she tried to get the words out. "Felix accused their opponent of cheating and the man pulled a knife. And Toby leapt between them . . . The knife . . ."

"The knife?"

"Pierced Toby's chest," Ellen sobbed. "The Danziger man had my address. I've just had this letter telling me . . . He wrote you as well," she added as she pulled a crumpled envelope from her pocket.

DEAR BRIONY (Felix Danziger wrote),

Although we've never met, Toby often talked of you. When he was dying he asked me to give your family help if you ever needed it. Toby saved my life, so my son and I owe him a life-long debt of gratitude. Perhaps in the future either my son or myself will be able to fulfill our promise to Toby. I am so sorry, so terribly sorry about this tragic accident. The man concerned has been jailed, but that is no consolation to those of us who loved Toby and have now lost him forever.

Lost forever, Briony thought. Not only had she lost the only man she had ever loved, but now all her dreams of owning Drumcraig had vanished as well. She cried then, deep racking sobs that shook her body. "I wish I'd told Toby that Alexandra was his daughter," she moaned. "I vowed I wouldn't do that unless he came back to me."

Ellen's eyes widened. "Alexandra can't be Toby's child, lass. Don't talk so daft."

"Alexandra was conceived with Toby, I tell you."

"Nae, lass. I was housekeeper at Drumcraig when Master Toby got a bad case of mumps. The doctor said he'd never be able to have children."

"Well, the doctor was wrong!"

Ellen shook her head. "Toby was checked by several doctors; they all said the same. Then and later."

"But Ellen, by the time I married Angus I had missed two of my periods."

"A woman can miss her courses if she's worried about summat!" Ellen said firmly. "The Great War proved that."

Briony felt an icy chill begin deep inside her. Love with Toby had been coupled with guilt. And then at her Aunt Bessie's house she had been worried sick because Toby had not written to her. Another shaft of memory pierced her: the midwife mentioning that Alexandra was a tiny five-pound baby because she had arrived two months early. That would have been feasible if she had been Angus's baby, but at the time Briony had dismissed that notion.

Briony rose from her chair, her face stricken, as she tried to come to terms with the unpalatable truth: Alexandra was the product of that loveless coupling with Angus on her wedding night. Angus's child. Angus's child. The refrain beat at her brains till she put her hands over her ears and rushed out of the croft.

"Is there something wrong, mum?"

Alexandra had come home from school and was clutching her mother's waist in an attempt to comfort her.

"Don't touch me," Briony hissed. "Keep away from me."

IV

After the news of Toby's death Briony became obsessed with leaving Deeside and making a new start with Alexandra somewhere else. When she mentioned to David Elphinstone that she was looking for ways to augment her nest egg he told her he would pay her well if she let him make love to her. She overcame her scruples and agreed. One bonus of their affair was that he wanted her to spend more time at the castle and when he started saying that he loved her she began to nurture new dreams of becoming mistress of Drumcraig. But it was the spring of 1939 before she found the courage to speak to him about it.

He seemed preoccupied when she went into his studio. "I don't feel like painting or making love today, my dear. My brother and his wife have been killed in a car crash."

"I'm sorry." She sat down on the studio couch, a little puzzled by his concern since he'd fallen out with his brother years before. Yet here he was, his cheeks flushed, his distress all too clear.

"There's a problem," he said heavily. "The survivor of the crash is my 13-year-old nephew Tom and I've been made his guardian. I've had to ask him to come to live with me at Drumcraig. And I suppose I'll have to make him my heir as well. I don't know how I'll keep the boy occupied. Apparently, the only game he likes is chess."

"Perhaps I'd better go. Alexandra . . ."

David Elphinstone whirled round on her. "Alexandra! That could be the answer. I've spent hours teaching her to play chess. She can pit her wits against Tom."

"But he's 13 . . . Won't he feel it beneath him to play with a girl of 7?"

David Elphinstone rubbed his hands with glee. "I'm sure he will, but he'll get a shock when he discovers how good Alexandra is. Whilst you were sewing I was teaching her, and she's learned well. Don't look so worried, our arrangements won't need to be changed. I do love you . . ."

Briony seized the moment. "Then why don't I come and live at the castle permanently? I could divorce Angus and marry you . . ."

David Elphinstone clicked his tongue reprovingly. "No, no, my dear, that wouldn't do at all. Divorce would be very difficult—perhaps impossible—for a woman like yourself. Besides, our relationship is perfect the way it is."

Briony's dreams of owning Drumcraig dissolved yet again.

The following week she announced coolly that the fee for her "services" had doubled. David Elphinstone cocked an amused eyebrow, but gave her what she wanted. Briony calculated that by August her nest egg would have grown sufficiently to allow her to make her break for freedom. After the harvest Frank was going to Glasgow to start his apprenticeship in the shipyard. She and Alexandra would go with him.

SIXTEEN

I

Alexandra twiddled her toes under the blanket, aware that this was a special day. Usually she ran barefoot over the moors to save the cost of leather, but today her mother was allowing her to wear shoes. She glanced at her brown brogues by the side of her bed and hoped Mr. Elphinstone's nephew would be impressed. If he did not like her he might not want her to come to the castle and that would be awful. She loved Drumcraig. She'd heard its story so often it was like a family fairy tale and she kept hoping that one day it would have a happy ending. She was convinced that if the Meldrums ever owned the castle again she would turn into a princess instead of being a plain mousey schoolgirl.

A grunt from her father reminded Alexandra that it was time to get up. She jumped out of bed and within minutes was washed and dressed and racing to the privy across the yard. When she came back the hunger which seemed a continuous part of her existence was a sharp ache in her belly. She yearned for a boiled egg from one of their hens, but she knew better than to ask for it. Eggs were there to be sold, not to be eaten by the family. She helped her mother set the table and then they sat down to breakfast. Her father liked to eat by himself when everyone else was finished.

"I can't wait to start work at John Brown's shipyard," Frank was saying to her mother. "I hope I can make a go of it."

"Of course you can," her mother replied fondly and laid her hand on his arm.

"Stop making a namby-pamby of the lad! A kick up the arse is fit he needs!"

Alexandra turned round and saw her father standing in the doorway of the kitchen. He strode forward and slapped her mother's arm so hard that the plate of hot porridge spilled over Briony's lap, causing her to cry out in pain. Frank leapt out of his seat and grabbed his father by the scruff of the neck. Angus Meldrum was powerful, but so was Frank and they rolled over on the floor, arms and legs kicking, faces crimson with rage as they tussled for a stronghold. Then Frank landed a blow on his father's jaw that sent him reeling.

"For years I've watched you bullying everyone in this family," Frank shouted, "and I'm warning you. If you ever lay a hand on any of us again I'll kill you!"

"Ye'll be deid first!" Angus Meldrum yelled as he picked up his tools from the kitchen dresser and banged out of the house.

Frank rubbed his knuckles. "I've had to wait a long time to get my revenge."

"But when Angus comes home tonight . . ." Briony began.

"I won't be here. One of my mates has already offered to put me up till the end of August."

"I hate it when father is nasty," Alexandra sobbed.

"I've made you a new dress," her mother said brightly. "Why don't you put it on and then we'll walk across the moors to the castle? We want to be in good time. Mr. Elphinstone's nephew says he'll play chess with you."

II

Primroses nestled in rock crevices like patches of lemon sunshine, skylarks sang, and the whole countryside seemed to be celebrating springtime. Alexandra was picking bunches of tiny moorland blooms. "Teacher wants us to collect wild flowers and press them in a book," she informed her mother.

Briony's heart ached for her child as she remembered her tear-stained face at breakfast. But then, she thought wryly, her daughter had been listening to quarrels and fights ever since she'd been born; Stoneyground had never been a tranquil home. Briony had given her daughter the piece of polished Rubislaw granite that had once belonged to Fergus, and told her to cherish it. And to remember every time she looked at it that only the strong survive. Fortunately Alexandra seemed to be resilient and never stayed sad for long. She had disappeared into the bracken, but suddenly she emerged and pointed upwards.

"Mother, look!"

There, floating on the thermals was a golden eagle, its wingspan so vast that it cast a shadow over the hillside. In Skye Briony had grown used to seeing these magnificent birds, but they weren't so common in this part of Aberdeenshire. She remembered the time her father had taken her up into the Cuillins to show her an eyrie . . .

"Wasn't it huge?' Alexandra appeared at her side, tripping over a clump of heather in her excitement. "Perhaps that eagle came from the Cairngorms? Teacher says the source of the River Dee is in the Cairngorms. Guess where?" She danced about in front of her mother, eager to show off her knowledge.

"I've no idea," Briony replied gravely.

"From a spring on the plateau of Braeriach. Miss Roberts says there's snow there even in summertime."

"Well, if there's snow in the summer, I don't suppose there'll be any wild flowers up there."

"Oh, but there are," Alexandra protested. "Teacher says that on the edge of the snow you can sometimes see pink flowers. When I'm older I'm going up there to see them."

"And what else are you going to do when you're older?' Briony asked, amused at her daughter's intensity. Sometimes Alexandra was such a fierce little girl.

"I don't know. Miss Roberts says I should have ambition, but I haven't got any yet," Alexandra said anxiously.

Briony ruffled her daughter's hair and bent down to kiss her. At the moment Alexandra was a bit of an ugly duckling, but she loved her dearly. It was only when she remembered that her daughter was Angus's child that her love turned to hostility. She *must* try to fight that feeling.

"Look, bluebells," Alexandra shouted as she gestured to a haze of blue beside some trees. "I want to pick some."

Briony rested her back against a tree, enjoying the softness of the fern beneath her feet, and the soft rustling of the branches as they swayed with the wind.

"Could I wear this dress to school one day?" Alexandra begged as they neared the castle. "I'd like Miss Roberts to see it."

Briony grimaced. Miss Roberts again. Her daughter was at the stage when her teacher had become all-important.

"You like Miss Roberts a lot, don't you?"

Alexandra nodded. "I like it when she gives me extra tuition at her house and makes tea and cakes. The others say I'm her favorite. But there's nothing wrong in being a favorite, is there?" she asked, a pucker of worry creasing her brow.

"I'm sure you're her favorite because you're so eager to learn. And maybe Miss Roberts likes the company since she lives alone. She has a sister in Glasgow, hasn't she?"

"A twin sister who looks exactly like her," Alexandra said gleefully. "She told me about her last week. Her twin is a headmistress too. Isn't that strange?"

Briony nodded, but as the turrets of Drumcraig came into view she forgot all about Miss Roberts and her twin sister. As usual Ellen came rushing out to meet them. "I've just made some lemonade. Come into the kitchen and have a drink."

"What's Mr. Elphinstone's nephew like?" Alexandra asked anxiously.

Ellen drew her brows together. "That's not for me to say, miss. Off you go. They're waiting for you in the Great Hall."

III

"Glad to meet you," Tom Elphinstone said to Alexandra as he stretched out his hand. "My uncle says you're a whizz at chess. Would you like a game now?"

His uncle brought out a chess table with carved ivory chess pieces and stood with his arms folded as Tom set them up.

"You can make the first move," Tom said graciously.

Alexandra concentrated hard before moving her fingers decisively over the board. It was checkmate in fifteen minutes. David Elphinstone laughed at his nephew's dismay. "Good, isn't she? See if you can do better this time."

When they started the second game, Tom's smile vanished as quickly as his chess pieces. "I'd love a glass of water," he said suddenly.

"I'll get it for you." Alexandra pushed back her chair and ran down the room and out of the door. When she came back and looked at the board she realized Tom had moved her queen. She glanced up at his uncle, but David Elphinstone was gazing out of the window.

"Well?" Tom demanded in a challenging voice, Alexandra gulped and stuttered and then kept quiet. They played in silence for a few minutes until Tom called, "Checkmate!"

"Well done!" his uncle said approvingly. "Let's go on a tour of the castle. Alexandra will tell you all about it. When I realized how clever she was I started teaching her about furniture and furnishings and works of art."

Alexandra had enjoyed the hours she'd spent with Mr. Elphinstone learning about those things, but as she glanced at his nephew's face she saw that he wasn't pleased at the praise that was being heaped on her. When the tour was finished Mr. Elphinstone told Tom to escort her home across the moors.

"Ask Alexandra about the wild flowers. She knows all their names."

Alexandra glanced up at Tom warily as they began walking down the drive, but Tom kept his lips tightly shut and looked away from her. It was only when they neared the small loch in the middle of the moor that he voiced his thoughts. "Have you always been such a beasty little swot?" he said with a sneer.

"I'm not a swot!" she protested. "I've just got a good memory. Anyway, your uncle wanted me to learn everything about the castle."

"Well, now you have, you should shut up about it. And I don't want to play chess with you again."

"Are you frightened I'll beat you?" she asked, surprising him with her show of spirit.

"You were just lucky the first time."

"You cheated! You moved my queen when I went to get the water."

"So why didn't you tell my uncle?"

"I didn't want to get you into trouble," she stuttered.

"What a little prig you are!"

Alexandra turned away till she was standing on the edge of the loch.

"I wish I could leave you here," Tom muttered, "but my uncle wouldn't like it. Come on, pest," he said, tugging at her arm. "The sooner I get you home the sooner I'll be rid of you."

"I don't want to go with you."

"D'you think I want to go with you? An ugly little brat who has a skivvy for a mother!"

"Don't you *dare* say anything against my mother!" Alexandra shouted.

"Why not? She's just a common little maid who helps out with the sewing!"

Alexandra's eyes flashed and before Tom realized what was happening she had started pummeling him with her fists. He staggered backwards in surprise and tumbled into the loch.

"You little brat, I'll get you for this!"

Alexandra turned and fled across the moor. She hoped her mother was home.

                                IV

The walk on the moors with her daughter had given Briony pause for thought. If Miss Roberts was taking a special interest in Alexandra she might be concerned enough to help. Briony decided to walk to Peterculter and talk to her.

"I hope you don't mind my calling on you," she said when Miss Roberts answered the door of her cottage. "I'm Alexandra Meldrum's mother, and I need your advice."

Agatha Roberts was a tiny lady with grey hair tied back in a bun. She seemed insignificant till she started speaking; she had the deepest contralto voice Briony had ever heard.

"I'm so glad to see you, Mrs. Meldrum," she boomed. "Alexandra is a brilliant pupil, quite outstanding. Come in and have afternoon tea with me." She led Briony into a small, comfortably furnished parlor and busied herself serving tea and buttered scones.

Briony took a deep breath and began explaining some of the circumstances which had made her decide to leave home. Miss Roberts was distressed but sympathetic.

"Alexandra told me your sister was a headmistress in Glasgow," Briony ventured. "I wondered if there was any chance of Alexandra getting into her school?"

"My sister, Abigail, is always interested in gifted pupils. As I am. I shall phone her tonight and ask her about it."

Briony leant forward eagerly. "That would be wonderful! And there is something else," she added.

"Tell me about it," Miss Roberts said in such a commanding voice that Briony felt like standing to attention.

"I need a job," Briony confessed. "When you're speaking to your sister, could you ask her if she knows of anything that might be suitable for me? I have a nest egg to give us all a start, but I'll have to find a way of earning more money."

"Don't worry, Abigail and I will think of something. Come to think of it, Abigail mentioned that she was looking for a housekeeper. Would you be interested in a job like that?"

"Alexandra would be able to live with me?"

"Of course."

"Then the jobs sounds ideal. But please, I'd rather you didn't mention it to anyone. My husband is depending on me to help him bring in the harvest. Once that's over I can leave for Glasgow right away. But if he discovered my plans he might try to stop me. He's . . . a very violent man. I'm concerned about Alexandra; I want her to grow up where she'll be happy and safe."

"You are a very good mother to that child," Miss Agatha said briskly. "And I shall make a point of telling your daughter that. Alexandra should do well in Glasgow, mark my words."

PART IV

1951-58

SEVENTEEN

I

1 January 1951

Alexandra stretched out her hand to touch Robert. He grunted, but it was obvious that he was still in a deep sleep. Hardly surprising since they hadn't gone to bed till dawn. Alexandra felt she should have been exhausted as well. She had taken Robert's advice and opened the Pandora's box of her childhood. Instead of trying to banish disturbing images, she had forced herself to re-examine them.

Little things had come back to her. Miss Agatha had taken her aside one day and made a point of telling her what a good mother she had and how concerned Briony was about her welfare. That incident had been buried in Alexandra's subconscious along with all the things that had bothered her—like the men in her mother's life. Alexandra had been ashamed by Briony's candor about them.

Ashamed. Alexandra folded her hands together on the bedspread realizing at long last that this had been the real problem. For years she had been secretly repelled by the thought that her mother had loved a spineless charmer like Toby Armstrong, and had then married a brute like Angus Meldrum simply to save her respectability. And when her marriage hadn't worked out Briony had gone on to sell her body to build up her savings. In her innermost thoughts Alexandra had sometimes despised her mother for being so weak and foolish. But not this morning . . . After several hours of mental confrontation she was seeing things in a different light. Alexandra had always imagined that truth crept up on you slowly, but sometimes it was like a flash of lightning.

Some time during the early morning hours she had suddenly

wondered about the nature of love. It was easy enough to love someone you respected, but to continue loving a man who was flawed . . . Was that weakness or strength? What was it Shakespeare had said?

> . . . love is not love
> Which alters when it alteration finds,
> Or bends with the remover to remove.

And then there was the problem of Briony's marriage and her lack of money. Other women might have resigned themselves to their fate, but Briony had been made of sterner stuff. In order to make money for her children she had modeled for David Elphinstone even though she had heard he seduced his girls. Briony had even proposed marriage to him, an unbelievably courageous act for a woman in 1939! When he had turned down her proposal, Briony had just gritted her teeth and continued to offer her body as a means of increasing her savings and escaping from a man who delighted in physical abuse. Wasn't that wisdom rather than folly? And her motives had been altruistic. She had never craved anything for herself; she had wanted a better life for Alexandra and Frank. Even her resolution to regain Drumcraig Castle for the Meldrums had been prompted by the vow she had made her father . . .

In Glasgow Briony had been happy working as Abigail Roberts's housekeeper, but she had still yearned for a better future for Alexandra. Once again, instead of daydreaming or complaining she had seized the initiative. Briony told Miss Abigail that she had intended to become a schoolteacher before her father died and she felt it wasn't too late to start a new career. Patiently Briony explained that she could easily combine her job as a housekeeper with training as a teacher and she promised to work from dawn till dusk to achieve her aims. While Miss Abigail prevaricated, Briony phoned up Jordanhill College, was interviewed, and secured a place as a mature student.

As for her mother's ambivalent attitude to Alexandra: affection alternating with hostility . . . A few months before Briony was killed, she took Alexandra out for a long walk and made a

startling confession, one she said she would never have made
had Alexandra not been so advanced for her age. "You're only
11 years old," she said, "but your teachers say you look at life
in a grown-up way. So I'm going to treat you as a grown-up
and tell you something that has bothered me for years." Briony
went on to explain that she had been appalled when she realized Alexandra was the result of a wedding-night rape. It was
only when she thought she had lost Alexandra in the blitz that
Briony understood that she did not care *whose* child Alexandra
was—she loved her regardless.

Most mothers would have been wary of confessing such a
thing in case their offspring turned against them, but Briony
had not been afraid to tell the truth. Tears trickled down
Alexandra's cheeks. Why had she ever thought her mother
weak? Strength comes in different guises.

A hand cupped her face. Robert was awake and concerned.
"What's wrong?" he asked.

"Took your advice. Opened Pandora's box. And I discovered something. When you bury secrets that you imagine are
shameful they can fester inside you and seem worse than they
really are. Thinking it all through can put everything into perspective. That's what I've been doing this morning: putting
my past into perspective."

Alexandra turned on her side so that she could look Robert
full in the face. "Remind me some time to tell you about my
mother. She was fine and brave and strong. When she wanted
something she went for it . . . and I'm going to do the same!"

Robert's eyes softened. "That's my girl, face up to everything. Even your mother's death . . ."

"No!" Alexandra countered quickly. "That's the one exception. I never want to talk about the way my mother was killed,
it was too horrible . . ."

Robert held her tightly. For a while he too seemed to reflect,
then he shook off his serious expression and turned to her with
his familiar teasing smile. "You've done your mental stocktak-
ing. Don't you think that deserves a reward?"

He gave her no chance to answer because one hand was caressing her nipples and the other was teasing her pubic hair,
probing for the erogenous spot which drove her wild and made

her twine her long legs round his back and beg for more and
more and more . . .

Afterwards they lay contentedly side by side. "Hey," Robert
said suddenly. "Know what day this is? January the first. I've
a feeling this is going to be the best year of our lives."

He was wrong. It was the worst.

EIGHTEEN

The New Year started well for Alexandra. The Edinburgh tenement which Meldrums had renovated attracted favorable comment when it was completed. To Alexandra's delight, Boyd Brown was able to sell it for four times its purchase price. Alexandra immediately began looking at other properties in the Bannons Estate Agency files. She noticed a row of empty houses in Edinburgh which had been on the agency's books for months. They were in such poor condition that it looked as if they might have to be pulled down.

She phoned Malcolm to tell him about them. "Brian Bannon says I'll be able to pick them up very cheap."

"I'm sure you will," Malcolm said cautiously. "Very few people would want to buy a whole row of dilapidated houses."

"This could be the time to follow up my idea of buying aircraft hangars, disused railway carriages, and unwanted army accommodation units," Alexandra said slowly.

"I thought you didn't have enough capital for that."

"I have now, and I aim to get more financial backing."

She was surprised that Malcolm did not sound more excited, though he did promise to get his tradesmen to strip out wood, wire, plumbing, and electrical fittings from anything he could buy.

"What's the limit on my spending?" he asked.

"I'll talk it over with Boyd and Fyfe and come back to you."

Fyfe Walker was the accountant who had been recommended to her by Mrs. O'Malley. He was enthusiastic about the new project and suggested various ways of raising the necessary money to keep Alexandra's cash flow healthy. With his approval she approached a merchant bank in Edinburgh in the hope that they might be prepared to back her. When they agreed Alexandra wasn't sure whether to be relieved or terrified. "I feel I'm walking a financial tightrope," she said to Boyd when she went into his office to sign the necessary papers.

"Construction firms are masters of the high-wire act," he agreed, "but at least you've got a terrific team of building workers on your payroll. By the way, I've just had Malcolm on the phone. He wants you to come through to Edinburgh as soon as possible."

II

Malcolm's headquarters were a small office which Alexandra had rented the day after she bought her first tenement. She had hired a secretary who also acted as telephonist. When Malcolm wasn't running the office or taking orders, he was out and about cutting a swathe through officialdom and supervising the tradesmen.

"I'm not happy about the foreman," Malcolm said to Alexandra when they were having lunch in Jenner's in Princes Street. "I've got a new candidate lined up and I've also tracked down an old chum who is a superb cabinetmaker. I'd like to get your approval before I hire them."

Once again Alexandra was puzzled by his caution. "You don't need my approval, Malcolm. You're the one in charge of the tradesmen." She looked at him a little anxiously. "You are enjoying the job, aren't you?"

"I love the freedom to come and go as I please, but I'm a bit worried about these terraced houses . . ."

"I'm sure you can cope."

"I don't want too much responsibility," Malcolm said firmly. "The minute that happens I feel like a prisoner of war again. I must be frank, Alexandra: you can't go on playing the property game at a distance. If you intend to keep on expanding you'll need a new and bigger office, more staff, more equipment. You should be here in Edinburgh taking charge of everything. It's your business, not mine."

Alexandra was silent. She would have to give Malcolm's suggestion serious thought. Although she was the one who had brought the team together and secured loans from the banks, it was Malcolm who was organizing the day-to-day running of Meldrum Enterprises; she couldn't afford to lose him.

Malcolm was watching her. "I know you want to finish your degree. That takes us up to the end of June."

After that, Alexandra thought, she would be leaving university. And so would Robert. Robert was returning to Aberdeen to take his rightful place in Armstrongs. Was he expecting her to go with him? Six months, she thought. Six months to enjoy herself with Robert and forge such a strong bond between them that the future would resolve itself happily. Plenty of time . . .

III

The highlight of the first week of January was the torchlight procession to mark the fifth centenary of Glasgow University. Alexandra had been looking forward to it for months. In 1451 when the Old College was founded by Bishop Turnbull, Glasgow was just a small cathedral town in a good position near the only bridge over the lower Clyde. When Glasgow developed into an important mercantile center and then a great industrial city, the Old College in the High Street was seen to be too small, and the university transferred to Gilmorehill on the west side of the city.

The students' celebration started at dawn when a small company gathered at the birthplace of Bishop Turnbull. A torch was lit and carried by relays of runners to Glasgow Cathedral where the university's life had begun. Alexandra and Robert met at the cathedral and joined the students who had gathered there. It was a solemn occasion at first, but when they all sallied forth into the city with their leaders carrying torches everyone became caught up in a sweeping surge of excitement. Crowds turned out to watch, small boys ran alongside the procession and the students exulted in the knowledge that they were all taking part in a piece of history. From the sky Kelvin Way must have looked like a sea of heads illuminated by torches held aloft in strong arms.

Adam and Belinda had not taken part in the procession, but later that evening they went with Robert and Alexandra for a meal. "This is great. We four get on real well together," Belinda said. Alexandra had gradually become aware that Belinda was using the foursome as a means of getting close to Robert. She kept seeking his advice, and whenever Adam's back was turned she flirted shamelessly with his brother. So far Robert seemed immune to her charms. Alexandra hoped he would stay that way.

As January slipped into February Alexandra made no attempt to let Robert know that she had formed a property company. I'll tell him at Easter, she decided, but as Easter drew near it brought exams and they all became concerned about their studies. Robert immersed himself in conveyancing and family law; Alexandra spent days analyzing Plato, Butler, and Mill for her moral philosophy exams. She hated zoology, her compulsory science subject. The theory was fine, but she felt sick every time she was asked to dissect a frog or a dogfish.

Despite the study program she managed to see Robert two or three times a week. Whenever she heard the telephone ring in her room she would drop everything and pick it up, hoping that it would be Robert's deep voice saying, "Hello, Alex!" Since he never used the abbreviation of her name in public, the nickname had acquired an intimate resonance.

Once the term exams were over Adam went off to the south of France with Belinda for the Easter holiday, and Aunt Ethel decided to visit a cousin in Wales. Robert was jubilant. He invited Alexandra to come and stay with him. "And by the way, after a couple of weeks in Jordanhill I'm taking you abroad for two days," he announced. Alexandra loved being ordered around and cherished. She informed her business associates that she was going on holiday and moved in with Robert the morning Aunt Ethel left.

IV

"I think I'll make a steak pie for lunch," Alexandra announced as she surveyed the contents of Aunt Ethel's kitchen larder. "Robert, be a love and go to the shops and buy the meat."

When he returned, the parcel in his hand, Alexandra was rolling out pastry in the kitchen. She was wearing one of Aunt Ethel's aprons, her cheeks were flushed from the heat of the oven, and there was a blob of flour on her nose.

"This is what it must be like being married," Robert said with a satisfied smile, as he wiped the flour from her nose with his hanky. "I can see you'll enjoy being a stay-at-home wife."

"Not a hope!" Alexandra retorted cheerfully as she washed and cut up the meat. "I'm going to be a career woman."

Robert smiled indulgently, obviously not believing her. Now, Alexandra thought, I've got to tell him now. She put the steak pie in the oven and wiped her hands. "Did you see that picture in the papers yesterday?" she asked, trying to sound as casual as possible. "The woman who's a property tycoon in America? How would you like to live with someone like that?"

"I wouldn't. I can't have a wife who's my rival. A subsidiary company of Armstrongs is in construction and property, and that's the one I'm interested in developing."

Alexandra felt as if she had been kicked in the stomach. She'd understood that trawling and shipbuilding were the bases of the Armstrong business; she hadn't realized they had a property company as well. Robert took the dishcloth out of her hands and kissed her and her doubts evaporated in the conviction that he loved her enough to want her happiness.

In the days that followed she cooked other meals for Robert and in between baking and studying and making love they walked, talked, listened to music, or played tennis at Woodend Tennis Club. In the evenings when it was dark they often slipped through the railings of Jordanhill College and walked in the grounds. They played tag amongst the trees, tried to track down the wild life and counted the stars, but whatever game they played in the woods it always ended the same way. Robert would press her back against a tree and begin undressing her.

When her breasts swung free he would look at them in the moonlight, tracing the blue veins with his fingers, kissing the deep pink of the areolas, marveling at the marble whiteness of her skin. Then he would cover her up quickly so that she wouldn't catch cold and they would wander hand in hand over the mossy carpet of leaves. But very soon he would reach for her again and uncover her thighs and expose the soft hair between. When they could bear the suspense no longer he plunged into her, driving so hard that she felt his maleness was reaching to her innermost core.

Once when they drew apart, breathless from their efforts, Alexandra shook her head. "We're crazy. There's a perfectly good bed in the house where we can do this in comfort." But even as she said it she knew comfort did not matter. Making love in the house wasn't enough. Like animals they wanted to imprint their scent wherever they went.

V

For Robert too it was an idyllic time. When Alexandra had moved into the Jordanhill house he worried about his Drumcraig nightmare, but when he did waken up one night shouting that he "didn't mean to push her," Alexandra just told him crossly that he shouldn't have eaten so much cheese for supper and if he ever pushed her she would push him back. After that she went straight back to sleep.

Towards the end of their second week in Jordanhill he commanded Alexandra to lay out everything she needed for a day and two nights abroad.

"Just as well you warned me in plenty of time to get a passport," Alexandra said. "Stop being so mysterious. Where are we going?"

"Paris."

VI

Paris was wreathed in a morning mist which made Notre Dame and the Eiffel Tower seem like ethereal images drifting in and out of focus. The taxi drew up outside a *pension* in Montmartre. As Robert paid the driver Alexandra stood on the pavement taking in the scents and sounds of the city: car horns, Gauloises cigarettes, sibilant French accents, brewing coffee, freshly baked bread. The *pension* was one of those tiny Parisian treasures which few tourists ever have the good fortune to find. A black-garbed lady welcomed them warmly and led them upstairs to a bedroom which overlooked the square where artists came to paint. They had so little to unpack they were soon downstairs again, emerging out into the square to savor coffee and croissants.

"Let's take a trip on a *bateau mouche*," Robert suggested, "then we can visit Notre Dame, go to the top of the Eiffel Tower, visit the Louvre . . ."

At the Louvre Robert stood in front of the "Mona Lisa" and wondered aloud at its fame. "You can't tell whether she's happy or sad."

"She's mysterious," Alexandra murmured. "Whichever way you look at her she seems to be gazing right back at you. Come on, I want to see the Flemish and Dutch masters."

"An expert, are you?" Robert teased.

"Wish I was. I'm just glad that someone made me appreciate beautiful paintings when I was young."

"David Elphinstone of Drumcraig? He certainly owned some fabulous paintings. Just as well he stored them before the castle was turned into a hostel for evacuees. They would have wrecked the lot. Billy and Lennie Karmigan were real hell-raisers when they lived with us. My mother was glad to see the back of them."

"I became quite friendly with the Karmigans," Alexandra said with a smile.

"Did you? How on earth did that happen?" Robert asked curiously

"I met them when David Elphinstone invited me to the Lodge for the summer holidays. By then the Karmigans had been turfed out of your home and sent to Drumcraig with other evacuees. I came across them in the grounds one day. They were fizzing mad because your brother had seen them stashing their ill-gotten gains—underneath the floorboards of a hut on Aberdeen esplanade, incidentally. Adam swiped the lot. Fifty pounds. I helped them get it back from him."

"How did you manage that?" Robert asked incredulously. "I've never managed to get anything back from Adam in my life."

"I noticed some writing paper in Mr. Elphinstone's study which his solicitor had sent. Some of the sheets had the firm's heading at the top. I wrote a legal-sounding letter to Adam purporting to be from the solicitor. I said the firm had obtained evidence that Adam had stolen £50 from the Karmigans, and that unless he delivered it in a sealed envelope to Drumcraig Castle the firm would prosecute. *And* they would report the matter to the headmaster of his school."

"Don't tell me Adam fell for that?"

"All the way. He arrived at Drumcraig the following Saturday and left a brown-paper parcel for the Karmigans. It was a book with £50 in its pages. When Billy and Lennie realized my ploy had been successful they gave me the kind of awed look they usually reserved for Celtic football players!"

Robert laughed out loud and was given a stern glance by a crowd of art critics who were assessing some of the Louvre art treasures.

"The Karmigans said I was their friend for life," Alexandra went on, "but I don't suppose I'll ever see them again."

"I'll make a confession to you," Robert said as they strolled down a long corridor. "When we started going out together, I was worried in case the memory of Drumcraig Castle would shadow your life. And maybe mine," he added uneasily. "But in all the time I've known you you've never mentioned the castle. And you hardly bothered replying when Adam tried to provoke you about it at New Year. I'm so glad you've managed to come to terms with what happened on the night of the evacuees' party . . ."

Alexandra made no reply, but Robert did not notice the disturbed quality of her silence.

"I've had this recurring nightmare about Drumcraig," Robert began, "but perhaps you don't want to hear about it . . ."

"No, I certainly do not," Alexandra said promptly and diverted his attention by pointing out a Titian that she liked.

When they felt they'd had their fill of culture they made their way back towards Montmartre where they had a *plat du jour* in a café before retiring to their room in the tiny *pension*. They slipped off their clothes and stood by the window letting the moonlight play on their naked bodies as they watched the crowds below.

Robert gently flicked Alexandra's thighs with his fingers and at once she felt the familiar fire. She pressed herself against him, coiling her legs around his waist, guiding him into her. Pushing. Panting. Straining for fulfillment. when they were both sated she broke away and pulled him to the armchair by the bed. "Sit down," she said softly.

Alexandra stood over him for a moment or two, then slid down on top of him and they began making love all over again.

"You're in a strange mood tonight," Robert said huskily when he eventually led her towards their bed. "I've never seen you so desperate for love."

"I can't get enough of you, Robert," she panted, sweat streaming down her face, eyes wild, mouth hungry as she kissed every part of his body.

"You're insatiable," Robert teased before he finally fell asleep.

Alexandra lay awake, her heart pounding, her hands trembling. Lovemaking hadn't driven out her demons. She wished fervently that Robert had not mentioned Drumcraig, the Karmigans, and the night of the evacuees' party. She had kept its memory at bay for so long, but now it was reaching out for her with octopus arms, encircling her, terrifying her, holding her so tight she had no means of escape . . .

NINETEEN

I

Drumcraig Castle, 1943
The field of wild daffodils shimmered and swayed in the sunlight as the woman and child moved amongst them. "I love Drumcraig in the springtime," Briony said as she bent down to cut more flowers, "and this spring seems specially wonderful now that the news is good."

The tide had finally turned. The Russians were beginning to drive the Germans out of the Soviet Union, the Eighth Army were still forcing Rommel to retreat and the industrial arsenal of the Ruhr was being systematically destroyed by the RAF. Best of all, the threat of invasion seemed to be over: Churchill had recently announced in the Commons that the church bells could be rung again. Admittedly the blackout was still being rigorously enforced, but the previous week the anti-aircraft guns in Aberdeen had been sent south. If the Germans were going to bomb anywhere in Britain it wouldn't be Aberdeen.

"It's a pity Mr. Elphinstone won't come to the evacuees' party," Alexandra remarked.

"He thinks the evacuees are disgusting. He can't understand why you go out of your way to be nice to those awful Karmigan brothers when you come here on holiday. And talking of the little devils, here they come! Running for their lives from the look of it."

"Hey Alexandra," Billy gasped as he came up to her, "if that prissy old English teacher comes looking for us, tell her you never saw us."

"What have you done now?"

Billy scratched his head. "See, there was this stink bomb I made. I wanted to see what old prune-face would do if I let it off in her classroom."

"Billy, you're a wee rogue, so you are!" Alexandra declared.

"Och, you're always saying that. Mind now, don't split on us," Billy chortled as he fled for the woods.

Alexandra could see that her mother was about to give her another lecture on befriending the Karmigans, so she quickly changed the subject. "Have we picked enough daffodils?"

"More than enough. We'd better take them to the castle and start arranging them in vases."

"The evacuees' party should be fun," Alexandra said, "but I bet they'll be more interested in the food than the flowers."

They began walking back towards the castle. Drumcraig still rose tall and slender towards the sky, its turrets and windows embellishing the beauty of its soft pink granite. But if the exterior had not changed it was a different story inside. When the castle had been requisitioned, David Elphinstone had put his furniture, furnishings, paintings, and *objets d'art* into store. Toilets and dining areas had been installed on the ground floor, the Great Hall on the first floor had been transformed into a dormitory with beds for the evacuees, and the rooms on the other floors had been converted into classrooms, offices, and sleeping accommodation.

"When I see Drumcraig in its present state I'm glad we're staying at the Lodge," Briony remarked as they pushed open the castle door. They had been coming to the Lodge for a fortnight in spring and summer ever since the Clydebank blitz.

The Lodge was a small mansion a mile from the castle and, although it held no enchantment for Briony, it was a comfortable house and she couldn't help thinking that Ellen would have found it much easier to run than the castle. Ellen had died of pneumonia in the autumn of 1939. Since then David Elphinstone had employed a number of housekeepers. His current one always went off on holiday before Briony and Alexandra arrived, as did his nephew. Alexandra had not seen Tom Elphinstone since she had left Aberdeen, nor did she want to. From all accounts the disagreeable boy had grown into a disagreeable young man who toadied to his uncle in public and laughed at him behind his back.

"Here, let me hold your bucket," Alexandra said to her mother and swung it over her arm as they went into the castle kitchen where two maids were busy cleaning dishes for the party. They smiled a welcome and helped them look for containers for the daffodils. When all the vases were filled Briony decided to go to the classroom upstairs and give the teachers a hand. She had nearly finished her teacher-training course at Jordanhill and welcomed the experience of working with the evacuees.

At Soesterberg near Utrecht in Holland, twenty-five aircraft of the Kampf-Geschwader Group 2 were awaiting instructions for their target for that evening. The German pilots joked and grumbled and laid bets with each other that it would be London again. They were surprised when they received orders to proceed to Stavanger.

When the evacuees trooped into the Great Hall they gasped with astonishment at the decorations, balloons, and crackers. On the other side of the huge room a large trestle table was piled with food, but before the children could get it a teacher clapped her hands. "First we're having some party games. I want you all organized in teams."

For the next hour Briony and Alexandra ran round the room trying to help the rest of the staff. Several times Alexandra bumped into Robert Armstrong and he gave her a friendly smile. Adam, taking his cue from his mother, went out of his way to be as rude as possible.

At Stavanger the orders from Luftwaffe headquarters came through. The Dornier 217s which had flown in from Utrecht were armed, refuelled and loaded with two tons of bombs before they soared off into the night. Their crews had been told their destination. It was Aberdeen in the north east of Scotland.

"Can we have the food now?" one of the evacuees shouted. The teachers nodded and the children dived for the big refectory table. They gazed in awe at the plates of sliced chicken, the casseroles of home-made stew, the platters of vegetables, the bowls of fruit, the cakes sweetened with carrots in place of sugar, and the bottles of lemonade and milk.

"Most of these children never see food like this in peacetime, never mind wartime," one of the teachers muttered as they all helped preside over the table and make sure that each evacuee had a fair share of what was on offer. The food and drink seemed to disappear at an alarming rate. When the feast was finished the children were sent to the top of the castle to play Hide and Seek. The teachers helped by Robert and Adam removed the refectory table and manhandled the beds back in position. Party debris was taken back down to the kitchen, dishes were washed and dried, cutlery was collected.

A siren had been specially fitted to the castle tower when the evacuees had moved in and there had been plenty of air-raid rehearsals, but when the siren started wailing no one could believe it was for real.

"The mechanism must be faulty," one of the teachers said. "I mean, this couldn't be a proper air raid, the war's nearly over . . ."

"We can't take a chance on it," someone else said agitatedly. At that moment the lights went out.

"The children have gone up to the top of the castle to play Hide and Seek. They'll be terrified in the dark," Briony said in alarm. "I'll go and help them. Alexandra, you wait at the front door and lead everyone out to the shelter."

The next half-hour was chaotic as the staff searched the castle, rounded up any children they could see, and shouted at the ones who seemed to think this was just a joke. They tried to stem the rush as the evacuees finally realized the danger and came tumbling down the stairs, pushing, shoving, and shouting. Their screams added to the cacophony of sound from the siren as they rushed through the open door and followed Alexandra along to the ice house which had been converted into an air-raid shelter.

Alexandra was alarmed when she could not find her mother. Robert and Adam were amongst the last to come into the shelter, closely followed by Billy and Lennie Karmigan. Briony Meldrum wasn't with them.

"I'm going to look for my mother," Alexandra said.

The teachers refused to let her leave the shelter. "Don't worry, dear," they said soothingly. "The air raid probably won't last long." Everyone nodded. But they were wrong. Since the war had started, Aberdeen, like many other northeast towns, had suffered from hit-and-run raiders, but this time the bombers had come for a longer visit. The Luftwaffe roared over the city looking for the biggest buildings. The Gordon Barracks and the Royal Mental Hospital suffered direct hits, Middlefield School and Causewayend Church were set alight, and bungalows and tenements were torn apart.

"I think that's a plane right above us," someone shouted. Suddenly there was a tremendous explosion which rocked the walls and floor of their shelter, dislodged some of the bricks, and sent plaster and dust spilling over them.

When the All Clear sounded there was an orderly move to the door, then a collective gasp as they looked at Drumcraig Castle. The whole building was ablaze and the fire seemed to be growing fiercer by the minute. Without stopping to think Alexandra ran towards the inferno. A teacher raced after her and practically threw her to the ground. "What d'you think you're doing?"

"My mother's in there—I'm going in to get her."

"You'd never get through the flames." The teacher kept a tight grip on Alexandra's arm as the other members of staff shrieked instructions to the rest of the children.

"Back, stay back. Children! Follow Miss Brown to the field beyond the castle and wait there till help arrives."

"I'm staying here," Alexandra said fiercely and after one look at her face the teacher nodded.

Someone ran down the road to the Lodge to phone the fire brigade in Aberdeen and the other members of staff rushed to the sheds where the firefighting equipment was stored. As hoses were trained on the flames, the teachers formed a human chain and threw buckets of water on the lower windows in a vain attempt to curb the conflagration. The heat turned the water to steam and as the fabric of the castle began to disintegrate, the fire fighters had to draw back.

"Mother!" Alexandra screamed in a panic. Smoke obscured her vision as she strained her eyes to see if anyone was moving behind the windows. Glass shattered on the first floor and for one brief moment Alexandra thought she glimpsed a familiar face.

"Mother!" Alexandra screamed again.

There was a roar as the windows of the Great Hall exploded outwards. The watchers put their arms over their heads, trying to protect themselves from the falling glass. The wind whooshed in through the empty space and fanned the flames inside: a million red and gold and scarlet demons dancing through the old castle, destroying everything in sight. The castle groaned and glowed and trembled. Like a soul in torment.

It took a day to put out the smoldering fires and search through the wreckage. The teachers tried to dissuade Alexandra from seeing her mother's body, but she insisted.

"Until I see the . . . I won't believe she's dead."

But nothing had prepared her for the sight of the corpse. The features on her mother's face had melted into a giant blob and her body had been reduced to a rubbery charred mass of bones and muscles.

"No!" Alexandra screamed in horror, unable to believe that this was her beloved mother. "No! No! No!"

When they finally quietened her, the doctor injected something into her arm which made her sleep.

II

Paris, 1951
"No!" Alexandra screamed. "No! No! No!"

"Alexandra, it's all right, it's all right!"

She had been lying rigidly in bed, eyes open, mouth dry, as she relived the events of that terrible night in 1943. It was the vivid image of her mother's corpse that had made her scream in protest. She turned her head and saw Robert's anxious face beside her in the bed. She clung to him, soaking his body with tears.

Robert held her tightly and stroked her hair. "My love, don't cry," he whispered. "I'm here to look after you. I'll protect you from your demons."

If she married Robert he would always be there to comfort her, Alexandra thought. Lovers came and went; husbands tended to stay. And she loved Robert so much . . . She couldn't bear the thought of losing him. If he were really serious about wanting her as a wife she would agree to it. She would find some way of convincing him that she could combine marriage with a career.

* * *

They spent the next day sightseeing, making love, and laughing. Alexandra felt she had never laughed as much in her entire life. Robert was good for her. In the afternoon he went off on his own for a while. He came back carrying a parcel, but refused to tell Alexandra what was in it. At midnight when they were in their room Robert finally handed it to Alexandra. "I bought you a present to make this evening special."

Alexandra opened the wrapping and gasped as she drew out the most beautiful black nightdress she had ever seen: a gauzy shimmering affair of black satin, lace and ribbons.

"It's exquisite," she whispered. When she put it on, the cobwebbed lace and satin clung to her creamy skin. The moonlight played on her chestnut hair making it gleam like champagne.

"Will you marry me, Alexandra?" Robert asked gravely.

"Yes, yes, I will," she said almost in tears, and threw her arms around his neck.

After a while he disentangled her arms. "I've got another present for you." He took a signet ring out of a small box and slipped it on to the third finger of her left hand. "I daren't tell my father about us until the exams are over, but once I have my law degree he'll be so pleased he won't be in any mood to raise objections, or protest that we're too young."

"A secret engagement," Alexandra sighed, enchanted with the romance of it all. "I love you, Robert. I'll remember this day for the rest of my life."

And she did. Because it was soon afterwards that it all started to go wrong . . .

TWENTY

I

Belinda shivered as she stood on the pavement waiting for the traffic to clear before she crossed University Avenue. After two weeks of sun in the south of France she was feeling the cold. The engagement ring Adam had given her at the start of the holiday hadn't resolved her doubts by the end of it. One evening Adam had got really drunk she'd asked him what he was going to do when they got married.

"Live off your money, my darling," he had hiccuped. "I'm counting on your father to find me a nice sin . . . sina . . . sinecure!" he had finished triumphantly.

It wasn't good enough, Belinda decided, as she crossed the road and ran up the steps to the Reading Room. She shouldn't have accepted that darned ring and rushed into an engagement with Adam. She wanted to marry someone who would love her even if she were penniless. Who was she kidding! She wanted to marry Robert Armstrong. She'd gotten engaged to Adam out of pique because Robert was so wrapped up with Alexandra. She had to face that fact and *do* something about it. Soon. Fast.

Once she was inside the library Belinda looked round wondering where to sit. She saw Alexandra studying at a table facing the entrance. There was no one at the desk beside her. Belinda walked towards her. "Hi, Alexandra," she said cheerfully when she reached the desk where she was sitting. "Adam says there's a dinner-dance at the Marlborough on Saturday. Why don't you and Robert . . ."

"Sorry, we're busy. I don't think Adam will mind too much."

Belinda studied Alexandra for a moment and then sat down

beside her. "I can see you're in the mood for candour today. So tell me why you dislike Adam?"

Alexandra raised her eyes heavenwards. "Adam has gone out of his way to be nasty to me ever since we first met. So let's just say that if I had to choose between Attila the Hun or Adam, I'd choose good old Attila!"

"You sure aren't pulling your punches! So tell me one more thing. Have you ever heard Adam or any of his friends suggest that he might be marrying me for my money? I want the truth!"

"Since I'm studying philosophy right now, my answer is a question: what *is* truth? Maybe it's relative in this case, maybe not. I have my own very personal view of Adam. You shouldn't let it stop you marrying him."

"You still haven't answered my question. Have you ever heard Adam say anything which made you think . . ."

"I heard the question the first time and I'm not going to answer it. I'm not in the business of spreading gossip. Now d'you mind? I have a lot of work to do and I told Robert I'd come to Jordanhill around three."

Belinda's rage at Alexandra's dismissive tone was superseded by her own feeling of wounded pride. It was obvious from Alexandra's reaction that she *had* heard allegations about Adam intending to marry for money. And Alexandra had believed them; it was written all over her face and threaded through her evasive answers. Maybe everyone thought Adam was marrying for money. And Adam himself? He'd practically admitted it on holiday when he was drunk.

Belinda seethed. Darn it, she was a great catch even without her money. To hell with her engagement! Come to think of it, maybe she could use a broken engagement as a way of enlisting Robert's sympathy. And why wait? She would go to Aunt Ethel's house this afternoon *before* Alexandra was expected. And she might try to stage some kind of scene; something that would make Alexandra think Robert was being unfaithful. If she could just cause a rift between the lovebirds . . .

Adam was suntanned and smiling when he came racing up the Reading Room steps. The holiday in the south of France had been a foretaste of his future. Belinda's father had made it clear that he would smooth out any of his financial problems.

Adam felt incredibly lucky. Not only was he marrying money, but he loved the girl who had it. Couldn't live without her. He allowed himself a moment of pity for Robert who would have to spend the rest of his life slaving away in Aberdeen in Armstrongs.

He glanced round the Reading Room and walked over to the desk where he saw Belinda bent over her books. A girl was sitting beside her, but since she had her back turned to him he couldn't see who it was for a moment. When he realized it was Alexandra Meldrum he felt a twinge of unease. The Meldrums were bad luck for the Armstrongs; always had been, according to his parents and grandparents. He gave a curt nod to Alexandra and bent forward to kiss Belinda. To his surprise Belinda averted her face.

"What's up?" he asked. "You're looking at me as if you'd never seen me before."

"Let's take a walk."

Alexandra worked on for another hour, glad that Belinda and Adam had left. She was finding it difficult to write a balanced essay on the merits and demerits of Plato's *Republic*. Was life really just the dark tunnel before the light of another existence?

She felt a movement at her side and turned round to find Adam in the seat beside her. His face was white, his eyes blazing. "I thought you'd like to know that Belinda has broken off our engagement. She seems to have got it into her head that I'm marrying her for her money."

"And aren't you?" Alexandra couldn't resist asking.

"As it happens I'm not," Adam replied, teeth clenched. "I've spent the last hour trying to convince her, but she won't believe me. You've made a thorough job of assassinating my character."

Alexandra sighed. "If it's truth time I don't mind admitting I can't stand you, Adam. But when Belinda asked me outright if I thought you were marrying her for her money I refused to answer."

"It can't be a coincidence that Belinda breaks off her engagement to me just after she's had a heart-to-heart with you?"

"Believe what you like, Adam. I'm going to Jordanhill to see Robert."

Adam continued to stare at her and Alexandra was aware that he was racking his brain, trying to find some way of wounding her. "Did you know Robert has nightmares?" he said suddenly.

"Everyone has nightmares from time to time."

"But not about Drumcraig Castle. And the night of the fire."

The book that Alexandra was holding slipped from her fingers.

"Robert confided in me," Adam continued. "He told me he dreams he caused your mother's death."

"You're lying!" Alexandra said angrily as she stood up and gathered her books together.

"Then why would Robert shout out in his nightmare: 'I didn't mean to push her!'?"

Alexandra felt a giant claw grasping at her innards. When she had been staying with Robert in Jordanhill he'd had a nightmare. And had used those very words. She pushed past Adam and ran to the Reading Room door, praying that it wasn't true.

Robert had decided to study in his room at Aunt Ethel's for his business law exam. When the front-door bell rang he ran downstairs and opened the door. "Belinda, you're crying! Have you and Adam had a row?"

"It's worse than that!"

"Come into the sitting room. Aunt Ethel's at the shops."

"She might come back early," Belinda sobbed. "Couldn't we go up to your bedroom? I must talk to you privately."

In the bedroom Robert guided Belinda to a chair. "What's wrong?"

"I've given Adam back his ring. When I got home from holiday I overheard some of his friends saying he was marrying me for my money."

"You don't want to believe that kind of gossip."

"Alexandra believes it. I've just had a long chat with her in the Reading Room." Briony began crying once more and leant against him.

He grimaced when he saw Belinda's mouth was smeared: she must have left a lipstick stain on the collar of his shirt. He'd better get that off before Alexandra arrived or there'd be trouble. "Come now," he said, with an anxious glance at the clock. "This is just a lovers' quarrel; you'll make it up . . ."

"No," Belinda protested. "It's all over. But when I said that to Adam he was so angry he made me frightened, so I came to you, Robert." She gasped when she heard the front door bang. "If that's Adam I don't want to see him."

"I'll deal with him."

"Promise you'll come back to the bedroom and talk to me?"

"I promise," Robert said soothingly as he left the room and ran downstairs. He wondered what on earth he'd say to Adam, but it was Alexandra who stood in the hall, door key in her hand.

Alexandra looked at the man she loved: tall, strong-featured, with wavy dark hair spilling over his forehead. The peaty-brown eyes which so often blazed with passion were studying her with concern.

"My love," he said, as he pulled her into his arms, "why are you looking so tragic?"

"I want to make love to you," she said, desperately needing the reassurance of his closeness. "Let's go up to your room."

Robert pulled her back as she turned towards the stairs and led her instead towards the couch in the drawing room. "Let's stay down here. What's happened to upset you?"

Alexandra sat down on the couch and repeated Adam's explanation of his brother's nightmare. "Robert, tell me it isn't true?"

"I don't know if it's true, Alex," he said, anguish etched on his face. "When you grazed your knee on the night of the party I told you then I'd bumped my head and was feeling a bit woozy. All I can recall after that is . . . helping your mother look for the Karmigan brothers at the top of the castle. Running downstairs. Throwing out my arm to stop a boy falling. But in my nightmare my arm pushed your mother as well. I wake up sweating, wondering why I didn't raise the alarm or look for her."

Alexandra's throat was so dry she could barely speak. "Surely someone would have heard her scream?"

"*Everyone* was screaming and shouting, and the siren was wailing . . . A single cry wouldn't have made itself heard."

"But someone must have seen my mother fall?" Alexandra's voice was hoarse with pleading.

"The castle was pitch-dark. In the crush no one would have noticed a body slipping over the edge of the stairwell."

The imagery he conjured up was too vivid for Alexandra to bear and she covered her face with her hands. When Robert tried to comfort her she drew away from him, because several facts stood out clearly. Although Robert claimed that he could not remember what had happened, he seemed to have a gut feeling that he had pushed her mother, but he hadn't raised the alarm, hadn't tried to find her. No wonder he was still having nightmares about it.

When he touched her again Alexandra jumped up from the couch, her nerves shattered. "Keep away from me," she shouted, tears streaming down her face. "Don't come near me!"

Belinda had been waiting upstairs, wondering when to make her move. At first there had been silence, then the sound of raised voices and someone crying. Good, she thought, they're having a quarrel. Let's see if I can help it along a little. She took off her shoes, socks and jeans, and removed her blouse, letting her rounded breasts bounce free. Hmm, she thought, as she glanced in the mirror. I look a tad too tidy to suggest a furtive bedroom romp with Robert. Quickly she tousled her hair, smudged her lipstick and for good measure put a few scratch marks on her neck.

She went out to the landing and began tiptoeing down the stairs. The voices in the sitting room were becoming louder and she heard Alexandra shouting. Terrific, Belinda thought, this is my moment! As she strolled into the sitting room she glimpsed Alexandra by the window, but she looked straight at Robert who was sitting on the couch looking stricken. "Robert, you said you'd be coming back upstairs to the bedroom . . ."

Belinda turned slowly, pretending that she had seen Alexandra for the first time. "Oh hell, that's torn it!" she cried, trying to sound embarrassed and guilty at the same time.

"Succinctly put," Alexandra said in a voice that could have cut concrete. She looked closely at Robert. "And it's only now I notice you've got lipstick on your collar, Robert. No wonder you didn't want to go up to the bedroom . . ."

Robert jumped up from the couch and, striding across to where Alexandra was standing, seized her roughly by the shoulders. "It's not what you think! I don't know why Belinda's looking as if she's just got out of bed. She came here to talk to me about her broken engagement. She wanted my advice!"

"In the bedroom? You don't expect me to *believe* that!" Alexandra yelled. "You're a double-dealing bastard, Robert Armstrong. Just like your brother. I hate you both, *hate you* . . ."

Robert put his hands over her mouth. "Shut up! You've jumped to all the wrong conclusions. Now listen . . ."

"I'm not going to listen to you ever again. We're finished. There may have been some doubt about it before Belinda walked into this room, but there's none now."

Belinda stood at one side of the room, hardly able to believe her luck. It's over between them, she thought gleefully, as she watched Alexandra tear a signet ring from her finger and throw it at Robert's feet. As Alexandra stormed towards the door she stopped in front of Belinda and slapped her face. "He was mine, you bitch, mine!"

When Robert began chasing after Alexandra, Belinda ran upstairs. She'd better be dressed by the time Robert came back. He would be furious with her, but she had her story good and ready. She would say she had fallen asleep on his bed and had stumbled downstairs without realizing that Alexandra was with him. And she would remind him that she had been speaking the truth: he *had* promised to come back to the bedroom. She'd apologize, she'd grovel. And later when he had got over the loss of Alexandra he'd come to her for consolation. She'd get Robert in the end. Daddy's girl always got what she wanted, Belinda thought smugly.

TWENTY-ONE

I

A week after Alexandra gave Robert back his ring she heard that David Elphinstone had died peacefully in his sleep and been buried in the grounds of the estate. The news gave impetus to her decision to make a pilgrimage and confront the last of her ghosts from the past.

When she arrived on Deeside she left her hired car at Peterculter and walked up to Stoneyground Croft. Her eyebrows arched in amazement when she caught her first glimpse of the house where she had been born. The dingy gray cottage had been transformed into a sparkling white villa. The old loft had been extended to form what looked like two new bedrooms, and a conservatory had been built on to the kitchen. All the windows were outlined in black; some had flower boxes, others boasted wrought-iron balconies. A paved courtyard complete with miniature trees and tubs of flowers made Stoneyground seem like a hacienda in Spain. Alexandra wasn't sure if she cared for some aspects of the conversion, but she knew her mother would have been thrilled with it. The thought prompted her first decision: some day she'd buy Stoneyground Croft. Why? Just because . . .

Alexandra looked out over the moors, remembering how she'd run across them barefoot to save her shoes . . .

When she got back to her car she switched on the engine and began making her way towards Balmoral where she lingered over an evening meal. She did not want to go to Drumcraig in the daylight. When it was dark she drove the long way round to Drumcraig Castle and parked the car by the moor. She had put on stout walking shoes so that she could scramble up the path to the hill overlooking the castle.

A flag was fluttering from the flagpole which meant that

Tom Elphinstone was in residence. Alexandra was glad she hadn't driven up to the front door. She could imagine the reception she would have received from the new laird. Up here she was safe from his prying eyes and waspish tongue. She fingered Briony's piece of Rubislaw granite, finding comfort in the smoothness of the stone.

Alexandra turned her gaze upwards. The sky was oceans-deep dark. The stars were brilliantly carved chips of ice. It was cold on the hilltop, but Alexandra savored the chill of the wind as it scythed through her bones. In this harsh north-east corner of Scotland you had to be strong to survive. The Picts and Vikings and other raiders had tried to destroy the spirit of the people, but they had failed. The people had been honed and shaped by their environment and they had grown stronger. Her mother had been strong too; and she might have been alive today had it not been for Robert Armstrong . . .

Alexandra felt the bitter taste of gall in her mouth. She had loved Robert. Passionately. And all the time he had been concealing his own part in her mother's tragic death, and his love affair with Belinda Belgrove . . . Unbidden, the image of Belinda's lipstick on Robert's shirt rose up to taunt her. Damn Robert! Damn all the Armstrongs! They had caused trouble for the Meldrums for generations. Drumcraig Castle had been a ruined pile of stones when Fergus, her grandfather, had first seen it and he had spent years of his life rebuilding it until it became the most beautiful castle in Scotland. His cousin had signed a disposition conveying the castle to him, but the Armstrongs had cheated him out of his inheritance.

Briony had made a solemn vow to her father that she would restore the castle to the Meldrums, the rightful owners. Now Alexandra made the same vow in memory of her mother. She would get it back.

And she would extract retribution from the Armstrongs . . .

TWENTY-TWO

I

1951–58
Alexandra walked out of the doctor's consulting room in a daze. She was expecting Robert's child. An abortion? No. She could never dispose of her child as if it were an unwanted piece of baggage. She would go through to Edinburgh and ask Malcolm Semple if he would consider taking over Meldrums before and after the birth.

Malcolm refused categorically and then electrified her by offering another solution: marriage. He said he would be more than willing to give her baby his name. Alexandra protested that she liked him enormously but did not love him. Malcolm's answer was that he had love enough for both of them. He made marriage seem like a friendly business proposition and she was in such a state of emotional turmoil that she accepted.

Alexandra wore a pale-blue suit and a feather hat for the civil ceremony in Edinburgh. Daisy was the bridesmaid, Frank was the best man. After the wedding the four of them repaired to the North British Hotel for a celebration dinner.

Alexandra was adamant that she did not want anyone to know about her marriage until graduation day. "Everyone would think it strange that I rushed into marriage with Malcolm when I've been so friendly with Robert. I don't want to spend my last days at university fending off awkward questions."

Especially from Robert. She was determined that he would never find out he was the father of her baby.

Alexandra embraced Daisy warmly before she left on her honeymoon. "You're a real pal, Daisy. Sometimes I feel like throttling that brother of mine. You go out to the pictures with him, you encourage him with his political ambitions, yet he's too dumb to see that you'd be a better girlfriend than any of his fancy females!"

Daisy grunted. "We were having fish and chips the other night and do you know what he said? That he thought of me like a sister. I felt like shoving the fish in his face!"

"Don't give up! One day Frank will realize he loves you."

"We'll probably be in an old-folks' home by then," Daisy quipped. "Promise me you'll try and enjoy your honey-moon . . ."

Alexandra imagined Malcolm might choose a hotel in Edinburgh or Glasgow, but instead he took her to the George V Hotel in Paris.

"Don't you remember my promise to you on the night of the Clydebank blitz? I said I'd take you to some place abroad where you could wear a long dress, and wine and dine and dance."

Alexandra was touched by this gesture and by his consideration when they went to bed for the first time. Once they were undressed he lay beside her, talking quietly until she began to relax. Only then did he begin kissing and exploring her body. She felt consumed with guilt because she lay in bed and longed for Robert. Guilt shadowed her days as well as her nights because so many of the places they visited evoked memories of the weekend she'd become engaged. Her only consolation was that Malcolm appeared to be enjoying himself.

They returned to Glasgow to be in plenty of time for Alexandra to sit her degree exams. The minute they were over she rushed away without speaking to anyone. Graduation day was another ordeal, as was the interview with a journalist. Alexandra agreed to it only because it would give Meldrums the publicity the company needed. She knew Robert would probably read the feature and would realize she had been deceiving him. But, after all, he had deceived her with Belinda.

II

Her first home with Malcolm in Edinburgh was a tiny house in Ann Street across the Water of Leith. The painter Henry Raeburn had given the whole street to his wife for her birthday and the doll-like scale of the buildings captured Alexandra's imagination.

Although she wasn't in love with Malcolm, the first few months of her marriage were happier than she had anticipated. She had made up her mind to be a good wife, and to divide her time between home and business so that Malcolm wasn't neglected.

At first they both worked from the small office in the Haymarket which she had set up when she made Malcolm her building manager; a role which she soon changed to Managing Director, with herself as Chairman. She made her accountant Fyfe Walker the Financial Director.

The row of terraced houses in Edinburgh had turned out to be a watershed in the fortunes of Meldrum Enterprises. Since Alexandra wanted to make money from them quickly, she had hired a team of tradesmen for each house and offered them substantial bonuses if they could finish the work quickly. It was a gamble because the wages for so many men ate into her capital and if the houses took a long time to sell, her capital would keep diminishing. But when the properties had been renovated, she had a stroke of luck. A London estate agent bought the complete row for a sum that staggered her bankers. Alexandra hastened to point out that she was now in a different league from the girl who thought it would be fun to buy and sell houses, and she capitalized on their admiration for her success by asking for another sizeable loan.

Soon after that Alexandra moved the headquarters of Meldrum Enterprises into spacious office premises near Princes Street, and appointed a Sales Director and a Marketing and Publicity Director to cope with the growing number of properties which the company was acquiring. A few months later she set up an additional office in Glasgow. Malcolm protested that Meldrums was expanding too fast and he wouldn't be able to cope if it got any bigger, but Alexandra didn't take his complaints seriously. She knew he was just concerned because she worked so hard.

"Pregnant women don't sit at home with their feet up these days," she said. "Honestly, Malcolm, you shouldn't worry about me."

All the same, as she neared the end of her pregnancy she

couldn't help wondering if Malcolm would resent a baby which had been fathered by Robert Armstrong.

Her fears proved groundless. The minute the baby clasped Malcolm's finger with her hand he seemed to feel an instant bonding with little Catherine. It was Malcolm who revelled in all the rituals of feeding, changing, soothing, and pram-pushing, and, though Alexandra often complained if Catherine disturbed their night's sleep, Malcolm never did.

Once Catherine was 3, Alexandra decided to look for a bigger home for them all. She found one in Joppa, a suburb of Edinburgh where there were spacious houses beside the seaside. At the back of the house in John Street was a garden enclosed by high stone walls covered with rambling roses. Alexandra breathed in the sea air and the scent of the flowers and thought how pleasant it would be for her child to grow up in this environment. Malcolm was delighted with it as well and built Catherine a Wendy House in the garden where she could play in all weathers. At weekends when Catherine's nanny went home to her family they ate out on the patio. If it rained they sometimes crept into the Wendy House and had a picnic there.

"Stay home with me," Catherine shouted when Alexandra left for business each morning, but she explained she had to go and make pennies.

Meldrum Enterprises continued to prosper over the years. "We've got a good spread of properties throughout Scotland," Alexandra pointed out at one board meeting in early spring 1958.

"Too many!" Malcolm argued.

"I wouldn't agree with that." The speaker was Mason Laidlaw, Malcolm's deputy. "We're careful not to forge ahead with new projects till we get money in from completed ones."

"I think it's time we dipped a toe in the London market," Alexandra said. "Mason, I think you and I should go down with Malcolm and have a look round."

"I've got good contacts in London," Mason replied immediately.

Alexandra wanted to tour London with her team to assess the housing market, but once she was there she became interested in some bomb sites which other builders were reluctant to develop. "They're ideally placed for commuters going to and from work," she said thoughtfully.

Mason looked at her. "You're thinking of a shopping precinct?"

"I haven't got anything definite in mind, but land is going to be at a premium in London, so let's buy the sites."

"Buy, buy, buy. One day we'll all be bankrupt," Malcolm warned gloomily. "Which reminds me: you're not really serious about submitting a tender for that KP office development in Glasgow?" He studied her face. "Armstrong Construction are going to tender for it. That's enough to make you want to compete, isn't it? I wish you'd get rid of your hang-up about the Armstrongs."

"How can I do that when they're business rivals?"

"It's more than business, it's personal. And since Adam moved into Drumcraig Castle . . ."

"I'd rather not talk about that," Alexandra said quickly and changed the subject by pointing out the new shops in the King's Road. But Malcolm had guessed correctly: it was the news about Armstrongs' intentions that had made her determined to put in a rival bid. Francis Bacon had said revenge was a kind of wild justice. It would be wild justice indeed if she managed to outbid Armstrongs.

TWENTY-THREE

I

1958

As dusk settled on the city of Amsterdam lights began to pierce the purple haze and café owners tuned in to love songs on their transistors so that tourists would be beguiled into a romantic mood. They knew perfectly well, of course, that romance was the last thing on the minds of the people who came to this part of the city. Most of them were wanting to assuage more basic urges.

Adam gazed at the girls displayed in the windows as they laughed and pointed and beckoned to him. Some of them pretended indifference, but under their heavily made-up lashes, their eyes were as sharp as those of the pimps who protected them and the policemen who had them under surveillance. In the red-light district of Amsterdam everyone watched each other.

Adam felt excitement gather in the pit of his stomach at the thought of what lay ahead. He'd seduced dozens of girls, but tonight promised something different. Tom Elphinstone was taking him to a private club which specialized in sado-masochism.

Tom was five years older than Adam and had shown no interest in him when they'd met as boys in Aberdeen. However, when Adam joined the King's Own Scottish Borderers for his national service he discovered that Tom Elphinstone was serving out the remainder of a short-term commission. The two men found they had the same taste for off-duty fun and games and they became firm friends.

On one of their nights out just before their service was completed Adam had been in a foul mood. "What am I going to do, Tom? I've no home to go to. Robert has seen to that."

Robert had married Belinda Belgrove a month after he graduated, then he'd gone off to do his national service leaving Belinda installed with her father-in-law in the Armstrong family home in Rubislaw Terrace. She had hired a firm of decorators and instructed them to strip the house and then redecorate it to her taste. Her father-in-law had been so blinded by her blonde beauty that he hadn't objected. Belinda had even had the gall to convert Adam's old room into a nursery for the baby which she was expecting the following April.

"You can have the spare room, Adam," she'd said, completely unconcerned by his anger.

"Stuff the spare room!" he'd blazed at her. "On my next leave I'll stay with Tom Elphinstone."

"You're very welcome to stay with me again," Tom volunteered as he listened to Adam's grumbles. "In fact, why don't you come and live at the castle? There are seven floors in Drumcraig. No problem in giving you a flat of your own. Free board and lodging. How's that?"

"And in return?"

Tom gave him a sly grin. "Well, dear chap, I'm having fun speculating with the money my uncle left me, but some of my business dealings sail a bit close to the wind, know what I mean? Your knowledge of the law might keep me out of trouble."

"I took a law degree, but I'm not a practicing lawyer."

"A practicing lawyer wouldn't approve of some of my little ploys. Oh, you'd be very useful to me, Adam, in all kinds of ways. And think of the sport we'd have! Organizing wild parties, visiting hot spots abroad. Much better fun if you've a chum with you."

His father had been furious when Adam announced he was moving in with Tom Elphinstone, Robert was relieved, and Belinda, surprisingly, seemed disappointed. The arrangement with Tom worked very well and, after a day slogging in Armstrongs, Adam was only too delighted to retreat to Drumcraig where he could smoke and drink and womanize without his father spoiling his fun. Tom kept his promise to take Adam to taste exotic pleasures abroad. The private club in Amsterdam was the latest escapade.

"I'm thinking of investing in the club," Tom said as he

stretched his legs and ordered another cognac. "Check it out for me with the manager."

Adam nodded. There was no point in telling Tom that it was a risky form of investment. He had discovered that Tom got his kicks from living dangerously.

"The last time I was there I found the girls very . . . imaginative," Tom went on. "Beautiful, too. Though not as ravishing as your ex. The beautiful millionairess! You lost out on that one, Adam."

Adam kept his face straight. He had discovered another facet of Tom's character: he winkled out your Achilles heel and then kicked it. Adam had learned how to cope: the trick was not to show that it hurt.

"Belinda's not a millionairess any longer," he replied with some satisfaction. "Her father's company has gone bust and he's lost all his money." He was delighted that Robert didn't have access to extra millions anymore. It eased the pain of losing Belinda. But only a little . . .

Meanwhile he was executing his own form of vengeance on his brother. Just before he left on this holiday he'd suggested to his father that Robert's obsession with the construction arm of Armstrongs was a waste of time and money. His brother was so angry Adam thought he might burst a blood vessel. "You don't deserve a directorship in this firm," Robert fumed. "If I could sack you, I would."

"But you can't," Adam replied slyly. "And since I agree with father all the time, he thinks the sun shines out my ears. He even gave his blessing to my holiday with Tom."

His father hadn't known, of course, that the week's holiday would be spent touring the brothels in the red-light district of Amsterdam.

"Time for fun!" Tom announced now. "Be a good chap and pay the bill!"

Adam did not flinch at the condescending tone. Being treated like an unpaid lackey from time to time was a small price to pay for the freedom he enjoyed at Drumcraig. He summoned the waiter and, once money had changed hands, he followed Tom along the street to a narrow lane where houses of varying sizes huddled together. At the end of the row a detached house stood apart from the rest. It had a faded exterior and beige shutters: an uninspiring, anonymous facade. Tom walked forward to the door and when he rang the bell a grille opened and a voice demanded proof of identity. Tom showed his club membership card and after a few minutes the heavy door was opened and a turbaned doorkeeper bade them enter.

The hallway was covered with thick black carpeting, as smooth and dark as the velvet which covered walls festooned with mirrors and erotic pictures. Adam heard piped music, soft voices, and laughter as four beautiful girls came dancing towards them: one white, one cream, one coffee-colored, one dark as mahogany. Apart from black eyemasks the girl were naked. They were carrying whips. The black girl's teeth flashed in a smile. Aberdeen was never like this, Adam mused, as he allowed his senses to enjoy the ambience of scented lust.

The girl took his arm. She led him through to a room dominated by a bed covered in black satin and commanded him to lie down. As she bent over and started undressing him, his eyes were drawn to the erect purple nipples on her dark breasts. Her skin felt soft, satiny . . . but he felt the strength in her hands and arms. As she raised the whip above her head Adam prepared to give himself up to the pain and pleasure Tom had promised.

Tom certainly knew the best places. He'd told Adam that Amsterdam was pretty fair, but said the Patpong district of Bangkok was mind-blowing. That's where they'd go the next time!

II

It had been a tiring day. Robert was standing in front of his father's desk trying to make him understand that the Armstrong shipyard needed modernizing. William Armstrong's face was pinched with anger. "A law degree followed by national service doesn't make you a business expert! I've allowed you to keep developing the construction arm of Armstrongs against my better judgment. If you don't get the tender for that Glasgow development you'll have wasted weeks of the firm's time and money, so don't compound your folly by trying to make me alter my policy about the shipyard. You can't change things overnight."

Robert raised his eyes heavenwards. He'd been working in

Armstrongs for years, but his father talked as if he'd joined the firm the previous day. Other shipyards were upgrading their yards and if Armstrongs didn't do that as well they'd be left behind. By 1959 John Lewis predicted they'd be building eighteen ships of 31,500 gross tons in total. What would Armstrongs be building?

Robert thumped his fist on his father's desk. "Can't you appreciate that the demand for trawlers and tramp steamers has been overtaken by orders for tankers and ore carriers? And that customers are wanting bigger ships?"

"Why are you agitated? Our trawler fleet is making a profit."

"But the shipyard is making a loss."

"It'll pick up again. In the past . . ."

"Father, we have to think of the future. There's talk of cellular container ships and roll-on roll-off ferries. That could take a lot of custom away from ports like Aberdeen and mean a subsequent decrease in the demand for new trawlers being built."

"You're painting too black a picture. Our order book is full."

"The Clyde shipyards had a full order book after the war. But look what has happened since Germany and Japan became competitive again. Some Scottish yards have started making a loss. I hear even John Brown's are having problems."

"Aberdeen isn't in the same position as the Clyde," William protested. "Anyway the shipbuilders on the Clyde are aware of the situation."

"And like you," Robert said pointedly, "they're terrified of introducing new building methods or new ideas in case they interrupt production. Some Clyde shipbuilders are being shortsighted. And so are you!"

"I won't listen one minute longer. Kindly show some respect for my age and authority!"

Robert took a deep breath and left the room without saying another word. He went into his office, made a few calls, wrote some notes for a meeting, and finally picked up his jacket and made for the front door. If he stayed in the building one minute longer he'd hand in his resignation. And no doubt that would bring Adam scurrying back from holiday to step into his shoes, Robert thought grimly as he strode towards the harbor. He'd never had a good relationship with his brother, but it had deteriorated since his marriage to Belinda.

Robert inhaled deeply when he reached the fishing harbour and let the tang of the sea fill his nostrils. He loved to stand here and listen to the shouts of the fishermen, the creaking and clanking of the boats, the mewling cry of the gulls. The breeze whipping in from the North Sea invigorated him.

His thoughts turned to his brother. He would have to keep remembering that Adam could not be trusted. In Glasgow he'd made the mistake of confiding the details of his nightmare. Adam had then proceeded to tell Alexandra, knowing full well the misery that would result from his disclosure.

Robert turned away from the harbor as he recalled that awful day when Alexandra had stormed out of the house in Jordanhill. He had tried phoning, writing, and calling, but she steadfastly refused to see him or respond in any way. He would have persevered if it had only been the misunderstanding over Belinda which had caused their quarrel. But yawning between them was the abyss of her mother's death and the part he might have played in it.

On graduation day a press photographer took a picture of Alexandra wearing her gown and clutching her MA scroll. The photograph appeared in the papers under the headline: "Meldrum Enterprises boss is Master of Arts." The ensuing article described the growing success of Meldrum Enterprises, success which Alexandra said could not have been achieved without the help of her building manager, lawyer, stockbroker, and accountant.

The pain of it still hurt. Alexandra had never mentioned these names to him. Not one. All the time they'd been lovers she'd been leading a double life. But it was the last paragraph which delivered the most stunning blow of all: the journalist revealed that Alexandra had married her building manager Malcolm Semple a month before she graduated.

Robert was hardly able to believe what he was reading. Just a few weeks after they had quarreled Alexandra had married someone else? Just like that? He was in such a state of despair that he married Belinda Belgrove a month later. At least she loved him. It seemed obvious now that Alexandra's professed love had only been a charade. When he went to do his national service, it was Belinda's photograph that he carried in his wallet. Their son Cameron was born nine months after the wedding.

They were happy enough, Robert thought, as he began walking away from the harbor, happier than he had any right to be after the debacle with Alexandra. Even now, he marvelled at the extent of her perfidy. He often wondered if the wound she had inflicted on him would ever heal.

"Fine day, Robert. Fit aboot your bonnie wifie? Every time she walks doon here men fair fall o'er their feet gawking at her!"

The speaker was Willie Parks, a trawling skipper who worked for Armstrongs. They stood for a while exchanging chitchat and discussing the changing face of the fishing industry. During the war when demand for fish was at a premium, profits had soared, but the old problems were reappearing: overfishing in the near and middle waters, transport difficulties . . . "Some of the trawlers in yon harbor are as auld as my auld granny. And she's past it," Willie remarked. "The Armstrong fleet's fine and up to date, but I can't say the same for your shipyard."

"I've been arguing with my father about that very thing, Willie. But you know what he's like, he wants to stick to the old ways."

"Aye, laddie, ye'll have a hard job shifting him. Now mind and give my regards to that wifie of yours."

"I'll do that. She's at home cooking my dinner. And if I don't hurry home I'll be late." He was lucky to have a wife like Belinda. He must try not to think about Alexandra. And yet how could he avoid it? Meldrum Enterprises was frequently mentioned in the press. They had achieved success buying dilapidated houses and tenements and restoring them for the private sector. Meldrums' construction company was expanding, but not as fast as Armstrongs'. If Armstrongs won the KP contract to build an office block, that would move the company from the minor to the major league. They should win it; their price had been pitched at the right level for the development company. He might even find out tonight. His lawyer Macfarlane Gibson had promised to phone him if he heard any rumors about the outcome. Robert's moods had been seesawing up and down all day as his tension mounted, but as he reached his house in Rubislaw Terrace he began to feel cheerful again. He wondered what there would be for dinner.

III

Belinda was humming as she put the finishing touches to the meal she had prepared for Robert. In the early months of their marriage Robert had arranged for her to go to cookery classes and she had enjoyed them enormously. She was still stunned by the news that her father had lost all his money in a series of disastrous investments. Boy, had that been some shock! One day, rich. Zap! Next day, poor.

Funny the way it had all turned out. Her father said that in the circumstances she'd fallen on her feet marrying a prosperous man like Robert. And in a way she had. She liked this stone house with its spacious rooms and she thought Aberdeen was quaint. Robert became annoyed when she described his home town as quaint. He seemed to believe that Aberdeen was a bustling city. She'd fallen about laughing when he said that. Jesus, nothing happened in Aberdeen apart from the trawlers sailing out to sea and then sailing back again with their catches. Talk about life in the slow lane! And the shops weren't exactly Bloomingdale's or Macy's. Some of them could have fitted into the deck of the beach house her father used to own. Used to, honey, used to. Keep remembering that.

Against all the odds she was reasonably happy living in this gray seaside town, though lately she'd begun to feel a bit bored. If it weren't for her son the days would be very long. To everyone's surprise—including her own—she discovered that she adored babies, and ever since Cameron had been born she'd longed for another. A baby girl to complement her baby son would make life perfect, but so far she hadn't conceived.

She blamed it on Armstrongs. Robert was so preoccupied and tired that by the time he came to bed at night he wasn't in the mood for sex. Kisses and loving, yes. Sex, no. Since Robert never seemed to worry about the infrequency of their lovemaking, she wondered if he were undersexed. Yet he gave the lie to that supposition on the occasions he did feel in the mood. At times like these he could be wild crazy in bed. Talk about passion, he was like a man possessed. Tonight she was going to *make* him feel in the mood and for once business wasn't going to interfere. She *needed* sex!

She kissed Robert warmly when he came in and led him through to the dining room which was set with the best silver and crystal. She had even placed a posy of fresh flowers in the center and a single rose on each side plate.

"What's this in aid of?" Robert asked.

"Civilization. Just because we're living in a remote part of England doesn't mean we should forget our table manners."

"If any Scot hears you calling Aberdeen a remote part of England you'll lose more than your table manners!"

"What makes the Scots so touchy?"

"Years of insults from the English!"

She laughed. "Okay, smart guy, now listen good. I've gone to a lot of trouble to set up an intimate evening *à deux*. Tonight I want you to concentrate on your wife."

Robert bent forward and kissed her. "I'll go and wash and change, and let you set up your seductive dinner."

When Belinda went through to the kitchen she nearly tripped over her 6-year-old son. "Cameron! What are you doing here? I put you to bed an hour ago."

"I want another bar of chocolate. I ate the one you gave me this morning."

Belinda hesitated. She knew she spoiled her son, but she found it difficult to resist the big brown eyes which were the mirror images of Robert's.

Cameron was looking up at her. "If you don't give me chocolate I'll scream," he said. "And then daddy will know I'm up and I'll get a row. And so will you."

Belinda did not want a row, not tonight. She extracted a Milky Bar from the fridge and pressed it into his hand. "Quick, upstairs, and don't let daddy see you."

He planted a sticky kiss on her cheek. "I love you, mommy. Best of everyone."

"I love you too, sugar. Run, I'll be right behind you."

Once she saw him safely in bed she ran downstairs to the sitting room. She plumped up the cushions and was busy stoking the fire when Robert came in.

"Want your usual?" he asked. He poured her a gin and tonic and then gave himself a liberal helping of whisky. "I need this—I've spent the day arguing with my father, cussed old blighter that he is. Thank God, he's out at a dinner!"

"What were you fighting about this time?"

"His attitude. He used to be an adventurous man, now he just wants to play safe. I can't understand it."

Belinda relaxed back in her chair and sipped the iced gin appreciatively. "Maybe it's the effects of the war. I've been reading an old issue of *Time* magazine. They did a series of interviews with graduates of the Class of '55 at Ivy League colleges. Their dreams seemed to be suburbia and a safe job."

Robert considered this for a while. "That's interesting. Reminds me of that book . . . forgotten the title. No, wait. *The Organization Man*. There seems to be this feeling in the States that people who went through the war came out of it wanting security more than anything else in the world. Well, that's my father!"

"The man in the gray flannel suit?"

"Precisely. Belinda, why don't we have conversations like this more often?"

"Because you're too tied up with work. Not another mention of your father or business this evening. Promise?"

"I promise. What's for dinner? I'm starving."

The rest of the evening passed pleasantly and Belinda was gratified by Robert's evident enjoyment of the soup, steak pie, and apple pudding: simple fare but his favorites. Afterwards they sipped coffee and liqueurs, and Belinda put on some dreamy Strauss waltzes and snuggled up beside him on the couch. When Robert began stroking her hair and kissing her forehead Belinda whispered in his ear, "Let's go to bed!"

He came into the bedroom carrying two glasses of champagne. He put one on Belinda's bedside table and began sipping the other as he surveyed her naked body stretched out waiting for him.

"Beautiful," he said as he began sprinkling her skin with drops of champagne. He put down his glass and began licking the liquid from her skin. He had just started to kiss her pubic hair when the phone trilled.

"Don't answer it," Belinda said plaintively.

"I must. It might be a call from Macfarlane Gibson. I told him to ring me if he heard anything. Whatever the hours."

He picked up the phone eagerly, but as he listened his face

lengthened. "Yes, I understand that. But how the hell were we undercut by such a small margin? Yes, I suppose that's possible. Thanks for letting me know."

Belinda watched Robert anxiously as he put down the phone. Obviously Armstrongs had lost the tender. He was taking it very well, she thought. He was even going to finish the champagne. Suddenly Robert hurled the champagne glass against the wall, smashing it into a thousand pieces. "That bloody woman!"

Belinda sat up in alarm. "Who are you talking about?"

"Alexandra Semple. Or Alexandra Meldrum as she prefers to be known. Call the bloody bitch any name you fancy. To lose the contract to Meldrum Enterprises . . ."

Belinda wiped the rest of the champagne from her body and put on her nightdress. There would be no sex tonight, she thought bitterly. Or in the next few days. Robert took a long time to get over business failures. Frustrated and angry, Belinda settled herself for sleep. If she couldn't get sex from her husband she'd damn well get it elsewhere. She'd been playing the perfect wife and mother too long. Time to try another role.

IV

When Alexandra opened her eyes she smiled as she remembered that Meldrums had won the contract. Robert would be humiliated. For a moment she felt a twinge of sympathy for him, but she banished it. Why should she feel any emotion except hate for a man who had repaid her loving by treachery? And as for his brother . . . Alexandra's gritted her teeth as she pictured Adam lording it in Drumcraig Castle with Tom Elphinstone. She had already instructed her lawyer to make an offer for the castle, but Tom hadn't even deigned to reply. She would keep trying. She wouldn't be happy until Drumcraig was in Meldrum hands again.

Malcolm rubbed his eyes sleepily as Alexandra nestled into his side and whispered in his ear, "Meldrums won the contract."

He kissed her. "Congratulations. I had a feeling this might happen, and like a boy scout I'm prepared."

He jumped out of bed and disappeared into his dressing

room. He came back into the room a few minutes later carrying a tray with a bottle, two glasses, and an ice bucket.

Alexandra clasped her hands together in delight. "Champagne for breakfast! I haven't had that since our honeymoon!"

As he uncorked the bottle and began pouring the Bollinger into two crystal glasses, Alexandra leant back against the pillows, her eyes dreamy. "I didn't believe you when you said we were going to Paris for our honeymoon. You've been good to me."

He handed her a glass. "That's because I love you."

"And I've made you happy, haven't I?"

"At home you always make me happy. At business you scare me to death!"

"I'd be worried if I thought you meant that! Aren't you going to propose a toast?"

Malcolm perched on the edge of the bed and raised his glass to her. "Here's to the worst mother in the world!"

He laughed when he saw her outraged expression. "Calm down, my sweet, I'm only repeating the remark you made yourself. Catherine is well looked after. Nanny and the daily housekeeper spoil her outrageously."

"But I adore Catherine," Alexandra protested, thinking of her 6-year-old daughter. Catherine was dark-haired, stubborn, and utterly adorable. Apart from the star-shaped mole on the inside of her wrist . . . Every time Alexandra looked at it she remembered that Catherine was Robert's child. "I give Catherine lots of attention when I'm here," she said defensively.

"Yes, but I have to be honest and tell you . . ."

"That I'm not here enough? Does Catherine resent that?"

"Yes, but not as much as she resents the times you promise to take her somewhere and then cancel because of business."

"I've promised we'll go to the zoo this Saturday," Alexandra recalled. "Please don't let me forget."

"I'll try. But when the business red light flashes, my darling, you develop tunnel vision. Have some more champagne!"

"Will it help my tunnel vision?"

"I doubt it. But it might make you invite me back to bed."

"What a lovely idea! Put down that glass immediately."

Malcolm slipped off his pajamas as Alexandra wriggled out of her nightie. She tasted of lemon and apple blossom, he thought, as he began kissing the chestnut hair which hung rich and shining against the creamy breasts he loved to fondle.

"You're a chameleon," he whispered. "So brisk and remote with me in the office; so warm and wonderful to me in bed."

Afterwards they lay contentedly side by side, but when she made a move to rise he held her back. "It's only seven o'clock. Early. Stay a while. These days we hardly ever have time to talk."

Alexandra's green eyes were contrite. "At times I feel so guilty, but there's so much happening and this new development is going to mean an awful lot of extra work. For everyone. You might even have to stay in Glasgow to keep an eye on . . ."

"Alexandra," Malcolm said softly. "Let's stop pretending."

She frowned. "What are you talking about?"

He turned in the bed and took her face between his hands. "Listen to me. This is important. I enjoyed helping you run the business for the first few years, but it's become too much for me. I warned you early on that I wasn't ambitious, didn't want too much responsibility. Now I'm drowning in it. I want out!"

Alexandra pushed his hands away and sat up in bed. "Malcolm, you can't mean that!"

"I do. I'm Managing Director in name only. For the last few years other members of the board have been assuming responsibilities that I've sidestepped. People turn to Mason Laidlaw for direction. I'm out of my depth in the business that Meldrums has become. I'd be happier back in my old trade."

"Cabinet-making?"

"That's right. You know the shop near the Royal Mile where I used to work? I wandered into Paddy's Antiques the other day and discovered some of my old chums still there— fashioning fine furniture. I stroked the wood of the tables and chairs, admired the craftsmanship, and realized I'd far rather be there than in Meldrums."

Alexandra put out her hand to touch him. "I'm so sorry, Malcolm. I've been blind, too caught up with Meldrums . . ."

"Don't reproach yourself. The fault is mine, not yours."

"So what . . . would you like to do?" she asked huskily.

Malcolm got up from the bed and offered Alexandra more

champagne. When she shook her head he filled his own glass and sat down again beside her.

"Ideally, I'd like my old job back. I even asked Paddy if he'd have me, but at the moment he can't afford to take on new staff."

"But you'll carry on working in Meldrums till you find something else?"

"No, my darling, I won't. The KP contract means you'll have to reorganize, take on new staff, expand . . . The sooner you appoint Mason Laidlaw as Managing Director of the group, the better. He'll make all the new staff changes that you need." He leaned forward and kissed her. "Are you very disappointed in me?" he asked as he drained his glass and bent over her.

She put her arms round his neck. "I'm upset because I didn't realize you'd been so miserable. I'll find a way of making you happy."

A month later when Malcolm came in after a walk in the park, Alexandra handed him a set of keys. "You wanted to work in Paddy's Antiques. You can. I've bought it for you!"

Malcolm stared at her. If he owned the shop he'd have to be responsible for the men, the money, the materials. Once again he would have to worry about balance sheets, profit and loss, and all the other problems of ownership. He opened his mouth to protest that the last thing he wanted was to own anything, but when he saw the anxiety and love in Alexandra's eyes he couldn't do it.

"How did you persuade Paddy to sell?" he asked, trying to show enthusiasm.

"Shopowners are usually open to offers . . ."

Malcolm held her gaze. "Especially if they're offered far more than the shop's worth?"

Alexandra nodded. "I don't think Paddy's made much money recently. He told me the only reason he's held on so long is that he likes working with wood."

"So what will he do now?"

Alexandra hesitated. "Well, I did say that I was sure you'd let him stay on. He jumped at the idea."

Yes, he would, Malcolm thought enviously. Paddy would

have the enjoyment of the antiques shop without the responsibility.

That night when they went to bed Alexandra turned to him for love. But for the first time in his life Malcolm was impotent.

PART V

1967–71

TWENTY-FOUR

I

1967

Robert was leaving Aberdeen early to drive down to Glasgow to a business luncheon. He was surprised when Belinda got up and made him breakfast, and decided she must be up to something. His wife thought he was unaware of her affairs; she was wrong. Aberdeen was such a small city, men in power usually got to know what was happening. Especially to their wives.

He should have been jealous and indignant when he found out about her infidelities, but it had simply added to his disillusionment. He had discovered that behind Belinda's doll-like prettiness lay a hard, calculating woman who lied and cheated whenever it suited her. As a result, when she lay naked in bed wanting him to make love to her, his body responded, but his brain reneged and consequently his lovemaking lacked fire. He knew it. She knew it. And there wasn't a damn thing he could do about it.

At first he wondered why Belinda stayed married to him. Then she revealed that she still cherished hopes of having another child.

"We make beautiful babies," she'd said to him. "Look at our son, Cameron. So dark, so handsome. I want a beautiful daughter."

And what Belinda wants, Belinda gets. Well, that had once been the case, but no longer. Although he still made love to his wife occasionally he hadn't managed to father another child with her. So why had she risen early to make his breakfast and kiss him goodbye? With many wives that would have been the natural thing to do, but with Belinda it was unnatural: she liked to sleep late.

When he reached Glasgow, Robert drove towards Clydeside. He was lunching on a schooner that had been turned into a riverside club. As he walked towards the *Carrick*, Robert reflected that it was typical of the contrariness inherent in many a Scottish character that the influential banker who had invited him was a man who often proclaimed that he couldn't stand the sea.

"What'll you have?" Muirhead Davidson asked when Robert spotted him.

"Whiskey and water, please. I'm afraid I'm a bit early."

"Delighted to see you. We can have a chat till the others come. Hold on, there's our newest MP on Clydeside. I know him, decent chap!" Muirhead beckoned to someone half-hidden behind a pillar and when he came towards them Robert realized it was Frank Meldrum. When Robert had been going out with Alexandra, Frank had been a joiner in John Brown's. Since then his influence in the unions had grown steadily and eventually he had been selected as the Labour candidate in a recent parliamentary bye-election. He had surprised everyone by winning it.

"Congratulations!" Robert said and held out his hand. He couldn't imagine what Alexandra had told Frank about the break-up of their affair, but Frank showed no sign of embarrassment.

"Thanks," he said. "I'm still a bit dazed by it all."

"And so are the Tories!" Muirhead said ruefully. "You gave us all a shock. Come on, have a drink with us."

"Well . . . I'm meeting two of my constituents for lunch, but they're not here yet. All right, I'll have a small whisky."

"Good lad! I heard you getting a pasting on the radio the other night about Labour's plan for expansion in Scotland."

"It was a good plan," Frank said defensively. "Labour wanted to modernize and reorganize the old industries, and help new ones like cars and electronics, but with the financial crisis . . . Well, of course, Harold Wilson had to defend sterling."

"There's no 'of course' about it," Muirhead Davidson protested. "Look what's happened in Scotland as a result of Wilson's deflationary measures: 50,000 people emigrated in 1966 and unemployment is soaring!"

Robert contributed very little to the argument; he was much more interested in studying Alexandra's half-brother. Frank still had an air of rugged honesty, but his years in politics had enriched his knowledge and his skill in argument. He would make a good MP. We could have been friends, Robert thought regretfully, as Frank left to join his constituents.

"Now where's the rest of my lunch party?" Muirhead asked, looking round the room. "Sir Eric Yarrow couldn't make it. Pity. Charming chap. Ah, here come the Norman brothers!"

Andrew and Drew Norman were shipbuilders on the Clyde. A few minutes later the party was completed when they were joined by two trade unionists and Big Duggie, an outspoken shop steward. Andrew Norman was soon launched on the matter that was preoccupying all of them: current problems in the shipbuilding industry.

"The unions don't seem to understand that our rivals in other countries are being helped by their governments. German shipbuilders have special taxation relief, Japan is aided by low interest on loans, and Sweden and Holland are getting long-term credit."

"And then everyone wonders why companies choose these countries to build their ships," Drew Norman added. "And when they ram the point home by adding that shipbuilders abroad are offering lower quotations and shorter delivery times, the bosses are accused of being disloyal to the Clyde."

"Aye and so they are!" Big Duggie declared. "Bosses think more of ships than the men who build them and in the Clyde shipyards relations between management and unions are generally poor."

"That's a sweeping generalization," Robert said reprovingly. "I've toured the Yarrows yard many times, and the unions and management there work splendidly together. Just as Armstrongs do."

Muirhead Davidson turned to Big Duggie and the two trade unionists. "Speaking as a banker I'm very concerned about the state of shipbuilding in Scotland. Look at the Fairfield Company, one of the famous names on the Clyde. Bankrupt. Had to be rescued by the government. Who's going to be next?"

"How are you surviving in Aberdeen, Robert?" Andrew Norman asked. "A few years ago you told me the future of your shipyard looked a bit dodgy."

"It was, but I finally managed to persuade my brother and

my father to modernize. We still build trawlers, but we're now chasing contracts for merchant shipping and ferries."

"The Clyde yards are never going to buck the trend until they're more flexible about wages and working hours," Drew Norman was saying, with a challenging look at Big Duggie. He had obviously decided to make the shop steward his main target.

"Most of the trouble in the yards *comes* from the management," Big Duggie replied angrily. "See Scandinavia? There're no separate canteens for management and workers in that country. Catch youse Clydeside bosses behaving like that. Nae chance!"

Robert sighed. "Why is it that when you blame a Scot he always says someone else is at fault?"

"Let's continue this discussion over lunch," Muirhead said, and led them towards the dining room. "How's your son?" he asked Robert as they sat at a table overlooking the river and ordered asparagus soup, steak and salad.

"Cameron? He's 15 and longing to go to San Francisco on the hippie trail. In the meantime, while he waits to grow up, his aim is to get to Woburn Abbey where the Duke of Bedford is holding a festival for the flower children!"

The men round about him laughed at his expression of disgust, but the smile on Robert's face was a little strained as he picked up his spoon and began to take his soup. It had been a proud day for him when Cameron followed in his footsteps and enrolled at Robert Gordon's College in Aberdeen, but since then, days of pride in his son had been few and far between. Cameron had become a spoilt brat of a boy, always getting into trouble at school for smoking, swearing and flouting authority. Unfortunately Cameron knew that however badly he behaved his mother would make excuses and give him any money he wanted.

"Maybe they should bring the flower children down to the Clyde," Muirhead Davidson joked as they settled down to their meal. "They couldn't build the ships, but they could throw flowers at the workers and make them smile."

There was an outburst of laughter and, though arguments continued over lunch, when the party eventually broke up everyone seemed in an amiable mood.

* * *

Before driving back to Aberdeen Robert decided to call in at the Glasgow office of Armstrongs. Despite the initial setback when Armstrongs lost the contract for the KP office development, their other construction projects were doing well. Much better, Robert suspected, than Meldrums whose aggressive bidding must have left them with narrow profit margins. Robert felt his face muscles tense. Sometimes he felt Alexandra was shadowing his every move at business and then trying to get ahead of him. As well as building up her construction company, Alexandra had made a major move into commercial and office development.

"One of these days Alexandra Semple's ambition is going to outpace her capital," he remarked to Harry Rosemary, the office manager of his Glasgow operation. They were sitting in Harry's office going over the accounts.

Harry shook his head. "If commercial development doesn't work out for Meldrums, Alexandra will pull them in another direction."

Robert looked up from the papers laid out neatly before him on the desk. "I didn't know you were on first-name terms with her?"

Harry shifted uncomfortably in his seat. "I've had several long chats with her lately."

"And?" Robert asked, sensing trouble.

"And she's offered me a job in Meldrums. I'm sorry, Robert. I was about to tell you: I'm handing in my resignation."

"I'll give you more money."

"It's not the money, I'm being offered a main board directorship."

II

Robert was so angry he found it difficult to concentrate on the road as he drove back to Aberdeen. Not content with winning contracts from under his nose, Alexandra was trying to steal some of his best staff. He tightened his grip on the wheel. He wasn't going to let her get away with it. If Alexandra continued on her present course she'd soon be putting him out of business.

Unless he put her out of business first . . . Now there was a thought, Robert reflected. He'd discuss it with Adam; in this matter at least they would be united. Robert swore as a motorist braked too sharply in front of him. Adam was another problem in his life. His brother's initial discontent had given way to ambition and he was trying to persuade their father that he would make a better Chairman-elect than Robert. These days board meetings were fraught.

When he reached Aberdeen Robert wondered what new devilment his wife was planning; he wasn't in the mood for Belinda's ploys. Still, he thought wearily, as his car crunched on the gravel of the driveway of his home, they would probably keep up the pretense of being happily married. That was the way in the north east. Some of his friends' marriages were as big a sham as his own, but they rarely considered divorce. Especially if they had a wife who looked like Belinda. She was in her mid-thirties now, but with her slim figure and flowing blonde hair she could have passed as a teenager.

During the evening he could see that Belinda was making an effort to please him. The only note of discord was when his son appeared. Robert gazed disapprovingly at the long hair flowing to Cameron's shoulders and at the blue earrings which matched the peacock jacket his son was flaunting.

"You look like a poofter!" Robert said shortly.

"How many poofters do you know, father?"

"Don't you dare cheek me, young man! Isn't it time you started behaving like an adult? One day you're going to inherit the Armstrong empire . . ."

"I may as well tell you now that I wouldn't touch Armstrongs with a barge pole . . ."

Robert pushed his chair back and was about to move towards his son when Belinda laid a restraining hand on his arm. "Robert, please. Cameron's only 15. He's just having fun while he's growing up. Lots of other boys behave the way he does."

"But they don't get carpeted at school for smoking and drinking."

Cameron groaned. "I'm off to a party. I'll be late."

It was obvious that for once Belinda was really annoyed with her son; he'd completely spoilt the atmosphere she'd built up so carefully. Once Cameron left she kept refilling Robert's wine glass. He knew she was hoping the alcohol would put him in a better mood and in truth he found himself mellowing as the evening wore on.

"After an evening like this I begin to think there's still hope for our marriage," he said as he stroked her hair in the sitting room after dinner.

"Lots of hope," she whispered. "Now why don't you get ready for bed and wait for me. I have a surprise for you."

Robert lay in the big double bed, the day's events racing round his head like a merry-go-round that wouldn't stop, but he sat up when his wife walked into the room. "Christ, where did you get that!" he exclaimed.

Belinda was wearing a black lace nightdress which he hadn't seen before. It reminded him immediately of the one he'd bought for Alexandra to wear in Paris. Belinda's nipples pushed against the flimsy material, just as Alexandra's had done . . .

Belinda slipped into bed beside him. "Make love to me, Robert. Make love the way you used to when we were first married. Then I'll want to stay married to you."

Robert felt rage racing through him as he reached out his hands and tore the nightdress off her shoulders, ripping the fine lace as he pulled it from her body and threw it on the floor. He began kissing her, rough bruising kisses that were meant to hurt. He pushed her legs apart and drove into her, plunging deeper and deeper. "Babies!" he muttered, sweat streaming from his brow. "That's what you want and that's what you'll get!" He had never felt so savage, so possessed. Curses mingled with his kisses, caresses became coarse tokens of lust, and all the time a hot tide of passion rose between them carrying them forward until it engulfed them both and she shouted out his name.

Robert shouted out too, but in his final moment of ecstasy it was Alexandra's name he called and there was such pain and anguish in his voice that it numbed every bone of the woman lying beneath him. He fell asleep almost immediately, but Belinda lay in the dark, miserable and angry. She'd thought Robert had forgotten his passion for Alexandra, but all these years it had been eating away at him. God, how she hated her. Hated him. She wanted revenge on them both. She twisted and turned in bed, trying to think of something that would humiliate Robert and anger Alexandra. By morning she knew exactly what she would do.

III

Frank had been disturbed by his meeting with Robert Armstrong. Alexandra had long before told him the whole story about the fire and Robert's confession about the accident, but somehow it had seemed out of character. Nor had Robert appeared to be the kind of man who would proclaim his love for Alexandra whilst dallying with Belinda.

He wished everyone would forget the past. Whenever Daisy asked him about his parents he changed the subject. How could he tell her he'd killed his own father? He wouldn't think about it; it would take away from the success of his lunch-time encounter with his constituents, two intelligent men who lived on one of the biggest housing estates in the area where he had been elected MP. They had put forward a suggestion that appealed to him: they wanted to form an organization to promote better housing without waiting for government help. During lunch they had drawn up ideas for him to convey to the Housing Minister.

Frank was anxious to hear Daisy's opinion, but it was a few weeks before he had a chance to talk to her. Good old Daisy, Frank thought, as he turned the car towards Whitecraigs. Once she had graduated as a doctor and served a year as intern in a city hospital, Daisy had joined her father's medical practice in the Gorbals. Fortunately for him she had maintained her interest in politics and in Frank's career, and they were the best of chums.

Daisy was looking out for him when he drew in to the entrance of the villa in Whitecraigs. He smiled as he remembered how the luxury of her home had once intimidated him. He no longer gave it a moment's thought. He owned a home himself now: a four-roomed flat in a tree-lined avenue in Glasgow's west end. As usual Daisy was wearing baggy trousers and a shapeless sweater. "Hello there," she called. "You can have a quick cup of coffee in the kitchen, but then you'll have to scoot. I've just had a call to go to Cumberland Street—a patient's baby is on the way."

While she was preparing the coffee Frank told her about his constituents' scheme and they had a lively discussion about it. In passing he mentioned that Robert Armstrong had been lunching at the *Carrick* and he had spoken to him.

"Well, I suppose it was inevitable that you two would meet again," Daisy said as she poured out the coffee. She handed Frank a cup and perched on a stool as she talked to him. "In any case, industrialists like Robert should keep lines of communication open to politicians who might help them. I keep seeing Robert's picture in the papers," she went on. "I must say he's aging well. Handsome. Not a gray hair in that black mane of his. A formidable bastard from all accounts!"

"He would have made Alexandra a far better husband than Malcolm Semple," Frank said with such force that Daisy choked on her coffee.

"Since when have you joined the Robert Armstrong fan club?" she spluttered.

"I haven't. Forget Robert Armstrong. I came to talk to you about Malcolm Semple. My informants say he's well on his way to becoming an alcoholic. He goes to the seediest pubs in Edinburgh and often has to be helped home."

"Trust an MP to hear rumors," Daisy said dryly.

"The worst of being in the public eye is that people think rumors about your in-laws will embarrass you. I'm not bothered about me or Malcolm, I'm concerned about Alexandra. She refuses to discuss it with me. Keeps saying it isn't a problem."

Daisy put down her coffee cup. "She freezes up whenever I ask, so I don't."

"Malcolm was arrested for being drunk and disorderly last week," Frank said worriedly.

"I didn't see it mentioned in the papers."

"I managed to keep the incident quiet."

"So what are you intending to do?"

"I've come to you for advice."

"I think you should go through to Edinburgh and see him. When I tried to talk to him about his drinking he changed the subject."

"We've drifted apart. I doubt if he'd listen."

"I think you have to try," Daisy said candidly.

IV

Frank parked the car by Waverley station and walked up to the old town. The tall tenements in the Royal Mile seemed to face each other across the road like fishwives gossiping about old times. Some of the buildings had been there for hundreds of years and the closes and wynds were still redolent with the atmosphere of the past. Paddy's Antiques had been a small shop tucked into the corner of a tenement, but once Alexandra had bought it she changed the name to Meldrum Reproduction Furniture. Frank peered in through the mullioned windows. There were no tradesmen about, but in a corner of the shop he spied Malcolm polishing a table.

Frank braced himself and pushed open the door, making his way past tables, chairs, chests, escritoires: furniture of the highest quality. "This is a fine place you've got here," Frank said jovially. "Quite an achievement for you."

"I haven't achieved anything," Malcolm replied brusquely, showing no surprise at Frank's sudden appearance. "I just work in the shop. It's Alexandra who has transformed it into a nationwide chain."

"But you're Chairman . . ."

"Come off it, Frank. I'm Chairman in name only. You and everyone else knows that Meldrum Reproduction Furniture is run by the Managing Director. I'm happy to leave Morton Cockburn to make all the decisions."

"You look awful," Frank said candidly as he took in Malcolm's haggard face and worried eyes. His fair hair had turned gray. "Look, I came here today because I'm concerned about you. Are you drinking too much because you think you can't measure up to your wife?"

For the first time there was the glimmer of a smile on Malcolm's face. "Do me a favor! Is there any man who could measure up to Alexandra?"

Robert Armstrong, Frank thought immediately. He frowned. "Is there anything anyone can do to help?"

Suddenly Malcolm's eyes showed his anguish. "I wish there was, old son. I only wish there was. But I've got myself in a mess . . . Still, I'll find a way out of it."

Frank stepped closer. "Surely I can . . ."

Malcolm stepped back in alarm. "If you try and interfere,

Alexandra will get hurt. I mean that. You'll have to leave. I want to shut up shop."

Frank walked slowly back to his car, feeling a gloom that had nothing to do with the onset of dusk. There was more to Malcolm's problem than drink. He was frightened of something. Or someone. He stood irresolutely on the pavement, every instinct commanding him to go straight up to Alexandra's home and talk it over with her. But Malcolm had been so insistent. So convincing. Best not to meddle.

TWENTY-FIVE

I

Malcolm would never have met the prostitute if he had not been drunk. He would never have responded to her solicitations if he hadn't thought she could cure his impotence. And she would never have acted the way she did if she hadn't become greedy.

Later he would mull events over in his mind and wonder how he could have prevented the situation getting out of hand, but in the end he decided that he had simply been unlucky. The fact that he had no real reason for self pity made it worse. Although he had grumbled about Alexandra to Frank, he had no cause. It wasn't her fault that nothing worked and he couldn't find a niche for himself.

Worst of all was his impotence. After nine years of failing to make love to his wife he had given up trying. It was his discontented frame of mind that led him to the pub and, once he discovered that six or seven whiskies blotted out his worries, he became a regular at the Ploughman in Edinburgh's east end. Sometimes he spent half the day there. He was such a good customer someone invariably offered to drive him home; home being a magnificent mansion in Barnton, an exclusive suburb of Edinburgh.

On the Friday when his troubles began he foolishly decided to take the car and on an impulse went to a new pub called The Admiral's Inn. When he reeled out of the pub after closing time he stood beside his car, trying to fit his key into the lock.

"Want any help, dearie?"

He screwed up his eyes and saw a girl standing next to him. The first thought that struck him was that her hair was the same color as his wife's: brown with gold bits. The girl had a heavily made-up face, and she was wearing a bright-red miniskirt which was much shorter than any his daughter Catherine ever flaunted. Her legs were covered with sheer red stockings which seemed to shine in the light from the street lamp.

"Want a bit of fun?" she asked.

He shook his head sadly. "Cantsht . . . Can't. Do itsh any more."

"Impotent, are you?" she asked with a candor that made him shudder. "Well, Belle can fix that. Never met a fella yet who couldn't get it up by the time I've finished with him."

Some part of his brain registered the importance of what she was saying. "You cansh make me . . . do it? Fix me?"

" 'Course I can. Why don't I drive you home, luv? You're in no fit state to be behind the wheel."

"Men's shupposed to drive tarts somewhere. Not other way shabout," he said thickly, feeling that he had somehow got things mixed up.

"I know, dearie, but you couldn't pedal a bike, never mind a big car. And I happen to be a tart with a driving license. 'Cos my boyfriend has a car. Taught me hisself. So give us a fiver and I'll drive you home."

Malcolm looked at the girl doubtfully and then handed her a fiver. She propped him into the passenger seat and started the engine. "This car's a beaut!" she said as she ran her free hand over the walnut of the woodwork. "What d'you do, then?"

"Meldrum. Reproduct . . . Furniture. Charimansh," he said.

"Pull the other one, it's got bells on! Or should I say balls!" She giggled. "Where d'you live?"

He fumbled in his pocket and gave her one of his cards. She raised her eyebrows when she saw the address in Barnton, and when they drew up outside the gates of his house she forgot her poise and stared open-mouthed at the imposing mansion with fine gardens.

"Thought we'd go to your place for a bit of nookie. But this . . . cripes, you must be stinking rich. You married, luv?"

He nodded sadly. "Wonderfulsh wife. But can't do it . . ."

She regarded him thoughtfully. "Well, we can't go in there if your wife's waiting. I know a spot not far from here." She restarted the engine and drove quickly till she reached a path leading into a wood.

"This'll do nicely. Let's get you into the back of the car and out of your clothes. I *know* you're drunk, but so're most of my customers. I've had to learn how to make drunk men get it up—and I can. Don't worry, luv, you're in the hands of an expert."

An hour later she drew up outside the gates of his house. She kept the engine running, put the gears in neutral, and pulled on the handbrake. Malcolm was dazed but happy. The girl had fixed him. Made him do it. First time in years.

"There, that's the best you've had in a long time!" the girl cooed, straightening his tie and wiping some lipstick off his cheek. "And if you want it again, you just come to The Admiral's Inn on a Friday night. My name's Belle."

"Money," he said thickly, fumbling in his pocket and pulling out a ten-pound note. "That's all I've got on me."

"Don't worry, dearie, that'll do for now. I 'spect there's plenty more where that came from." She looked up at the closed gates in front of them. "Is there a thingy in your car that opens them? Has to be with a posh car like this."

He pointed to a knob on the dashboard and as she pressed it the gates slid open.

"Told you I knew about cars, didn't I?" Belle slipped out of the car and coaxed Malcolm across to the driving seat, positioning his feet on the pedals, and his hands on the steering wheel. "Your driveway slopes down to your front door," she said, "so when I pull off the handbrake the car will go forward. All you have to do it put on the brake when you get to your front door. Think you can manage it?"

"Eashy, eashy!" Malcolm muttered and the car glided slowly down the driveway. Belle concealed herself beside the gatepost to see what would happen. Since her boyfriend Sid had taught her to drive she'd often driven customers home. An extra service, she called it, and charged them accordingly. Sometimes Sid trailed behind her in his car if he thought her customers might give her trouble. And lately he'd started trying to sneak up and take a few shots with his camera of the men bonking her in the back seat. Said it would keep them quiet if they refused to pay. She was lucky having a minder like Sid. He hadn't come tonight, but maybe he'd come another time. It gave him a thrill to look at pics of the nobs having their jollies! Belle giggled as she saw Malcolm's car ride up the front step of his house and slide down again. Gawd, he wasn't half pissed. His missus would give him a right earful. He had begun honking his horn like mad.

A woman came rushing out of the entrance of the house and her high clear voice sounded concerned. "Malcolm, what possessed you to take the car? I've been so worried about you!"

And you'll be a lot more worried, my lady, by the time I'm through with your husband, Belle decided as she began walking towards the main road. She had found herself a pigeon just ripe for the plucking. Sid would be pleased. Very pleased indeed.

II

Malcolm began patronizing The Admiral's Inn every Friday where he indulged himself with whisky and Belle's company. She always took him to the path leading into a wood. It was usually deserted, but once he noticed another car parked nearby.

"Probably another courting couple," Belle said reassuringly. She kept him so busy he forgot all about it until flashes of light filled the car interior. He tried to jerk his head up, but since he was lying on his back with Belle's hair trailing over his eyes he couldn't see.

"Shut your eyes," Belle hissed quickly. "It's a nosey parker with a torch."

Malcolm glared at the intruder and shook his fist. Then he closed his eyes and gave himself up to the pleasure of Belle's body. When he dared to glance out the window again, he saw that the other car and the nosey parker seemed to have gone. He refused to go back to that spot the next time. Belle didn't seem worried. "We can go where you like, dearie."

For the first few months Malcolm was too delighted by his restored virility to be aware of any threat. Then Belle started demanding more money. "I've changed your life," she asserted after once again bringing him to a climax in the back of the car. "Reward time. I want you to bring me £100—in cash."

Malcolm stared at her aghast. "That's far too much!"

"If you don't bring it to the Inn, I'll tell your wife. Know where you live, don't I?"

He cashed a check and paid her. After that he stayed away from The Admiral's Inn, but it wasn't so easy to get rid of Belle. To Malcolm's horror she appeared at the furniture shop in the Royal Mile on Saturday when Catherine was helping. He watched transfixed as Belle chatted happily to her. After a while Belle strolled over to him. "I was asking your daughter to look out for a nest of tables for me. Ever such a nice girl she is. She says her daddy's the expert on wood. I can see she's a real daddy's girl."

"Why are you here?" he whispered, unable to conceal his agitation.

"I want £500: to be given to me at The Admiral's Inn next Friday. A final payment," she added encouragingly.

"You promise it's final and you won't bother me again?"

" 'Course I do!"

He cashed a check and paid her, hardly able to believe that his ordeal was over. Alexandra was delighted when he announced that he was going to stop drinking and Catherine gave him an especially warm hug. Although Catherine had been very much aware of his alcoholic binges she had never uttered one word of reproach or criticism. She was a daddy's girl all right. He had tended and cherished her since she was a baby and nothing seemed to spoil the love and respect they bore for each other.

On one occasion when he was helping her with an English essay she flung her arms round him and told him he was the best father in the world.

"Don't put me on a pedestal," he warned her. "I'm not worthy of it. I tried to succeed as a business man, and I couldn't cope. I must be a great disappointment to your mother."

"Well, you'll never disappoint me," she said.

He hoped the words wouldn't come back to haunt him, but as time passed and there was no further word from Belle he began to relax.

III

When Meldrum Reproduction Furniture was about to be launched in France Alexandra was interviewed in the *Scots-*

man about her ever-burgeoning empire. Meldrum shops were being stocked in five French cities, and staff were being hired. Alexandra and Morton Cockburn the Managing Director of MRF had arranged to visit the Paris branch to discuss problems about security.

"Come to Paris with us," Alexandra suggested to Malcolm. "You're Chairman of MRF and maybe . . ."

". . . I can start acting like one?" Malcolm chuckled. "You never give up hope, do you? Sorry, my love, I may have reformed, but I still don't want any responsibility. But tell you what . . . I'll come to Paris and we can make a holiday of it, and perhaps spend a couple of days in London on the way out?"

"Damn!" Alexandra said suddenly. "I've got business meetings all day Friday, I won't be able to leave till late. But you could spend the day in London shopping for new clothes. Let's update your image."

The prospect appealed to Malcolm. "I'll catch the early train from Waverley station. That will give me time to stroll round the shops in the afternoon."

"And I'll book an evening flight and meet you between ten and eleven at the Waldorf," Alexandra replied eagerly. "Wait a minute, we've forgotten Catherine."

Catherine was a weekly boarder at St. George's in Edinburgh and she came home on Friday evening for the weekend. If Alexandra and Malcolm happened to be out, they always contrived to have someone in the house so that Catherine wasn't on her own. Lately their daughter had become resentful about these "babysitters," maintaining that she was old enough to look after herself.

"Can't you ask Mrs. Sloan to stay over?" Malcolm asked. Mrs. Sloan was the daily housekeeper who cooked and cleaned.

"She's not free this weekend."

"We'll ask Catherine to invite one of her chums over."

"I don't like the crowd Catherine's mixing with these days. She's brought some really weird friends home lately."

"It's the swinging Sixties, lots of teenagers look weird. Anyway Catherine's 15 and going to art school in two years. You can't treat her like a baby. You have to trust her."

"Well, I don't," Alexandra said flatly. "All right, I'll suggest she invites a friend and I'll warn her not to entertain any notions of having a party."

"You worry too much. Let's start looking forward to Paris."

IV

As Malcolm walked down the Waverley Steps to Waverley station on the day he was due to catch the train to London, he felt more light-hearted than he had in years. At the foot of the steps he happened to turn his head and to his consternation saw Belle walking behind him.

"Sid and I have been watching your house," she announced by way of greeting when she caught up with him. "Saw your wife driving you to Princes Street. When she kissed you goodbye and drove off on her own, we thought, 'Right, got him!' "

"Keep away from me."

"Want me to shout it out? Best move into this dark corner where we can have a nice little chat and the crowds can't see us."

"I won't chat to you. And I won't give you any more money."

As he studied Belle's brassy brown hair and heavily made-up face he wondered how on earth he could have had sex with her. But then of course it had been dark, he had been unhappy, and he had been drunk.

"My boyfriend, Sid, picked up a copy of the *Scotsman* in the pub. Spotted that article about you and your missus and your daughter Catherine. I mean, we knows you was rich, but blimey, the paper said you was filthy rich. So Sid decided we should squeeze you for a little more."

"I'm not interested in anything you have to say!"

"Please yourself," Belle said with a shrug. "I can always ask your daughter. Met her in the shop, remember? Your wife said in that interview that your daughter was the apple of your eye. Ain't that nice! And my, wouldn't Catherine be shocked if she heard what her daddy had been up to?"

"She wouldn't believe you," Malcolm said thickly, as he glanced round uneasily, hoping that none of his friends were amongst the crowds who were flocking through Waverley station.

"Oh yes she would. Remember one time we were in the back of the car? Doing all sorts of shocking things we were! Another car was parked farther up the lane."

Malcolm remembered the car, the sudden flashes of light which he thought came from a torch, and Belle's admonition to keep his eyes averted.

"My Sid was the nosey parker," Belle said smugly. "He was ever so naughty taking flash pictures through the back window . . . They came out quite well," she added conversationally. When she thrust the pictures under his nose Malcolm wanted to vomit. The photographs weren't of a good quality, but there was no mistaking his car numberplate, his face, and what Belle was doing to him. Catherine professed to be so swinging that nothing shocked her, but those pictures of him cavorting in the back of the car with a prostitute . . . Catherine would be disgusted. She'd want nothing more to do with him.

"Me and Sid want £10,000," Belle said calmly. "Final payment."

"You said that last time! I've got a train to catch," Malcolm said desperately. "I've got to go."

"Well, go. When you come back, I'll be waiting. At your shop, or your house. Somewhere."

Malcolm caught the London train with a minute to spare. He was sweating as it pulled out of Waverley and it wasn't just because he hadn't had time to buy a ticket. Even if he paid the money to Belle there would be a demand for more. They would keep squeezing him until he had nothing left and his empty bank balance would be discovered. After that, Belle and her Sid would start working on Alexandra. Although Alexandra was a shrewd, tough business woman she had a soft center and wouldn't be able to bear seeing Malcolm disgraced and Catherine disillusioned. She'd bankrupt herself before that happened and her carefully cherished empire would collapse.

He couldn't let that happen. Alexandra had been a good wife to him and he loved her. Always had done. Their marriage breakdown was his fault not hers. And his impotence . . . Dear God, he'd forgotten that. If Alexandra ever found out he'd been able to perform with a prostitute but not with her, her humiliation would be complete. He would have to get rid of Belle—or think of another solution that would save his family from disgrace.

V

As Alexandra was about to leave the office to drive to the airport the phone rang. It was Jacques, the manager of Meldrum Reproduction Furniture in Paris. He was upset: the shop had been burgled. Alexandra immediately began phoning lawyers, policemen, and insurers and by the time she'd finished with them all she realized she'd missed her flight to London. As she put out a finger to buzz her secretary she remembered she had left. Alexandra glanced at the clock on her desk, surprised at how the hours had fled. She tried to phone Catherine, but got the engaged sound. Drat the girl, she'd left it off the hook.

Malcolm would be disappointed that she'd missed the flight. Alexandra sat back in her chair and allowed her mind to roam back over the years of her marriage. Happy ones, initially. She'd been so thrilled with Malcolm's competent handling of Meldrum Enterprises that it came as a great shock to her when he indicated that he'd had enough. She'd spoken to their doctor about it.

"Usually a man gets executive 'burnout' after years of stretching himself beyond his capabilities," the doctor explained. "But returning prisoners of war can be affected in the same way after only a short time in a responsible job."

"So how can I help my husband?" Alexandra had asked.

"Indulge him. Encourage him to return to his old trade if that's what he wants."

She had done that and had relieved Malcolm of responsibility whenever she saw that it irked him. Yet it hadn't been enough. Malcolm still hadn't been happy and eventually he had started drinking heavily. The doctor reassured her by suggesting that this latest phase might pass. And it had. In the last month Malcolm had been relaxed and confident. Except about sex. She had schooled herself not to think about that during the day, but sometimes at night her ache for physical fulfillment brought tears to her eyes.

Enough sentiment, Alexandra decided, as she looked at the correspondence on her desk. Meldrum Enterprises was more than enough fulfillment for any woman: a wide variety of companies, private property, commercial and industrial development, the furniture chain. And the areas that had once been bomb sites . . .

She hadn't been sure what to do with the bomb sites until someone mentioned in passing that too many cars were chasing too few parking spaces. She had decided there and then that this could be a unique opportunity to get ahead of the game. It had taken years to transform the sites into multi-story car parks, but the scheme had proved one of her biggest money-spinners.

Not all her ideas had worked, of course. When she left university and started buying and selling property she hadn't forgotten her small-time catering business and had tried to turn it into something bigger. It had failed abysmally. At that time Malcolm had proved a great comfort.

Alexandra looked at her watch. Ten o'clock. Malcolm would be expecting her. She dialed his room in the Waldorf and explained what had happened.

"I'll fly to London tomorrow morning and we can catch the first flight to Paris in the afternoon."

"I like Paris. Our honeymoon was fun, wasn't it?"

"Why, yes . . . Are you all right?" she asked.

"I love you, Alexandra. Always have done."

Instead of being warmed by his affectionate tone, Alexandra felt uneasy. "Malcolm, is something wrong?"

"Just with my voice—it's a bad line. How's Catherine?"

"Fine as far as I know, but the wretched girl's left the phone off the hook. She'll get the sharp edge of my tongue when I see her tonight. And for once her darling daddy won't be there to protect her."

"I've always protected Catherine, haven't I?" Malcolm said, his voice slurred.

"You've been drinking!"

"Just a little."

"Oh Malcolm, please don't start going on binges again!"

"No more binges," he agreed. "Night, my darling. I love you."

Alexandra was frowning when she put the receiver down. She signed a few papers, packed others in her briefcase and prepared to leave. She hesitated by the phone, concerned about her husband. When she dialed the Waldorf again the receptionist told her that Mr. Semple had just left. Alexandra sighed. Malcolm must have gone out to a pub.

VI

Malcolm asked the doorman to direct him to the nearest underground station. He bought a single ticket and went down the escalator. He knew exactly what he intended to do. He paced from platform to platform waiting until the crowd thinned and he was on his own. When the sign showed that a train was due he walked forward to the edge.

VII

It was a clear moonlit night and the fresh air dispelled the sleepiness that had begun to overtake Alexandra in the office. As she got into her car she scolded herself for worrying about Malcolm. Why assume the worst? After he'd been out for a drink he might come straight back to the hotel and go to bed.

As she drove across Edinburgh she tried to refocus her mind on her business activities. She loved trying to guess future trends. In business it wasn't enough to play the game; to succeed you had to be ahead of it! Yet however hard she applied that diktat she hadn't been able to acquire Drumcraig Castle. She had lost count of the times she had tried to persuade Tom Elphinstone to sell the castle to her. Each time he replied to her offers with derisory letters of rejection. Lately she'd become impatient. "I doubt if I'll ever acquire Drumcraig by conventional methods," she'd told Boyd Brown and Alan Gillian, "so if you ever hear any gossip about Tom Elphinstone or Drumcraig . . . let me know."

"How can gossip help you buy the castle?" Alan asked.

Alexandra had shrugged. "Who knows? Bait everything and something will bite!"

They had all laughed.

Alexandra was still smiling at the memory of that conversation as she approached her house in Barnton. The smile vanished from her face when she saw that the big gates were open and the driveway was packed with strange-looking cars, psychedelic vans, and motorbikes. When she opened the front door her eardrums were assaulted by a wave of sound, her nostrils detected strange scents, and her eyes smarted from the smoky atmosphere. She staggered to one side, only to be clasped in the arms of a girl draped in a sari. She looked closer and saw it was a man with a large gold curtain ring in one ear. His eyes were glazed.

"Peace!" he said solemnly.

"War!" Alexandra declared and fought her way through a swaying crowd to the living room, only to find that it had a new wall-to-wall carpet: people! She peered at the faces to see if Catherine were amongst them and found herself being pulled to the floor by a bearded hippie. "Wanna joint? I got good grass and I dig older chicks."

"Well, go dig in the back yard—and bury yourself!" she snarled. She pulled herself up and made her way to the hall. At the top of the stairs the main hazard was a man with a reefer in one hand, a guitar in the other and a cigarette dangling from his mouth.

"Wanna pass round the reefer?" he asked as she scowled at him.

"Go get Catherine!"

"Catherine? Don't know that chick."

"She's your hostess. And don't you dare smoke a joint in my house." She snatched the reefer from his lips, stuck it into a glass of wine which was standing on a table, and then threw his guitar out of the window.

"Hey, you some crazy lady!" he yelled.

A girl in trailing robes and an Indian headband came out of the bathroom and groaned. "That's no lady, that's my mother. Mum, why d'you have to come and spoil everything? We were all having a really great time. The party . . ."

"The party's over."

"Mum, don't embarrass me. This scene won't last much longer."

"You're damn right it won't!" Alexandra shouted. "Now do you throw them out, or will I?"

"Okay, okay," Catherine replied. She picked up a large bell standing on a table and began clanging it and screaming, "*Fire! Fire! Fire!*" Fifteen minutes later everyone had left.

Alexandra surveyed the chaos of dirty glasses, cigarettes, paper hats, cups with tea and coffee spilling onto the carpet. The phone was off the hook. She replaced it.

"I'll clear everything up!" Catherine said. "And look, mother, before you say a word, I'm sorry."

"Damn right you are! I bet you're sorry you've been found out."

"Can't I even apologize without you taking it the wrong way?"

"What way am I supposed to take it? I forbid you to have a party in our absence and then come home unexpectedly and find you've disobeyed me!"

"Obey, disobey . . . Those words are anachronistic. For heaven's sake, how do you want me to behave? Like a younger version of you! Well, thanks, but no thanks. I want my life to have some fun. All you think about is work. That's more important to you than anything."

"That's not true!"

"Oh yeah? What about all the times you promised to take me to the zoo, or the pictures, or the park, and then had to cancel? In this house, business comes first."

"If it weren't for business you wouldn't be living in a house like this!" Alexandra shouted.

"Who *wants* to live in a house like this?" Catherine shouted back.

Alexandra realized she was making matters worse. "Catherine," she said patiently, "I do want you to have fun, but drugs are dangerous."

"They're thinking of legalizing marijuana, mother. And getting pleasantly spaced is no big deal."

"The Rolling Stones are facing trial for drug use!"

"I bet their convictions will be quashed. Dad wouldn't have made a fuss like this," Catherine stormed. "He'd have laughed and helped me to clear up . . ."

The loud ringing of the phone made her stop in mid-speech.

"That'll be your father," Alexandra said. "He's in London." In her hurry to get to the phone she knocked over a tray of glasses and sent them crashing to the floor.

"I'll get it," Catherine said impatiently and picked up the receiver. She turned to her mother with a strange expression on her face. "It's the police. In London. They want to talk to you."

Alexandra grasped the receiver. "Yes, this is Mrs. Semple speaking. Yes, Mrs. Malcolm Semple. What is it? Has something happened to my husband? You found his Access card on his . . ." As she listened the color drained from her cheeks and she sank to the floor, still holding the receiver in her hand. "Yes, I'll contact my lawyer straight away. He'll make all . . . Thank you . . ."

"What is it?" Catherine asked, alarmed by the way her mother seemed to be aging in front of her eyes. "Has something happened to daddy?"

"He's had an accident," Alexandra whispered. "He was in an underground station . . . and fell in front of a train."

Catherine sank to the floor beside her. "But he's not badly hurt, is he? I mean . . . mummy, he's not . . ."

"He's dead, my poor darling, dead. Killed instantly."

Catherine screamed and went on screaming until Alexandra muffled her daughter's face against her breast. Then they wept in each other's arms amidst the debris of the party.

TWENTY-SIX

I

There was a mystery about Malcolm's death. Alexandra sensed it—and so did the press. She acted quickly to scotch further innuendo by giving an interview.

"I spoke to my husband in his room at the Waldorf on the night of his tragic accident. He was very happy and looking forward to our trip to Paris, but he did say that he'd eaten something earlier that had disagreed with him. He thought exercise and night air might clear his head. Unfortunately when he was waiting for a tube he seems to have had a dizzy spell and toppled in front of a train."

The postmortem revealed evidence of a heavy meal which might or might not have caused dizziness. The coroner recorded "Death by misadventure."

After the funeral there was another flurry of attention from some newspapers, but this time it was focused on Alexandra and the expansion of the Meldrum empire in France and possibly in the States. Her picture appeared under the headline: "The barefoot millionairess." Much was made of her humble beginnings in Aberdeenshire as the "barefoot crofter's child" who had become a millionairess. Comparisons were drawn with the Forbes who had risen from humble origins in Aberdeenshire to become one of the wealthiest families in America.

"I hate it!" Catherine cried. "Every time we go into Edinburgh there's always someone who recognizes you and stares."

"Why don't we go away somewhere?" Alexandra suggested.

"If we go together, people will notice you. Oh mum, I don't mean to be unkind, but I'm so miserable."

Alexandra tried to comfort her daughter, but Catherine drifted around the house like an unhappy ghost.

"I'm really worried about her," Alexandra confided to Daisy over the phone. "She needs to get away from here."

"She's planning to go to art school, isn't she?" Daisy said thoughtfully. "I've got an idea. I saw an advert for a fort-night's painting holiday in Florence—leaving next week. They still had some places vacant. I'll take her."

"But what about your medical practice? How will it get on without you?"

"More people might survive!" Daisy quipped in typically sardonic style. "There's no problem," Daisy went on, "father can get someone to fill in for me. Anyway, I'd like to go to Florence. I might meet a sexy Italian who'll sweep me off my feet and make mad passionate love to me. Fat chance of that happening with Frank."

"I don't know why you still go out with him after all this time. Seventeen years . . ."

"I don't go out with him as a girlfriend. He thinks of me as his chum and men keep their chums for life. Don't worry, I joke about Frank, but I've long since given up hope. Now, about this painting lark, why don't I drop in on you and ask Catherine myself?"

Catherine smiled for the first time since her father's death when she heard Daisy's proposal. "Florence! Gosh, that would be great!"

"Are you going to be all right on your own?" Daisy asked Alexandra anxiously. "You've been so concerned about Catherine you haven't had time to indulge your own grief. Speaking as a doctor I'd suggest you have a good long howl."

Alexandra found it easy to follow Daisy's advice once she'd driven them to the airport and returned to her house in Barn-ton. The tears began streaming down her face as soon as she crossed the threshold and by evening she felt exhausted. Why had Malcolm committed suicide? That it *was* suicide she had no doubt. Her statement to the press had been a farrago of lies. Malcolm hadn't told her he'd felt dizzy, hadn't mentioned that he wanted fresh air. And Alexandra did not find it credible that he would have lost his balance on an underground platform.

She looked round and realized that it was dark and she hadn't eaten since breakfast. There was no one in the house but herself. Mrs. Sloan was an admirable daily housekeeper, but Alexandra was beginning to realize that if she had living-in help the house wouldn't seem so lonely. She foraged in the kitchen and made herself sandwiches and a cup of coffee which she took through to the study.

Her desk was still piled with letters of condolence. Alexandra opened some of them after she'd finished eating and drinking, but she hadn't the heart to begin replying. A flash of red caught her eye and she pulled the envelope towards her. Her name and address were childishly scrawled in red ink and the letter was marked "Personal." Alexandra read the contents with growing disbelief. Someone wanted to talk to her on a matter concerning her late husband. The sender had photographs to prove that she had known him intimately. Very intimately. He owed her money. A lot of money. The letter went on to suggest that Mrs. Semple should deliver a note to The Admiral's Inn arranging a meeting place. It was signed "Belle."

Alexandra went across to the cocktail cabinet and poured herself a stiff brandy. She was breathing rapidly and she could feel her heart pounding. Malcolm owed some woman called Belle a lot of money? Was this a clue to his strange behavior the night he died? She sat nursing her brandy, thinking about it. Then she picked up the phone and dialed the home number of Sam Sweeney, a private detective who had been useful to Meldrums on various occasions. She asked him to find out as much as possible about a woman called Belle who patronized a pub called The Admiral's Inn.

"And Sam? This is very urgent. You'll be paid extra for speed."

Two days later Sam Sweeney came to the house with his report. Alexandra studied it and penned a short note inviting Belle to take a taxi to her house in Barnton at ten o'clock on Monday morning. She said she wouldn't discuss anything with her unless she brought the negatives as well as the proofs. Alexandra handed the note to Sam and instructed him to deliver it to The Admiral's Inn.

"Why don't you let me handle this for you, Mrs. Semple?" Sam's face was concerned. He was a small man with a slight stoop and an air of fragility, but his appearance was deceptive.

Meldrums had discovered that Sam Sweeney had a black belt in judo. He was also extraordinarily sharp and very discreet.

"Thanks, Sam, but this is something I have to do myself."

II

Alexandra considered her wardrobe carefully before Belle was due to arrive; she did not want to appear to be either feminine or vulnerable. She picked out a black chunky pants suit with heavy chain belts round the waist. Malcolm had contended that the outfit made her look like a refugee from a motorbike gang.

The doorbell rang. Alexandra waited a few minutes in the study and let it ring again before she answered. The woman on the doorstep had brown hair which had been badly dyed and her heavily painted face, too-tight clothes and brassy manner proclaimed her profession. Alexandra invited her into the study and pointed to a chair beside a small bookcase. "If you've something to say, say it quickly and get out!" she said briskly without any preliminaries.

Belle bristled. " 'Ere, not so fast! Your husband and me was good friends. Know what I mean? We had a *special* relationship!" She frowned. "I read that he'd gone and died. I was sorry about that. 'Cos he's made me pregnant, see! And now I've no one to support me and the poor kid I'm expecting."

"Tough!"

Belle gasped. "Ain't you shocked?"

"Why should I be? You're a prostitute, aren't you?"

"What would you know about it?"

"I have my sources. So don't think you can con me into believing you're pregnant. It's just a ploy to get money, and it won't work!"

Belle glared at her. "Hoity-toity, ain't ya? Well, maybe this will make you change your mind? You said you wanted to see the pictures. Well, here they are!" With a flourish she produced some photographs which she held out to Alexandra.

Alexandra made no move to take them. "These photographs could be fakes. I said I wanted you to bring the negatives as well, and if you haven't, you may as well go away."

She stood up and warmed her back at the fire, seemingly unconcerned. Belle hesitated, then pushed her hand into her bag and took out another envelope which she placed on the table. Alexandra bent down and extracted the negatives which showed pictures of Malcolm in obscene poses. Belle looked at her with a calculating smile. "He was drunk when I first met 'im. Confided in me. Said he couldn't get it up. I said I could fix that."

So that was it. Poor Malcolm. It must have been tempting for him to imagine that someone could cure his impotence.

"And I succeeded," Belle said proudly.

Where I failed, Alexandra thought, with a twist of pain. "These negatives aren't very good," she said. "Underexposed."

Belle's eyes widened. "Well, you're a cool one, I must say. You won't be so cool when I show these to the newspapers."

"Show these to every newspaper in the country if you like. I don't care tuppence for your threats."

"But you do care for your daughter," Belle said triumphantly. "I met her in the shop once. Your husband turned ever such a funny color when I said I'd show these to her if he didn't pay up."

Alexandra could have wept. Malcolm had always basked in Catherine's adoration; he wouldn't have been able to bear the thought of that devotion turning to disgust. He'd rather have killed himself—which is precisely what he had done; hoping it would save his family from disgrace. Alexandra strove to keep her tone conversational. "So . . . you were blackmailing my husband. How much were you demanding?"

Belle looked at her warily, obviously wondering if she had won. "Ten thousand quid—to set me up for life. But seeing as you've been so cheeky and the newspaper articles say you're so rich . . . I'm upping the ante. Twenty thousand. And you won't hear another word from me . . ."

"You're right about that," Alexandra said and tossed the photographs and negatives in the fire.

Belle jumped to her feet. "Don't think that's the end of it."

"It's not!"

Alexandra walked forward and put her hand into a space in the bookcase near where Belle was sitting. She pulled out a tape recorder, pressed the reverse button and then switched it on. She stood holding it in her hand as their conversation was replayed. "I switched this on before you came into the study."

"But how did you know . . . ?"

"I hired a private detective. I know everything about you and Sid."

"Don't you try to threaten me," Belle blustered.

Alexandra advanced till she was face to face with Belle. "I'll threaten you from here to kingdom come if you ever approach me or my daughter again!" she shouted. "You cow! You must have made my poor husband's life miserable with your blackmail threats. That's why he killed himself."

Alexandra slapped Belle's face, then grasped her by the collar and started shaking her. "You're guilty of murder as well as blackmail! Stay here one minute longer and I'll call the police."

Belle was dumbfounded by the force of Alexandra's rage and terrified that she would call the police. She backed away and ran from the house as if all the hounds of hell were after her. When she heard the front door bang Alexandra collapsed on a chair, overwhelmed by a storm of weeping. At last she knew the truth about Malcolm's suicide. But God, how it hurt!

Another phase of her life had passed. She must gather her strength to face a new one—and without Malcolm's love and support. Drearily she picked up the mail which she had earlier pushed aside. There were no more envelopes marked in red ink, but there was one with a New York postmark. She opened it listlessly, and saw that the letter was signed "Felix Danziger."

The name struck an instant chord. Toby Armstrong, the great love of her mother's life, had emigrated to America where he'd gambled away any money he managed to earn. He had saved Felix Danziger's life and lost his own when he'd intervened in a gambling dispute. Alexandra never thought she would hear from the Danzigers and she wondered what had possessed Felix Danziger's son, apparently also named Felix, to sit down and write to her twenty-nine years on . . . Intrigued, she settled down to read the letter properly.

DEAR MRS. SEMPLE (Felix wrote),

I happened to pick up a paper which carried an article captioned: "The barefoot millionairess." When I read that feature I realized you must be Briony Meldrum's daughter. I have to confess that at that juncture I felt both guilt and relief: relief to hear that you'd done so well; guilt because I hadn't fulfilled my father's promise to your mother to keep in touch with the Meldrums and lend them a hand if they needed it.

After Toby's death, my father prospered and set up a small minerals company which I inherited when he died. I've built Danziger Minerals into a sizeable empire. My personal life hasn't been so hot: married twice, divorced twice. Seems strange, doesn't it? We've each ended up with millions, but haven't exactly struck it lucky on the home front. I was sorry to hear about your husband's tragic accident.

The newspaper article suggested that you were about to expand into the property scene in the States. Well, I'm not in real estate, but I'm a wise old guy and probably have the kind of contacts you need. So why don't you come to New York for a visit and mix business with pleasure? I'd sure love to meet a "barefoot millionairess."

Alexandra shook her head. The media had seized on the fact that she'd once run barefoot to save her shoes and now she seemed tagged with it. It was embarrassing . . . Still, it had brought her to the attention of Felix Danziger. He sounded a nice old guy. One of these days she might take him up on that invitation.

TWENTY-SEVEN

I

20 September 1967

Alexandra and Daisy stood side by side on a high vantage point overlooking the crowd of 100,000 people who had assembled in John Brown's shipyard. They were there to witness the launch of the last great passenger liner to be built on the Clyde, a ceremony to be performed by the Queen. A shipyard on a working day can be an inferno of noise and ugliness, but when a ship is about to be launched, a mysterious alchemy transforms bleakness into beauty, and strident clamor is replaced by a susurration which sweeps backwards and forwards over the spectators as they try to guess what the new ship will be called, a secret which is not revealed to the onlookers until the actual moment of the launch.

The papers had reported that the wind was a cause for concern: at rehearsals on the previous day it had gusted at twenty-five miles per hour. If it increased by another three knots, the launch might have to be postponed. Yet absence of wind would present another problem: unless there was a bit of a breeze from the west, the level of the tide would not be brought up to the required height. But on this momentous morning Scotland breathed a sigh of relief as the weathermen announced that the winds were just right for the launch.

Alexandra turned to Daisy. "Come on, what's all this mystery about a boyfriend and marriage? Frank sounded very upset about it."

"He did?" Daisy muttered. "Catherine's plan must be working."

"What's Catherine got to do with it?"

"We were talking about Frank when we went to Florence on that painting holiday. I happened to mention that I'd never be anything more than Frank's mate and was so firmly on the shelf I was glued to it. Catherine went all broody after I said that, and then astounded me by arguing that Frank could be in love with me, but just couldn't, or wouldn't admit it to himself."

"I've thought the same," Alexandra said, "but I haven't known how to make him take off his blinkers."

"Your darling daughter decided drastic measures were called for. Refusing to go out with him was phase one of her plan for me."

"And phase two?"

"Phase two might shock you rigid, so don't ask."

"At least tell me when it's happening?"

Daisy gulped. "Tonight! Well, if you must know," she grinned weakly, "I said I was going out with a man I might marry, but Frank could call round for coffee about ten. It will be the first time I've seen him in weeks."

"No wonder he's sounding edgy."

"*He's* edgy! I'm practically paralytic at the thought of carrying out your daughter's suggestion. Let's drop the subject. Talk about something else—the ship, the weather. Malcolm's death," she added cautiously, looking at her friend with concern.

"No, I can't bear to discuss that," Alexandra said sadly.

"Everyone says the sun's going to come out," Daisy remarked, trying to cheer her up.

Sunshine would be a good omen, Alexandra thought. People were hoping that this launch would be a symbolic turn of the tide for Clydeside. The Sixties shipbuilding slump was continuing. The Fairfield Shipbuilding and Engineering Company had been rescued from bankruptcy by a consortium of state and private enterprise interests which aimed to integrate management and labor in a radically new way, but though an incentive scheme had increased productivity for a while the shipyard was still having problems. Ross Belch, the Managing Director of Lithgows on the lower Clyde, maintained that the government would have to do more. "You can't build an industry without a strong home market."

Salvation had beckoned with the shipbuilding industry bill which promised cheap credit to shipowners building in a UK yard. This solved one problem but the Geddes Report had still to be implemented. Clyde shipbuilding was to be reorganized into two groups: Scott Lithgow based on Greenock and Port Glasgow, and Upper Clyde based on Govan, Linthouse, Scotstoun and Clydebank. Unity was to be the keyword and there was hope that the new liner would herald a new era for Clyde shipbuilding and for Scotland.

Frank had told Alexandra that a lot depended on an improvement in relations between unions and management, which were generally poor on Clydeside. The exception was Yarrows, the famous naval shipyard. Much of their success was due to their charismatic chairman Sir Eric Yarrow whom *The Times* had called a "shrewd example of the younger generation of Scots shipbuilders." The Yarrows shop stewards had even held a unique press conference at which they informed curious journalists that labor relations in Yarrows were second to none on the Clyde or anywhere in Britain. Sir Eric Yarrow had told them that his door was always open. In Scotland, and particularly in the Labour stronghold of Clydeside, such words of praise from shop stewards were so unprecedented that they made an impact not just in shipbuilding but in other spheres of business and industry.

Alexandra had paid heed as well. She had taken a long thoughtful look at the labor relations in her own companies and had set up a series of meetings between workers and management throughout the group. She then issued instructions that complaints had to be aired, workers' grievances looked into very thoroughly, and management had to take their cue from Sir Eric Yarrow's open-door policy. She made it known that her door, too, was always open. When Daisy heard about it she teased Alexandra and told her she must fancy the debonair shipbuilder, but Frank wasn't prepared to joke about the matter. The situation on the Clyde was serious, and if shipbuilding kept being bedevilled by restrictive practices any new era heralded by this launch would be as disastrous as the last.

"There's Frank!" Daisy exclaimed. Alexandra felt a shaft of pity as she looked at the love on her friend's face. She doubted if any plan of Catherine's would lure Frank to Daisy's side. Her half-brother was a very physical man and he liked girlfriends who exuded potent sex appeal, a quality that Daisy seemed to lack.

Alexandra watched Frank as he walked with a group of

VIPs on to the raised platform from which the Queen would perform the ceremony. Since he had been elected as MP Frank had become quite a celebrity, his opinions continually sought by the media. Once the platform party were settled, the air of expectancy in the crowd heightened as everyone waited for the arrival of the Queen and the royal party.

"It's going to be one of the most luxurious liners in the world," someone remarked nearby, drawing everyone's attention to the great ship guarded by her cohort of cranes. "Cruises for the rich."

"And work for the poor," Daisy whispered to Alexandra. To the people of Clydebank the building of a great ship meant shoes for their children's feet and food in the larder. When work had stopped on the *Queen Mary* in 1931 half the total wages in the town had been cut off. Two years and four months later when they heard work was to start again the men had streamed down the streets in their thousands, singing and dancing, pipe bands playing. Work on the *Queen Mary* had started in the years of depression; the *Queen Elizabeth* was launched in the shadow of war. Now here was a new ship and the prospect of a new idea for Clydeside: shipyards working together instead of fighting each other for orders.

"I wonder if the new deal will work?" Alexandra mused aloud. She knew that Frank had his doubts. Different rates were being paid for the same job in different yards, there were variations in labor practice and of course there was the big problem of persuading Yarrow Shipbuilders, which was making a profit, to merge with the others which were making a loss. Yarrow and Company had finally agreed to join provided they controlled forty-nine per cent of their subsidiary, Yarrow Shipbuilders.

"Did you see that report in the papers about Frank?" Alexandra asked.

"Hinting that he may get into the next cabinet?"

"They could do with someone like Frank in the cabinet," Alexandra continued. "I mean, the present lot aren't doing very well for Scotland, are they, Daisy? Our shipping and coal industries are declining, railway lines have been cut by Beeching, the steel industry's in a mess, people are emigrating . . ."

"But Labour *have* brought new growth to Scotland," Daisy protested.

"See here," a woman on their right interrupted. "If youse yins want to natter about politics, do it somewhere else. We's are wanting to enjoy the launch."

"Awa and bile yer heid!" Daisy retorted in her best Gorbals accent, leaving her protagonist open-mouthed.

Alexandra felt merriment bubbling up inside her; an unusual emotion these days. Since Malcolm had committed suicide, Daisy was the only one who could make her laugh. Alexandra tried not to mention Malcolm in the hope that her sense of loss would gradually diminish, but the manner of his death was a millstone she knew she would carry for the rest of her life . . . Most nights she cried herself to sleep, overcome with guilt and regret that she hadn't been able to help her husband. If only she hadn't been so preoccupied with business . . . If only she'd known how miserable he was . . . If only, if only . . .

Alexandra and Daisy stopped talking as the royal standard was unfurled over the launching platform and the Queen appeared. She was wearing a matching coat and dress in turquoise wool topped by a swathed hat. In a few minutes everyone would know the name of the new ship. Suggestions had ranged from *Winston Churchill* to *John F. Kennedy*, but when Cunard had issued a last-minute invitation to Princess Margaret to come to the launch, odds on her name being chosen had shortened from twenty-five to one to four to one.

Alexandra nudged Daisy as she looked at the petite princess sitting on the platform. "I'll lay you 500 to one that it's *Princess Margaret*."

"Is this one of your devious methods of trying to give me some of the money you've made over the past fifteen years? Forget it! I'll lay you 500 to one it's *Prince Charles*. And if it isn't I can't pay you!"

But they were both wrong.

"I name this ship *Queen Elizabeth II*. May God bless her and all who sail in her!"

The Queen stepped forward to cut the ribbons holding the bottle of vintage champagne and pressed the button controlling the release mechanism. The ship seemed to move a fraction of an inch and then for the longest minute anyone could remember it stayed still.

"Give us a shove," someone shouted from its deck, and the

shipyard director seemed about to do that as he climbed on to the platform alongside the ship's cradle. There was a great grinding and roaring from her drag chains as the ship's weight took charge before she floated effortlessly into the water to the cheers of the crowd and the hooting and blaring of sirens.

II

The day had not started well for Frank. He had sent all his washing to the laundry and found himself without a white shirt an hour before he was due at Clydebank for the official lunch with the Queen. Luckily he was able to borrow a shirt from a friend, but his troubles weren't over: he was caught in a traffic jam on his way to Clydebank. When he arrived he barely had time to snatch a drink before he was accosted by a steel magnate who took him to task for encouraging Colvilles to build the strip mill at Ravenscraig.

"A disaster from the onset—there's not enough demand for sheet steel in Scotland. Interest rates and freight charges have made sales to the south uneconomic. You politicians have to take your share of the blame. If you people hadn't awarded another strip mill to Wales," he went on, "there would have been more demand for the output of Ravenscraig. It's all your fault!"

Frank managed to escape when he was introduced very briefly to the Queen. She was smaller than he had imagined, but much lovelier than her pictures, and her complexion really was peaches and cream. In her speech at the lunch for the VIPs the Queen said with obvious sincerity that the *Queen Mary* and the *Queen Elizabeth* were better known and loved than any other ships in the world and she had always had a special affection for them because they had been named after her mother and grandmother.

Frank should have been filled with excitement at his involvement in such an important event for Clydeside, but he felt unmoved by it, indeed he had never felt so low. It was all Daisy O'Malley's fault. After seventeen years of friendship she had suddenly lost interest in seeing him and when he had taken her to task she had announced that there was a man in her life whom she wanted to marry. He should have been happy for her, but he wasn't. He felt betrayed. Why hadn't she told him about this man some time before? And who was he? Somehow the idea of someone else sharing Daisy's life was repugnant to him. And yet he had no claim on her. She was just a friend, a chum, his mate ... When he saw her that evening he must put his selfishness aside and let her know that he was pleased at her news.

III

It was ten o'clock before Frank presented himself on the doorstep of Daisy's house in Whitecraigs. He shifted uneasily on the doorstep when no one answered the bell. Was Daisy still out with this ... this man she wanted to marry? He was relieved when she opened the door wearing trousers and an old T-shirt.

"You didn't go out with your new boyfriend like that, did you?"

There was no answering smile on Daisy's face and she seemed unaccountably nervous as she led him into the small study overlooking the garden. It was his favorite room in the house, simply furnished with a comfortable couch and a couple of armchairs. Although it was only September, he noticed that there was a blazing fire in the hearth.

"Phew! It's hot in here." Frank took off his jacket and tie before he sat down in the big armchair. As Daisy poured out the coffee they chatted about the launch.

"I was so proud to see you up there with the VIPs," she said.

"I'd never have become an MP if you hadn't encouraged me.'

"It's a pity your parents aren't alive. They'd have been proud of you today."

"My father proud of me? That's a joke!" Frank said bitterly.

Daisy put down her coffee cup. "Whenever your father is mentioned your face darkens. I've never pried, but tonight ... well, let's just say that after our long friendship I feel hurt you can't confide in me."

"You'd be shocked," Frank said, his face grim.

"Try me."

When he started talking, Frank had no intention of telling

Daisy the whole truth, but somehow once he began he couldn't stop. It all came out: the beatings, the hate, the appalling brutality his father had meted out to Briony Meldrum, culminating in the day they brought in the harvest . . .

IV

August 1939

The sun rose shyly, hesitating behind an opaque sky as if uncertain whether to put in an appearance. As the cloud drifted away, the orb in the sky turned from pale gold to searing yellow. By eleven o'clock it was blazing down on the fields where the Meldrums were harvesting the corn. The steady swish of the scythe had a rhythmic cadence as Angus Meldrum swept it from side to side, making sure that the grain fell neatly. Frank and Briony followed in his footsteps, gathering the corn into bundles and then using stalks of straw to bind them into a sheaf. Frank felt there was a therapy in the monotony of it and he was conscious that the tableau they made in the field echoed back over the centuries. On just such a day, in just such a place . . . The residue of folk memory gave Frank pride in his work despite his hatred of his father. He watched carefully as Briony tidied the ends of each sheaf and then laid them all in the same direction.

At midday they put down their implements and Briony walked back to the croft, reappearing a few minutes later with a wicker basket covered by a tablecloth. Underneath it were the floured baps and honey ale which she had prepared. Silently she handed her husband his share, then she walked across to where Frank was sitting and squatted down beside him. They were both apprehensive. That morning Angus had fought with a tinker who had tried to sell him some baskets and his face was covered in bruises.

"Angus has found out about David Elphinstone," Briony whispered.

Frank was aware of his stepmother's relationship with the Laird of Drumcraig, but he was concerned to hear that his father knew about it as well.

"He's in a really nasty mood. I'm frightened, Frank."

He patted her hand. "Don't worry, we'll be away from here

the minute the harvest is in. I don't know why you waited for it," he added.

"I know how much the harvest means to him," Briony said slowly. "I couldn't just walk off with you and leave him stranded."

"He'll have no such scruples about ill-using you," Frank replied grimly. "Look at him, he's drunk all that ale already."

"What are you two whispering about?" Angus shouted. "Frank, fetch me more ale."

"Get it yourself!"

Angus rose unsteadily to his feet and advanced to where they sat. He had an empty bottle in one hand and an iron bar in the other. "If you want a fight, I'm ready for you," he said aggressively.

"Frank, fetch him the ale," Briony intervened. "No more fights."

Frank hesitated and then went striding down the field towards the house. He was nearly there when an electrifying scream pierced the silence of the morning. In blind panic Frank raced back along the field. His father was drunk and dangerous; he should never have left him alone with Briony.

"I watched you yesterday on the moors with Elphinstone," he heard his father yelling. "Going to run away with him, are you? Well, he won't want you if you're crippled."

Dear God, let me be in time, Frank prayed silently, his lungs straining for more air as he pounded over the ground. He threw himself at his father and managed to push him to the side before the downward thrust of the iron bar reached Briony's legs. His father yelled in frustration, kicking out, slashing and cursing, but Frank's muscles had been strengthened by years of exercising and his hatred was at fever pitch. He wrestled the iron bar out of his father's grasp with one hand and used the other to aim a blow at his jaw. It had such venom behind it that his father rocketed back on to the boulder behind him and lay still. Frank turned to his stepmother. "Let's get out of here before the old bastard tries something else."

"Frank," Briony said in a hushed voice. "His eyes . . . They're wide open . . ."

Frank stepped across a pile of stones and gazed down at his father. He wasn't moving. Warily Frank bent over him and felt for his pulse. When he turned round his face was like chalk. "He's dead. I've killed him!"

At the inquest the pathologist said he'd found a bruise on Angus Meldrum's jaw and numerous contusions consistent with a bare-fist fight. He noted that his wife had seen the deceased fighting with a tinker on the day of the harvest. Although the police had failed to locate the tinker his presence was not considered necessary. The pathologist stated that death had been caused by the deceased's skull being pierced by his backward fall on to a pointed boulder. The coroner brought in a verdict of misadventure.

V

"The coroner's verdict was wrong," Frank said, as he finished his story. He walked across to the window so that he would not have to look in Daisy's eyes. "My father may have died accidentally, but I meant to kill him. By my book that makes me a murderer. Remember that night when you were delivering a baby in the Gorbals? You said you wanted to help the women and children, but you hated being near men who had blood on their hands . . . Now you know—I'm one of them."

He felt a glass of whisky being pressed into his hand. "Come and sit down," Daisy said. She guided him towards a chair and pushed him into it.

"You're the only one I've ever told," Frank muttered in a low voice, his head bent. "Alexandra thinks her father's death was an accident."

"But it was!" Daisy protested. "In any case, it can be argued that right and wrong are relative values. Would it have been morally wrong to kill your father in order to save your stepmother's life? I don't think so. You can't be condemned for acting the way you did."

She knelt at his side and pulled his face into the crook of her arm. "Why don't you have a good cry and get it out of your system?"

"Men aren't supposed to cry," Frank said in a muffled voice.

"I'm the doctor here. And I say men *should* cry more often. Oh Frank, my love, I feel heart-sorry for you." Daisy kissed the side of his cheek and held him close, and after a minute she felt his shoulders heaving. She kept hugging him till he was still.

"Made a right fool of myself, haven't I?" Frank said eventually. "But at least it was with you, Daisy. You're my best pal."

The words shattered Daisy's feeling of wellbeing and made her recall the original purpose of her invitation to Frank. And Catherine's plan.

"You've got that millstone off your neck, so let's celebrate," she said briskly. "I'll get some champagne from the fridge."

She came back carrying a bottle and began removing the cork in the deliberately awkward way Catherine had demonstrated. The champagne spurted out in a silver stream which soaked Frank's shirt and her own sweater. Before Frank had time to do more than brush away the liquid, she had dashed through to the kitchen and brought back another bottle of champagne which she proceeded to manhandle in the same inept way. Frank got up from his chair, trying to wipe the liquid from his shirt. "What *are* you doing, old thing? You're acting crazy."

"I'm not an old thing," Daisy snorted furiously. "I'm a woman, and I've been in love with you for seventeen years."

As Frank gaped at her, Daisy's voice rose several octaves. "I confided in Catherine on our holiday. She said . . . that if I soaked us both with champagne we'd have to remove our clothes to dry them. You see, she saw me naked in the shower . . . She said she bet I had a better body than most of your girlfriends, and if you saw it . . . Well, never mind. But just for the hell of it, you can *see* my beautiful body, Frank Meldrum. And then you can bloody well get out of my life!"

Daisy stripped off her sweater and jeans revealing that she had been wearing nothing underneath. Then she lay back on the couch, with her eyes tightly shut. "Go, Frank. Just go!"

The silence in the room was broken by a strange sound, halfway between a groan and a sigh. Daisy felt Frank's hand begin to trace the rosy areolas of her breasts with his fingers. Instinctively her nipples hardened and she heard Frank draw in his breath again as he began pulling off his own clothes with one hand while he held her down with the other.

"I don't want you escaping!" Frank muttered.

Escaping! Daisy thought hysterically. Wild horses couldn't

drag her away. She felt Frank's naked body on top of hers as he began kissing, touching, fondling, caressing. This can't be happening, I'm dreaming, she thought as she wrapped herself round him. Afterwards they lay in each other's arms, still joined together. Daisy was too happy to move and too frightened to speak. She felt sure she couldn't have measured up to the nubile blonde girlfriends Frank had dated over the years; she must have been a terrible disappointment to him.

Oh God, what will he say? Daisy wondered moments later, anxiety eating at her. And what on earth can *I* say to save my pride. But in the event pride did not come into it. After a few more minutes Frank said with a note of wonder in his voice, "I must have loved you for years, Daisy O'Malley. I think we'd better get married. Don't you?"

TWENTY-EIGHT

I

Ever since Robert had called out Alexandra's name at the moment of orgasm, Belinda had fixed her sights on exacting revenge: a revenge that would cause maximum distress to both Robert and Alexandra. When Robert announced that he was going to London with his father on a business trip for a few days she realized it was time to put her plan into action. She called out a firm of carriers to estimate the cost of transferring all her personal belongings, clothes, furniture, and furnishings, and fixed the date of the removal. She also gave them strict instructions not to telephone her at Rubislaw Terrace before then.

"If by any chance my plans have to be changed, I'll call you," she informed them briskly. But her plans did not have to be changed and, half an hour after Robert and his father had driven off towards London, the carriers arrived. Belinda was careful not to take away anything that belonged to her father-in-law, but she wasn't so picky about items that had been joint wedding presents, or gifts that she and Robert had exchanged. If she liked them, she took them. It wasn't legal, of course, but she knew perfectly well that Robert would never resort to the law to get them back. When the removal was complete and her belongings had been delivered to her new home, Belinda drove back to Aberdeen to wait for Robert's return from London. Revenge was like justice: it wasn't enough to be done, it had to be *seen* to be done.

She was watching at the window when Robert's car drew up at the front door. Belinda knew he would be alone because he had mentioned that his father intended to remain in London for another few days. As far as she was concerned that made everything real neat: when her father-in-law came back she would spin him a sob story that would put him on her side. She'd already prepared the ground with some not-so-subtle hints and had managed to cry on his shoulder at one point. The old man was a pushover if you fluttered your eyelashes at him.

"Hi!" she said as Robert came through the front door. "Had a good trip?"

"Tiring." He gave her a quizzical glance. "You look like the cat that got the cream . . ."

"Not the cream, honey! Just the bits and pieces that belong to me. And maybe a few that belong to you as well." She gestured with her free hand to indicate the absence of some pieces of furniture and the empty spaces on the walls where mirrors and pictures had been hanging.

"What are you up to now?" Robert asked wearily.

"The carriers took away my belongings last week. I'm leaving you! And I'm taking Cameron with me. He's already installed in his new home."

Robert put down the grip he had been holding. "If you're expecting me to be surprised, I'm not—especially after the way you've snapped and snarled at me lately."

"Can you blame me?" she asked, her voice tight with anger. "Why would I want to stay when you called out another woman's name in my bed?"

"Once. I did it once. And that was because I'd met up with Frank Meldrum. Oh, and lots of other things that made me think of her."

"Once is enough!" Belinda said angrily. "It explained a lot: the times you were remote from me, your lack of passion . . . You've never got over Alexandra, have you? You're still in love with her."

"Are you crazy? I can't stand Alexandra Semple. Ever since she set up in business she's been nibbling away at my empire. Meldrums are Armstrongs' biggest rivals!"

Exasperated, Robert shrugged off his coat and strode through to the sitting room where he made for the cocktail cabinet. Only it wasn't there. Belinda chortled at his expression of fury and pointed him to the decanter tray sitting on the sideboard. He poured himself a drink and carried it over to his chair by the fire.

Belinda followed him. "Don't you want to hold on to your

son? Aren't you going to try to persuade me to change my mind?"

He shrugged. "I've never been able to make you change your mind. As for Cameron, he's made no secret of the fact that he prefers mummy to daddy."

"You don't really care, do you?" she said bitterly as she perched on the arm of the chair opposite him

"I married you, didn't I?"

"That was because I snowballed you into it,." Belinda turned her head to the window. "I was happy in this old house for a few years. We seemed to get along real well. I knew you didn't love me, of course, but I thought in time . . ." She turned back to look at Robert, her eyes narrowed. "But you found it more and more difficult to keep up the pretense, didn't you?"

"Oh, for God's sake, leave it alone, will you?" Robert said, banging down his whisky glass. "I'm not in a mood to analyze the breakdown of our marriage. If you want a divorce I'll make no objections, as long as you'll give me access to Cameron. He might not care for *me*, but he's still my son."

Belinda felt her fury mounting as she surveyed him. She had been right: Robert wasn't fazed at all by her leaving him. But she was about to launch a little grenade into his lap that would shake him up good.

"I'm not going to divorce you, Robert; that would be too clean, too respectable. I fancy a little scandal—something that will make you a laughing stock. So . . . I'm going to move in with Adam at Drumcraig Castle."

This time she got the reaction she wanted. Robert put down his drink, his face suffused with anger as he leapt out of his chair and came towards her. "Going from one brother to another . . . You'll drag all our names in the mud! And taking Cameron with you!"

Belinda smiled, enjoying herself now. "Oh yes, the gossips will have a field day. They'll think Adam is better in the sack than you are. And they're right!"

Robert seized her by the shoulders and pulled her to her feet. "Are you telling me you've been sleeping with him?"

"Yes. For weeks and weeks and weeks. You thought you knew all about my affairs, didn't you? But I managed to keep this one quiet—till now." She laughed in his face. "Your sure hate the thought of being cuckolded by your own brother, don't you? And someone else we both know is going to hate the fact that I'll be living in Drumcraig Castle."

Belinda wrenched free from Robert's grasp and picked up the telephone by the window. She dialed a number and then nodded. "Alexandra? I reckoned you'd be home by this time of night. Remember that New Year's Eve many moons ago when Adam revealed that you were obsessed by Drumcraig Castle? Well, honey, I have bad news for you, I'm moving into it."

"You vindictive bitch!" Robert said softly and before she could stop him he slapped her hard across the face. Grimfaced, he strode from the room and stormed out of the house, slamming the door behind him. Belinda heard the squeal of tires as he drove off into the night.

"That'll teach you, you bastard!" Belinda shouted. And it would teach Alexandra as well. She hoped she felt sick as a dog.

II

New York, 1968
Although Alexandra had been intrigued by Felix Danziger's letter, it was 1968 before she visited New York to set up the delayed expansion of her property empire to the States. After an exchange of letters with Felix she arranged her flight and booked a room at the Pierre in Manhattan. At Kennedy airport a chauffeured Cadillac was waiting to transport her to the headquarters of Danziger Minerals in New York.

Despite the dull weather Alexandra was excited by her first glimpses of the city. As the Cadillac approached Manhattan she glanced through the windows at the towering skyscrapers: improbable confections of glittering glass and concrete which looked as if they'd been painted on the skyline in monochrome.

At the headquarters of Danziger Minerals she was met by Felix Danziger's secretary and escorted to the executive lift which zoomed up to a penthouse suite dominated by vast windows overlooking the river. The furniture was modernistic, black and white Bauhaus style. Across what seemed to be acres of space a man was walking towards her, his hands outstretched. "Hi there, and welcome to New York. Come and sit over here and let me mix you a drink."

While he busied himself at a drinks cabinet in the corner Alexandra tried to recover her equilibrium. For some reason Felix Danziger's letter had conjured up an image of a frail old man mulling over the past and wanting to make amends for his neglect, but there was nothing frail about Felix Danziger. He was a burly-looking man in his late forties with a square face and an aggressive chin. When he handed over Alexandra's drink his eyes seemed to devour every bit of her.

What have I got myself into, she wondered, as he gave her another slow appraising glance. Felix seemed to sense her discomfort and immediately set about putting her at ease by talking about the past.

"Toby Armstrong was my father's great buddy," Felix told her. "When he came to our house he used to sit drinking with him and spinning tales about Aberdeen. When his old housekeeper put him in touch with your mother again, he would read out bits of her letters to us. I think you'll be amazed at how much I overheard about your childhood," he added, his eyes twinkling, "and about Drumcraig Castle."

"He talked about Drumcraig?"

"Frequently. Said it meant nothing to him until after he'd lost it. So what's happened to the castle? And to the Armstrong-Meldrum feud?"

Alexandra found herself telling him about Tom Elphinstone and Belinda's news that she was moving into the castle with Adam.

"I'm determined to regain Drumcraig for the Meldrums," Alexandra confessed. "I want to keep that vow I made when my mother died."

"Here's hoping you will!" Felix said, raising his glass to her.

Alexandra found herself relaxing as she talked. Their shared knowledge of the past made him seem like an old friend instead of a new acquaintance. When she decided she ought to check in to her hotel Felix told her he'd placed one of his limos and a chauffeur at her disposal for her stay. Alexandra thought she'd be too excited to sleep, but the journey had exhausted her.

The next morning she woke up feeling refreshed and looking forward to her lunch with Felix at The Four Seasons. Over the *mélange* of seafood followed by grilled trout, they talked about possible ways of expanding Meldrums into the States.

"Have you heard of Abraham Levitt?" Felix asked. He explained that after the Second World War Levitt realized that war veterans would be looking for cheap homes, so he decided to build no-deposit small houses which would sell at $9,000. They proved such a success that he built bigger and better Levitt towns in New Jersey. "If I were in your position I'd aim at something similar—the principle, not the practice. I'm suggesting you set up a property company in Manhattan and hire guys to scout the country looking for areas with potential."

"By 'potential,' you mean places that stand a good chance of being developed?"

"Sure. Hell, that's all some developers do: buy up land and sit on it till it grows in value."

"And when it does," Alexandra said thoughtfully, "Meldrums could go into the construction business, as we've done in Britain."

"Wouldn't advise it," Felix said as he attacked his trout. "Too many legal complications for a firm like yours, and as for labor relations . . . It's a different ball game over here, Alexandra. If I were you I'd stick to buying and selling land. That'll give you a product that appreciates in value without capital being continually spent on it."

"I like that idea. It would mean I could tailor my acquisitions to my capital very neatly; though I might have to wait years before I realize a profit."

"No problem," Felix said easily, as he signaled to the waiter to bring the sweet trolley. "Since I own the controlling share in Danzigers I can arrange favorable loans for you."

"But why would you?" Alexandra asked so directly that he blinked.

"Would you believe me if I tell you it's because I want to repay that overdue debt?"

"No."

He laughed. "Aw, shucks, you're right. I'd forgotten all about my promise to my father until I read that article. How can I explain my motives? When you're a 'seen-it-all, done-it-all' guy like me you're always ferreting around for new stimuli, and when I saw your picture in the paper it gave me ideas.

Helping you could give me a new interest—with no strings attached," he added quickly as he studied the expression on her face.

"Seems to me I'm getting the best side of this bargain, so I accept," Alexandra said quickly.

"Great! Let's shake on it!"

His handshake was warm, firm, decisive: qualities which he displayed to the full in the hectic few days that followed as he helped her start the process that would lead to the setting-up of Meldrum Manhattan. In between seeing attorneys, accountants, and government agencies, Felix managed to whisk her off to enjoy the sights of New York and escort her to lunch or dinner.

"You've been marvelous," Alexandra said to him gratefully on their last night together. They were sitting in Felix's den in his Fifth Avenue apartment.

"I'm just an old wheeler-dealer," he said amiably.

"One smart enough to get in on the ground floor with the natural gas finds," Alexandra commented.

In 1959 a Shell-Esso combine had struck gas at Groningen in the north-east Netherlands and the oilmen began to explore the possibility of the Dutch gasfield extending across the North Sea to Britain. BP made the first big gas strike in the UK section of the North Sea and their success was followed by a second big strike by an American company, Continental Oil. By 1966 the Shell-Esso combine had struck it rich. And so had Felix Danziger.

"Wish Meldrums had done the same," Alexandra said regretfully. "What really bugs me is that Frank *told* me about the two rigs that John Brown's were building. When they struck gas on the famous 'fairway' leading to the Dutch coast I could have kicked myself."

"You can't be ahead of the game all the time."

"You're just trying to console me because I missed out. Did I tell you that Robert Armstrong persuaded his board to invest heavily in gas?"

"Sure did—with that same tight smile that comes over your face whenever that guy's name is mentioned. Did you two ever have something going?" Felix asked curiously.

Alexandra was about to give him a firm denial. Then she shrugged. "When we were students at Glasgow University."

"And now you're the best of enemies?"

"Our companies are growing fast in the same areas. One of these days there's not going to be room for both of us."

"Oh boy, that old feud runs deep and strong!"

"So deep that I get angry whenever I think Robert Armstrong has got ahead of me. As he has with natural gas. There's a rumor that it's going to provide a third of the UK's energy. If that's the case, Armstrongs will be in for a bonanza."

"Stay cool! I invested heavily initially, but I've pulled back a bit. David Barran, the Deputy Chairman of Shell, came to New York last November," Felix recalled. "Know what he said? He warned everyone not to pitch their expectations too high about the potential impact of natural gas. So if the Armstrongs have put all their eggs in that basket, they may get their fingers burned—if you'll excuse me mixing my metaphors!"

Alexandra laughed. "I suppose it's too late for Meldrums to invest now?"

"If I were you I'd forget gas and start snooping around for oil. Shell are exploring the north-east coast of Scotland."

"Most people think they're hunting for fool's gold!"

"They've found gas. Who's to say they won't find oil? Our geologists say there's as good a chance off the Scottish coast as anywhere else. Let me tell you about Phillips. They've been working off the Norwegian coast backed by a consortium with Belgian, French, Norwegian and Italian interests."

"Prospecting for oil?"

"So far with no success. But it would be a good time to buy in because their drilling budget has run away with $30 million and head office in the U.S. is getting scratchy about it. Some people are beginning to doubt the wisdom of spending so much money in a remote area off Norway."

"It's a good time to buy in, but it's a bit risky. I like it. You're beginning to know me, Felix."

"I'd like to know you even better," he said softly and kissed her gently on the lips.

Alexandra drew away from him. "It's been years since anyone . . ."

"Not even your husband?"

"Malcolm . . . had a problem."

"My only problem is keeping my hands off you," Felix said as he looked at her. "Since the moment I saw you I've wanted you. You've felt it too. I've seen your hands tremble when I've touched you, watched you shiver when I brushed against your breast. If ever there's a woman who's needing to be taken to bed it's you, Alexandra!"

Without further ado he hauled her to her feet and guided her towards his bedroom.

"Felix, I don't know, I'm not sure . . ."

"I'm sure," he said decisively.

When they were naked she began to speak, but he pressed him palm over her mouth and pushed her gently down on the big double bed. Alexandra felt flickers of desire sparking through her as he caressed her breasts, but when his fingers probed between her legs the flickers exploded into a fireball and she became a woman possessed, offering her body up to him with a passion that left them both breathless.

"Jesus!" he said as he lay back for a rest.

Gently she kissed away the beads of sweat around his eyes. Then her lips moved downwards till she was at his center, kissing, pulling, arousing . . . pressing him into her again, tightening her vaginal muscles till once again they found a rhythm that rocked the bed and their senses.

Afterwards Alexandra lay back, sated, a golden glow seeping into all her secret places. "You were right," she said, "I needed that." They both burst out laughing at the understatement, then moved together again.

When he kissed her goodbye at the airport he whispered in her ear, "Don't forget what I said about the possibility of oil being discovered off Scotland. Guess right on this one, babe, and you'll *really* make a fortune!"

III

The weather was chilly when Alexandra returned from the States, but she felt warm and alive and invigorated. There was a note from Catherine saying that she was still staying with one of her friends. When her daughter finally returned to the house in Barnton, Alexandra was relieved to see she was looking much better.

"I don't know how you can bear to stay on in this house," Catherine said as they sat in the lounge after dinner. "You should make a fresh start somewhere else. By the way, something really exciting's come up. Remember I mentioned a crowd who are going backpacking round Europe for the Easter holidays? Well, one of the girls is ill and I've been invited in her place."

"But Catherine, it's not that long since your trip to Florence."

"So? If it's money that's worrying you I've got my savings," Catherine said aggressively.

Alexandra got up from her chair and sat down on the couch beside her daughter. "You know money's not a problem. Your father left you . . . "

"I don't want to talk about him," Catherine said, putting her hands over her ears. "I just want to get away—to some place where no one will mention his name!"

"I can understand that. Perhaps it would be a good idea for you to travel abroad."

"What about you?" Catherine asked.

Alexandra hesitated. It was still too early to mention Felix to her daughter. "I think I'll go up to Aberdeen at Easter. I can work from our office there. A . . . friend suggested I check up the oil prospects off the north-east coast."

IV

Alexandra stood at the harbor in Aberdeen and gazed out across the limitless expanse of the North Sea. Was it really possible that oil might lie beneath those cold inhospitable waters? Most Aberdonians viewed the oil companies' surveys as a waste of money. Alexandra turned her back on the harbor and began walking towards Union Street. Bannons had one of their estate agency offices near the center of the town. It was time to pay them a visit and look over their properties for sale.

Brian Bannon beamed at her when she opened the agency door. "Every time I read something about you I tell anyone who'll listen that I gave you your start in property."

"You taught me a lot, Brian. How are things?" she asked as he led her into a big room at the back of the agency.

"Bannons have agencies all over Britain now. They're small but profitable—except for the Aberdeen branch. It's not doing well at all. I'll sell it to you if you like."

"I dipped my toe in the estate agency business once and I bombed!"

"Ah, but think of the experience you've gained since then," he joked. "Meldrums seems to be adept at turning round ailing businesses."

"Are you trying to con me into buying an ailing business? Actually I'm surprised Bannons Aberdeen isn't doing well. I've been checking up on land and property in the Grampian region and I'm astonished at how low the prices are."

"Aberdonians don't seem to have the cash to buy much at the moment. I've had one of those huge mansions in Queen's Road on the market for the past year."

"Queen's Road? When I was a little girl I used to think the houses there were palaces. Mark you, some of them are pretty big."

"So is this Highgate House!" Brian said as he pushed some particulars in front of her. "It got its name from its high gates."

"How many rooms?"

"About twenty. The west wing has six bedrooms, two drawing rooms, and a dining room: all very spacious. And there's a small sitting room and study. The east wing has six rooms; they're big as well. It used to be two semi-detached mansions, then a family converted it into one house, though they kept the separate back and front doors."

Which would be very useful, Alexandra mused, if Catherine ever wanted a flat of her own. Catherine could stay in the east wing, she could stay in the west, and they would each have independence.

"There's also a guest suite of three rooms on the ground floor, and servants' residential quarters over the kitchen." Brian shrugged. "A magnificent house, but not in very good condition, I'm afraid."

"You mean: 'Property with interesting potential,'" Alexandra teased.

"I see you haven't forgotten the estate agency jargon." He stopped talking when he saw Alexandra studying the details very closely. "The asking price is a thief's bargain, but you can't seriously be interested in a place that size?"

"My headquarters are in Edinburgh. All the same," Alexandra said dreamily, "it looks impressive, doesn't it?"

"Tell you what," Brian said. "I'll take you to see it if you promise to think about buying Bannons Aberdeen. I want it off my hands. I don't see much potential up here, but you can probably make it work!"

V

"Well?" Felix asked when he phoned her at Meldrums' Edinburgh office. "Do the Aberdonians think there's oil off their coastline?"

"They think the surveyors need their brains oiled for even suggesting such a thing!"

"So you came away empty-handed?"

"Not exactly," Alexandra said happily. "I acquired an ailing estate agency office and a dilapidated twenty-roomed house in Queen's Road. My mother would have been thrilled. She had nothing, nothing."

"I've only known you a short time, Alexandra, but I can see that your past still looms too large in your life. Can't you let it go?"

"I don't want to. There are still too many scores to settle!"

TWENTY-NINE

I

1970

William hadn't been feeling well for months. Although he was losing weight and seemed to have a permanent cough, he refused to see a doctor on the premise that his malaise would pass. But when he collapsed one morning as he was walking to the office, matters were taken out of his hands. He was rushed into hospital where he underwent a battery of tests. Lung cancer was diagnosed.

"How long have I got?" he asked the specialist. "I want the truth."

"Difficult to say. The cancer has metastasized—spread through your body."

"Then I'm done for," William said resignedly. He called Robert and Adam to his bedside and gave them the news. "It's up to you two now. You'll be in charge of Armstrongs when I die."

Robert frowned. "You always said that I would be Chairman. I've been senior to Adam ever since we joined the firm."

"I'm too tired to think," William groaned, his face gray. "Be democratic. Let the board decide."

"A good idea, father," Adam agreed, his eyes alight.

II

Robert stood by the window of his office, hands thrust into his pockets, desolate at the prospect of his father's impending death. He looked down at the street where people were clutching their hats as a fresh breeze blew in from the north. On a day like this he longed to be at sea with one of the trawlers in the Armstrong fleet instead of spending so much time behind a desk. There was nothing like the buck and heave of a ship in a choppy sea to make you feel gloriously alive. The Armstrong trawlers were still reaping rich dividends for their owners and the skippers were saying that 1970 might be the best year since the war. Only the inshore fleet were complaining. They were objecting to the high costs of fish-handling by the dockers registered in the Dock Labour Scheme. Robert had heard that the inshore fishermen were threatening to boycott Aberdeen and use Peterhead instead. He hoped that wouldn't happen.

Reluctantly Robert turned back to his desk and his analysis of the Armstrong empire, which now had a wide diversity of interests. Apart from the shipyard, the trawling fleet, and the ships' chandlers there were subsidiaries for property, construction, commercial and industrial development, fish-processing and curing. The ships' chandlers weren't doing well, but he was optimistic about their future, unlike Adam, who was determined to push through the sale of the chandlers simply because Robert opposed it.

Since their father's pronouncement that the board should decide who was to be the next Chairman Adam had become increasingly aggressive. Robert balled his fingers into a fist. His father had been ill and confused when he'd made that edict, but Robert had no power to go against it. Adam had made sure of that by passing on the information to every member of the board.

Robert perused the papers in front of him. He was the one who had persuaded the board to invest in natural gas, but unfortunately the prospect of low gas prices had diminished the operators' enthusiasm and he was now beginning to wonder if oil were the better prospect. Adam disagreed. He had stated at a board meeting that even if oil were found under the North Sea the cost of extracting it could prove prohibitive. Most Aberdonians agreed with him and looked skeptically at the survey ships which had started appearing off their coast. "Richt daft-looking things," they said dismissively. Yet in 1969 an American company, Amoco, partnered by the Gas Council, had moved a rig 180 miles east of Aberdeen and there were rumors about an oil strike. Throughout the months that followed other rigs persisted with their search despite being battered by wind and waves.

Robert was impressed that Shell-Esso and BP seemed so determined to find oil off the north-east coast of Scotland. Admittedly Phillips had struck oil in the North Sea off the coast of Norway, but whether or not the Ekofisk oilfield would prove commercially viable was a question that no one had yet answered.

Robert looked up as his door was pushed open after a perfunctory knock. It was Adam with some papers. He came round to Robert's shoulder and glanced at the data on oil companies spread out on the desk. "Still trying to make up your mind? Very indecisive, aren't you?"

"Only in some matters," Robert replied crisply. "I lost no time in suing Belinda for divorce!"

"And I lost no time in marrying her," Adam retorted smugly.

III

When Adam arrived back at Drumcraig he found Belinda curled up in the big armchair in their drawing room on the sixth floor of the castle. He was glad to see that Cameron, as usual, was out somewhere. Adam couldn't stand the boy—a spoilt brat if ever there was one. He felt the familiar pull of passion as he looked at his wife. Belinda's blonde hair was tousled, her cheeks were glowing and her eyes shone with health and energy. She no longer looked like a teenager, but she could have passed for a girl in her twenties.

"Kiss, kiss," she said as he bent over her. To his surprise she pulled him closer. "I was just thinking . . . Wouldn't it be wonderful if you could persuade Tom to part with Drumcraig?"

"He'll never sell it."

"Not willingly, no. But if we encourage him to spend all his money, one of these days he'll be short of cash. I'll never leave you if you own Drumcraig, Adam. Worth a thought, isn't it?"

Prising Drumcraig away from Tom Elphinstone would be quite an achievement, Adam mused: one that would give pleasure to Belinda and pain to Alexandra Meldrum. It was certainly worth a thought.

IV

Funchal, the capital of Madeira, lies in a spacious bay backed by steep hills in which nestle the typical houses of the region: sparkling white, red-roofed, and set in glossy green vegetation lit by the brilliance of tropical flowers: scarlet poinsettias, pink, purple and white bougainvillaea, and flaming peach strelitzias.

Alexandra had come on a brief holiday to Madeira the previous year and had been so enchanted by this island of flowers that she had bought a hillside villa which the Portuguese call a *quinta*. The locals had told her to be sure to come back in the spring when the jacarandas were in bloom. Alexandra decided to invite Alan Gillian and Boyd Brown and their wives to share part of her spring holiday, and she flew out with Catherine to put the *quinta* in order before her guests arrived.

"Look at the jacarandas!" she said to Catherine as they drove through Funchal. Violet-blue flowers blossomed amidst the delicate green foliage which hung like a canopy over Funchal's main street.

Catherine was captivated by Madeira and the day after they arrived she set up her easel in the garden. On one side of the *quinta* was a magnificent view of Funchal and the rocky coastline, on the other a steep cliff towered to the sky. Catherine was painting the cliff and the miniature figures which moved up and down the precipitous face tending tiny strips of land. On Madeira arable ground was so scarce it was never wasted. Alexandra lay in a recliner watching her daughter paint. She was enjoying the scents of the sugar cactus and vanilla bush beside her chair. After an hour or so in the sun she mentioned that she was thirsty.

"I'll get a drink for you," Catherine volunteered.

From the shade of her sunhat Alexandra watched her bikini-clad daughter lope across the grass to the house. She was a long-legged girl with flowing hair that gleamed blue and black in the sunlight. Just like Briony Meldrum: Catherine was the image of her grandmother. She came back with the drinks and sat in a chair beside her mother. "This beats attending classes!"

"I thought you liked art school."

"I did at first, but now I'm bored. I've told them I'm leaving in June."

Alexandra sat up so abruptly she knocked her sunhat to the ground. "This is the first I've heard of it."

Catherine grinned. "I knew you'd blow your top so I delayed telling you till we got here."

"But Catherine, you'll only have been there a year!"

"I know. And that's enough. Painting is a great hobby, mum, but I've discovered that I don't want to make a career of it. I'm 18 now. God, I'll be 19 this December!"

"Would you think of joining me in Meldrums?" Alexandra asked tentatively. Her daughter had never shown any interest in working for the family business, but Alexandra kept hoping she might change her mind.

"Not now. Not ever. There's more to life than money."

"That's easy to say when you've never been without any. If you'd been as poor as I . . ."

"Please don't rerun *that* record! So you were poor and you wanted to get rich. My generation are different. We want to change things."

"What are you going to do?" Alexandra asked.

"Go round the world. I want to find out what life's all about: there has to be a meaning to it all. And before you ask, I don't need you to finance me."

"So how are you going to live?"

"Cooking, cleaning . . . that kind of thing. I thought I might write some articles. And paint. I've already sold two seascapes."

"Why didn't you *tell* me?" Alexandra asked in an aggrieved tone.

Catherine shrugged. "It's no big deal."

Alexandra was silent. Were other teenagers as uncommunicative with their parents as Catherine was with her?

"If you go on this world trip, when will you come home?"

"Who knows! Cameron Armstrong told me his chum spent a year travelling, but some people stay abroad for five years."

Alexandra tried to keep her voice calm. "When did you meet Cameron Armstrong?"

"Ages ago at a party. Boy, is he a *creep*!"

"You didn't like him?"

"He's not together."

Alexandra relaxed. At least that was something to be thankful for. If her daughter had taken up with Robert's son that could have caused problems. He was, after all, Catherine's half-brother. She would have told her daughter the truth years ago but for the fact that Catherine had adored Malcolm and would have been devastated to discover he wasn't her father. Alexandra glanced at Catherine, aware that Robert would have been proud of his beautiful daughter. And would probably have been better at handling her than I've been, she thought.

The jasmine rustled as a tiny lizard searched amidst its foliage and when Alexandra picked a crumb from the table it darted out and nibbled from her hand. The lizards were tame, the garden peaceful. Alexandra closed her eyes and dozed in the sun.

The house party was a great success. The Gillians and Boyds toured the island, swam in the lido at the Savoy Hotel, and took Alexandra and Catherine to dine at Reid's. On the last day of their visit Marjorie Gillian and Rosemary Boyd announced that they wanted to buy some presents in Funchal.

"Go the the Casa do Turista," Alexandra suggested. "It's an Aladdin's cave of a shop in an old Portuguese house off the main street. It's got exquisite embroideries, ceramics, linen, souvenirs . . . Ask for Nina; she runs the place. She'll tell you what to buy. By the way, there's free wine-tasting there . . ."

"Oh no!" Boyd groaned. "Wine will make the girls want to buy more. Well, I'm not going on a shopping spree."

"I'm opting out too!" Alan said firmly. "Catherine?"

"I'm taking my easel to Camara de Lobos. Churchill used to paint the view there. I'd like to see it."

"So would I," Boyd said. "Tell you what, Alan and I will go with you and leave our wives to their shopping."

"I'll join the painting safari,"' Alexandra decided.

Camara de Lobos was a tiny fishing village on the outskirts of Funchal. Catherine set up her easel at a spot which was supposed to have been Churchill's favorite viewpoint. Black fishing nets were draped across the beach, exotic banana plantations formed a backdrop, and in the distance loomed the purple shadow of Cabo Giaro, one of the highest sea cliffs in the world.

While Catherine painted, Alexandra sat in the café sipping iced drinks with Boyd and Alan. Alan's white hair and piercing blue eyes were still unusual enough to make people stare in admiration at him. Very few people ever stared at Boyd. He had always classed himself as an "ugly bugger," but Alexandra decided that age had improved his looks; his silver hair made him seem distinguished. She'd first met Alan and Boyd when she was 19—twenty years before. They were on the board of Meldrums now and were close friends.

"You're looking thoughtful," Boyd said presently. "Dreaming of Drumcraig?"

"As ever." Alan and Boyd had each tried to help her achieve her heart's desire, but Tom Elphinstone had remained obdurate: Drumcraig Castle wasn't for sale at any price, especially to Alexandra.

"Felix is coming out soon. I thought you'd be dreaming about him," Alan said with a suggestive wink.

Alexandra grinned. Since Malcolm had become a Meldrums consultant, Boyd and Alan had frequently traveled to New York to discuss business with him. They were well aware of Alexandra's special relationship with him and weren't above teasing her about it.

"Felix would have been here earlier," she said, "but he wants to be present at the Petrofina shareholders' meeting in Brussels."

Alan nodded. "Ah yes, the Ekofisk field. All the oilmen say it's commercially viable, but today we should hear firm figures."

"Meldrums have committed a lot of money to it—another high-risk investment," Boyd said edgily.

Alexandra leant forward and patted Boyd's hand. "Being a member of the Meldrums board can't be easy for you. I know I take too many chances for your liking."

"You do," he agreed, "but since you seem to be right nine times out of ten I've learned to respect your judgment. I admit I err on the side of caution."

"Whereas I prefer to live dangerously," Alan joked. "That's why we make a wonderful team."

He was right, Alexandra reflected. The calibre of the Meldrum main board was excellent, but Alan and Boyd were undoubtedly her chief lieutenants. Felix, of course, was in a category of his own. He was continuing to help her with Meldrum Manhattan which had become a flourishing subsidiary of her main company; land was being bought and sold, and profits were high. Alexandra flew out to New York at least once a month and whenever she was there Felix entertained her lavishly during the day and made love to her in the evenings. These nights of passion released a thousand tensions and she welcomed them, but regretted that passion had never turned into love.

She glanced at her watch. The Petrofina meeting would still be in progress, but she wanted to be back at the *quinta* waiting for Felix's phone call. Boyd and Alan realized she was restless and paid the bill. Catherine glanced up briefly from her painting when she saw them all preparing to leave and said she'd prefer to stay.

"I wonder if our wives have returned from their shopping trip," Alan speculated aloud as Alexandra turned the car into the driveway leading up to the *quinta*.

The house was empty apart from the two servants who were busy concocting lunch. The two men wandered out on to the verandah and Alexandra went up to her bedroom. She was in the middle of washing her face when the telephone rang. She grabbed a towel to dry her hands and picked up the receiver.

"That was Felix," she announced as she rushed out on to the patio where Alan and Boyd were relaxing. "The President of Belgian Petrofina concern has . . . just told the shareholders that the Ekofisk well has been tested at 7,000 barrels of oil per day. Lots of other technical data, but the bottom line is that Ekofisk is three times better than they'd hoped. Wonderful!"

The two men smiled and came forward to kiss her. "This calls for a drink!"

Alexandra's eyes were glittering. "Felix said on the phone that the major oil companies have already committed money and resources in forward planning in Scotland. And so should we!"

Boyd looked at her warily. "So?"

"We already have an office in place. And an estate agency. But we'll have to expand much faster than I'd originally . . ."

"Whoa!" Boyd exclaimed. "Don't expand too fast or Meldrums will start having cash-flow problems."

By evening the Boyds and Gillians had returned to Scotland with Catherine, and Alexandra was on the patio of the *quinta* wrapped in Felix's arms. Despite the vigor of Felix's personality he was a gentle lover and he never forgot her needs in pursuit of his own. Alexandra felt tears pricking her eyelids as she looked at the firefly flicker of lights in Funchal bay. She wished so much that she could love Felix as he deserved, but with him she never experienced that ecstasy that she'd had with Robert Armstrong. But then she'd been in love with Robert . . .

"Tell you what!" Felix said suddenly. "Why don't we celebrate by spending a few days in Paris? We'll sail up the Seine in a *bateau mouche*, wine and dine royally, and I'll buy you a painting in Montmartre."

Alexandra unfolded herself from his arms. "I think I'd rather give Montmartre a miss."

"Ghosts?" he asked shrewdly. "Isn't it time you banished them?"

"Maybe you're right. Love me again, Felix, love me!"

Afterwards he kissed her gently. "There now, did I banish your ghosts?"

"Of course!" she replied at once; and if it was said too quickly for truth he did not seem to notice.

V

It was midnight and the streets of Aberdeen were deserted. Robert was lying beside Melanie Bradford, his secretary and his new mistress. She was a desirable girl and very affectionate, but once they'd made love he had no wish to linger beside her. Since he was aware that she would have been offended by a too-hasty departure he usually folded her in his arms and thought of other things: the latest deal at Armstrongs; whether he would play golf at the weekend; Alexandra Meldrum . . .

He and Adam had hatched out a scenario for the takeover of Meldrums. They appreciated that they would have to go about it very carefully since Alexandra had become a woman of consequence and her brother Frank was an increasingly influential MP. Annoyingly, when journalists mentioned Frank Meldrum they often referred to his connection with Alexandra Semple, "the barefoot millionairess" as she was dubbed by the press. It was all good publicity for Meldrums. Still, there was an election coming up, Robert mused, as he hugged Melanie closer to him. Maybe Frank Meldrum would lose his seat. Robert felt he would have enough problems trying to take over Alexandra's company without having to contend with Frank Meldrum MP hovering in the background.

VI

June 1970

The rain was sheeting down so hard Frank felt it icing his face. He hurried to the hall where he was making the last speech of his election campaign. He wasn't optimistic about Labour's prospects. Although they had managed to nationalize steel and build new towns, hospitals, houses, bridges, and airports, the heavy industries in Scotland were in the doldrums.

Shipbuilding was a prime example of a dream that had failed. The *Queen Elizabeth II* had been plagued with so many setbacks since her launch in 1967 that she'd left on her first commercial voyage months late, and Upper Clyde Shipbuilders, the consortium that had been vaunted as heralding a new era of cooperation between unions and management, was in trouble. There would be questions about UCS tonight, for sure, and how was he going to answer them? With a politician's bland assurance that all would be well? Or with the truth? Frank had a feeling that if he told the truth he'd lose his seat and his party bosses would see that he wasn't reselected.

From the mixed reception which greeted him on arrival at the hall Frank knew he was in for trouble. He managed to state the case for Labour as succinctly as possible, but inevitably he was heckled about rising unemployment and the sad state of Upper Clyde Shipbuilders.

"The government now has a forty-nine per cent share in UCS, so why is it doing so badly?" a voice yelled from the back of the hall.

"UCS inherited £12 million worth of losses on existing contracts," Frank began . . .

"To which it added nearly £10 million of its own!" the heckler replied.

Frank was prevented from speaking again and again. Eventually he lost his temper and banged his papers down on the podium in front of him. "It's my opinion—and I stress it's personal—that UCS are taking too narrow margins on contracts because they know the government will pay the bill. Management are at fault, but so are the unions," he went on. "Some are too bloody-minded to appreciate that their demands could wreck hopes for prosperity. Eric Yarrow is right. Unless trade unions and management show more flexibility, shipbuilding on the Clyde won't survive!"

There was stunned silence before uproar broke out as the union men present voiced their disapproval of his disloyalty. Frank saw his constituency Chairman glare at him, but he didn't care. He was tired of lies and half-truths and if his candor had ruined his election chances, so be it! All he wanted now was to get home to Daisy. She was the center of his life and every day he thanked God he'd found out he loved her before it was too late.

VII

Daisy was looking out for Frank at the window of their flat in Hyndland. After their marriage she had kept on working as a doctor in her father's practice in the Gorbals until he decided to retire.

"Won't dad be bored?" she had asked her mother.

"No. Your father and I are going to emigrate to Australia. It's where I was born and it's where I want to die. We'll miss you, Daisy, but you've got Frank, and we know you'll both come out and visit us. I hope Alexandra will, as well. I feel very proud that I was one of the first to see her potential."

"I'd forgotten you backed her," Daisy said absently.

"Not for very long. After a year or two she didn't need my help. Are you going to keep on working, Daisy?" she went on.

At first Daisy had thought she would continue working in the Gorbals practice, but she gave it up when she found she was expecting a baby. Now she patted her tummy protectively as she looked out of the window; her baby was due in December.

She caught sight of Frank trudging up the road and ran to the door to greet him. "Was it bad?" she asked.

"I've blown it, Daisy girl—told truths instead of lies."

"At least the election campaign is over. You go and sit by the fire and watch the news, and I'll pour you a beer."

The pundits on television were predicting that Harold Wilson would be re-elected. They were wrong. On 19 June the Tories were in power, Edward Heath was installed at 10 Downing Street, and the inquest had already begun at Labour Party headquarters. The only consolation for Frank was that he was returned with an increased majority and was billed as one of the few politicians who was man enough to tell unpalatable truths.

Frank's confidence in himself was restored and as Daisy began to acquire that special bloom which so often goes hand in hand with pregnancy he felt life couldn't be better. His only worry concerned Alexandra. Every time he picked up the paper he read of another acquisition she had made, and lately she'd been working so hard that she looked strained and tired. He made up his mind to give her a good talking-to. But he wasn't given the chance to give her any lectures: the next time Alexandra phoned she took his breath away by announcing that she had just got engaged to Felix Danziger.

VIII

The first oil strike in British waters was Amoco's Montrose Field in 1969, but by the summer of 1970 it began to look as if other oilmen's dreams were coming true was well. Phillips reported an oil field in the North Sea's Scottish waters and BP moved one of their rigs 110 miles north east of Aberdeen.

"I can't believe it!" Alexandra said to Felix when he made one of his frequent phone calls from New York. "The rigs are coming nearer and nearer. They'll be drilling in the harbor next!"

"There's a whisper that BP have suggested sharing drilling costs with other groups. That should be a bad sign, but I had lunch with a bunch of oilmen in Texas yesterday and they're optimistic."

Alexandra's grasp on the phone tightened. She had persuaded her board to invest heavily in oil and oil-related developments. If BP made a big strike Aberdeen's fortunes could be transformed overnight and oilmen would flock to the city from all over the world. The thought of it made her bones tingle.

"When are you coming to the States to marry me?" Felix asked.

"Oh Felix . . . I can't come right now. I've just transferred my headquarters from Edinburgh to Aberdeen and moved into the house I bought two years ago in Queen's Road. If it's all going to happen in the north east I want to be on the spot."

"Sound like the moves a career lady would make. Only, where do I fit into the picture?"

"It doesn't make any difference to our plans. We're engaged and we agreed that when we get married . . ."

"I know. We agreed that marriage wouldn't make any difference to your career, but what kind of marriage is it going to be? You at one end of the Atlantic, me at the other . . ."

"Some couples manage it . . ."

"And pretty rare birds they are too!"

"Well, so are we!" she replied spiritedly.

Felix laughed. "I suppose you're right. Anyway, have I any choice? Now how about fixing a date for the wedding?"

"Let's wait awhile. We haven't been engaged for long."

"Okay, okay. I suppose I shouldn't push my luck about a date."

"You're so understanding, Felix." Too understanding, she thought suddenly.

"You'll keep me posted about the BP well," she went on anxiously. "Your friends in New York seem to hear news first."

"London's pretty hot too. So is the Hague. Royal Dutch Shell seems to know if anyone breaks wind!"

It was October before Felix heard a rumor that BP's well in block 21/10 was looking good. A few days later BP issued a cautious statement that "indications of hydrocarbons had been found," but they dismissed reports of a big oil find as mere speculation.

"Oh no!" Alexandra wailed, worried about Meldrums' massive investment. "Please tell me you're still hopeful, Felix."

"I am. Oil companies like BP have to be careful how they

word their press releases. If they weren't, they could cause turmoil on the markets. Have patience."

Alexandra put down the phone, anxiety making her clasp her hands tightly together. She wished Catherine were still at home, but once Catherine had helped her move house to Aberdeen she had taken off on her backpacking trip round the world. Work had been the best antidote to the moody blues that followed Catherine's departure, but it did not help her tension now as the days passed and there was still no announcement from BP. Alexandra felt so restless after a particularly worrying board meeting that she phoned Daisy. Daisy was in her seventh month of pregnancy and complained of feeling weary. She confessed that she was also a little scared. As a doctor, she knew the risks of having a first baby at the age of 39.

"Come and stay with me," Alexandra suggested.

"Not possible. Frank needs me."

"How is Frank?"

"Worried about Upper Clyde Shipbuilders now that Yarrows have left it."

"He can't have been too surprised. After Yarrows merged with UCS their profits began dwindling."

"Frank appreciates that, but he's really concerned about the future of UCS. If it has one!"

"Surely the government will never let it go to the wall?"

"I think the government are beginning to think of it as a lame duck. I mean, do *you* believe they'll subsidize it for much longer?"

"Frankly, I haven't been thinking too much about UCS lately; I'm much too concerned about Meldrums' investments in oil and oil-related businesses."

"What about Armstrongs?" Daisy asked. "Are your rivals turning their sights towards oil too?"

"I don't know, but I hear old Mr. Armstrong is dying and no one knows who's going to succeed him as Chairman."

IX

William Armstrong's funeral was one of the biggest Aberdeen had seen in years and after it was over Robert felt a great sense of loss. He wished he'd made a bigger effort to draw close to his father, but he knew regrets were useless, nor did he have time to indulge in them. A new Chairman of Armstrongs had to be appointed.

At the board meeting the subject of investment in North Sea oil was the first item on the agenda. Robert drew the board's attention to BP's well in block 21/10 and their hopes for it as a pointer for the future.

"It's all pie in the sky," Adam declared contemptuously. "Not all that long ago the Chairman of BP said to Reuters that he didn't expect there to be a major oilfield in the North Sea. Anyway, BP have dismissed speculation about a big find. So I vote that we sell the shipyard, the chandlers, and the land. We've been offered such good prices for all of them we'd be crazy to keep them."

Robert gestured to his secretary and she began distributing sheets of facts and figures to the board members. "My sources are optimistic about BP's chances of making a big oil strike in block 21/10. If they do, the shipyard, chandlers, and land will be invaluable for oil and oil-related developments. My decision is to postpone selling them."

Adam leapt to his feet. "Members of the board have expressed doubts to me about some of your decisions, isn't that right, Ker?" He nodded to Ker Howie, the Marketing Director.

"There's something in what Adam says," Ker agreed. "I trust Adam's judgment."

Dickie Peacock, the Sales Director, stood up. "If there's even the slightest possibility of an oil boom on our doorstep we should follow Robert's advice."

So, Robert thought, battle lines were being drawn up, but before he could speak, Adam once more commanded the board's attention.

"I think the board should delay electing a Chairman for another month. We should know by then whether BP have struck oil in commercial quantities. If they haven't, I suggest my brother's judgment will have proved faulty. And since by then we'll have lost the buyer for the shipyard, the chandlers, and the land, perhaps the board will wonder whether Robert should be elected Chairman."

"We will indeed!" Ker Howie echoed.

The discussion swayed back and forth for another hour, but at the end of it the board agreed to delay election of a new Chairman.

Robert was in a rage when he returned to his room. It was damnable the way Adam had managed to manipulate the board. It looked as if the chairmanship of Armstrongs was going to depend on whether or not BP found oil in block 21/10. That night when he took Melanie Bradford to bed he made love to her more savagely than he'd ever done before. "I'm sorry," he apologized, "I shouldn't take my frustration out on you."

"Don't apologize, I enjoyed it," Melanie purred. "Robert, now that you're divorced, have you thought about marrying again?"

X

Alexandra was glancing through the property section of the *Glasgow Herald* when she noticed a stately home for sale in the Trossachs, that vast area of woodland, mountain and loch twenty miles from Glasgow. The mansion looked like Buckingham Palace.

"Needs renovation," the advertisement stated: "Ideal for conversion into a palatial hotel."

Alexandra rolled the phrase round her tongue. Palatial Hotels? No. Country House Hotels? No, she was sure she had seen that used by someone else. Meldrum Trossachs? Yes, she liked that. And Meldrum Trossachs could be followed by Meldrum Loch Lomond, Meldrum Deeside, Meldrum London, maybe even Meldrum New York? She pushed the paper away, beginning to regret that she had used so much capital expanding her base in Aberdeenshire.

The phone rang. She picked it up and jerked to attention

when she heard the anticipation in Felix's voice. "The grapevine in New York is murmuring that BP are about to announce a huge oilfield—block 21/10. Don't get too excited. Not yet. I've contacted BP head office in London, but they're giving nothing away."

"So it's still speculation . . ."

"Not according to my information! Rumor says that they're just waiting for the New York Stock Exchange to close. When it does they might make an announcement. Got to go, honey." He hung up.

At 20.30 hours when the New York Stock Exchange closed, BP made their announcement: "The 21/10 well produced sweet oil of 37 degree API gravity at a rate of about 4,700 b./d. through a 56/54 surface choke on a $1\frac{1}{2}$ hour test." Alexandra did not understand a word of the technical jargon, but she honed in on the word "sweet"—and the upbeat tone of the press release. Felix phoned a little while later to confirm her hopes: BP had struck it rich. And so had Meldrum Enterprises and Danziger Minerals. The following week she noticed an announcement in the papers that Robert had been made the new Chairman of Armstrongs . . .

XI

The oil bonanza had begun. In the following months Shell-Esso found oil further south and the Hamilton Consortium in which the British-owned Burmah Oil Group had a stake made a good strike 180 miles east of Aberdeen. The rich Forties field was found to extend into the neighboring Shell-Esso block and within twelve months the North Sea was producing 2 million barrels a day, with over 1 million coming from waters round Scotland.

Alexandra had instructed Alan Gillian to sell all her oil shares whenever the market hit a new peak. By the end of the year Meldrum Enterprises were celebrating a massive profit and the first hotel in her projected chain, Meldrum Trossachs, was already being renovated.

"At this precise moment I feel I can succeed at anything!" she said joyously to Felix.

"Don't get over-committed!" he warned. "You know what happens to people when they suffer from hubris. Overweening pride," he added, seeing her puzzled look.

Later, that phrase came back to haunt her.

THIRTY

I

1971

"I think he's saying 'Daddy'!"

Daisy looked at her husband indulgently. "He's only six months old, Frank. If he's saying 'Daddy' he's a genius!"

To everyone's relief, it had been an easy birth and young Archibald Frank Meldrum was developing so fast that he was delighting his parents every day. Frank was particularly thrilled with his son's progress and Daisy sometimes wondered how her husband would have remained sane if he hadn't had young Archie to make him laugh. Nineteen seventy-one was proving a bad year for Scotland.

The Rolls-Royce engineering factory at Hillington near Glasgow was one of the major casualties: when it went into liquidation thousands found themselves unemployed. This debacle was no sooner over than it became evident that the crisis on the Clyde was worsening. At the beginning of the year a spokesman for Upper Clyde Shipbuilders had claimed that there was no cash crisis; by June, UCS were unable to pay their employees' wages for the following week.

Frank came home one evening and slumped into an armchair. "I think UCS is about to go into liquidation."

Daisy found it hard to believe. The Clyde was world famous for shipbuilding: it couldn't collapse! "Can't anything be done?"

"The unions were asked to take a cut in wages and they refused; just as the suppliers refused to freeze the company's debts. The company need an immediate injection of 5 to 6 million pounds from the government, but I doubt if they'll get it."

His doubts were confirmed and when a provisional liquidator was appointed he announced that the debts of UCS amounted to 28 million pounds. The Scottish people were shocked and saddened.

In July the situation on the Clyde took an unexpected turn. When John Brown's shipyard faced closure the workers locked the gates against the management and stated that they were now in charge of the yard: the term "work-in" slipped into Scottish phraseology.

"Jimmy Reid has a golden tongue," Frank commented as he listened to the shop steward who was one of the leaders of the work-in. "He's arguing that Clyde shipbuilding is a touchstone for the social and economic life of Scotland. He's right. The closing-down of the upper Clyde shipyards is as bad a blow to the nation's consciousness as the Clearances."

As the summer dragged on there seemed no ready-made solution to the crisis in Clyde shipbuilding and by the middle of August attention turned to London where Scotland's newest industry was under the spotlight. Frank was amazed to hear that Alexandra intended to be right in the middle of it.

II

The basement cinema of the Trade and Industry department's offices in London could qualify for the least glamorous meeting place in Britain, but on August 21, 1971 some of the richest men in the world—including Paul Getty—were gathering there for the auction of the North Sea drilling leases. Amidst the dark-suited oilmen trooping through the entrance, a woman stood out like a bird of paradise amidst a crowd of penguins. She was wearing a Chanel linen skirt and jacket in a bright emerald green which matched her eyes, and every now and then she ran her fingers through her magnificent mane of chestnut hair. Heads turned in her direction and necks craned. Some knew her, of course, but to others she was a stranger: an exotic bird who had surely alighted in the wrong place. It was evident that she was nervous, but then so were many of the assembled company. Although the system of selling concessions to the highest financial bidder was widely used to allocate drilling tracts in the United States, this was the first auction to be held in Europe.

When Felix had mentioned the auction to Alexandra he told her that the government were offering 421 concessions.

"How do the government decide which ones to choose?"

"On a discretionary basis. They assess the work programs submitted. This isn't a problem for giant companies like Shell and BP because they've already spent a great deal of money on surveys, but independents have to bid blind, or use the grapevine to glean information about what's happening. Then there are the *big* blocks, a different scenario altogether."

"How big?"

"Around 100 square miles. Success goes to the highest bidder. It's a guessing game and if you guess right you could be into the big time."

"I'm out of my depth," Alexandra said dryly, "but my gut feeling is that I want to be part of it. Bidding for a block, I mean."

Felix had contacts with oilmen throughout the world, but his most reliable source was a geologist in New York who knew some of the top people in Shell. He had found out that Shell had had "encouraging results" from a block they'd been drilling north east of the Shetlands. The more Felix asked around the more he became convinced that Shell was on to something. In the 1950s George Williams of Shell had found a lot of oil in Nigeria at a time when just about everyone else had given up hope.

"But how do we know Shell will bid for that block?"

"We don't. Hell, this industry breeds more rumors than a bunch of fishwives. Sometimes you just play your hunch. So what's yours?"

"My deceased grandmother!" Alexandra replied at once. "Her father, Captain Hoseason, came from a county family in Shetland."

"Fascinating!" Felix said dryly. "Is that relevant?"

Alexandra gave him a dazzling smile. "Since my roots are there, my hunch is identical to yours: go for the Shetland tract."

A new consortium, Danziger Meldrum International, was formed, finances were arranged and finally the day of the auction arrived.

When Alexandra sat down beside Felix she glanced along the row and saw Paul Getty looking thoughtful. She fingered the gilt buttons on her Chanel outfit and tried to steady her nerves by gazing down at her feet.

"Something wrong with your shoes?" Felix whispered. "You're studying them like a balance sheet."

Alexandra smiled. Maybe her shoes were a balance sheet of sorts. The fine-leather Italian court shoes she was wearing could have kept Stoneyground Croft and its inhabitants for a month.

"I wonder which block Paul Getty wants."

"Everyone's been promised a fair deal," Felix murmured.

Although many companies and consortiums had applied, Mr. Beckett, the undersecretary in charge of petroleum affairs at the Department of Trade and Industry, had made it clear that this was not to be an auction for the giant oil companies alone; he wanted small independents to take part as well.

At 2 p.m. Mr. Beckett came on to the platform and explained how he would run the auction: he would open the envelopes containing the tenders one by one and would then announce the value of each successful bid. There were whispers and coughs as he began announcing the bids and calling out the sums of money which had been involved in procuring them. As promised, the small independents were given their fair share. While a big American consortium had to pay over 500,000 pounds for the block they wanted, a Canadian oil group secured theirs for a little over 3,000 pounds. BP in conjunction with a German oil group had to pay 3.4 million pounds for their oil-prospect permit.

Paul Getty had teamed up with the Occidental Petroleum Company for a stake in the North Sea. He didn't look very happy when his $5 million bid was beaten for the concession he wanted. Another envelope was opened and this time the successful bidder was the Danziger Meldrum consortium. Alexandra and Felix smiled happily, but they knew congratulations were premature. Acquiring a concession was one thing, finding oil in it was another matter altogether. But if Shell made a sizeable bid, that would mean there was every prospect of lots of oil in that area and the Danziger Meldrum consortium would share in the bonanza since their block was nearby.

"Look at Beckett's face," Felix whispered. "I bet this is the Shell bid coming up. 5 million pounds would be a good indicator. Eight even better," he commented.

In his quiet dry voice Mr. Beckett announced that Shell had been successful in securing a single 100-square-mile tract designated 211/21 located seventy miles north east of the Shetland Isles. As everyone waited to hear the price for that block there wasn't even a murmur in the hall.

"Twenty-one million and fifty thousand pounds!" he declared.

The audience were stunned. If Shell were willing to pay out that kind of money they must think the block off Shetland was worth a fortune. Alexandra and Felix were overjoyed: the Danziger Meldrum block was in the same vicinity!

"Marvelous news!" Felix said to Alexandra. "I'm just sorry you have to fly back to Aberdeen."

Alexandra's mood of exhilaration lasted all the way to the airport where she was suddenly confronted by Adam Armstrong. "I read that article about you in *The Times* today. Pleased with all your fame and fortune, are you? Maybe you won't be so happy when you hear you've lost your chance to buy Drumcraig," Adam added. "By the time I come back from Bangkok I'll be the new owner of the castle."

III

In the Patpong area of Bangkok, music throbbed, smells assailed the olfactory organs and neon signs invited customers to come and see live sex shows and enjoy erotic massage. Through the open doorways of the clubs barebreasted go-go dancers swayed and writhed, beckoning with seductive fingers. The vendors who lined each side of the street were as usual taking advantage of gawking tourists by offering unbelievable bargains from their stalls: fake Gucci, fake Chanel, fake anything.

Adam's eye was caught by the gleam of a beautiful bowl. "Authentic Ming!" an old Thai lady promised.

He examined it. Although ninety-nine percent of any antiques on offer were rubbish, now and again a genuine Chinese dynasty bowl was salvaged from the river at Sukhothai, but not this one, he decided. The vendor's disappointment turned to joy when Adam noticed a jade monkey in a gold cage and decided Belinda might find it amusing.

He'd had to work hard lately to keep his wife amused now that there were so many diversions in Aberdeen. Oilmen and tycoons mingled with businessmen and tourists from all over the world. Belinda adored the new vibrancy in Aberdeen and frequently went out on her own. She even taunted Adam about her lovers and threatened to fly back to the States with one of them, but she stayed—because of Drumcraig Castle. Adam had learned that Belinda tended to keep a terrier-like grip on her obsessions. Fortunately for him Drumcraig was still one of them. She had encouraged Tom Elphinstone to spend freely in the hope that when his finances became depleted he might allow them to buy the castle, but although Tom had sold all the valuable pictures in the castle he still seemed to have plenty of money.

It was a mystery and Adam had come to the conclusion that the answer to it lay in Thailand. Tom was a regular visitor to Bangkok and when he returned from one of his jaunts he was always flush with ready cash.

"Want a girl? Very young," a voice prompted at his side.

"I got better one. Much younger," a rival called.

Adam brushed away the fingers clutching at his sleeve. Walking the gauntlet of the Patpong pimps held no appeal for him on this particular evening. He was making for Tom Elphinstone's favorite haunt: a notorious club which laid on extravagantly erotic performances.

Adam bent his head as he went through the doorway and nodded at the owner who led him upstairs. In this darkened room naked girls paraded round the room offering drinks to the guests, but all eyes were on the stage where a beautiful Thai girl was using sparklers to burst the blown-up balloons protruding from the vagina of her partner. Adam was amazed at the strength of the muscles which enabled the girl to perform such a feat. When this act finished another girl took the spotlight and began pressing pieces of broken glass up inside her. Adam had seen this act before and knew that somehow she would be able to bring them out again without a show of blood. It was a high-risk performance, but that was the attraction of Patpong.

"Not seen you in long time, Mr. Adam."

The tall Thai woman standing in front of him was the

Madame who controlled the girls. On his first visit here he had saved her from being knifed by a drunken psychopath.

"You owe me a favor," he said without preamble.

"I not forget. Anything you ask."

He drew her to the quietest corner of the club and began questioning her about Tom Elphinstone. He was aware that Tom came to the club at least once a month and sampled all it had to offer, but he wanted to know if anyone gave Tom anything before he left.

"How would I know such a thing, Mr. Adam?"

"You know everything that goes on in this club."

"But even if such a thing happened . . .if I told you . . .I would get into trouble. The owner, too. And the police . . ."

"I promise that I will tell no one. I also promise that Mr. Tom will be able to carry on his business here without hindrance."

The black, almond eyes sharpened. "Then why you ask?"

"My knowledge will be a weapon I can use. Just for one night."

The almond eyes gazed at him for long minutes before she started whispering in his ear.

Adam smiled. "Thank you."

"Favor repaid. Not see you here again."

It was a warning and Adam felt chilled by its menace.

IV

The following evening Adam made his way to the First Class lounge of Thai airlines and waited for Tom Elphinstone. The Thai had told him the number of Tom's flight. Tom looked astonished when Adam waved to him from the far corner of the lounge and made his way towards him. "I thought you'd given up vice since you married," Tom sneered.

"I have."

"So what are you doing in Bangkok?"

"I have evidence that you're smuggling drugs out of Thailand and I'm about to report you to the police."

"Don't joke about such things."

"I'm not joking. I happen to know you've concealed drugs

in a length of Thai silk in that suitcase you're carrying. Each month you find somewhere different to hide them."

Tom's face had lost all its color. "Look here, Adam, what do you want?"

"Drumcraig Castle. I'm willing to pay you 100,000 pounds for it."

"Alexandra Semple would pay me three times that," Tom snorted. "Anyway, I'm not selling."

"Yes, you are. I arranged for a lawyer to draw up the necessary documents, and I've got them right here in my briefcase. All you have to do is add your signature. If you don't, I'll notify the police, and you could serve out a life sentence in a Thai jail."

"I can't believe what I'm hearing," Tom said hoarsely. "When I think of how I've shared my home with you, taken you everywhere with me, paid for our jaunts together . . .we're friends . . ."

"I feel hellish about this, Tom, but the bottom line is that Belinda means more to me than you do, and Belinda wants Drumcraig."

Tom refused to believe that Adam meant to carry out his threat: he stalked out of the lounge and made his way into the center of the terminal. Adam followed him.

"Are you going to sign?" Adam asked.

"No!"

To Tom's horror Adam signalled a passing policeman.

"Jesus Christ!" Tom said hoarsely.

"Anything wrong?" the policeman asked as he came up to them.

"I panicked when I thought I'd lost my passport," Adam said quickly, "but I had it all the time." He produced it from his pocket.

"Give it to me." The Thai policeman checked it quickly and turned his attention to Tom. "Let me see your passport as well."

Tom was sweating heavily as he fumbled in his pocket and produced his passport. The Thai policeman looked through it, then handed it back before walking away. Tom sat down on the nearest chair and mopped his brow.

"Maybe you won't get a life sentence," Adam remarked conversationally, "sometimes they execute drug smugglers.

Want to risk it? Or want to sign?" he asked as he thrust the papers into Tom's hand.

Beads of perspiration dripped on to the papers as Tom signed them. "You're a bastard," he moaned. "I hope that castle brings you nothing but misery and that Belinda chucks you for someone else."

PART VI

1975-80

THIRTY-ONE

I

Puerto Rico, May 1975

The reef was skyscraper tall. Catherine hovered at the top of it, then plunged downwards towards the sea bed past swaying sea fans and coral branches, marvelling at the way the rainbow-colored fish sharing her sea-space never seemed to touch her. Down in this underwater world there was no yesterday, no to-morrow; she loved it. She saw a shadow darken the water—another scuba-diver. She pushed with her feet and headed in the opposite direction; when she was scuba diving she wanted to be alone. She spotted a large fish resplendently striped in green and yellow and let herself drift in its wake until her muscles were tired.

Slowly she began to move upwards towards the surface, los-ing the feeling of weightlessness as she began to rise to where she could stand on her feet. She hadn't been aware of the scuba-tanks in the water, but as she struggled towards the shore they pressed down on her back.

"Give you a hand?"

"Thanks!"

Once the tanks were off her back she looked up at the man who had helped her; flirtatious eyes gleamed from a tanned face. Another randy Puerto Rican, she thought.

"Chad Grenville!" he said with an American accent.

"Catherine Semple."

"English?"

"Scottish. My mother lives in Aberdeen."

"A good place to live?"

"I wouldn't know. Haven't been home for five years."

"Family quarrel?"

"Nope!" Catherine shook out her hair and ran her fingers through it to make it dry. "I just took off."

Whenever she phoned Scotland her mother tried hard to do the "tolerant-parent" bit, but Catherine could tell she wanted her home. But for what? The minute she was back in Scotland her mother would start lobbying to get her to join Meldrums, and that was the last thing she wanted. She was blissfully happy working her way round the world and she had expressly forbidden her mother to send out any funds. Half the fun was learning how to live off your wits; she had spent the last five years being cook, cleaner, waitress, and babyminder. She sold paintings, wrote articles, and once she'd made enough money she moved on someplace else. She was a free spirit: no ties, no problems.

Catherine looked up and realized the tanned American was still standing beside her. He was six foot tall and had a muscular body. Used to working outdoors?

"So what's your line?" she asked.

"Vagrant. Itinerant rig worker. Maybe I'll try Scotland next," he added, a glint in his dark-blue eyes. "Anything's better than going back stateside to work for my dad!"

Catherine felt the first stirrings of empathy. "What does your father do?"

"All kinds of things—paint, engineering, property. He's thinking about getting into oil as well."

"Everyone in Scotland seems to be scrabbling to become rich on it; my mother for one. She wants me to join the family firm."

"But you felt stifled by the idea? Attagirl!"

This time she smiled at him. Maybe he wasn't so bad after all.

"Why don't we discuss our parents' failings over dinner?" he suggested.

"I didn't think vagrants could afford dinner."

"Maybe not in there," he said pointing to the Caribe Hilton in the background, "but I know a little restaurant in the old quarter of San Juan where they bake wine-flavored lobster in a shrimp-and-egg crust spiced with garlic."

"You Yanks are always thinking about your stomachs!"

"Not *all* the time," he replied, his tone suggestive.

"I don't sleep around," Catherine said flatly, as she intercepted his assessing eye.

"Are you always this frank with vagrants?"

"Always."

"And what if they don't believe you?"

"I tell them I'm recovering from syphilis."

Chad threw back his head and roared with laughter. "I'm going to enjoy your company, Catherine Semple!"

Catherine grinned. Chad Grenville had possibilities. The only other man who'd intrigued her half as much was Cameron Armstrong. She'd told her mother that when she'd first met Cameron she'd thought him a creep. But after that she'd kept bumping into him at parties and dances, and the more she saw of him the more she liked him. Since her mother was still obsessed with the old feud between the Meldrums and the Armstrongs, Catherine had decided to say nothing about her growing friendship with one of the opposition. But there was something about Cameron that drew her; the empathy between them was hard to pinpoint, but it was there. When they went out together on their own she felt totally relaxed and happy.

They'd had a long chat just before she left for her trip round the world. Cameron had told her that he was going to Canada for some real adventure. "Aberdeen is dead from the neck up," he'd said disgustedly. "The sooner I get away the better—and I'm never coming back!"

But something must have happened to change his mind. Catherine had met someone in Puerto Rico who knew Cameron Armstrong and they'd told her he was going back to Aberdeen.

II

Cameron was camping out in the Rockies with a group of students from Vancouver when they began talking about oil and the big new fields being discovered off the mainland of Scotland. "Man, Aberdeen's the new Yukon!" they all agreed. "That's where it's all happening!"

It was a phrase that Cameron was to hear again and again as more oil was discovered and he began to wonder why he was trying to find excitement in Canada when it seemed there was more than enough for everyone back in Aberdeen. His father was pleased when Cameron returned home and even suggested that his son should stay with him in Rubislaw Terrace. That was one option Cameron discarded right away, nor was he attracted by the idea of living with his mother and Adam Armstrong in Drumcraig Castle on Deeside. He'd tried that and found it boring. Besides, he and Adam hated each other.

Aberdeen was the place to be; it had become a swinging city, an international venue. Just what he wanted.

He had heard that in the mid-Sixties more people had left Aberdeen than almost any other place in Britain. Now the emigration trend was being reversed. Men in stetsons walked up the main street and the hotels were crowded with oilmen, journalists, and financiers. Bars, shops, restaurants, and hotels were being built to accommodate the population explosion.

He did not find it difficult to get a job. Although rig managers needed men experienced in the oil business, they also needed a large pool of unskilled laborers. Many of the rig workers were coal miners, steel men or shipyard workers who had become redundant. There were even some fishermen who had once worked on Armstrong trawlers. "The sillar's better and so's the food," they confided gleefully to Cameron. Some of the men left after a few weeks, others stayed on for six months, or settled into the rigs as a permanent way of life.

Cameron joined the rig Dolphin 200, which was positioned a hundred miles out in the North Sea, and developed such an aptitude for his job that he eventually graduated from roustabout to roughneck. The money was good and the rent he paid for a shared flat in Aberdeen hardly dented it. On the rigs he found comradeship, excitement, and a pioneering sense of adventure. Everyone said it was akin to space exploration.

The analogy with space was the one that frequently tripped off the tongues of the good-time girls who hung around the bars. "You're all like Captain Kirk in the Starship *Enterprise*," the girls would joke, though when the men went off with the girls they could hardly say they were going where no man had gone before!

One evening Cameron found himself sitting at a bar with a blonde on one arm and a brunette on the other. The girls were students who had come up from Edinburgh to see what all the fuss was about. They seemed to be impressed with his macho air and the way he threw his money about. He couldn't make up his mind which girl he liked best and when he wakened up the next morning in a strange hotel he found he had taken both of them to bed. He closed his eyes and wondered if this was really the sedate little fishing town where he'd grown up.

"Stay with us," they pleaded.

"Out! he said, once he had paid their bill. "I'm going back on the rig today."

He drove to the heliport and caught the chopper out to Dolphin 200 where he joined the crew who were about to "change the bit." Lengths of pipe were being hauled up and multi-hinged tongs were being clamped round their bases. The derrick loomed above: a skyscraper with a projecting platform jutting out in front of it. A derrick man stood on its edge, poised to lasso each section of pipe with his rope. Once he had secured it, the clamps were released and the pipe stand could be stacked with the others. It would have been arduous work under normal circumstances, but on this particular day the wind was gusting and the platform decks were being lashed with rain and sleet.

"God-damn mother-fuckers, watch what you're doing!" the driller shouted as one of the floormen slipped on the greasy floor. Cameron grinned. The driller was a Texan with a tongue like a whiplash for the men working on the drill floor. The toolpusher was another whose language was salty. None of the bossmen found it easy shaping up a polyglot band of assorted nationalities: American, Canadian, Australian, French, Dutch, Irish, and British. Some had worked in the oil industry before, but most had come to Aberdeen attracted by the tales of high wages and fast living.

Another section of the drill string was pulled back up the hole and Cameron began cleaning it. He wasn't bothered by the noise of the generators and the machinery, and the ever-present sense of danger lent an added spice to the job. Cameron enjoyed the backbreaking work. His mother had told him he wasn't strong enough and his father had forecast that he would give up after a few months; he was enjoying proving them wrong.

He glanced across the derrick floor to where the new drill bit was waiting. It looked like a giant's knuckleduster, but there would be no oil without it. At a signal from the driller they dragged the new bit across the deck. An earsplitting scream pierced the noise of machinery. Cameron whipped his head round. A roughneck had slipped and fallen heavily against a sharp wire which sliced off part of his hand. Cameron stared at the blood as the medics moved in. Had a main artery been severed? If a man died on the rig someone had to break the news to his relatives back on the beach. The beach was what rig workers called the land. It pointed up the difference between them and ordinary mortals; a difference the women seemed to appreciate.

Cameron had a girl lined up for his next leave. He'd give her a whirl and then look for someone new. Or maybe he'd try and discover if Catherine Semple had come back from her travels . . . He wondered if her mother had managed to persuade her to join the family business. From what he'd read about Alexandra Meldrum in the papers she sounded just as bad as his father. No wonder Catherine had tried to escape from her clutches!

III

November 1975

Alexandra found herself humming as she drove out of Glasgow and took the northbound road. The sun seemed to be making a special effort to shine as if mindful of the fact that the following day was to be one of the most important occasions in the history of Scotland—and a momentous one for Britain. The Prime Minster, the cabinet, and everyone who was anyone were all traveling to Aberdeen to see the Queen press the button that would officially launch Britain as a major oil-producing nation.

The road from Glasgow to Aberdeen was a familiar one to Alexandra. Although she lived and worked in Aberdeen, she had just spent a profitable few days in Glasgow seeing officials at the Offshore Supplies Office, which had been set up in 1973 to make sure that United Kingdom companies got a slice of the North Sea oil cake. It had proved a bigger one than anyone had anticipated.

The discovery of BP's Forties field in 1970 had been followed by Shell-Esso's Brent Field. By the end of 1973 eleven more fields had been discovered that were eventually brought into production: Shell-Esso's Auk, Dunlin, and South Cormorant, Occidental's Piper, BNOC's Thistle and Mobil's Beryl. In 1974 there were six more including Statfjord which straddled the boundary between the UK and the Norwegian sector.

But even after the presence of oil in the North Sea had been confirmed, for a long while there was continuing concern about its profitability, especially as the international price of crude was only $2.50 per barrel. Then the Yom Kippur war and OPEC pushed the price up to $11 a barrel by 1975 and that had the immediate effect of making half the discovered oil reserves commercially viable.

The first oil had come ashore earlier in 1975 from the small Argyll field, but the BP Forties field was in a different league since it would reputedly provide a quarter of Britain's oil needs.

Alexandra tried to concentrate on her driving, but her mood became more somber as her thoughts turned towards Meldrums' financial commitments in this new mineral wealth. Two years after the Danziger Meldrum consortium had made a successful bid for a block in the North Sea they had struck oil. Alexandra was overjoyed until she learned that this was just the beginning of the process; the value of the field had to be appraised before any oil could be extracted. The appraisals confirmed the presence of vast quantities of oil, but that in itself posed a problem because it was estimated that it would cost many more millions to develop than the consortium could afford.

Felix approached Barnico, a Texan drilling conglomerate with oil interests, who offered to loan cash in exchange for equity. Barnico then became the operator in the consortium with seven other venture partners including Danziger Meldrum. Unfortunately there had then been problems with drilling and disagreements about the type of production platform needed to extract the oil. Felix was phoning this evening to let her know Barnico's decision about which to use. It was all very worrying because Alexandra was anxious to have a return on her investment as soon as possible. Sometimes she felt quite sick when she thought of the vast amounts of money pouring from the Meldrum coffers into oil exploration. Fortunately the majority of the companies in the Meldrum Enterprises group were making healthy profits.

Alexandra glanced out at the cottages and houses which lined the road. Ever since she had worked in Bannons Estate Agency in Glasgow she had delighted in buying and selling property, but when she had purchased the Aberdeen branch of Bannons she'd had no intention of buying the whole group. It was Brian Bannon himself who had suggested the idea. He'd been suffering from angina and wanted to take things a little easier. After some hesitation Alexandra agreed, but only on condition that Brian and his wife remain on the board as consultant directors. Meldrum Estate Agencies had branches all over Britain and were reaping rich dividends. No problems there.

But if the estate agencies had proved a good buy, Alexandra's efforts to become a hotelier were proving less successful. She had bought six magnificent stately homes in different parts of the country and turned them into luxury hotels, but only the Meldrum Trossachs was showing reasonable profits. The others were plagued with a variety of problems ranging from dry rot and woodworm to faulty masonry and leaking roofs; they were a constant drain on her resources. Fyfe Walker, Meldrums' Financial Director, kept urging her to cut her losses and sell them. Alexandra hated admitting failure and obstinately hoped she could still turn Meldrum hotels into profit-making ventures.

Nor did she want to sell the Meldrum Reproduction Furniture shops, though they too were becoming financial liabilities as it became more and more difficult to find the cabinet-makers who could turn out the quality furniture that had once sold so well. Harry Rosemary, the Marketing Director, wanted to launch a big new advertising campaign for the furniture shops in a bid to win back the custom they had lost: another huge capital outlay.

The cloud shifted as Alexandra drove along the Perth Road to Dundee and then northwards to Aberdeen. As she thought about her native city she recalled Felix's forecast that it could become the largest oil-related center in Europe. It had all come true. Not only did the city play host to Americans, Dutch, French, Germans, Italians, and Norwegians, but many foreign companies had their European headquarters in Aberdeen and some controlled their Middle East operations from there as well.

Felix had predicted that this would happen and he had been proved right. Alexandra smiled a trifle wryly. Felix had all the answers. Except in bed . . .

Making love to him had released all her tensions, but had not brought her the contentment she craved. At times when she was in bed with Felix she found herself thinking of other things; perhaps that was why she had kept postponing the date of their wedding. In the end Felix tired of her excuses and forced her to admit that she really did not want to be tied down. Though marriage was no longer on the cards, happily they were still good friends as well as business associates.

Dear Felix, Alexandra thought wistfully, why couldn't I fall in love with him? But then she hadn't been able to love Malcolm that way either. Maybe there was something deficient in her make-up.

What a stupid train of thought, she said to herself sternly as the small coastal towns of the north east flashed past. She couldn't help noticing that some of the familiar landmarks were changing. Alexandra had always had a soft spot for the old fishing village of Ferryden, but it had been pulled down and rebuilt to accommodate onshore oil facilities.

She glanced out of the car window at the North Sea thinking how strange it was that a substance discovered beneath its bed was changing not just Aberdeen but many other parts of Scotland as well. Shetland, once a backwater, had become the thriving hub of a new oil-exploration center and supply base, and instant villages had been created to house the workers; consequently locals who hadn't had two pennies to rub together had suddenly found themselves with more money than they knew what to do with.

Peterhead was another dramatic example of change: with all the construction work that had taken place there, the transformation of its economy and landscape was startling. Other areas in Scotland had prospered as well. On the east coast, steel platforms had been built and in many places the shouts of fishermen now had to compete with the clanging of metal as the countryside accommodated the requirements of pipeline landfalls and the terminal and storage facilities associated with them. Even the magnificent mountains and romantic islands of the west coast had attracted the construction builders of the oil industry.

And Edinburgh, of course, as well as being the capital of Scotland, had become a booming financial headquarters with new banks, offices and insurance agencies to finance and administer energy-related projects costing millions.

As Alexandra passed the small villages of the north-east coast she wondered what the local folk thought of the many changes which North Sea oil discoveries had initiated. She had heard that the villagers of Gourdon had long since abandoned the old steam drifters for motor fishing vessels, but they hadn't forsaken the old ways. The fishermen's wives still baited the hooks for their husbands each day and wheeled them in "prams" to the quay.

The old ways, Alexandra mused. She felt sure that whatever happened with oil there would always be fishermen and crofters who carried on the traditions of their ancestors. She was comforted by the thought that when the last dregs of oil had been taken from the North Sea, Scotland's moors, mountains, lochs, and forests would still be there. Nature would triumph over man's puny efforts to change the landscape. Or would it?

She was passing through the Howe of the Mearns now, a fat fertile land unlike the upland hill slopes of her father's croft where the ground had been dour and unforgiving. Did the soil make the man or was it the other way round? All she knew was that her childhood would have been vastly different if Stoneyground Croft had not lived up to its name.

Three miles beyond Catterline was Dunottar Castle. Alexandra stopped the car and got out to stretch her legs. Dunottar was perched dramatically on a wedding-cake rock jutting out from the shore. When the mist swirled round the grey stumps of stone they looked like monster's fingers rising from the sea bed. Even in sunlight Dunottar Castle made her shiver. Unlike Drumcraig. Alexandra closed her eyes and the image of Drumcraig Castle floated before her, rose-pink, slender, bewitching.

And owned by Adam Armstrong . . . He had said publicly that he wanted to remain there for as long as he lived. But she wasn't going to give up her dream, Alexandra vowed as she walked back to the car and switched on the engine. She'd find some way of getting it back.

She hadn't been driving for long when the sign for Stone-haven caught her eye. Not far to go now; Stonehaven was only twenty miles from Aberdeen. She had begun investing there in the Sixties. When the houses and cottages were renovated and modernized she had intended selling them as holiday homes, but once the oil strikes began off the mainland of Scotland, the little towns and villages on the north-east coast became commuter suburbs for Aberdeen. Alexandra was delighted to discover that when any of her properties fell vacant she could lease them out at a high price to the cash-rich incomers. The money from the leases had enabled her to buy more land and property.

The house in Queen's Road which had become her home was the purchase that had given her the most pleasure. It was far too big for someone living on her own, but she kept hoping that some day Catherine might come back and share it with her. Alexandra found herself pressing harder on the accelerator as she recollected the last conversation she'd had with her daughter. Just before she rang off Catherine had added that she intended to return to Scotland soon. It was the first time she had mentioned the idea since she left home. Alexandra had kept her voice light as she had told her daughter that she'd be delighted to see her anytime. Anytime at all.

"I think I know what I want to do with my life," Catherine had said. "You'll be surprised, mother, really surprised. No, it's not painting. Or Meldrums. I'll tell you when I see you. By the way, I'll have a boyfriend with me."

"Who is he?" Alexandra had asked, an edge of anxiety creeping into her voice.

Catherine had chuckled. "Relax, mother, you'll approve. He's an American I met in Puerto Rico. He's coming back with me to Aberdeen so that he can get a job on one of the oil rigs."

The road journey from Glasgow to Aberdeen had taken four hours. As Alexandra got out of the car at Queen's Road she stretched and yawned before locking up the car and letting herself into the house. She threw off her coat in the hall before wandering into the adjoining conservatory. One pot of geraniums seemed to be wilting. She nipped off the dead flowers and withered leaves, and gave the plant a good watering before going through to her study where she picked up the *Glasgow*

Herald, the *Scotsman* and the Aberdeen *Press and Journal* which Betsy had laid out for her. In Edinburgh she'd had help in the house every day, but once she had moved to Aberdeen she employed living-in staff: a cook, a maid and a housekeeper. Betsy was her housekeeper, a forthright Aberdonian who wasn't at all in awe of her new mistress and indeed at times treated her like a wayward daughter. She was a big-bosomed woman with short brown hair. Now she came bustling into the study with a frown on her face.

"A fine lady like you shouldn't have to open her own door," she said disapprovingly. "You should have rung!"

"It feels more like home when I open the door myself," Alexandra replied with a smile. "What's the weather been like?"

"Far better in Aberdeen than down in that Glasgow place. Cook's made you a good dinner and I hope you'll eat every bit of it. You'll need all your strength for yon shindig tomorrow."

Alexandra smiled again. Only Betsy could have described the opening of the Forties field by the Queen as "yon shindig!"

IV

Dyce

Robert Armstrong looked round the excited throng and thought to himself that Dyce was the bridesmaid who had suddenly become the bride. This was the day when the Queen was bypassing Aberdeen and coming out to the suburb of Dyce to perform the opening ceremony for the Forties oilfield. When he had been growing up in Aberdeen, Dyce had been a quiet little village. It became busier when it acquired the status of an airport for passenger planes, but it had never attracted much attention until the oilmen came.

Robert reckoned the transformation of the airport's role illustrated very dramatically the impact of oil on the region with its doubling and redoubling of passenger services and the influx of helicopter fleets to supply the oil rigs with men and materials. People were forecasting that Dyce would one day become the biggest helicopter base in Europe. To add icing to

Dyce's cake, BP had built their Petroleum Development Office there.

Today, however, interest was focused on the enormous circus-like tent with the red and blue dais in the middle where the Queen would stand to perform the opening ceremony. Assisting the Grampian Police Band was the regimental band of the Gordon Highlanders which had been flown home from Singapore for the occasion. As Robert glanced round he could see that the foreigners amongst the audience were loving the pomp and circumstance of the occasion. Ten overseas countries had oilmen working in the north east; amongst them were 5,000 Americans, 800 Dutchmen and nearly 900 French, each with their own schools and social clubs.

"You need some cheerleaders out there to whip up the excitement!" a voice said at his side. Robert grinned at Shane Meecher, a Texan millionaire who had come to Aberdeen to buy himself a slice of the action. "Stephanie used to be a cheerleader. D'you know that?" Shane asked.

"That doesn't surprise me," Robert replied. Stephanie was Shane's glamorous dark-haired daughter and had become Robert's latest girlfriend. He'd abandoned Melanie Bradford once she'd started pressurizing him about marriage. Fortunately Stephanie wasn't enticed by the sound of wedding bells; all she wanted was fun.

"Where is that durned daughter of mine?" Shane asked. "She's a wild one, Robert. I'm hoping you can leash her in a bit!"

Robert made no comment. He had no intention of putting a leash on Stephanie. She was lending a bit of excitement to his private life. Tonight he was taking her for dinner to the Petroleum Club, a beautiful old house on Deeside where people in the oil industry could wine and dine in elegant surroundings.

"There's your brother," Shane remarked as he caught sight of Adam and Belinda walking into the tent. "A fine-looking couple."

"And well-suited," Robert replied smoothly. And by God, they were! Devious, self-seeking, ambitious. If he'd ever had any illusions about Adam they had long since disappeared. They kept up a friendly front in public for the sake of business, but in private they no longer concealed their dislike of each other. Belinda was wearing an expensive-looking outfit in ice blue. She was still very pretty, but Robert felt no sense of loss. His marriage had been a mistake and he had been relieved when it ended.

He glanced round the marquee and saw Alexandra sitting with her brother and his wife. Alexandra's hair shone like champagne and he could see that her eyes were sparkling. She was beautiful. For a fleeting moment he remembered chasing her in the woods round Jordanhill. She had been so passionate, so wild. Where had she gone, that lovely lively girl who'd given him so much pleasure?

But she had been treacherous too, he reminded himself, as he mulled over his plans for taking over her company. The groundwork had been completed: all he had to do was wait for the right moment, and it was fast approaching. From what he'd heard Meldrum Enterprises were having cash-flow problems.

Alexandra and Daisy were discussing clothes. Daisy had smartened up since she had married, and now she was wearing a dress and coat in a becoming shade of violet which softened her angular features. Alexandra was wearing an Yves St. Laurent suit in black. It was beautifully cut, but it did not emphasize the femininity of her curves or highlight her coloring.

"That suit may be high fashion," Daisy said with the candor of an old friend, "but it does nothing for you."

"I can't work up any interest in clothes these days."

"That's because you've no man in your life. If you're not going to marry Felix it's time you bloody well looked for someone else."

Frank heard Daisy's last remark and gave her a reproving frown, but he knew he'd never reform the forthright way of speaking which had stood her in such good stead when she was working in the Gorbals. It was strange, Frank mused, to think that the old Gorbals was disappearing. Demolition had begun in 1972 and many of the locals had been moved to high rises in the suburbs. The man on Frank's right gave him a nudge. "What d'you think of Margaret Thatcher?"

It was the question everyone had been asking him since she had been elected leader of the Conservatives. "She's much prettier than Ted Heath!"

It was Frank's stock reply and it usually managed to shut people up, but to his dismay his neighbor wanted to confront him about government policies. One of the problems about an occasion like this was that people had plenty of time to "nobble" you while they were waiting. If you were a Labour politician surrounded by Conservatives usually they nobbled you with piranha teeth! His aggressive neighbor had launched himself on a long spiel about Upper Clyde Shipbuilders and the state of the shipbuilding industry. Following the collapse of the UCS only two yards had survived apart from Yarrows: Govan Shipbuilders and John Brown's shipyard at Clydebank. With government help, the latter was eventually taken over by an American company, Marathon, who wanted to build oil rigs. Govan Shipbuilders had absorbed nearly 80 million pounds of public money and other yards were losing heavily as well. Only Yarrows' future seemed secure.

"The whole of the shipbuilding industry in Scotland is heading for bankruptcy!" Frank's neighbor declared. "It's Labour's fault!"

Frank made the point that it was the rising price of oil that had caused the shipbuilding industry to fall into the doldrums. Oil was now so expensive no one wanted to order ships which consumed vast quantities of the black gold. When he saw his neighbor wasn't convinced he tried to deflect his wrath by mentioning that in the first half of the Seventies, Scotland had outperformed the UK economy. The emigration trend had been reversed as well.

"Labour can't take credit for Scotland's performance when it's the oil boom that has transformed the economy," his neighbor said truculently. "It's Scotland's oil," he went on forcefully, "so why are you lot letting the English control it?"

Frank stifled a groan and prayed for the early appearance of Donny B. MacLeod, the television personality who was scheduled to warm up the crowd before the Queen's arrival. The man on his left was obviously bracing himself for another onslaught, but to Frank's relief Donny MacLeod came on stage and launched into a routine of jokes and topical comments.

The arrival of the Grampian Police Pipe Band and the Gordon Highlanders Band heralded the approach of the Queen, the Duke of Edinburgh, and Prince Andrew.

"The Queen's wearing emerald green," Daisy whispered to Alexandra. "That outfit would suit you perfectly."

"Should I ask her if I can borrow it?" Alexandra joked as everyone stood up for the National Anthem.

The Queen seemed relaxed and happy as she talked to flag-waving children from local schools before going into the main BP operations center. Everything was already in place. All that remained was for the Queen to press a button which would officially launch the flow of oil from the Forties oilfield. The crowd listened attentively as speeches were made about this bright omen for Britain's future and at last the Queen was ready to perform the opening ceremony.

"Is that all?" Alexandra whispered as the Queen stepped forward. Frank and Daisy knew exactly what she meant. Pressing a button seemed a ridiculously insignificant way of inaugurating the new oil age.

V

There is a velvet quality to country dark that one never finds in a city. As Robert drove along the Deeside road he thought how lucky he was to live in a place which had such easy access to vast tracts of moorland and mountain. The leaves had long since turned from green to amber and were dropping from the trees and gathering in piles at the roadside, swirling up in protest as cars disturbed their peace. As the headlights of Robert's car shone on a copse, the shadow of an owl was illuminated for a brief moment before vanishing into the night.

The dining room of the Petroleum Club had a vista of lawns, shrubs, trees, and distant mountains. Robert and Stephanie sat by the window and enjoyed the stars and a meal of southern fried chicken and salad followed by chocolate pudding. Afterwards they went through to the lounge to have coffee. Robert studied Stephanie. From the way her nipples peaked against the fine material of her red shirtwaister dress he knew she wasn't wearing any bra. Nor would she have on any knickers despite the November chill. Stephanie said she always felt sexier without her underwear.

"Have you seen the new conference room?" she asked when she had finished her coffee. "Daddy showed it to me tonight just before he flew off down to London. I'm gonna have another look at it." She got up from her seat and strode off down the corridor.

Robert paid the bill and followed her, but when he peered

into the dimly lit conference room there was no sign of her. A yellow cloth was draped over a couch which had just been delivered and Stephanie's head suddenly emerged from one end of it. When she threw back the cloth Robert saw that she was lying spreadeagled on her red dress and was completely naked. "I'm waiting for you, honey," she said invitingly. "I want it now!"

"Someone might come in!"

"I know. It'd give them a helluva thrill."

Robert needed no further invitation. He jammed a chair under the door handle, and pulled off his clothes before lowering himself down beside her. Their bodies merged in a tumultuous flash of passion and they both came very quickly. Half an hour later they were back in the lounge enjoying another cup of coffee.

Lust suited him perfectly, Robert thought; he didn't need love.

VI

Alexandra was in the small sitting room of her house in Queen's Road, dispensing after-dinner liqueurs to Daisy and Frank. Instead of being preoccupied with the day's events she found herself thinking about Robert Armstrong. From her seat at the launch of the Forties field she'd had a good view of him. He was more handsome than ever; money and power had added to his aura. Once when he'd looked across at her something flickered in his eyes before he looked away again. Unaccountably that brief glance had upset her. Perhaps Daisy was right. It was time she took another lover.

She was relieved when the phone disturbed her train of thought. It was Felix ringing from New York. "Barnico have decided to go for a floating production facility instead of a fixed platform. They'll use an offshore tanker-loading system to transport the oil ashore."

"Is this good news or bad news?" Alexandra asked.

"It will mean lower production costs, which has to be good news . . ."

"And the bad news?"

"Before all that happens they've got to submit plans to the

Department of Energy, then they've got to go to tender for the installation platform, and by the time *that's* built . . ."

"It will be years before we go onstream," Alexandra groaned.

"Relax, honey. I know you're worried about your financial situation. So I've a suggestion to make: I've arranged that Danziger Minerals will secure more loans for you. They'll be repayable on demand, but we'll let you roll up interest on favorable terms."

"I can't tell you how grateful I am! Didn't your board object?"

"My cousin Cornelius wasn't keen on the idea."

Cornelius Danziger was Felix's only surviving relative, and heir to his empire. Alexandra disliked Cornelius and suspected the feeling was mutual.

"Don't worry about my cousin!" Felix went on. "He may be Vice President of Danzigers, but he can't afford to go against me."

Alexandra felt enormously relieved when she put down the phone. Fyfe Walker, her Financial Director, had warned her that if she kept expanding she might endanger her empire. He would be delighted to hear about Felix's loans; the reprieve meant that Meldrums would have time to consolidate. Hard on the heels of that thought came another: it would be a different story when Felix's cousin took over . . . Still, that was a long way off. Felix was in splendid health and thoroughly enjoyed dashing about the globe keeping an eye on his vast empire. As long as he was Chairman of Danziger Minerals Alexandra felt she didn't need to worry . . .

THIRTY-TWO

I

Catherine came back to Aberdeen just before her twenty-fourth birthday and installed herself in a wing of Highgate House. She wanted Chad to move in with her, but he insisted on being independent and bought himself a four-roomed apartment not far from Queen's Road.

"Why won't you tell me about your new career?" Alexandra asked after her daughter had been home for a few weeks.

"I've been waiting for a telegram. It came today, so let's get together tonight."

"If this is going to be a celebration dinner perhaps I should ask Cook to prepare something fancy," Alexandra remarked.

Catherine held up her hand. "I've had enough of exotic foods. Plain Scottish fare—that's what I want."

Ruby Leslie, the Highgate cook, prepared a deliciously thick Scotch broth, followed by roast ribs of Aberdeen Angus beef served with jacket potatoes, fresh peas, and cabbage. Apple pie and cream was the dessert.

"Marvelous!" Catherine proclaimed after the meal was finished. She followed her mother through to the small room off the hall which she had christened "the snug" because of the intimate ambience created by the wood-panelled walls, red-velvet upholstery and softly lit table lamps.

Catherine sat in one of the Parker Knoll chairs by the side of a blazing log fire. "It's good to be home," she said as she stretched her legs and relaxed.

"Catherine! Don't keep me in suspense," Alexandra said impatiently as she settled herself in a chair opposite her daughter. "I know you've been working your way round the world, but what kind of career . . .?"

Catherine smiled. "I've cooked, cleaned and done all kinds

of jobs. The most productive—and most satisfying—was writing articles about my experiences. Look, here are some of my press cuttings from American newspapers and magazines."

Alexandra's eyes widened as she skimmed through articles on parasailing in Barbados, rafting on the Rio Grande, swimming up a Sicilian gorge, cruising round Australia's Great Barrier Reef. "I'd no idea you had a flair for this kind of thing!"

"Neither did I till I met a newspaper editor at a party in the States. He asked me to write some travel articles for him and when I submitted them he said I had real talent. I was knocked out by his praise, *and* by the money he paid me. That's how it all began."

"So travel writing is your forte?"

"Not anymore. I've moved on." Catherine handed over another pile of press cuttings. "Take a look at these pieces. There, read that one."

The article, written in a hard-hitting, trenchant style, was on the Mafia in Sicily and the government's attempts to deal with it. Alexandra leafed through some of the other articles and saw they ranged from conservation problems to guerrilla warfare.

"From travel writer to investigative journalist . . .I'm really impressed. But why didn't you let me know?"

"I thought the first few acceptances were just luck, and when I got more published I decided it would be fun to get really established and surprise you."

"You've certainly succeeded in doing that! Why American publications?"

"They have a bigger appetite for material. My ultimate aim was to become a contributing editor to an American magazine, writing seven or eight articles a year. That pays really well, believe me. But I didn't seem to be in the running for a job like that until I told an editor that I was returning home to Aberdeen. I got the contract today," Catherine went on happily. "My assignment is to report back to New York on Scotland in general and the oil scene in particular. I'm going to be based here, I reckon."

Alexandra leant forward in her chair, her eyes bright. "Oh darling! You've no idea how thrilled I am."

"You're not too disappointed that I'm not joining Meldrums?"

"I'm delighted you seem to have found your vocation. I just want you to be happy."

"And you like Chad, don't you?"

"I like him a lot," Alexandra replied warmly, "and I admire his determination to learn every aspect of the oil business before he joins his father's firm. Grenvilles of Houston is well-respected."

"How d'you know that?"

Alexandra hesitated. "I could lie to you, but I won't. When I heard you were bringing a Houston boy called Chad Grenville home to Scotland I asked Felix to make some inquiries."

"Mother!"

Alexandra held up her hands. "I know! I know! But you'll be equally protective when you marry and have children of your own. And talking of marriage, are you and Chad . . .?"

Catherine shook her head. "I'm far too caught up in my career to be interested in marriage and Chad has things to do as well. He wants to spend a few more years being independent before he settles down to work for his father. Did I tell you he's already got himself a job on the Seafarer rig?"

"But he's only just arrived!"

"Chad's a fast mover. You watch him. He'll be an offshore installations manager on one of the platforms within months."

"I doubt it, Catherine. That's a job that needs experience."

"Which he has! He's a qualified engineer and before he left the States to go bum . . .round the world he worked for four years with an offshore company in Texas." Alexandra's interest sharpened. In the oil business, potential leaders were cherished like prizefighters. She'd tip off the consortium to keep a check on Chad's progress.

"Mum, you'll never guess who else is working on the Seafarer: Cameron Armstrong is one of the roughnecks. The minute he heard I was back in Aberdeen he called round here to see me. You just missed him."

Alexandra felt her insides dissolving. "When you first met Cameron you said you hated him."

"That was yonks ago! We became very friendly just before I left on my world trip and we started writing to each other. When I told Cameron I'd brought a boyfriend home with me he wasn't pleased. I think he's got a crush on me."

"I don't want you to become friends with Cameron Armstrong!" Alexandra protested before she could stop herself.

"Mother, don't start trying to interfere with my life!"

"Won't you trust me if I tell you there's a very good reason for my attitude?"

"What is it?"

Alexandra averted her eyes. "I can't tell you."

Catherine groaned. "Oh my God, it's the stupid family feud again! Well, let me tell you something: neither Cameron nor I care tuppence for it. Relax. Cameron may be keen on me, but as far as I'm concerned we're just good friends."

Alexandra struggled to keep her self-control. "I'm sorry, I didn't mean to spoil our celebratory dinner together, but I don't want Cameron Armstrong in Highgate House."

II

Catherine was furious. She certainly wasn't going to give up Cameron's friendship on her mother's say-so, but on the other hand she didn't want to antagonize her mother; she was enjoying their new close relationship. She was lying on the floor in Chad's flat playing records with him when the solution came to her. It was simple. She would meet Cameron in cafés or bars that she knew her mother never frequented. And if necessary they could spend evenings together in *his* flat.

"You're going off to the rig tomorrow, aren't you?" she asked Chad.

"Sure. Why?"

"When you're here I devote my free time to you. But when you're working I like to make arrangements to see other friends."

"Such as?"

"Cameron Armstrong, for one."

"Oh Christ, that asshole! It's bad enough working with him offshore . . .I don't like that guy, Catherine!"

"Neither does my mother. She nearly had a fit when I said I'd become friendly with Cameron. She's barred him from Highgate!"

"Your mother's a very intelligent lady," Chad commented.

"Oh stuff! She just doesn't want Cameron around because of the old Armstrong-Meldrum feud."

"Can you blame her? Armstrongs and Meldrums are business rivals. Anyway, some of the guys think Cameron's a bit of a weirdo."

"Rubbish," Catherine protested. "I feel sorry for Cameron. He's estranged from his mother and rarely sees his father and I'm sure he's lonely."

"Tough shit! He's not the type of friend I'd choose for you."

"I reserve the right to choose my own friends," Catherine said stiffly.

"Oh, do what you like. But watch out for that guy, he's trouble!"

"You're the one who's dangerous," Catherine said as she pushed the records out of the way and pulled Chad down on top of her. "Why are you wearing so many clothes? Take them off!"

"Now that's a suggestion I like," Chad said and within moments he had stripped off his own clothes and Catherine's as well.

He looked at her as she lay on the floor. "I'm a hair-fetishist," he said as he spread the shining black strands in a fan shape across her breasts. "I like your bush too, though there's too much of it. Stay still and close your eyes."

He jumped up from the floor and Catherine heard him moving around the bathroom. When he flopped down beside her she was startled to see that he had a razor in his hand. "Why d'you want that?"

"Because I'm going to give your bush a beauty treatment—trim it till it's heart-shaped. I once saw a nude sunbather with one, and I've never forgotten it."

"You're crazy," Catherine giggled, but she lay back obediently and let him shave her pubic hair. When she opened her eyes again Chad was gazing at her appreciatively. "I knew it was going to be sexy. When you're all dressed up at some social function . . .I'll look at you and think of this and get a hard-on. Talking of which . . ."

He took her in his arms and gasped. "Your jaggy hairs are tickling me. What a fantastic turn-on," he said as he began driving into her. Catherine felt herself caught up in the excitement of making love without any foreplay beforehand.

"Too fast?" Chad asked hoarsely.

"No, no," she said urgently. "Don't stop, please . . .please," she screamed as they began to climax at the same time.

As they lay twined together Catherine began stroking Chad's body. His skin had been toughened and browned by years in the sun and his right thigh had a long deep scar which was the result of an oil-rig accident. He picked up her hand and kissed the star-shaped mole on the inside of her wrist before trailing his lips down her arm and on to her breasts.

"Promise me you'll be careful on the rigs," she whispered.

"Sure I will. The North Sea doesn't give you second chances."

As she lifted her hips once more he plunged deep into her, each consumed by the physical need to relieve the passion that was always smoldering between them.

"Don't you think it's time you made an honest man of me?" Chad said as they were lying peacefully side by side.

"Why bother getting married? I want a career."

Chad pulled her closer. Once they were married and started to raise a family Catherine wouldn't have time for a career. He wanted a good old-fashioned wife who stayed home and baked cookies!

III

Robert thumped his fist on his desk as he realized that his takeover plans for Meldrums were no longer feasible. "You told me Meldrums had a cash-flow problem!"

"They had, but they've been bailed out by the Danziger corporation in New York. Felix Danziger is reputedly Alexandra's lover," Adam added.

"I'm not interested in Alexandra Semple's love-life," Robert replied coldly, "just the state of the Meldrum finances. Let's talk about our trawlers."

European Economic Community quota regulations, restrictions imposed by Iceland, the Faroes and Norway, and escalating costs of fuel had led to the decline of the middle-distance trawler fleet.

"We should convert some of our trawlers to service the oil industry," Robert said to his brother.

"I don't agree," Adam said at once.

"Well, I do!"

"We'll see what the board have to say," Adam replied angrily before he left.

Robert studied the papers in front of him. He felt quite sure the board would back him. Once his judgment about oil had been vindicated and he had been elected Chairman he had been able to effect all kinds of changes. Now he wanted Armstrongs to start servicing the oil industry as their first priority: using shipyard space to provide the type of "one-stop-shop" operated by the Wood Group and Seaforth Marine. These companies were able to pipe fresh water and fuel oil from their bases straight to the quay. They had the facilities to provide everything a rig needed from mud and cement to supplies and equipment, and their profits were reputed to be enormous. If he could emulate their example, one day he'd be able to swallow Meldrums for breakfast.

THIRTY-THREE

I

1980

Catherine's column in the New York magazine was such a success that it became one of its most widely read features. In Britain, her reputation as a tough-talking knowledgeable journalist earned her columns in a daily and a Sunday paper and to cap it all she became a regular contributor to television.

Chad sat in the hospitality room waiting for Catherine's program to begin. Tonight she was on a current-affairs slot giving her views on the impact of North Sea oil on the Scottish economy. She was wearing a yellow pants suit which set off her waist-length black hair and she looked stunning. As Chad watched her he felt a pang as he remembered their undiluted glee the night he had trimmed her pubic hair. In time it had grown, but Chad had never felt the urge to repeat that bit of fun.

"People can't seem to agree on the benefits of the North Sea oil boom," Catherine was saying on the screen. "The North Sea produces high-grade light crude which is worth more on the world markets than the heavier crudes from Africa and the Middle East. But people who think Scotland has stumbled on an Aladdin's cave of wealth forget how traumatic this has been for a small nation. It hasn't been easy trying to adapt to the biggest change in our economy since the Industrial Revolution."

"So what's been the biggest drawback?"

"Well . . .some experts argue that the oil industry has been divisive to the Scottish economy with the west-coast wealth being diminished by the prosperity of the east, and the resultant gravitational pull making life difficult in the central belt."

The interviewer nodded. "And it hasn't turned the tide of unemployment in Scotland, has it?"

Catherine gave a rueful smile. "You wonder if there's *anything* that would do that! Still, let's not forget that 60,000 jobs have been created either directly or indirectly by the oil industry. *That's* certainly helped some of the thousands who've been thrown out of work by the recession in the traditional heavy industries."

The interviewer was a media celebrity from London and Chad could see that he was dazzled by Catherine's grasp of the economic implications of the oil boom. Chad was more in love with her than ever. If it hadn't been for Catherine he'd have gone back to Houston long since, but he'd hung on in Scotland hoping that he could persuade her to marry him and move back to the States with him.

Catherine was beautiful *and* brilliant, he acknowledged, as he watched her fielding further questions about the impact of oil on Scotland. Then the interviewer threw in a question about the thousands of Americans who had come to Scotland since oil was discovered. "How well d'you think they've integrated with the Scots?"

Catherine's eyes twinkled. "Since my boyfriend is American and he's not a million miles from here, I'd say the Americans have integrated really well. Actually, Scotland has more American-owned subsidiary companies than any other part of Britain. Let's face it, we wouldn't have made such fast progress in oil without American know-how."

"If Scotland has benefited so much from North Sea oil, why are the Scots always whining about not getting their fair share?"

"Because they say it's *their* oil! I have sympathy for that point of view, but I also realize that exploration and development cost billions. Scotland didn't have the money to get the oil out on their own."

"So the Scots should stop grumbling, shouldn't they?" the interviewer asked provocatively.

Catherine's brown eyes flashed. "Maybe they wouldn't grumble if Englishmen like you gave Scotland more credit for improving Britain's balance of payments. In 1974 Britain had to import all her oil. Now in 1980 we're self-sufficient for the first time in our history. By next year we'll be exporting oil and in a few more years we'll have a surplus."

Chad grimaced. Why did the Scots always try to take all the credit? What about the gas and oil in the southern and central basins? They had helped Britain's balance of payments as well. Still, he wasn't going to argue with Catherine. Not about that. It was her job that bugged him: it made her so busy she didn't want to settle down, and he was fed up with it. If she didn't agree to marry him soon he'd go back to the States on his own.

II

When the interview was over, Catherine and Chad had a meal in one of Aberdeen's new restaurants, but afterwards Chad surprised Catherine by saying he wanted an early night. "Is there something wrong?" she asked, worried by his remoteness.

"Not really. Everything's just the same. Isn't it?"

Catherine said nothing. She knew perfectly well what Chad meant. Her position was unchanged: she loved Chad, but she didn't want to give up her career for marriage. And that's what he wanted.

"Aren't you going to invite me back to your flat?" she said uncertainly.

"You need an early night as much as I do. Anyway, I've got to get up early—I'm flying out to the platform on the first chopper."

Barnico Zulu, the floating production facility, commissioned by the consortium which included Danziger Meldrum, was now firmly in place on the North Sea and Chad was its offshore installations manager.

"Chad, what's happening to us?" Catherine asked sadly as he kissed her goodnight on the doorstep of Highgate House.

"Nothing's happening, honey. That's the problem."

Catherine watched him walk away down the road without a backward glance and felt unaccountably lonely. Maybe she was just tired. She looked up at Highgate House and saw a light in her mother's study. She took off her coat in the hall and was about to go upstairs when she decided to visit the west wing and find out why her mother was working so late.

"Still at it? It's past midnight, mum." Catherine realized with sudden alarm that her mother looked very tired. "Is there some problem?"

"Money, that's the problem. The time lag between discovery, platform-ordering and production . . ."

"But the floating production platform is in place now . . ."

"Yes, that's true, but cash profits take time to come through."

"I thought Felix Danziger's company had lent you masses of money to tide you over."

"They did."

Catherine walked across and perched on the edge of her mother's chair. "So why are you looking so anxious?"

"Because the loans are enormous. I don't like Meldrums being so dependent on them, especially as they're repayable on demand."

"But Felix is your friend. He'd never embarrass you financially."

"No, but his cousin Cornelius would!"

"Well, in that case why don't you get Felix to change the agreement you have with him so that the loans aren't repayable on demand?"

"I suggested that to Felix and he put it to his board, but Cornelius managed to persuade them that it would be a bad idea."

"Can't Felix use other methods to make Cornelius fall in line?"

"I suppose he could."

"Well then, suggest it next time you see him."

"I could do. He's flying out to the platform tomorrow. He'll stay with me for a few days before going back to the States."

Alexandra shivered and Catherine put a protective arm round her. "It's a funny old world, isn't it, mum? For years we seemed to needle each other constantly; now we're the best of friends. Don't worry about Felix. When he phones you tomorrow you'll become your cheerful self again."

III

When Chad Grenville gazed down on production platforms from the air he sometimes thought they resembled giant Meccano sets which had been left in the middle of the ocean. The derrick on Barnico Zulu rose skyward like the Eiffel Tower and the cranes surrounding it protruded at awkward angles from an amorphous collection of equipment. Not everyone relished the challenge of working in an environment which could change from Mediterranean calm to a terrifying scenario of howling gales and mountainous waves. There was a high drop-out factor. But since Chad was Houston-born and -bred he was toughened to the hazards of working in the oil business and he was proving a popular and highly efficient offshore installations manager.

He was having his morning meeting with the men who helped him run the platform: the engineers who looked after the machinery and building work, and the supervisors who were in charge of everything from catering to helicopters. Once it was over, he made an inspection of the platform. It was one of those days when fog swirled everywhere, blanking out one corner, then drifting to another like a hesitant dinner party guest wondering where to settle. Helicopters had been grounded and leave cancelled, isolating the rig in its own private world. Chad was used to the vagaries of the weather, but he reserved a special antipathy for fog: it blocked vision and deadened anticipation in an environment which needed both for survival.

He ran lightly up the steps leading to a position where he could get a good view of the anchor wires through his binoculars. They looked fine and dandy. He could see that Cameron Armstrong and the other scaffolders were working well. They perched precariously beneath the module deck, their world bounded by the floor of the module above them and the sea foaming beneath. Scaffolders tended to be loners who delighted in danger. Was that why Armstrong had changed from roughnecking to scaffolding?

Chad pursed his lips. He couldn't stand Cameron bloody Armstrong and wished fervently that the latter hadn't applied for the job on Barnico Zulu. He was uneasy as well about the special relationship Cameron seemed to enjoy with Catherine.

They went around together when Chad was away. What did Catherine see in the guy? Cameron was a sadist. Once, when a rigger had been blasted off his feet by a jet of high-pressure water and had screamed in agony, Cameron had actually laughed. When Chad had told Catherine that story she refused to believe it; instead she reminded him that Cameron had saved several men's lives when he had pushed them out of the way of a falling crane.

Winston Churchill had once said that Russia was "a riddle wrapped in a mystery inside an enigma." Chad thought that a perfect description of Cameron Armstrong. A man capable of heroism or murder? The last was supposition on Chad's part, but he kept wondering about it. He wondered too about the strange bond between Cameron and Catherine, disturbed by the knowledge that it seemed to be getting stronger. Thrusting that disquieting thought from his mind Chad concentrated on the platform, the weather, and the impending visit of Felix Danziger. As the morning wore on the fog began to disperse. Danziger would be delayed, but he'd still be able to come out to the platform.

IV

Felix was looking forward to spending a day on the platform and then seeing Alexandra in the evening, but thirty minutes into the flight the chopper suddenly lurched to one side and smoke began drifting into the cabin. He turned to his neighbor. "What the hell's going on?"

The pilot's voice came over the intercom. He sounded perfectly calm as he told the passengers that he had been having a few problems and was going to make a controlled landing in the sea. He added that the coastguard helicopters had been scrambled and would be on the scene shortly. Felix heard a stuttering sound and realized there was something wrong with the Sikorsky's engines. The pilot confirmed his fears by announcing an emergency drill for landing. The drill had been well-rehearsed by the crew and passengers on the plane, but eyes reflected disbelief that for once this drill was for real. As the chopper began to weave unsteadily towards the ocean, faces grew pale, and fists were clenched.

"Brace! Brace! Brace!" came the command and everyone straightened in their seats. Felix felt the breath knocked out of him as the Sikorsky crashed into a sea that was dangerously stormy. Within moments seat belts were unfastened, life rafts thrown into the water, and the men on board scrambled out as fast as they could.

Felix was one of the last to leave. He was about to slide out into the sea when the Sikorsky was hit by a huge wave and turned over. Felix's head smashed against the side and split open like an over-ripe pumpkin. His body was winched aboard the coastguard helicopter, but it was too late to save him.

The North Sea had claimed another victim.

V

The top executives in Meldrums flew to New York for the funeral. Alexandra kept thinking how fond she had been of Felix, and what a good friend he had been even after she had refused to marry him. She couldn't understand why she hadn't been able to cry since his death.

As the plane approached Kennedy airport Catherine squeezed her arm. "I'm here for you, mum," she whispered. And then at last Alexandra felt the tears come.

THIRTY-FOUR

I

Alexandra was studying the company balance sheet in her office in Aberdeen when the call came from New York. "I'm sure Felix told you that he'd made me his heir," Cornelius Danziger said quietly. "The board have just elected me President of Danziger Minerals."

Alexandra felt apprehension nip at her nerve ends as she waited for Cornelius to tell her that the special relationship between Meldrums and Danzigers was at an end. To her surprise Cornelius chatted amiably about their two companies and their commitment to the consortium. "As far as the loans are concerned, Alexandra, I'm quite content to carry on with them at the moment."

"That's . . .very generous of you, Cornelius. I never thought for a moment, I mean . . .Well, let's just say you've caught me by surprise."

"Just thought I'd reassure you. And I hope I'll see you in New York sometime," he added before he rang off. Alexandra felt she'd received an unexpected Christmas present. She'd completely misjudged Cornelius.

II

When he put down the phone Cornelius took out a cigar from the silver box on his cousin's desk. Initially he had tried to curry favor with Felix's mistress, but the bitch had made no secret of her dislike for him. And now she was going to pay for it. He glanced at the last letter that Alexandra had sent to Felix. There was a full page about Armstrongs.

"They won't have a chance of bidding for Meldrums whilst

you're still backing me," she had written to Felix. "I'm so grateful."

Cornelius drew deeply on his cigar and puffed some smoke towards the ceiling before opening the drawer where Felix kept his confidential documents. He pulled out Meldrums' latest balance sheet which Alexandra had sent to his cousin, then he picked up the phone and dialed Adam Armstrong's number in Aberdeen. He'd met Adam on several occasions in New York and had gathered that Adam hated Alexandra as much as he did. Cornelius smiled. Acquiring Meldrums would be much easier for Armstrongs once he put them in the picture about Meldrums' finances and his own intentions.

III

Felix Danziger's death was the first shock Catherine received. Chad's announcement was the second. He took her out to dinner and told her that he was flying to Texas immediately to see his parents. "I've bummed around long enough, Catherine, and since you've no intention of marrying me I think I'm going to make a new life for myself in the States. I'll discuss it with dad, then fly back here and serve out my notice."

"What about me?" Catherine asked, stunned by his news.

"Your career comes first with you, Catherine. You'll manage without me," he said as he kissed her goodnight.

Catherine lay in her bed at Highgate House. She revelled in her career, but life without Chad . . .Suddenly she got up and began dressing. She slipped out of the house and ran all the way down the avenue till she reached Chad's flat. She rang the bell and thumped on the door until it was opened.

Chad was in his pajamas and his eyes were sleepy. "Jesus Christ, what are you doing here? When I left you, you said you were going straight to bed!"

"Aren't you going to let me in?"

He stood aside as she walked before him into the small lounge, but she did not sit down. Instead she rounded on him, her eyes flashing. "I just came round to tell you that you're a wimp! Why didn't you try and force me to confess that I *do* want to marry you? You just accepted what I said and were prepared to leave it at that! Well, I'm not!"

Chad scratched his head in bewilderment. "So what are you going to do?"

"I'm going round to the travel agent's first thing tomorrow morning to buy two tickets for Houston, one for myself and one for my mother. She needs a break. And . . .well, it's about time I met my future in-laws!"

Chad gave a great whoop and lifted her off her feet before whirling her round in a circle and giving her a long passionate kiss. "You really mean it?"

"I do. Felix's death has made me rethink my priorities. Sure, I love my career, but not half as much as I love you, Chad!"

IV

The visit to Houston was to end on a note of high drama, but initially the omens seemed promising. Chad's father sent a stretch limo and driver to meet them at the airport. Alexandra and Catherine found the air-conditioning very welcome after the waves of heat which assaulted them the minute they stepped off the plane. Chad looked after the luggage, settled them into the Cadillac and suggested they lean back in the seats. Alexandra smiled at him indulgently. She had a feeling he was going to make a terrific husband for Catherine and she hoped his parents would feel the same way about her daughter.

She sat back and dozed. When she opened her eyes she could see the skyscrapers of Houston through the car window. "If the tenements in Glasgow looked like that no one would want to pull them down," she said softly.

"Everything's so big," Catherine explained.

"Forty miles across," Chad replied. "Same as from Aberdeen to Huntley. Look, there's the Astrodome."

"They play basketball there?" Catherine asked straightfaced.

Chad was horrified. "The Astros are the baseball team . . ." he began. Then he saw the twinkle in Catherine's eye. "You're winding me up, wench!"

An hour later the car turned into a driveway guarded by two imposing pillars. A mile further on they saw a magnificent white house.

"Wow-ee!" Catherine exclaimed. "Your home looks gorgeous!"

The driver drew the car to a halt and Chad helped them out. His parents were waiting to greet them. Marnie Grenville was a tall silver-haired lady with a kindly smile. Her husband, Willard, had white hair, a deep tan, and a truculent manner. "All this fuss," he grumbled.

"Don't pay any attention to dad," Chad said. "He tries to pretend that he doesn't like visitors, but he loves 'em."

He gave his mother and father a hug and then introduced his guests.

"We're real pleased to welcome you," Marnie said. "Now why don't y'all go up to your rooms to freshen up, and then join us in the drawing room for drinks."

Alexandra was the first to come downstairs. The drawing room, like everything else she had seen since she touched down in Houston, was vast. It was decorated in shades of *eau de nil* which were echoed in the rugs scattered on the polished hardwood floors. As she sipped the margarita that Willard had handed to her, Alexandra admired the paintings hanging on the walls and began to chat to Marnie about antiques. When Chad and Catherine came down hand in hand Willard snorted. "I suppose you two will be billin' and cooin' all week! Just don't let's have any misbehavin' ".

"Don't worry, Mr. Grenville," Catherine said smartly, "if Chad steps out of line I'll kick his ass!"

Willard cackled with approving laughter as he poured her a drink. "I want to have a long talk with your mother," he announced. "Though I don't approve of women messing about in the oil business," he added. "Most of them should have stayed home!"

Marnie was outraged at her husband's rudeness to his guests. "You inherited your business, Willard. From what Chad tells me, Alexandra built hers up from a hayseed. That's some achievement. I bet you're just jealous!"

"I'm not a jealous man!" he spluttered.

"Oh yes, you are, Willard Grenville!" his wife replied spiritedly. "You get sick as a dog whenever you think Turnbulls are going to steal a march on you. Turnbulls are his greatest rivals in the States," she added for Alexandra's benefit. "You behave yourself, Willard, or you'll get the sharp edge of my tongue!"

"Got that already!" he replied grumpily.

Alexandra couldn't help laughing. She'd seen the twinkle in

Willard's eyes and knew he was provoking his wife deliberately.

"Don't worry about your husband," she said reassuringly to Marnie. "I'm sure we'll find we have a lot in common. After all Texas and Aberdeenshire have a special relationship." When oil had been discovered off the north-east coast of Scotland seventy-two Scottish businessmen had joined the first offshore oil industry trade mission to Houston, and this had resulted in many business projects.

"I can see we'll have to separate these two," Chad sighed, amused at his father's volte-face, "otherwise they'll talk business all the time."

Willard winked at Alexandra. "Wouldn't dream of it. I'll take Alexandra to the oil technology conference and after that she'll be treated to some southern hospitality."

"And I want to take Catherine shopping," Marnie insisted. "You'll love the Galeria shopping mall. It's got balconies overlooking the ice rink and joggers on the roof track. And of course you'll want to visit Nieman Marcus. That's the biggest store for miles!"

"Well, I'm durned if I'm going shopping," Willard said crossly. "I've got sightseeing plans for you."

"And I've got plans to take Catherine to a sandwich bar. She can try the six-deckers at Whistlers," Chad said. "And maybe when you oldies are in bed Catherine and I will go out on the town and treat ourselves to gumbo soup and red snapper."

"Sounds like a real busy time ahead," Marnie commented, "but y'all remember I've fixed a party for Thursday!"

V

Thursday's party was to introduce Catherine and Alexandra to the Grenvilles' social circle. Trestle tables were replete with cold cuts and a bewildering array of vegetables; barbecue pits sizzled and flashed as king-sized steaks were grilled, and waiters bustled amongst the guests dispensing drinks. Although dress was supposed to be casual Catherine couldn't help noticing the designer outfits as guests danced in a wooden-floored marquee. There was plenty of light too from flashing diamonds, including the solitaire which now rested on the third finger of Catherine's left hand. She kept holding it up to the light to admire it. For Catherine the evening passed all too quickly. "It's been wonderful!" she said to Chad after the guests had left and the band had gone home. "I'm too excited to go to bed. We don't need music to dance, do we?"

"Sure don't, honey," Chad said as he kissed her cheek.

"Where's my mother?" Catherine asked as they drifted round the dance floor.

"Where she's been ever since she arrived: head to head with dad. They're over there." He indicated Alexandra and Willard still deep in conversation at one of the tables.

"She seems to admire him, but my God, don't they argue! Look at them. Yak, yak, yak. Hey, looks as if mum's been called away to the phone."

"Keep dancing. She'll be back soon."

Half an hour later Catherine realized her mother still hadn't reappeared. "Something's wrong; let's go find her."

"There's a light on in dad's study," Chad said. "We'll try there first."

Alexandra was holding the phone, looking shocked. "I'll take the first flight out tomorrow, Boyd. Bye."

"Mum!" Catherine protested. "We were going to stay till the end of the week."

"You can wait, Catherine, but I've got to leave right away."

"What's happened?"

"Cornelius fooled me. He's just phoned Boyd. Unless Meldrums can pay off the balance within four weeks Danzigers are going to call in the loans. And that's not all. By some strange coincidence Armstrongs have just made a dawn raid on Meldrums . . ."

"A dawn raid . . ." Catherine echoed faintly. She knew what that meant: when one company suddenly bought lots of shares in a rival company it was often the first move in a full-scale takeover bid.

Chad moved forward slightly. "How many shares have Armstrongs bought?"

"Fourteen per cent! Strange, isn't it, that Armstrongs have made their move at the exact moment Cornelius called in the loans? Makes me wonder if there's been collusion somewhere along the line. I'm sorry to spoil the visit, Chad, but I really will have to leave first thing in the morning."

"We'll come with you, mum. You'll need our help."

Alexandra stood up. Her eyes burned in a face that was as white as the walls. "Thanks, Catherine, but I have to warn you that the kind of help I need right now is a miracle. At this precise moment the chances of saving Meldrums seem remote. I'd better pack and then go to bed. Chad, would you make excuses for me to your parents?"

"I'll come up with you, mum," Catherine said quickly. She kissed Chad goodnight. "You may as well go to bed, I'd better keep mum company."

Chad did not go to bed. Once his mother had retired for the night he buttonholed his father and asked him to come into the study where he told him about Alexandra's phone call.

"That's bad news," Willard said, rubbing his chin with his fingers. "Alexandra's a feisty lady. It'd be a durned shame if Meldrums was swallowed up by this Armstrong outfit."

"It needn't be," Chad said thoughtfully. "When there's a dawn raid on a company it needs a 'white knight.' That's the jargon, isn't it?"

"Sure is. But don't look at me, son."

"But dad, you said a while back that Grenvilles wanted to expand their oil and property interests?"

"In the States, not in Scotland!"

"There's Meldrum Manhattan. And Meldrum Europe. And as for Scotland, that production platform in the North Sea is sitting on a pool of oil which could be worth a fortune. And Meldrums have a stake in it."

Willard rubbed his chin thoughtfully. "I have to admit I like the idea of that oil . . ." He sat for a while in silence. Then he shook his head. "Son, I'm sorry. When I talked to you about expansion I meant takeover bids for whole companies."

"Catherine's mother would never go for that. The last thing she wants is to sell her company—to you, dad, or to anyone!"

"Frankly, boy, I don't think she's going to have much choice. Looks as if that Armstrong outfit will take her company whether she likes it or not!"

VI

The next few weeks were a nightmare as it became clear that Armstrongs were indeed about to mount a full-scale takeover bid for Meldrums. Chad talked to his father on the phone several times a day, but he couldn't persuade him to change his mind. Alexandra was closeted with bankers, stockbrokers, and financial advisors, but they weren't hopeful. Armstrongs hadn't expanded as far and as fast as Meldrums and were cash-rich; they had vast amounts of capital at their disposal.

"I feel so useless," Catherine said to Chad one evening when they were lying in bed together. "I've never shown much interest in Meldrums, but since I've become so close to my mother I feel for her. She'll be desolate if she loses her company to Armstrongs."

Chad sighed. "The maddening thing is that Grenvilles have plenty of capital. It's a pity dad's not interested. Now if it were Turnbulls, that would be different."

"Turnbulls? Oh yes, I remember your mother saying he got eaten up with anxiety in case Turnbulls outsmarted him. Hey, that's an idea!" Catherine pushed her hair out of her eyes and sat up in bed. "Why don't you get in touch with Turnbulls and suggest they might like to buy a stake in Meldrums?"

Chad turned on his side and looked at her. "Your mother told me she didn't like the Turnbull set-up. She might not be keen to let them . . ."

"Don't you see?" Catherine said excitedly. "If you tell your father that Turnbulls are interested, he might . . ."

Chad leapt out of bed and punched his fist in the air. "You got it, baby! If my old man even *thinks* Turnbulls are interested, he'll change his mind about Meldrums pretty durn quick!"

Chad knew exactly how to handle his father. When he was on the phone to him he was careful to speak casually when he mentioned that Turnbulls seemed interested in Meldrums. Within the hour his father was back on the phone saying that he would be arriving in Aberdeen the next day.

VII

A meeting was arranged with lawyers from both sides, but Willard wanted to have his say first. "I'm not interested in a slice of the cake. I'm willing to come to Meldrums' rescue if I'm appointed President of the company which will be called Grenville International. The Meldrum name will be dropped."

"No, it won't!" Alexandra retorted vehemently. "The Meldrum name stays, or it's no deal. And I insist on being joint Chief Executive."

"I won't be 'joint' with anyone, especially a woman!" Willard stormed.

"It's not going to work," Catherine wailed to Chad when they heard news of the boardroom row.

Chad patted her hand. " 'Course it will. You wouldn't expect your mother and my father to reach an agreement easily, would you?"

"But I thought they respected each other?" Catherine said despairingly.

"They do, but they're both cussed and neither of them wants to relinquish power. They'll fight it out and then there'll be a compromise. And what's more," he said suddenly, "I know the very one that might appeal to both of them. I'll suggest it over lunch."

The steaks were underdone and when Chad saw his father and Alexandra chewing away like mad he decided this was a good moment to launch his proposal. He suggested that his father should become President of the merged company, Alexandra would be Vice President, and the name would be Grenville Meldrum International.

"I don't know why you two are still bickering," Chad added. "When I marry Catherine our families will be merged anyway, and surely I'll be the next President-elect of Grenville Meldrums?"

Alexandra smiled. "I'd forgotten that. Well, Willard, if you're happy with your son's suggestion, let's shake on it and our lawyers can get to work."

Willard glared at her. "Durned if those children of ours haven't bested us!" he said. And held out his hand.

"There's only one other condition I'd like included," Alexandra went on, "an unofficial one."

Willard looked at her suspiciously. "You're wanting more power?"

"No, Willard," Alexandra replied, "this is not a demand, it's a request. When the time is ripe I want you to help me make a takeover bid for Armstrongs. Adam bought the Meldrum castle, Robert tried to buy the Meldrum empire. I want my revenge . . ."

PART VII

1986-68

THIRTY-FIVE

I

1986

The canopy over the four-poster bed trembled as the two figures writhed and swayed, perspiring with passion as they came to their climax. Afterwards Belinda reached out to the bedside table and poured a strong measure of gin into a crystal tumbler.

"Maybe you not take so much. Or when your husband come home, he guess you been with lover."

"He doesn't need to guess, he knows!"

Hans edged off the bed. "You serious?"

"Sure! After sixteen years of marriage Adam doesn't expect me to be faithful." Although Belinda was in her mid-fifties, she continued to defy nature by looking slim, sexy, and provocative. And, like many of the film stars she admired, her appetite for sexual conquest was undiminished. Now she drained her glass and then turned to Hans once more. She pushed her hands beneath her bottom and raised her legs till they were twined round one of the bedposts. Hans was stroking her breasts when he felt himself being manhandled off the bed and on to the floor.

"Get your filthy hands off my wife!"

"Hi, Adam," Belinda said, without changing her position. "Say hello to Hans. He's been giving me a good time."

Hans picked up his clothes and fled.

"Have you no shame? Dutch, French, American . . . You don't care who you take to bed."

Belinda lowered her legs and smiled sweetly at her husband. "Damn right! I'm not fussy about oilmen's nationality. As long as they're amusing. And generous," she added as her eyes slid to the dressing table where an expensive gold necklace lay in its box. Adam picked up the necklace and threw it out of the open window. Belinda jumped off the bed and ran towards him, pounding his chest with her fists. "You'll have to buy me another!"

"I can't afford . . ."

"Can't afford this, can't afford that," Belinda mimicked. "That's all I hear from you these days," she added, as she began pulling on a dress. "For the first few years of our marriage life was such fun—trips to Monte Carlo and Paris, champagne parties, expensive presents."

"I'm glad you remember," Adam said bitterly. "I pandered to all your whims, gave you everything you wanted."

"I know you did. And I was happy. You were real good to me."

As Adam watched his wife brushing her blonde hair he felt his anger dissolving. She'd always been a spoiled rich girl. When Belinda wanted something she did everything in her power to get it—Robert, himself, lovers, presents—but eventually she became bored and wanted something else. Her one enduring passion had been Drumcraig Castle, but now it seemed she was bored with that too. Or was she just irritated by the amount of money they had to spend on the place? Adam thrust his hands in his pockets and walked to the window. As one of the major shareholders in Armstrongs he benefited from huge bonuses as well as a substantial yearly salary, but it wasn't enough to maintain Belinda's extravagant tastes and the upkeep of Drumcraig. Tom Elphinstone hadn't spent a penny on the fabric of the castle and eventually his sins of omission began to bear fruit. Masonry crumbled, doors and windows leaked and the castle had to be rerooted. Worst of all was the outbreak of dry rot. No sooner had one room been renovated and redecorated than spores appeared in another. Adam had borrowed heavily from the bank to pay for it and was still deeply in debt.

"If I weren't so short of money . . ."

"Bo-ring! Bo-ring!" Belinda taunted as she began putting on her make-up. "I can't understand why you gave up gambling? You used to do well at it."

"I lost my lucky streak. When that happens you keep away from the tables."

"So try something else," Belinda said as she applied her

mascara. "Make money on the stock market like some of our friends, then you won't have to go droning on about dry rot. There," she said as she surveyed herself in the mirror. "How do I look?"

She still looked lovely, Adam acknowledged; that was the problem. However badly she treated him he was still addicted to her.

Adam made the phone call while he was having a late breakfast the following morning. His broker's response was less than enthusiastic. "Traded options? That's high risk, Adam."

"Yes, but I know people who've made lots of money that way."

Adam put down the receiver and had another cup of tea while he glanced through the paper. On the television page there was a photograph of Catherine Grenville. She'd become even more of a celebrity since she'd married the son of Willard Grenville. These days when she wasn't writing articles, she was fronting the *Face to Face* current affairs program on television. Adam blinked: according to this paper the subject of her interview tonight was his brother Robert.

II

Robert Armstrong contemplated the girl who was interviewing him. Alexandra's daughter hadn't inherited her mother's green eyes or her chestnut hair. Catherine's eyes were a warm shade of brown and a black cloud of hair flowed round her shoulders, providing a pleasing contrast to her acid-yellow minidress. She wasn't like her father, Robert thought absently, Malcolm Semple had been fair. He tried to concentrate as he realized that the interview had begun and they were on screen.

"The discovery of oil has made a huge impact on Scotland, but has it been bad or good for the country?" Catherine began.

Robert glanced down at the birthmark mole on his wrist. What a question to throw at him without previous notice! But if this chit of a girl thought she'd thrown him off balance she was wrong.

"It hasn't all been favorable," he said firmly. "Traditional industries have found it difficult to compete against the high wages of the oil industry, and local people have sometimes been priced out of the property market. There's also been aggravation with the fishing industry, broken marriages caused by the oil-rig schedules, horrifying accidents . . . But on the other hand look at the plus side. Apart from the obvious benefits to the economy there have been many roll-on effects. Like the building of the world's largest survival center. It was Shell who suggested that to Robert Gordon's Institute of Technology."

As Robert gave other examples, he became aware that Catherine tended to arch one eyebrow when he gave an answer that surprised her. She reminded him of someone, but it was an imprecise image on the edge of his consciousness which he could not define. It was certainly spoiling his concentration. He was irritated by this girl who was young enough to be his daughter. Catherine had been born in December 1951; the date was burned on his memory. He had been devastated when he had seen the announcement in the papers because he realized that Alexandra must have been in Malcolm's bed as far back as April. It was in April that he'd taken Alexandra to Paris and proposed. And she'd accepted.

"Shall I repeat my question, Mr. Armstrong?" Catherine was saying.

Someone had warned him that it was fatal to daydream if you were on television. He made an effort to smooth over the awkward moment. "Perhaps you should rephrase it?" he suggested.

Catherine's eyes were steely. "In recent years, Armstrongs, unlike some of their competitors, have concentrated almost entirely on oil and oil-related services. For example, you've expended a huge amount of capital on your new 'one-stop-shop' installation at Aberdeen harbor, haven't you?"

"Yes," Robert replied shortly, "but I'm confident that it will prove a good investment." And if it didn't, he thought, Armstrongs would be in trouble. The cost had been way over budget.

"So I presume you have no fears of the oil bubble bursting?"

"None at all!" Robert replied. "When oil dropped from a peak of $40 a barrel in 1980 to $30 in 1985 everyone was worried, but the industry has learned to accept that though there are sometimes dramatic falls in price there are equally dramatic rises. One can't panic. The future prospects continue to look good. There's talk of the Gannet/Kittiwake field being developed at over 2.5 billion pounds and even the high-cost frontier areas west of Shetland are said to be targeted. Having said that, I should add that the oil industry remains very cost-conscious."

As he spoke confidently he wondered why this girl was unsettling him. Suddenly he realized who she reminded him of: himself.

"Could we turn for a moment to the question of safety in the North Sea?" Catherine was asking. "After the Alexander Kielland disaster in 1980, the following year 400 men had to be airlifted to safety after a crack was found in the Borgland Dolphin semi-submersible. And in 1983 two men died and six were injured after an explosion on the Cormorant Alpha platform. When there's so much high-tech gadgetry available, why so many accidents? That's the question some politicians are asking."

"Politicians!" Robert growled. "Half of them don't know what they're talking about. They're just trying to score political points. They should go out to the rigs and platforms before they start making pronouncements about safety and conditions!"

Robert saw Catherine stiffen and remembered too late that her uncle Frank was one of the politicians who had been sounding off about rig safety. Robert wondered if Catherine would declare her interest or take the easy option and switch the subject.

"I think your accusation is unfair and unjustified," Catherine retorted, anger making her eyes flash. "Frank Meldrum is one of the campaigning MPs. But he isn't just making speeches, he's going on a trip with a party of VIPs, to inspect a floating production platform which is ahead of its time, one of the safest in the North Sea. Have you been out on it?" she asked politely.

Robert couldn't help smiling to himself. Catherine knew perfectly well that he hadn't been near the Barnico Zulu production platform in which her mother's company had a vested interest.

"No, I haven't," he replied evenly, "but I'd welcome an invitation to inspect it. Have *you* seen it?" he asked, hoping to put her at a disadvantage.

Catherine smiled sweetly. "I've been asked to travel out with the inspection party."

"Well, in that case you'll be better informed than I am."

The interview ended. Once they were off screen he could see the anger in Catherine's eyes. "I'm sorry I made that remark about politicians," he said quickly. "I intended no insult against your uncle. He's one of the best MPs on either side of the house."

"Thank you." Catherine appeared to be slightly mollified by his generous apology, but her mouth was still tightly drawn.

"Since Armstrongs are a rival of Meldrums I'm surprised you suggested me for this program," Robert ventured.

"I didn't suggest you; that was my producer's doing," Catherine snapped. "I asked if someone else could do the interview."

Robert smiled wryly. "I'm glad you didn't chicken out, Catherine. I respect your skill and courage. And I'm sorry . . ."

"You've already apologized," Catherine said and held out her right hand to bid him goodbye.

"Would you like a drink before you go?" the girl in hospitality asked.

He felt like asking for a double whisky. As he'd shaken Catherine's hand he'd noticed the star-shaped mole on her wrist. My God, Robert thought. Maybe she's not Malcolm's daughter. Maybe she's mine!

III

In a Dublin pub three men had been watching the *Face to Face* interview. "That was an interesting wee program," Liam O'Rafferty said thoughtfully. "A floating production platform that's supposed to be one of the safest in the North Sea . . ." He turned to the man on his left. "I don't suppose you'd be knowing its name?"

"Barnico Zulu," Mick replied immediately. "Sure, and they were all talking about it when I left Aberdeen last week. That's the one everyone wants to work on."

"And were they talking about celebrities visiting it?"

"Nary a word! But then I wasn't asking, was I?"

Liam clapped him on the back. "Sure, and wouldn't it be in-teresting to know when all those grand folks will be going out there? You go and bring over more drinks while I have a wee talk with Sean."

The man on his right still hadn't spoken. Liam looked at him quizzically. "Well, Sean me boy, what d'you think?"

Sean pursed his lips. "I'm thinking it would make big head-lines if anything happened to all those grand folk. Would make a right fool of the government, wouldn't it?"

"Now you wouldn't want to do that, would you, Sean?"

Sean smiled.

IV

When Chad stepped off the chopper at Dyce he thought, as he often did these days, that it would have been great to be return-ing home to a welcoming wife. Home was the east wing of Highgate House which had been Catherine's bachelor-girl flat. Chad had moved into it when they married. Before the wed-ding Catherine had asked if he would mind staying in Scotland until she finished her television and newspaper contracts. It wasn't what he wanted, but he felt that since she had made a major concession in agreeing to their marriage, he had to make one as well. For her part Catherine agreed that eventually they would emigrate to the States where Chad would help run his father's business.

But how long is "eventually," Chad wondered as he opened a six-pack and settled down in a chair to watch his wife on television. They had been married for five years and every time he mentioned going to the States Catherine begged him to stay in Scotland a little longer. Nor were there any signs of Catherine becoming pregnant. For Chad this was a big disap-pointment. Like many only children he had always anticipated having a big family of his own when he got married. Catherine had said that once they had children she would definitely give up her career and go back to the States with him.

Lately Chad had caught himself wondering if his wife was playing it straight. Was she taking the pill and keeping quiet about it? He felt she would be insulted if he asked her, especially if his suspicions were false, nor did he relish the idea of hunting through her drawers. But as he looked at her on television, so cool, so confident, so beautiful, he decided it was time to find out the truth; his doubts were eating at the fabric of their marriage.

Chad put down his tankard of beer and walked quickly through to their bedroom. He rifled through Catherine's drawers, taking care not to disturb her clothing. There was nothing to interest him. As he was leaving the bedroom his eye fell on a pair of shoes and matching purse which lay on their bed. It looked as if Catherine had changed her mind about which outfit to wear at the last minute. Slowly he picked up the purse and opened it. Inside was a handkerchief, lipstick, some money . . . and a packet of contraceptive pills. And they weren't old ones. The date on the packet was the previous week.

Chad expelled a long breath and sat down on the bed. So . . . Catherine *had* been deceiving him! He closed his eyes and punched the air in anger. Then he pushed the pills into his pocket as he went back downstairs to watch the remainder of Catherine's interview with Robert Armstrong. Robert was making acerbic remarks about politicians and journalists who sounded off about safety but had never been on a rig. Chad could see that Catherine was really riled about that. She blasted Robert for being unfair and informed him that Frank Meldrum was taking a party of VIPs on a fact-finding visit to a production platform.

Chad frowned. Catherine shouldn't have mentioned that. He was relieved when she didn't specify the date or the name of the platform, but when she added at the end that she was joining the inspection party Chad smiled grimly. He had been informed of Catherine's wishes by his boss, but he had no intention of allowing his wife on his platform.

When Catherine returned from the studios Chad told her that the inspection visit would go ahead as planned, but he would make sure she wasn't included.

"Don't be ridiculous, Chad. Barnico are the consortium owners and *they're* happy about it. I want to write an article and include some oilmen in a future *Face to Face* program. You're such an old-fashioned chauvinist. Other women have been out on rigs writing up stories and nothing's going to hold me back on this one."

"If I don't want you on the platform everyone will listen. On Barnico Zulu I'm the boss!"

Catherine whirled round, her black hair flying, her brown eyes hot with anger. "You wouldn't do that!"

"Just watch me! By the way, what does your mother think of this idea?"

"She's not keen, but she wouldn't dream of interfering in my career!"

"And what about my career? I should be in Houston running Grenville Meldrum."

Catherine kicked off her shoes and smoothed out the creases in the acid-yellow dress as she sat down. "Don't let's go into *that* again. Anyway, you said you wanted to stay on Zulu until all the teething problems were sorted out."

"That task's finished. It's time for me to return to Houston."

"But Chad, I've just started filming a new program . . ."

"You promised to go back to the States with me!"

"Yes, sure. When the babies start coming . . ."

"Not much chance of that happening when you're using these!" Chad replied angrily as he flung the contraceptive pills at her feet.

The color ebbed from Catherine's cheeks. "You went through my purse?"

"I wish I'd done it five years ago when you married me. That's how long you've been cheating me, isn't it?"

Catherine's face crumpled. "For the first three years of marriage I wanted to have a baby. But when I got the chance to star in my own program I was terrified of becoming pregnant. So I . . ."

Chad got up from his chair. "That settles it."

"What do you mean?"

"I mean I'm going back to the States."

"But what about me?"

"You've got your newspaper column, your television program and your fame . . . Which are obviously much more important to you than our marriage. So that's it. I'll divorce you and find someone else."

Catherine's mood changed from distress to anger. She jumped up, her eyes blazing. "You're trying to blackmail me!"

"I'm going to move into a hotel."

"See if I care!"

"I don't care either!" Chad shouted back. "I'll still be working out my contract when you come on that fact-finding tour of the platform, but if you fall overboard don't expect me to fish you out."

V

Of all the people who had been watching or taking part in Catherine's *Face to Face* program no one was more disturbed by it than Robert Armstrong. His concern that nerves had made him sound boring dwindled into insignificance against the enormity of the discovery that Catherine might be his daughter and Alexandra might not have been cheating on him after all. He could have made her pregnant in Paris and their quarrel might have stopped her telling him about it. Was that why she had married Malcolm Semple? To give her baby a name? Robert poured himself a double whisky and drained it quickly before pouring another.

He looked at the phone, debating how Alexandra would react if he suggested a meeting. He must be going soft. How could he even contemplate such a thing when he'd tried to take over Meldrums? Alexandra's precious company meant everything to her. He felt the same way about his own. In his interview with Catherine he had expressed complete confidence in the future of oil, but in truth he was deeply worried. The industry always needed standby boats and supply vessels, but he had bulldozed the board into investing in many other oil-related projects. If the oil boom continued Armstrongs would make billions, but if the price of oil kept falling his company could be in trouble.

VI

By the month of July the price of oil had plummeted to $9.50 a barrel and redundancies in the Grampian Region were running at 1,000 a month. Although Grenville Meldrum had invested heavily in North Sea oil they were buffered by the vast range of their interests in Scotland, Europe, and the States. They knew if they sat tight, oil prices would probably rise again and they would be able to capitalize on their investment. Armstrongs were in a much weaker position. Their one-stop-shop operation had drained their capital.

When Alexandra heard the rumors she took herself off to Houston to finalize the Grenville Meldrum bid for Armstrongs which had long since been prepared and ready.

A few days later Catherine flew out to the Barnico Zulu production platform with Frank and Daisy and a clutch of VIPs.

VII

Liam O'Rafferty smiled when he saw Sean and Mick walk into the Dublin pub. "Just off the plane from Aberdeen, are you?"

The other men nodded and sipped appreciatively at the pints which Liam lined up for them.

"No problems then?" Liam asked.

"A small one," Sean admitted. "Our roughneck on the platform . . ."

"Don't tell me he bungled it?"

"Would I be picking a bungler for a job like this? No, no, when Danny came off the platform he assured me he'd done the job just the way I asked. He'd put my explosive device in place and fixed the delayed-time control—and all without anyone noticing. Danny is very capable."

"But . . .?"

"But I'm afraid he's too sensitive. He began worrying about the number of people who would be killed. There's no room in the organization for a man like that. So . . . maybe it's as well he had a wee accident. I got rid of the body and told his landlady he'd gone back to Ireland. A terrible shame, it was."

"Terrible," Liam agreed. "Still and all, maybe it was for the best. Danny might have got a bit upset when he saw the results of his work. When they start picking up survivors . . ."

"Didn't I tell you?" Sean said slowly. "Since there are going to be grand folks aboard that platform I got Danny to fix a grand device—a special. You've nary a worry about survivors, Liam. There aren't going to *be* any!"

THIRTY-SIX

I

Alexandra woke early in her penthouse apartment in New York. She switched on the light and saw it was only five o'clock. It was too early to get up, but she was too excited to go back to sleep. She pulled the silk sheet closer to her face and snuggled down under it. She loved warmth. Frank felt the same way. It was probably a legacy of their upbringing in the chilly north east of Scotland where they had run barefoot across the moors to save the cost of shoes.

Her lips curved in a smile at the thought of the half-brother who was so dear to her. Today was the day he was out on the North Sea platform with her daughter; she was glad Frank was there to protect her. Not that Catherine appeared to need protecting. Her columns in New York magazines and papers, and her television series in Britain were famed for their courage. Catherine's visit to one of the safest oil production platforms in the North Sea would make good copy.

As would Alexandra's takeover bid for Armstrongs. She could imagine the headlines already: "Crofter's daughter becomes one of the richest tycoons in the world." In the process she would destroy the only man she had ever loved . . . But why should she feel guilty? It was time Robert Armstrong paid the price for his double treachery all those years ago. Time all the Armstrongs paid for the misery they had caused the Meldrums.

Alexandra glanced at the clock calendar on the bedside table. Friday the thirteenth. The date did not worry her. She felt this was one of those times in her life when nothing could go wrong.

Later she was appalled at her lack of prescience.

II

Chad studied the weather reports and then went outside the control room to assess the situation for himself. It was cold, but the skies were blue and there was very little wind. Pity. He'd hoped that the weather would be bad and the damned inspection visit would be cancelled. He didn't mind Frank Meldrum and the other men in the party, but he hated the idea of his wife being out on the production platform—even though he was estranged from her. It was the consortium's fault. They were starry-eyed at Catherine's fame and the good report they hoped she'd write on Barnico Zulu's advanced construction. He was surprised that Alexandra hadn't objected to her daughter coming out to the platform, but then, she probably had. Catherine would pay as little attention to her mother's warnings as she'd done to his. Catherine was too darned cussed to be a comfortable wife; that's why he intended divorcing her.

He went back into the control room and studied the layout of the platform. He had persuaded the consortium to take up the recommendations made after explosions on other rigs and platforms. The accommodation module was constructed of material that wasn't combustible and steel blast walls had been fitted next to the gas-compression chamber. These wouldn't prevent an explosion, but they might contain it. Might . . .

Ideally Chad felt there should be three platforms: one for living accommodation and electronic control; another for drilling and wellhead; and a third for the oil and gas processes. In Norway much larger single rigs were being built to provide breaks between hazardous and non-hazardous areas; that at least was a step in the right direction. He wanted Frank to bring these matters to the attention of the people in positions of power. Alexandra had been enthusiastic about the idea of separating living accommodation from the dangerous compression area, but the consortium had outvoted her on grounds of cost.

Chad went back outside. The platform was safer than a lot of the installations on the North Sea, but you couldn't provide for every contingency. He would be glad when this visit was over.

III

The flight from Kennedy to Heathrow was uneventful and Alexandra was able to catch the six o'clock plane to Aberdeen. She was beginning to feel tired. Willard Grenville had flown from Houston to New York and they had spent the last three days with lawyers and bankers checking every detail of the takeover bid for Armstrongs. There was nothing more she could do now, except wait out the remaining few days before the bid was made public. Willard was as impatient about the delay as she was, and equally upset by his son's separation from his wife. He threatened to come to Scotland and knock heads, but Alexandra had cautioned patience.

"Patience!" Willard snorted. "They've been apart for four months and that durned fool of a son of mine is talking about divorce! See if you can make them see sense."

Alexandra had tried, but had made no impression on either of them. Catherine wanted to continue her career in Scotland and was adamant that she didn't want to have a baby. Chad's dearest wish was to return to the States and start raising a large family. Alexandra closed her eyes, willing herself to try to find a solution, but instead she fell asleep. She was wakened by the captain's voice announcing their imminent arrival at Aberdeen airport. She looked down at the mountains, glens and forests. Aberdeenshire was chameleon country: bleak and grey one moment, pretty as a peacock's tail the next.

When the aircraft came to a halt she picked up her holdall and began strolling along the walkway to the baggage return.

It was dark before the taxi deposited her outside Highgate House, the granite mansion in Queen's Road that was now her home. It gleamed silver grey in the moonlight.

Betsy, her housekeeper, opened the door. "Come away in. You've missed all the good weather."

"You always say the same thing when I've been away," Alexandra said with a tired smile as she walked inside.

"Och well, it's true. Cook's got a nice chicken roasting . . ."

Alexandra held up her hand. "No, thank you. I ate on the plane."

"The fire's on in the small sitting room," her housekeeper went on. "Oh, and Miss Catherine left a message. It's on the table."

The log fire was blazing brightly in the sitting room. Alexandra warmed herself at it as she opened Catherine's letter.

"Just in case we're delayed I thought I'd write you a brief note. Hope all went well in New York. Weather permitting we should be back in Aberdeen some time after seven. See you then. Love you lots. Catherine."

Alexandra glanced at the clock on the mantelpiece: 9:45. What had happened? She picked up the evening paper and studied the weather forecast: it was good. That was a relief. She'd heard Chad talking about the fog that came swirling round the rigs and platforms, delaying flights, cutting them off from the outside world. She glanced out of the window and shivered. Her daughter, her brother, her best friend. She hated to think of them marooned on an oil platform. Even though Catherine's husband was in charge of it . . .

She poured herself a stiff brandy, switched on the television, and gave herself a scolding for worrying. Emotional umbilical cords were a problem. The fiery liquid reached deep down inside her and she found herself smiling at one of the adverts. She sat down on the couch and was kicking off her shoes when she heard the announcer saying something about a special news bulletin. As she turned up the sound on the control panel she was horrified to see pictures of the Barnico Zulu production platform. It was burning fiercely.

"There's been a major disaster in the North Sea," the newsreader said gravely . . .

THIRTY-SEVEN

I

Barnico Zulu platform, the North Sea

Catherine was interviewing one of the roughnecks when suddenly a huge explosion lifted her up in the air. She was flung against something hard and immediately lost consciousness. When she opened her eyes she looked round in bewilderment and saw that the platform was a hellish inferno of flames, melting metal, burning flesh, black smoke, and unendurable noise. There was no sign of Daisy or the supervisor.

"Chad!" she cried in anguish. "Please be safe, please don't die!"

"Stay where you are!" a voice commanded. Chad? She felt relief washing over her in great waves until she heard a high-pitched scream of agony. And then the voice was silent.

"No!" Catherine screamed. "Please stay alive, Chad!" she begged again.

She wiped tears and ash out of her eyes, but all she could see was a wall of flames barring her way. She would have to stay where she was. "Help! Help!" she shouted, but her voice was lost in the cacophony of sound which seemed to increase in volume by the minute. And then she had a new worry: the flames were coming closer. If she stayed where she was she would burn to death.

The coastguard had received a Mayday call from the support vessel reporting the explosion and an alert had been flashed to headquarters in Aberdeen. The first helicopter from Lossiemouth had been scrambled and was already making its way towards the scene.

* * *

Chad was frantic. He too had been lifted off his feet by the explosion, but when he recovered from the shock his first thought was for his wife. Christ, how could he hope to find her in this hellhole of smoke and fire! Heedless of danger he rushed through flames and stumbled over wreckage towards the area where she'd been standing. There was no sign of her or of Daisy.

He heard a feeble cry and dashed across to where Frank Meldrum lay on the platform floor, his head bloodied. Chad knelt beside him, shouting out in horror as a ball of flame came hurtling in their direction. As it passed he felt as if he were being incinerated and when he put his hand up to his head he discovered his hard hat had been blown off and his hair was on fire. He smothered the flames with his sleeve and dragged Frank to a safer spot at the edge of the platform.

"I'll look after him," a rigger volunteered. Chad nodded and then raced towards the control center to find out if anything could be done to stop the fire getting completely out of hand.

Frank struggled dazedly to his feet. "What happened?"

"Explosion!" the rigger yelled back. "We can't get up to the helideck. I reckon we ought to . . . Watch out!" he screamed as part of the deck began collapsing beneath them. Frank felt himself slithering down, down, down . . . He saw the sea and the next minute he was hurtling towards it.

"Frank!" Daisy yelled again and again, but there was no answering shout. Tears streamed down her face. If anything happened to Frank she wouldn't want to live. And Catherine, where was Catherine? Daisy looked desperately around her; she was surrounded by a group of men who were trying to put on life jackets.

"Frank!" she yelled again.

"He won't hear you, miss, wherever he is," one of the men said sympathetically. "We can hardly hear each other and we're crammed tight together."

"Where do we go?" she shouted.

"We're supposed to make our way towards our muster station, but we can't get to it."

"I'm going to look for my husband and niece," Daisy said determinedly as she pushed past them. Twisted metal and machinery blocked her path at every turn and she fell back sob-

bing as a yawning chasm appeared. Far down below was the
sea.

"We should jump for it," someone shouted.

"Don't be a fool, no one can live, jumping from this
height," another man shouted back.

Daisy looked down and thought she could see a familiar
face in the foaming waves. "Frank!" she yelled. And then she
jumped.

The Nimrod aircraft which had been scrambled from Kinloss
reported seeing flames from forty miles away. They estimated
the flames were 200 feet high.

The deck tilted and suddenly Catherine saw a gap in the fire
and rushed through it. "Chad!" she shouted. She was appalled
at the devastation all round her. Lumps of iron were hurtling
through the air, windows were shattering in the heat, and steel
bulkheads were falling like playing cards.

"Chad!" she screamed again as she stumbled over something soft and realized it was a body. Tears rained down her
soot-streaked face, blood oozed from wounds on her legs and
arms. She watched a man clinging to a steel beam. It snapped
like a twig and he plunged downwards with a scream that
struck every nerve in her body.

"Chad!" she yelled once more and this time there was answering cry, and the next moment she felt an arm grip her and
she looked up at the blood-stained face of her husband. She
collapsed into his arms.

"Thank God you're alive!" he sobbed, and held her close.
"Come on, no time to lose." He took her arm and guided her
across the deck, yelling at her occasionally as bits of debris
hurtled past.

"Where are we going?"

"To the edge of the platform and then down to the sea!" But
as they inched forward they saw that this way was blocked as
well. Chad pulled Catherine back as a giant crane buckled and
toppled, gouging out great holes in the deck as it did so.

"The crane has formed a bridge to the outside of the rig. We
can use it as a ladder."

"I can't crawl along that," Catherine screamed.

"You can!" he commanded. They began inching their way

forward. The heat was suffocating and halfway along the ladder a piece of wood hit Catherine on the arm and she almost fell. Chad took a firm grip of her body and held her till she felt ready to go on again. When they reached the end of the crane he beckoned to her to start climbing down towards the water. It seemed an age before they reached the lower struts of the platform.

"Hold on," Chad yelled. "The rescue boats are coming in close. They've seen us. Once they get nearer, look for a spot that isn't on fire and jump."

"You'll be with me?"

"No. My place is here."

Catherine hesitated for one minute longer and then jumped. The water hit her like a sizzling hot towel and she ducked under the waves to avoid the flames. When she surfaced she saw the rescue boat and yelled at the top of her voice and began swimming towards it. Shattered remains from a lifeboat were all around her, but when she tried to cling to a piece of wreckage it turned over and she saw it was a badly burned body. She screamed and all the energy drained out of her. I don't care anymore, she thought, as she felt the waves pushing her back towards the burning platform.

A hand suddenly gripped her arm and began propelling her in the direction of the rescue boat, pushing her into the arms of the seamen who leant over to help her aboard. She turned round and saw that it was Cameron Armstrong who had saved her. The seamen were reaching out for him when an iron bar came hurtling down from the rig and smashed on to his head. Catherine screamed again hysterically as he sank beneath the waves.

"Help him, do something!" she shouted, but she knew her words were a useless protest against fate. The bar had hit Cameron with such force he would have been dead before he sank beneath the waves.

Catherine looked round wildly, but she couldn't see Frank or Daisy on the rescue boat. And Chad? She strained her eyes to look up at the platform. "Chad!" she shouted again, willing him to survive.

II

Alexandra was at Aberdeen Royal Infirmary where she had joined relatives hoping to find their loved ones. She held out her arms in welcome when she saw Daisy on a stretcher. She was badly cut and bruised and suffering from shock.

"Any sign of Frank?" Daisy croaked. When Alexandra shook her head Daisy closed her eyes.

"She'll feel better once she sees her husband," the doctor commented as they wheeled Daisy into one of the wards. As I will, once I've seen my daughter, Alexandra thought.

When Chad was brought in he was badly burned and unconscious. He was wrapped in an aluminum space blanket to help his body retain its heat, and plasma drips were being used to replenish his body fluids.

"Will he live?" Alexandra asked anxiously.

The doctor shrugged. At the beginning of the night he had been able to express sympathy towards relatives, but now he was too tired to do more than go through the motions. "Add the degree of burns to his age and that will give you a rough guide to his survival chances."

"He's thirty-seven."

"Well, he has twenty-percent burns so I'm afraid his chances of dying are around the fifty-seven-percent mark." As he watched her face fall he made a supreme effort to break through the tiredness barrier he was fighting. "Don't give up hope. I've seen worse cases than this pull through."

Alexandra sat on the nearest chair and put her head in her hands; she dreaded having to tell Catherine. But as the night wore on her perspective shifted and her only concern was whether or not Catherine herself had survived. When they brought in Cameron Armstrong's corpse her fears doubled. It was dawn before someone tugged at her arm. "Mrs. Semple, I think it's your daughter."

"Alive?" Alexandra asked, her throat so dry she could hardly speak.

"Alive. She's lost a lot of blood, but her injuries aren't life-threatening."

The tears flowed then, hot coursing tears of gratitude that

seemed to come from her depths. When they let her see Catherine, her daughter's lips parted in a question. "Chad?"

"Already here! He's badly burned, but he'll make it," Alexandra said with more conviction than she felt.

"Uncle Frank?"

Alexandra shook her head.

They brought Frank's body to the hospital in the morning but they advised Alexandra not to look at it. She insisted and forced herself to gaze down at the remains of her beloved half-brother. He was so badly cut and crushed that he was hardly recognizable. Alexandra let her tears fall unchecked as she said her private goodbyes to him. Her beloved half-brother. Big friendly Frank. Quick-tempered. Golden-hearted. Irreplaceable.

III

The next few weeks were anxious as Chad fought for his life and Daisy wished hers away. It was only the sight of her son which made Daisy decide she had to make the effort to live, and Alexandra made sure that Archie was at his mother's bedside every day. When Daisy was allowed home Alexandra insisted that she come to Queen's Road to recuperate.

Chad's recovery was less certain and for a few weeks his life hung in the balance. It was when he started asking about the cause of the accident that they realized he was going to make it.

The advanced construction of the platform and all its safety measures had prevented a major loss of life, but twenty people had been killed. At the inquiry the first pointers seemed to indicate a gas leak was the cause of the explosion, but when the experts examined all the evidence they realized it had been sabotage. Semtex had been put in the pipe leading to the gas-compression chamber and this had produced the same effect as an explosion from chemical causes.

One theory was that an itinerant worker had placed the incendiary device there before leaving on a crew change. Lists were checked of the men who had gone on leave shortly before the explosion, and only one man could not be traced: a roughneck from the south of England. When police went to the address he had given, his landlady said indignantly that he had gone back to Ireland without even paying the bill. His picture was circulated to agencies all over the world without results. The terrorist—and there was a strong feeling that he was one—had vanished.

THIRTY-EIGHT

I

Madeira, 1986

It was warm. The jacarandas were no longer in bloom, and the grapes had been plucked and transported to the shippers' wine lodges in Funchal. Once the juice had been extracted it would be left to ferment until it turned into alcohol and could be drawn into casks and placed in the heated chambers they called *estufas*.

Alexandra was sitting in the garden of the *quinta* with Catherine. They were lounging in deck chairs, sipping chilled Sercial, the golden wine which is the driest of all the Madeiran vintages. Catherine had acquired color in her cheeks and a new spring in her step since she had been reunited with Chad; the tragedy had made them realize how much they loved each other.

"Are you going back to television?" Alexandra asked as Catherine put down her glass and began studying the television pages of the *Daily Mail*.

"Not in Britain—maybe in the States. Though not for a while. I still want a career in journalism, but . . . out there on the platform I realized I wanted Chad more. And his children. The sooner the better! In fact . . ."

Alexandra's mouth dropped as she saw her daughter blushing. "You mean, you're not telling me that you're . . . ?"

Catherine laughed joyously. "That's right, mother. I'm expecting! Towards the end of October Chad felt well enough . . . And—well, I've just had it confirmed. The baby's due in July next year. Isn't it wonderful?"

She laughed again as her mother leapt up from her chair and embraced her. "Catherine, I'm so thrilled!"

"You won't mind being a granny?"

"I can hardly wait! And if it's a boy we'll have a new heir to an empire that's getting bigger every day."

"Mother!"

"So you're going back to the States with Chad?"

Catherine nodded. "Willard and Marnie can't wait to have us in Houston. I'll miss you, mum, I really will."

"I'll come out and visit."

"You'd better! Someone's got to keep Willard in order."

Alexandra pulled a face. Having Willard as her boss hadn't been easy and they argued endlessly. On the other hand they were each so competitive, ideas flew in all directions, and the merged companies seemed to be benefiting from the extra chemistry sparking from the top.

"Where's Aunt Daisy?" Catherine asked.

"In her room. She wanted to be alone."

Daisy made a visible effort to be pleased by Catherine's news, but since Frank's funeral her haunted, tragic eyes had torn at everyone's heart. That evening as she sat on the terrace having drinks with Alexandra she talked about Archie, her 15-year-old son. "I once said to you that I never had problems with Archie. Well, I've got them now. He's miserable, depressed, aggressive. I just haven't been able to get through to him since . . ."

Alexandra clasped her friend's hand, but said nothing.

Daisy's eyes were bleak. "Archie says he can't bear to remain in Scotland, so . . . I've come to a decision. My parents are in their eighties and want me and Archie to go and live with them in Australia. Archie visited them once in Melbourne. He liked it there."

"And you?"

"I think it might be best for both of us to make a new start away from all the memories."

"I'll miss you," Alexandra said huskily.

"You can come and visit us. You told me that Grenville Meldrum have sheep-farming interests in Australia."

"I'd visit you anyway. If there's anything you need, Daisy, anything at all . . ."

"You've been more than generous, Alexandra, settling an income on me and on Archie."

"It's the least I could do."

"What about Catherine and Chad?" Daisy asked.

"They're packing up and leaving for the States next month."

Daisy looked concerned. "I hate to think of you without anyone of your own. I just wish . . ."

"What?"

"Oh, idle thoughts—dating back to our university days. You were so much in love with Robert. Any chance of a reconciliation?"

"None."

"Catherine told me she'd never have made it back to the rescue boat but for Robert's son. I presume that's why you abandoned your takeover bid for Armstrongs?"

"Yes. A life for a life," Alexandra replied, thinking of the way her mother had died.

"So the Meldrum-Armstrong feud is finally over?"

"I doubt if it will ever be over, at least not while Adam Armstrong owns Drumcraig Castle. Did I tell you that I've hired a private detective to keep tabs on Adam? Sam Sweeney helped when Belle . . ." Alexandra paused, remembering that she had never mentioned to anyone that Malcolm had been blackmailed by a prostitute. "Sam has helped me with business queries," she finished vaguely.

"What do you hope to find out?"

"I want to know if and when Adam's vulnerable, and, more importantly, the minute he's even thinking of selling the castle."

Daisy shook her head. "Won't you give up this idea of getting back Drumcraig? You've carried it like a cross for as long as I can remember. I mean, is Adam any more likely to sell you the castle than Tom Elphinstone was?"

"No. Adam's known since university days that Drumcraig is my heart's desire. That's why in his warped way he'd do almost anything to prevent me getting it, but I'm not giving up hope."

Daisy gave a half-smile. "You used to complain that Catherine was stubborn. I can see where she gets it from!"

II

July 1987

Sam Sweeney came to give Alexandra a progress report one Saturday morning when rain was lashing the streets and the wind from the North Sea stung cheeks and fingers. Alexandra helped Sam off with his coat and took him into the room Catherine called "the snug." "Coffee or brandy?" she asked.

"Both!"

When Sam felt warmed, he got down to business. He had spent months compiling a list of Adam's friends, acquaintances and enemies, and tracing as many of them as possible. Alexandra noticed Tom Elphinstone's name. "Is he still friendly with Adam?"

"Not any more. He's living in Amsterdam and when he's drunk—which is often—he boasts that a friend cheated him out of his inheritance."

"Adam?"

"Yes. My hunch is that he was blackmailed."

"Tom's not the sort to stand for blackmail unless he was guilty. Those two deserved each other." Alexandra's eyes travelled further down the list of potential enemies. "Belinda? For heaven's sake, Adam's married to her!"

"Not so's you'd notice. I gather she's been quite hysterical since Cameron died. I was about to try to see her when I heard she'd run off to the States with an oil tycoon, who owns a string of houses including a *château* in France."

"Belinda was always keen on castles—and money, but I'm sorry she lost her son. I know how I'd have felt if it had been Catherine."

"There's another name on the list that might interest you," Sam went on in an attempt to distract her. "Cash Down Karmigan."

"That takes me back!" Alexandra exclaimed as she thought of the scruffy evacuee who had incurred Adam's enmity when they were children. "Why on earth did you bother tracing Billy?"

"You told me about his quarrels with Adam. Childhood enemies can be a great source of information. Unfortunately Billy hasn't seen Adam since he left Aberdeen, but he certainly hates his guts. He made a rude remark when he heard Adam was the owner of Drumcraig and said immediately that it was a Meldrum castle."

"Good old Billy!" Alexandra applauded.

"He said if you ever did manage to buy the castle he wanted to know, so that you could buy him a drink."

"I'll buy him enough drinks to drain the bar dry if I ever . . . In fact, I'll take a note of Billy's address and phone number. Sam, thanks for everything. And keep digging. One of these days . . ."

Alexandra stayed by the fire when Sam left and looked at the phone, willing it to ring. When Catherine and Chad had set up home in Houston Catherine had found out she was expecting twins. She wanted Alexandra to fly out the minute they were born.

Restlessly Alexandra picked up a copy of the *Financial Times*. There was something strange going on in the markets. Earlier in the year the world's leading finance ministers had drawn up the Louvre Accord in an attempt to stabilize exchange rates and prevent a damaging fall in the dollar. Willard Grenville hadn't been happy about the situation for some time and he'd had long arguments with Alexandra about how to react to this new financial situation. His view was that the equity markets would be fuelled at the expense of the bond markets.

The phone rang. Alexandra dropped her paper as she rushed to pick up the receiver. "Yes?" she said anxiously when she realized it was long-distance.

"Mum? It's me! I had the twins three hours ago. Chad said he'd call, but I wanted to tell you myself."

"Catherine, how wonderful! What did you have?"

"We're calling the girl Emma. And guess what we're calling the boy, the grandson who'll inherit the Grenville Meldrum empire? We're naming him after you, mum."

"But Alexandra's a girl's name."

"Of course it is. So we're calling him Alex. Bye now."

When Alexandra put down the phone she felt overwhelmed by emotions: relief that Catherine had survived the birth, gratitude that the twins had been delivered safely, and pride that they'd wanted to use her name for their son and heir. She poured herself a brandy and toasted Emma and Alex. Alex . . . Robert was the only one who had called her that.

Alexandra felt shaken. Once again the past had leapt out at her like a bandit: ambushing her when she least expected it.

THIRTY-NINE

I

Houston

Catherine and Chad were living in Greystones, a nine-roomed villa in the Grenville ranch grounds which had originally been built for the manager. When Catherine and Chad came to Houston he had moved to a smaller property on the estate. Marnie had been so thrilled at the prospect of having her son and his wife to stay so close to them that she had gone completely over the top on the decor of Greystones. Catherine arrived to find that she would be living in film-star luxury. Marnie told her daughter-in-law that she could change anything she wanted, but by that stage Catherine was heavily pregnant with the twins and would have been happy to let anyone brush her teeth never mind decorate and furnish her home.

Alexandra gasped when she saw the newly furbished Greystones. "This was the manager's house? Willard Grenville, you must be taking more than your fair share of the profits!"

Willard cackled with laughter.

"So what y'going to do about it?" he asked.

"You two hush your mouths, you've wakened the babies," Marnie said reprovingly as she led them up to Catherine's room. Chad was sitting by her side.

Catherine held out her arms. Alexandra felt choked with emotion as she embraced her daughter. "Well done, you clever girl," she whispered. "Now where are my grandchildren?"

Chad proudly showed her the twins lying in beautifully decorated cradles; they were both crying lustily. As Willard watched Alexandra cooing and gurgling over them he remarked that she was even softer in the head than he'd imagined. Alexandra grinned. The more she listened to Texans the more she became convinced that they had Scots ancestry.

"Doesn't Catherine look well?" Chad said when he escorted Alexandra to her room.

"Marvelous. So contented."

Chad gave her a quizzical look as he pushed open the door of the guest bedroom suite. "No way am I fooled that Catherine will settle down for ever to domesticity, but at least she's here on my folks' ranch ready to raise my kids."

"And if she decides to go back to television?"

"I'll just have to see she has so many kids she has no time for television," Chad joked. "How are Daisy and Archie settling down in Australia?" he asked on a more serious note.

"I had a letter from Daisy just before I left Aberdeen. She says young Archie is adapting well and enjoying swimming, surfing, and yachting, but of course Daisy is still desolate." Chad looked so somber that Alexandra touched his arm. "It wasn't your fault. Best to put it out of your mind. The twins will help."

"Sure will. I'm so hamhanded changing nappies that I make a bigger mess than the babies do!"

Alexandra laughed and the moment of tension passed.

II

Boyd Brown and Alan Gillian flew out for the christening which was held on a glorious day in August. After the church service there was a big gathering at the ranch. "I thought it'd be a great idea to invite anyone with Scots connections," Willard complained, "then I discovered I had to invite half of Houston. You Scots are like the Mafia, you're everywhere!"

"And aren't you lucky there's so many of us around to keep you on the right road," Alexandra retorted.

Willard snorted and went off to introduce some more of his guests to the twins. Tables had been laid out on the lawns and once the cake was cut and the speeches had been made everyone got down to the serious business of eating and drinking.

It was dusk before some of the guests left. Marnie bustled through to the kitchen to pay off the hired help and Alexandra sat with Willard, Boyd and Alan on the veranda. Inevitably the talk drifted towards money. "The trade deficit has already hit $156 billion," Willard remarked. "If the figures get worse governments will have to tighten fiscal policy. I don't like the look of the market one bit," he continued. "If the dollar goes into free fall there'll be an inflationary effect in the States and other countries will devalue. I predict another depression!"

"D'you think there's something in what he says?" Alexandra asked when Willard was called away to help his wife. Boyd was inclined to be optimistic, Alan Gillian took a more cautious view.

Two days later they all flew back to Scotland.

III

Edinburgh, September 1987

Alexandra had been advised to keep a watching brief on the market, but she decided to do more than that. She toured Edinburgh, Glasgow, and London, soliciting opinions from friends and acquaintances in the financial world. Once she was through, she had a conference with Alan Gillian and her merchant banker in Edinburgh.

"I've always had great respect for James Goldsmith's business acumen and there's a rumor that he's gradually been going liquid."

Alexandra did not mention that she'd heard a whisper that Robert Armstrong had insisted on the same course for Armstrongs.

Alan Gillian pursed his lips. "People always predict doom and gloom and most of the time it never happens. Boyd was bearish at the beginning of the year and went short."

"I know. He's very surprised at my line of thought, but I've made up my mind for my personal holdings."

"No problem. We'll fix that," her merchant banker agreed. "And Grenville Meldrum?"

"I'll have to discuss that with Willard and Chad."

"Do it from this office if you like. Want me to stay?" Alan went on.

She shook her head. "If Willard knows you're here he'll play up."

But Willard had a chill and it was Chad who answered the phone. Alexandra recalled that her son-in-law had once said he wasn't cut out for a desk job, but since he had taken over as

Assistant Vice President of Grenville Meldrum his conversion
to top management had been seamless.

Alexandra brought him up to date with her views and her
conclusions. "I think Grenville Meldrum should reduce their
exposure."

"You sound very sure about that," Chad said cautiously.

"I am. It's the short-term rise in interest rates that's influ-
encing me, plus the fact that Japan and Germany have reined
in their money supply. It looks as if there's going to be a
wholesale flight from the dollar. The Secretary of the Treasury
is bound to make a statement about that in the near future."

"Maybe we should wait and see what he says."

"No!" Alexandra said decisively. "I say we should close
these exposed positions right now."

"I've never heard you this positive about the market before,
Alexandra." He paused. "I'll get it going at this end."

IV

Alexandra was at the Meldrum Trossachs in October. She
wanted to have a look at the new jacuzzis and swimming pools
which had been installed, and she also wanted to discuss the
idea of a horse-riding school and a pigeon-shoot. There were
eight Meldrum Stately Home Hotels, but the Trossachs remained her favorite.

She took time out to climb the hill behind the hotel and
enjoy the vista of rolling moorland and mountain. The last
time she had come to the Trossachs had been in early summer
when the trees and bracken were still freshly minted green.
Now, autumn tints had shaded the landscape from old gold to
umber and the air had that unmistakable crispness that is the
precursor of winter. There was a definite change in the
weather, Alexandra decided, as she strode down the hill. A
wind had sprung up and the way it was bending the branches
of the trees looked like the beginnings of a storm.

Fortunately Alexandra was so tired her sleep was not disturbed and the following morning she woke early, but when
she turned on the news as she was getting dressed she heard
that a hurricane had swept through southern England. The
business news reported that the market-makers hadn't man-

aged to get into their City offices and the new electronic Stock Exchange dealing system—so bravely ushered in the year before—had been closed down for the day. Chad knew she was staying the night at the Meldrum Trossachs and he phoned her shortly after nine with an update from the States. It had been a bad week on Wall Street with the Dow Jones falling by record amounts. He read out a headline from *Barrons*, a leading U.S. business and financial paper: "Is this it? Did the bull market end? Has the bear market begun?"

Alexandra drove back to Aberdeen that morning, but kept in close touch with the international news. Over the weekend the news from the States got worse as investors became increasingly nervous over the rise in interest rates. On Sunday a senior official from the administration told the *New York Times* that the U.S. had already begun its policy of letting the dollar fall. In Britain traders expected the market to open sharply lower on the Monday. Everyone would be trying to catch up with the deals which they hadn't been able to make the previous Friday when the hurricane had forced the market to remain closed.

V

19 October 1987

Alexandra was in her office by seven o'clock on Monday morning. By eight o'clock the London market was in free fall and by nine the Stock Exchange were no longer guaranteeing the accuracy of prices on brokers' screens. Alexandra stayed by the screens, interrupting her viewing only to take calls from New York, Houston, and her brokers. No one seemed to be working normally. Everyone was transfixed by the television screens as history was made.

By mid-afternoon 50 billion pounds had been wiped off the value of shares in London and $500 billion had been wiped off the value in the States. Monday, 19 October, would go down in stockbroking history as Black Monday!

Grenville Meldrum had weathered the crash well, as had Armstrongs, but it had been a black, black Monday for Adam Armstrong. Sam Sweeney, Alexandra's private detective, had discovered through his numerous sources that Adam Armstrong had been writing "put options" on the FT-SE 100 index: betting heavily that shares would rise. Sam phoned to tell her that Adam Armstrong's positions hadn't been sold out, his losses had been permitted to run, and at the end of Black Monday he had lost 1 million pounds.

Alexandra felt her chest constricting as she put Boyd Brown in the picture. They had discussed a possible scenario in case a situation like this ever arose and had arranged to make the purchase of Drumcraig through David Judy, a London banker who happened to be Boyd's nephew.

"Adam has lost a million. Ask your nephew to offer a million for Drumcraig. Conditional on immediate acceptance," Alexandra said tersely. "And don't phone me till everything's signed and sealed."

Boyd whistled. "A million! I've a feeling we're about to witness a record-breaking conveyancing."

VI

December

Alexandra was in her Glasgow office when Boyd phoned her. "Congratulations, my dear and very old friend! You are now the legal owner of Drumcraig Castle. And by God, I admire your persistence!"

Alexandra had expected to laugh or cry or leap out of her chair at Boyd's news, but when he rang off she felt drained of emotion. She'd been almost 20 when she'd sat on the hill overlooking Drumcraig and vowed to get it back for the Meldrums—thirty-six years ago. A lifetime away. She probed her mind trying to analyze her lack of reaction and realized she was suffering from shock. She decided to call David Judy and thank him for his part in the proceedings.

"No problem," the cheerful young voice said at the other end of the line. "I enjoyed posing as a millionaire. By the way, Adam Armstrong's been trying to contact me about selling some of the furnishings in the castle. My secretary told him to phone back in five minutes. What do you want me to say to him?"

Alexandra realized she should be gracious in victory and not let Adam know so soon that he had been tricked. But: "Tell

Adam you sold the castle to me!" she replied. To hell with being gracious in victory! She pressed the buzzer for her secretary. "Mary, I don't feel up to the long drive north tonight. I think I'll stay in Glasgow. Can you book me into One Devonshire Gardens for bed and breakfast?" Clothes were no problem; she kept a ready-packed personal holdall in all her offices so that she could stay overnight at short notice.

VII

Alexandra checked into One Devonshire Gardens around eight. The hotel was small, exclusive, and had distinctive decor; a night spent in its relaxing ambience would put her in good fettle for an early morning drive to Aberdeen. Once she was settled in one of the comfortable bedrooms she wondered how on earth she was going to pass the time. She was far too excited to read or go over business papers. Idly she picked up her diary. As she was leafing through it she came across a number which made her smile. Of course. Why not?

The deep fruity voice that answered the phone made her hesitate. It didn't sound remotely like the cheeky evacuee she used to know. "Is that Billy Karmigan?" she asked hesitantly.

"This is Mr. William Karmigan. What can I do for you, ma'am?"

Alexandra couldn't resist it: "Hey Billy, you're a wee rogue, so you are!"

There was silence at the other end of the phone and then a shocked voice protested: "See, you! State yer business and then gerroff ma phone."

Alexandra chortled. "Billy, it's me, Alexandra Meldrum. Sam Sweeney gave me your number. He said you wanted to know if ever I managed to get Drumcraig away from Adam Armstrong. Well, I have!"

"That's bloody marvelous, that is," Billy exclaimed gleefully. "That Adam was a dirty rotten bastard, so he was."

"Billy, I'm staying the night at One Devonshire Gardens. It's a hotel . . ."

"Know it fine," Billy replied. "I take some of my customers there. I'm in the liquor business now. Prospering."

"I'm not surprised. Billy, I'd love to see you. Any chance of you coming round here this evening? I've got the castle so I'll keep my promise and buy you anything you want."

"Aye well, a wee pub would do fine!"

Alexandra laughed again. "You're just the tonic I need, Billy. See you in an hour."

As she placed the receiver in its rest the bell rang again and she sensed before she picked it up that it would be Adam. The minute he heard the news that she had bought the castle he would have started phoning round trying to find out where she was. She'd told her secretary to give him the number of the hotel. If Adam was going to vent his spleen on her she preferred it to happen tonight rather than in some public place. She wanted this business over and done with, and then perhaps she could forget about the Armstrongs.

"Think you're very smart, don't you!" Adam said in a voice that was thick with rage. "Fixing that banker. Making him buy the castle from me so that you could buy it back from him."

"You'd never have sold it to me, Adam."

"No, I wouldn't. I loathed you at university and my feelings haven't changed."

"So why are you phoning?" Alexandra asked.

"Did you know Drumcraig has a ghost? A lady in blue who wanders round the castle tapping on the windows—as if she's trying to get out and can't. Trapped by fire."

There had been rumors about a ghost at Drumcraig, but Alexandra hadn't heard that it was a lady in blue who tapped on windows. Her mother had been wearing blue on the night Drumcraig was set on fire by a German bomb. She would have been banging on all the windows trying to escape the blaze . . .

Alexandra shuddered and took a firm hold on herself. "If you think you're going to spoil my enjoyment of Drumcraig, Adam Armstrong, you're wrong! And if you're frightened by Drumcraig's ghost it's because you have a guilty conscience. I haven't!"

She clenched her hands and forced herself to say the words she was thinking. "If that blue lady is my mother she'll welcome me back to the castle and her ghost will finally be at peace!"

With that she banged down the phone and collapsed back in her chair. Pull yourself together, she told herself sternly as she heard a knock at the door and got up to answer it. When Billy

Karmigan greeted her his choice of words could not have been more unfortunate. "What's wrong? You look as if you've seen a ghost!"

Alexandra swayed and fainted. When she opened her eyes Billy was bending over her looking concerned. "I mean, I know I'm attractive," he said, "but ladies don't usually pass out when they see me!"

She gave a faint smile and allowed him to help her to her feet. "Sorry about that, Billy. Here, let me take a good look at you."

"You'd be better taking a good look at some brandy. I'll fix it," he said and went over to the cocktail cabinet in the corner.

Alexandra rubbed her eyes as she studied him. The cheeky wee evacuee was now a well-dressed fat man with a moustache.

"Get that down you and you'll feel better!" he said, placing a glass in her hand.

Two brandies helped her relax and she began telling Billy about Adam's phone call. She expected him to laugh at the very idea of her mother's ghost haunting the castle, but instead he shuddered. Without asking her leave he went over to the drinks cabinet, poured himself another double whisky and swallowed it neat. He poured more whisky in his glass and swallowed that back as well. When he turned to face her, Alexandra saw that he was shaking.

"If I'm not drunk I won't have the courage to say it!" Billy declared. "I always thought I was born without a conscience, but one event in my life has haunted me . . . the fire at Drumcraig."

Alexandra felt her chest tighten. That terrible day had caused her so much pain. Was there still more to come?

"I caused your mother's death," Billy said abruptly.

The brandy in Alexandra's glass spilled to the floor as her fingers lost their grip.

"No, Billy, it was Robert Armstrong who did that. He told me. He said there was a mad scramble in the dark to get out of the castle; Robert threw out an arm to stop a boy going over the steep edge of the spiral stairway and pushed my mother off at the same time. He admitted it." She clenched her fingers together and forced herself to go on. "I can believe it was an accident, but . . . Robert didn't bother to go back to look for her, just left her to die in that awful fire. That's what I couldn't forgive. Then. Now. Ever!"

"That isn't how it happened," Billy said carefully. "I remember every detail of that night. Because I was the one who pushed your mother. God help me, it was an accident, Alexandra, but me and Lennie never stopped to find out if she was hurt. It was Robert who yelled that he couldn't see her, Robert who tried to fight his way back to find her, but Adam wouldn't let him. And me and Lennie kept on running. Looking out for number one . . . When I heard your mother had been killed I was too scared to tell anyone what had happened. Thought I'd be up for murder."

Alexandra rose slowly from her chair and stood looking out at the traffic lights at Hyndland. She tried to concentrate on the cars and the people crossing the road in an attempt to block out the nightmare which had just been re-enacted for her.

"You were the first person who took an interest in us," Billy was saying. "That tragedy with your mother has always been on my conscience . . ."

"Robert said he couldn't remember clearly what happened," Alexandra said at length.

"Aye, that's because he'd had a knock on the head earlier. Don't blame Robert Armstrong, Alexandra, I was to blame!"

"No," Alexandra said tiredly as she came and sat down again. "The air raid was to blame. When there's a panic you can't always count on people to act responsibly. It was all just a ghastly accident. I met Robert when I was 11 years old," she added wistfully, "then at university . . . we fell in love. We were going to get married, until I stumbled on this thing with my mother. I thought he was to blame."

For a few minutes Alexandra found it difficult to speak. "Robert told me I shouldn't let the past warp the future, but I've been doing that ever since. I wish I'd given him the benefit of the doubt all those years ago . . ."

"Why didn't you?" Billy asked.

Alexandra sat very still as she remembered the tidal wave of jealousy that had swept over her when she'd seen Belinda in a half-clothed state. Belinda had acted like a mistress disturbed from lovemaking, and Alexandra had been so suffused with rage she wasn't willing to trust anything Robert said. Jealousy was such a powerful emotion. It clung to the mind like a creeper and was just as difficult to dislodge.

Billy looked at her curiously. "You're still in love with him, aren't you?"

Alexandra tried to laugh. "Robert hates me, Billy, and he thinks I hate him . . . But I suppose I've never stopped loving him. Only I didn't realize it till now, when it's too late . . ."

After Billy had gone Alexandra prepared for bed. She wouldn't think about Robert; that chapter in her life was closed. But at least a new one was about to begin. Some day soon she would drive to Deeside to claim Drumcraig Castle back for the Meldrums.

FORTY

I

The iron gates of Drumcraig Castle were magnificent, but they badly needed a coat of paint. The driveway was overgrown with weeds and wild flowers. The cathedral-high fir trees were leaning towards each other across the road, filtering out the light and sending sinister shadows dancing in every direction. Briony's words . . . Alexandra's mother had often described the approach to Drumcraig Castle and the day she had walked up that long driveway to apply for a job as housekeeper. When Briony had come to Drumcraig the sun had been shining. Now as Alexandra walked up the drive the sun was shining too, encouraging late-flowering plants to enjoy the unseasonal warmth.

While one part of Alexandra's mind darted back to the past, another contemplated the future. She would need to bring in squads of gardeners to clear away the weeds and plant new flowers. Rhododendrons always did well in this part of Scotland, and she would have masses and masses of azaleas: not just the more common pinks and purples, but all the exotic shades from yellow to peach. She stopped as she approached the bend in the road and she remembered her mother's words once more.

"The trees drew back as I reached the top of the hill and all at once I was confronted by a sweep of sky so densely blue it looked like fabric. And there, pinned to one corner of it like a brooch, was Drumcraig Castle."

The winter sky was paler, but the castle still seemed pinned to it: a slender rose skyscraper topped with turrets, gables, balustrades, and cupolas. It was beautiful. Fairytale beautiful. Alexandra walked forward to the door and touched the iron-studded wood. Then she fitted the key in the lock and began her journey back to the past.

The rooms were empty; the carpets, curtains, furniture, and furnishings had been removed, yet Alexandra was still filled with pride and pleasure. In the Great Hall she drew in her breath as her eyes ranged over the soaring stone vault, the huge fireplace, and the musicians' gallery. This would be her drawing room and she would find a beautiful Chinese carpet that would do justice to its ambience; there would be tapestries on the walls, antique lamps, fine paintings.

She hadn't been in the castle for years, but she felt as if she had just left it the day before. Alexandra decided she would locate her main study in the bedroom on the floor which looked down on the musicians' gallery. Her grandfather had followed tradition and built a concealed chamber above the gallery. She would turn that into a safe.

She felt an ache in her chest as she went up the steep stairway down which her mother had fallen; then it passed. Her mother was at peace now; her ghost laid to rest. She climbed up until she was on the fifth floor of the castle: the King's Room. She assessed it critically and wondered if this should be her bedroom. Seven floors to the castle: plenty of room for herself, and for Catherine and Chad and all their children when they came to visit her.

When Alexandra arrived at the top of the castle she clambered up the final steep steps on her hands and knees, blinking as she emerged into the sunlight. She walked to the edge of the parapet, trying to pick out the landmarks which had once been so familiar to her: Drum Castle, the turrets of Crathes Castle in the distance. She turned her eyes in the direction of the moorland hills to the north east of the Cairngorms. Somewhere up there was the source of the River Dee meandering its way down through glens, farmlands, and villages till it reached its mouth at Aberdeen. The clear mountain water of the Dee was virtually unpolluted from source to mouth; one of the very few rivers in Europe in that category. She must remember to mention that to Catherine; she had become keen on ecology.

How she missed her daughter . . . And Daisy.

Alexandra angled her face upwards towards the sun, marveling at its winter warmth. Even the stones on the parapet were hot. She brushed away some dust and sat down on the edge. She would go to her office in a little while, but meantime she wanted to sit here and hug the castle to her heart.

Only when the sun clouded over did she rise to her feet, taking one last look at the view before making her way down to the ground floor. The studded door banged behind her as she shut it, and she leant against the wood treasuring the thought that one day the castle would be a beautiful home again: the Meldrum home. If the blue lady still haunted the corridors she would have a smile on her face.

She had it all now: a happily married daughter, grandchildren, the castle, an internationally successful business . . . And though she hadn't bought out Armstrongs she had more than evened the score. It was strange the way you could strive for things all your life and then one day they just fell into your lap.

Yet she felt flat. Deflated.

What was it someone had once said? Achieving your dreams is one thing. Living with them is another.

FORTY-ONE

I

1988

Alexandra was flattered when Glasgow University intimated that they wanted to award her an honorary degree of Doctor of Law for her unique contribution to the oil and property world. The ceremony was to take place in December, but they suggested she might like to revisit her alma mater at a reunion weekend for graduates in July and be the star speaker in a debate fronted by a cabinet minister. Since Alexandra heartily disliked this particular member of the cabinet she decided it might be fun to speak against him.

When she arrived at the university, Cathy, the bright young graduate who was to be her official escort for the weekend, informed her that the cabinet minister had flu.

"So who's opposing me?"

"Robert Armstrong."

Alexandra recoiled. "I don't believe it!"

"We couldn't believe our good luck either," Cathy replied. "I don't know how he heard about the last-minute cancellation by the cabinet minister, but he did, and he phoned up and volunteered his services."

"But we're business rivals," Alexandra said faintly.

"He told us that. Said it would make for a great debate. Unless . . ." Cathy blushed in sudden confusion.

"Unless?" Alexandra asked peremptorily.

"He said it would make a great debate unless you weren't up to standing against him!"

"That wretched man has an inflated opinion of his own abilities. I'll make mincemeat of him," Alexandra snapped.

"Terrific!" Cathy said. "Now let me take you on a tour of

the university so that you can get the feel of the place again. Is there any special place you'd like to see?"

"No," Alexandra replied tightly.

"Then why don't I just take you to some of the landmarks we usually show visitors? I'll pretend you haven't been here before. We find that's a good way of refreshing someone's memory."

And it was. Alexandra stood before the memorial gates which had been unveiled in 1951 as part of the 500th birthday celebrations and looked again at the names inscribed on them of the twenty-eight men who had brought recognition and fame to the university during those years. Before degree exams she and her friends used to test their memories by seeing how quickly they could reel off the famous names: Adam Smith who wrote the *Wealth of Nations*, James Watt the modifier of the steam engine, Joseph Lister who introduced antiseptics to surgery . . .

She used to meet Robert Armstrong at the gates before walking down University Avenue to Byres Road for a quick lunch.

"The former Queen Margaret Union now houses the Students' Representative Society and John Smith's bookshop," Cathy said as they passed the building beside the main gatehouse which had once been affectionately known as QM: the women's union. "Let's go to the Professors' Square."

Alexandra had always liked the stately elegance of the large Victorian houses which had been built in the 1870s. At their front doors they still had the slabs that had made descent from horse-drawn carriages decorous. Robert had once stood on one of them and delivered a peroration about her beauty and intelligence.

"Numbers 5 to 9 have been reconstructed internally to form the Stair Building," Cathy said. "It's used for staff rooms and some teaching accommodation for the School of Law. Robert Armstrong studied law of course, but I doubt if the Stair Building would have been in use in his time. He might have used the pillar box, though." She pointed to the Victoria Regina pillar box.

Alexandra blinked. She had posted letters to him there.

"The lamps round the square are beautiful antique originals," Cathy was saying. And Robert Armstrong used to kiss me under them, Alexandra recalled. Damn the man! Memories of him were everywhere and somehow proximity to them was diluting her antagonism. That was a bad road to follow.

"Cathy, I've got a bit of a headache. I think I'll go and freshen up, and then perhaps have a rest before the debate."

II

The debating hall in the men's union was not the prettiest place in the university. Years of use and abuse had made it shabby and unwelcoming. When Alexandra stepped into it, resplendent in full evening dress as befitted a celebrity speaker, she couldn't help remembering the uncomfortable evenings at the "Saturday Palais." The Palais was a weekly dance where women lined one side of the hall and men the other. The women had complained bitterly that it was like a meat market, and some of the men weren't too diplomatic in their treatment of the "choice cuts." She saw Robert Armstrong advancing towards her, a welcoming smile on his face. "Looking forward to getting trounced, Alexandra?"

"I always look forward to putting pigheaded men in their place," she flashed back.

The debate was a disaster for Alexandra. Although everyone conceded that she argued her case brilliantly, the mood of the House was decidedly anti-government. The opposition won by an embarrassing majority and Robert Armstrong received a standing ovation.

"I suppose you'll pack up and go home now that you've been beaten," Robert said to her after the debate.

That was precisely what Alexandra had intended. The prospect of waiting till the following evening for the gala dinner in the Burrell Collection had lost its appeal.

"I'm looking forward to the rest of the weekend," she replied brightly, determined not to let him see how annoyed she was.

III

There are few art galleries in the world which have been more imaginatively designed than the Burrell Collection in Pollok

Country Park. Its setting in the corner of a meadow allows the neighboring trees to cast oblongs of light and shadow through the long enfilade of rooms and complement their contents. Alexandra had sometimes taken visitors from the States to the Burrell and they had gazed admiringly at the splendid edifice of red sandstone, Portland limestone, timber, and glass. They were invariably gratified to hear that some of the most spectacular portals and arches built into the fabric of the building had been purchased by Sir William Burrell in 1953 from the sale of the William Randolph Hearst Collection. Glasgow was justifiably proud that one of the most important museum buildings of this century was sited in the city. The university for their part were delighted when they heard that the gallery could be hired in the evenings for special occasions—like a graduate reunion dinner!

By the time the graduates had assembled at the Burrell, the visiting public had left and they had the gallery to themselves. After the dinner and the speeches they were free to wander round and admire the collection. Alexandra was relieved to be on her own. The weekend had brought back so many memories of her love affair with Robert Armstrong that every nerve in her body seemed to be in a state of tension.

She was admiring the Chinese ceramics when Robert came up behind her. "I'm glad you came this weekend," he said without preamble. "I saw the advertisement about the graduate weekend in a student magazine, then I phoned the minister who should have been opposing you."

"I understand he's got flu."

"He was fit as a fiddle when I spoke to him yesterday."

"Then why did he cancel?"

"Because I wanted to come in his place."

"And you persuaded him to let you do this?"

"Let's say a sizeable contribution to his party funds persuaded him!"

"That's immoral! Anyway, why did you want to take part in this debate?"

"Because you were in it. I couldn't think of a better way of commanding your attention." He gazed at her. "Your hair is shining under the lights. I always liked your hair."

Alexandra looked at him in astonishment and walked upstairs towards the collection of French Impressionist paintings.

"Did you know that William Burrell is thought to have bought his first picture when he was 16 and his father was supposedly surprised because he hadn't bought a cricket bat?"

"I have nothing to say to you, Robert. Leave me alone."

"Billy Karmigan warned me you'd be like this."

Alexandra rocked back on her heels. "When did you see Billy?"

"He invited me to meet him. He said he was on a conscience trip and had finally seen a way to make amends for the past. He told me all about the night of the fire at Drumcraig Castle. What you imagined happened. What I imagined happened . . ."

"I'm . . . sorry for some of the things I said, Robert. It seems you weren't to blame.

"I'm glad about that too," he said quietly. "And while we're on the subject, let me clear up one other matter. Belinda dreamt up that seduction scene at Aunt Ethel's house entirely for your benefit. I hadn't been to bed with Belinda. In fact I didn't go to bed with her until I heard you had married Malcolm Semple," Robert went on. He looked at her. "Sex is supposed to be a remedy for a broken heart, but it never cured mine . . . Probably never will!" he added softly.

As she felt tears spring to her eyes Alexandra moved away quickly before she disgraced herself. She hurried through the gallery aware that people were going in the opposite direction, aware that the gallery was about to close, but unable to face anyone. Wanting to be away from the crowds she turned quickly towards the deserted drawing room which had been reconstructed to show the lifestyle of Sir William Burrell when he had lived at Hutton Castle. She heard footsteps echoing down the corridor and realized Robert was following her. Reason fled, instinct took over, and she ducked behind one of the big pillars. She stood there, eyes tightly shut, not daring to move a muscle.

Even more shocking than Robert's implicit words of love had been her own reaction to them. Joy had flared through her body like a torch. It was the intensity of her feelings that had made her panic and run.

Alexandra forced herself to try to stay calm. If she stayed here long enough she would be the last to leave the gallery and she wouldn't have to face Robert again. She had been there for what seemed like endless minutes, eyes still tightly shut, when a voice whispered behind her, "They've all gone, Alex. You can come out now. The gallery's closed."

As Alexandra turned round Robert grasped her in his arms and kissed her; a rough bruising kiss that seemed to echo back through the years. She struggled at first and then the remembered sweetness of him flooded her senses and she found herself responding. When she tried to draw away again he pulled her closer and whispered in her ear, "It was said of the doomed French dynasty of the Bourbons that they had forgotten nothing and learned nothing. We don't want to be like that, Alex. Not anymore. We're getting too old for all this hatred and hostility."

Maybe he was right. The past had cast too long a shadow. She had studied philosophy at university, but hadn't taken it to heart. Kierkegaard had said, "Life can only be understood backwards; but it must be lived forwards."

Wanting more time to think and to explain her feelings to Robert, Alexandra drew back from him and ventured a few paces into the modeled re-creation of the Hutton Castle drawing room. Immediately a piercing siren began echoing through the building and footsteps came clattering from all directions.

"How appropriate!" Robert exclaimed. "You've just set off the burglar alarm!"

Alexandra gazed at him helplessly and then they both began to laugh. They were still laughing as they were escorted to the exit. Outside, Robert fumbled in his breast pocket and then handed something to her. It was the ring he'd given her in Paris.

"Here's to forever?" he asked hopefully.

"Let's settle for tomorrow!" she said and smiled at him, her heart full.

And then they walked out into the warm womb of the night.

Selected Bibliography

Addison, Paul *Now the War Is Over*. London: BBC and Jonathan Cape, 1985.

Allan, J. R. *Farmer's Boy*. London: Longman, 1975.

Alvarez, A. *Offshore*. London: Sceptre, 1986.

Anson, Peter *Fishermen and Fishing Ways*. London: EP Publishing (republication), 1975.

Berry, Simon and Whyte, Hamish *Glasgow Observed*. Edinburgh: John Donald Publishers, 1987.

Brogan, W. A. *Aberdeen*. Edinburgh: Scottish Academic Press, 1986.

Callow, Clive *Power From the Sea*. London: Gollancz/Scientific Book Club, 1973.

Cameron, David Kerr *William Gavin, Crofter Man*. London: Gollancz, 1980.

Crampsey, Bob *The Young Civilian*. Edinburgh: Mainstream, 1987.

Cunnison, J. and Gilfillan, J.B.S. *The Third Statistical Account of Scotland: Glasgow*. Glasgow: Collins, 1958.

Daiches, David, select. and introd. *Edinburgh*. London: Constable, 1986.

Fenton, Alexander *Country Life in Scotland*. Edinburgh: John Donald, 1987.

Finlayson, Iain *The Scots*. London: Constable, 1987.

Graham, Cuthbert *Aberdeen and Deeside*. London: Robert Hale, 1984.

Harris, Paul *Aberdeen at War*. Manchester: Press & Journal in association with Archive Publications, 1987.

Harvie, Christopher *No Gods and Precious Few Heroes*. London: Edward Arnold, 1987.

House, Jack *The Heart of Glasgow*. Glasgow: Richard Drew, 1987.

Jenner, Michael *Scotland Through the Ages*. London: Michael Joseph, 1987.

Johnson, Luke *The Crash of '87*. London: Weidenfeld & Nicolson, 1988.

Lenman, Bruce *An Economic History of Modern Scotland*. London: Batsford, 1977.

Lewis, Peter *A People's War*. London: Thames Methuen, 1986.

Lewis, Peter *The Fifties*. London: Heinemann, 1978.

Lund, Paul and Ludlum, Harry *Trawlers Go to War*. London: Foulsham, 1971.

Mackenzie, Hugh *The Third Statistical Account of Scotland: The City of Aberdeen*. Edinburgh: Oliver & Boyd, 1953.

Mackie, J. D. *A History of Scotland*. London: Penguin, 1964.

Macphail, I. M. *The Clydebank Blitz*. Clydebank: Clydebank Town Council, 1974.

Marren, Peter *A Natural History of Aberdeen*. Aberdeen: Robin Callander, Aberdeen People's Press, 1982.

Marwick, Arthur *The Pelican Social History of British Society since 1945*. London: Penguin, 1982.

Massie, Alan *Glasgow*. London: Barrie & Jenkins, 1989.

McGill, Jack *Crisis on the Clyde*. London: Davis Poynter, 1973.

McLaren, John *Sixty Years in an Aberdeen Granite Yard*. Aberdeen: Centre for Scottish Studies, N.D.

Morton, H.V. *In Search of Scotland*. London: Methuen, 1984.

Neal, Harry Edward *The Story of Offshore Oil*. New York: Julian Messner, 1977.

Robertson, George Gladstone *Gorbals Doctor*. London: Jarrolds, 1970.

Ross, Stewart *Scottish Castles*. Moffat: Lochar Publishing, 1990.

Saville, Richard, ed. *The Economic Development of Modern Scotland*. Edinburgh: John Donald, 1985.

Smout, T. C. *A Century of the Scottish People*. London: Fontana, 1986.

Smout, T. C. and Wood, Sydney *Scottish Voices*. London: Collins, 1990.

Thompson, Paul, with Wailey, Tony and Lummis, Trevor *Living the Fishing*. London: Routledge & Kegan Paul, 1983.

Turner, John R. *Scotland's North Sea Gateway*. Aberdeen: Aberdeen University Press, 1986.

Walker, Fred M. *Song of the Clyde*. New York and London: W. W. Norton & Company/Patrick Stephens Ltd, 1984.

Webster, Jack *A Grain of Truth*. Edinburgh: Paul Harris, 1981.

Webster, Jack *Another Grain of Truth*. London: Collins, 1988.

Wheeler, Robert and Whited, Maurine *From Prospect to Pipeline*. Houston, Texas: Gulf Publishing, 1981.